The Magpie

A Rufus Stone Detective Story

Book Three

by

K. J. Frost

GWL
PUBLISHING

First Published in 2020
by GWL Publishing
an imprint of Great War Literature Publishing LLP

Produced in United Kingdom

ISBN 978-1-910603-75-8 Paperback Edition

GWL Publishing
Forum House
Sterling Road
Chichester PO19 7DN

www.gwlpublishing.co.uk

Dedication

To S.L.

Chapter One

December 1939

My darling,

Thank you so much for yesterday's letter.

I can't tell you how relieved I was to hear that your exemption has been granted. I've been worried sick that you'd be taken from me, but to know that you'll be kept safe, it's the best news I've had in ages. I just wish I could be with you to celebrate.

I miss you too, my love, and obviously I agree that things would be so much better if we could telephone each other, but you're at work during the day and there always seems to be someone here in the evenings, and it wouldn't do to have our conversations overheard, would it? Especially not by 'his lordship'. We can't afford to get caught out – well, I certainly can't – and, in any case, I feel that can we say so much more in our letters, don't you? And then I can read them when I'm by myself, and think about how much I miss you… all of you.

I agree, our time together last Friday was so special, my darling. I wish we could have had longer too, but to feel your naked body next to mine, your hands caressing my skin, your lips all over me… and as for your tongue… oh God! It makes me shudder, just thinking about it, and those memories have filled my dreams every night since.

In answer to your question, I don't think it's going to be possible for me to spend the night with you anytime soon. I wish that wasn't the case, but I can't think of a good enough excuse to get away… unless you can? It would have to be something no-one suspected, and we'd have to be careful that no-one saw us together. But if either of us can think of anything, then yes, I'd love to. You know that. You know there's nothing I want more than to be able to take our time making love to each other, to fall asleep in your arms and wake up beside you. But in the meantime, we'll have to just make do with our lunchtimes and occasional afternoons, and treasure the memories.

Speaking of which, I should be able to get away for half an hour or so tomorrow at around 12.30. If I'm not there by quarter to, you'll know I can't make it. I hope I can though… I'm simply dying to seeing you.

Thinking of you always,

Your beloved,

Kitten xx

———•———

"Are you awake, dear?"

My mother comes into the bedroom and goes over to the window, pulling back the curtains and blackout to let in the weak December sunshine, ensuring that, if I wasn't already awake, I am now.

"Yes, Mother."

She comes back and looks down at me, her long brown hair restrained behind her head in a loose bun. She's already dressed, in her usual style, with a flowing dark blue skirt beneath a thin grey jumper, topped by a knee-length navy cardigan, and a teal coloured scarf around her neck. "It's Monday morning, Rufus," she says, as though I won't know what day it is, or that it's my first day back at work following a week's enforced recuperation at home, as a result of having been stabbed. Considering how much I love being a policeman, regarding it as a vocation, rather than a job, I'm hardly likely to have forgotten that today is the day I get to return to it. "Time to get up," she adds, with considerable, and completely unnecessary vigour.

"I'm not ten years old, Mother." I throw back the covers and sit up on the edge of the bed. Her ministrations each morning are wearing thin, especially as she seems to have forgotten that I'm no longer a child; I'm going to be thirty-three years old next month, although you'd never know it to listen to her mollycoddling.

2

I think what makes the situation worse is the knowledge that, while I appreciate that my broken arm – received in a car accident that predated the stabbing – means I do need help, I'm not sure I want that help to come in the form of my mother. Amelie, the woman I love more than anything else in the world, only lives around the corner. In fact, her house is visible from my bedroom window, and it serves as a constant reminder that her assistance, in helping me with getting dressed and undressed, would be a vast improvement on my mother's attentions.

"Then stop sulking like a ten year old and get up," Mother says, interrupting my much more pleasant train of thought, before going through to the bathroom.

I know better than to argue with her, and get to my feet, wandering over to the window and gazing out at Amelie's house. The rooftops are covered with a thin layer of December frost and I smile to myself, remembering our walk by the river yesterday and how cold we got… and how warm she felt in my arms when we sheltered from the fleeting snowfall beneath some trees, and I let her nestle inside my coat, her body close to mine.

"Of course, if you and Amelie were married, I wouldn't have to do this. As your wife, she could help you." Mother's voice rings out from behind me, intruding into my fond recollections, and I turn to face her.

"Being as I've only known her for eight weeks, I think to be married already would be quite an achievement, don't you?"

She smiles and shakes her head. "Not if you'd put your mind to it, dear." She turns and puffs up the pillows, pulling up the sheet and blanket and straightening them.

She and Aunt Dotty have been like this since they noticed my initial interest in Amelie; first matchmaking – although that wasn't strictly necessary, being as I fell in love with Amelie almost the moment I saw her – and now meddling, which is what they seem to do best.

"Even so," I point out, skirting around her and heading towards the bathroom, where I know she'll have run some water into the bath for me, "I think from first acquaintance to marriage in eight weeks would be asking a little too much."

"Perhaps," she muses, loud enough for me to hear her, "but if you at least asked her, then we could start making plans."

I come back into the bedroom and stand still, looking down at her.

"Mother…" She turns to face me. "When I ask Amelie to marry me, and if she accepts, then the planning will be done by us. I don't want you and Dotty, and Aunt Issa interfering. Is that clear?"

She smiles, her eyes sparkling. "You said 'when'."

I fold my arms and narrow my eyes at her. "That's not the point."

"Oh, I think it is, Rufus." She claps her hands together. "Now, go and have your bath. I'll be back in a minute to change your dressing, but first I need to go and tell Dotty…" She moves past me and starts along the landing.

"Tell her what?" I call after her.

"That you said 'when'," she replies.

"I also said 'if'," I point out and she stops dead, turning towards me.

"When did you say 'if'?" she asks, looking worried.

"Just now. I said 'if she accepts'."

A broad smile breaks out on her face and she waves away my comment. "Oh, you don't need to worry about that," she says and turns away again, scurrying into my aunt's room and closing the door behind her.

With Aunt Dotty and my mother under one roof for the first time in years, and Aunt Issa down in Somerset, telephoning to check up on my progress every other day, I suppose it was too much to ask that I might be allowed any privacy in my personal life. *Personal life?* I chuckle to myself… *heaven forbid.*

I make my way back into the bathroom and remove my pyjama bottoms – I never wear the tops – climbing into the bath and taking care of the small dressing that still covers the knife wound I received almost two weeks ago. The woman who did this to me is safely behind bars, her confession to my injury and the killing of another police officer, in revenge for the death of her lover, now a matter of record. The wound has healed really well, and the dressing is just for show, I think, but it's a timely reminder not to take anything for granted – like my life, or the people I love.

Once bathed, I return to my bedroom and dress myself, with the door firmly closed. I may not have found this very easy to start with, after I broke my arm – doing up buttons can be tricky with just one hand – but I've mastered it now, and prefer the independence of not having my mother doing everything for me. I've still got another three weeks until the plaster cast comes off and, as I wander over to the window again, I look outside and ponder on the two main reasons why I can't wait. The first of them is parked outside Aunt Dotty's house. It's a beautiful British racing green MG. My old one – which was bright red – was destroyed when I crashed it, and my mother decided to buy me a new one as an early birthday present. She also chose to get a drophead coupé version, which means that, unlike my earlier model, this one has a roof, and windows. It's the height of luxury and is much more practical for Amelie – or it will be, when I can drive it. The second reason for my impatience is Amelie herself. Although I can hold her, like I did yesterday, in the falling snow, it's been too long since I've been able to put my arms around her properly, and even as I stand here and look at her house, I ache for her.

I hear the dining room door open and close and realise that time's moving on and I need to have breakfast before my sergeant, Harry Thompson, arrives to collect me and drive me to work in Kingston. I leave my tie loose. It's one of the few things I still haven't mastered, but which I know my mother will do for me and, picking up my jacket, I make my way down the stairs.

"Good to see you again," Thompson says, holding the car door open for me. At six foot three, he's only an inch shorter than me, but where I have reddish-brown hair, his is blond. He's also of a more sturdy build, but we share the same sense of humour, which is a good thing, especially in our job.

He glances down at the brown-paper wrapped parcel I'm holding, raising his eyebrows, but I don't comment and neither does he.

"Can I expect this service every day?" I ask him, getting into the car and looking up at him.

"No," he replies, smiling, and then he walks around and climbs in beside me.

"How are you feeling?" he asks. We've been in touch during the last week, because I asked to be kept informed if anything important happened at work in my absence – which it didn't – but we haven't spoken since Thursday.

"A lot better, thank you. How's Julia?" I enquire, being as his wife is pregnant and is suffering from morning sickness.

"Better than she was," he replies, looking over at me. "Thanks for asking."

"Is your mother-in-law still helping?" Julia enlisted the assistance of her mother with their son, Christopher, because at one stage, she was struggling to leave the bathroom before midday.

He nods his head as he pulls the car away from the kerb. "Yes. Just for a day or two longer, I think. Although the sickness isn't so bad, Julia's still quite tired."

"Do you get on alright with her?" I ask. "Your mother-in-law, I mean… not Julia."

He smiles. "Yes, I do. I think she's the ideal mother-in-law, actually."

"How's that?"

"Well, she dotes on Christopher and loves babysitting, or even having him to stay, which means Julia and I get to have the occasional night to ourselves." He smirks and I shake my head, although I don't know why I'm surprised that a conversation with Harry would end up veering towards the bedroom. It's always been the same, for as long as I've known him. "And, she doesn't interfere in our lives," he adds.

"What more could a man ask?"

"Precisely."

"My mother could do with taking some lessons from her," I remark, without thinking and he glances across at me, before looking back at the road ahead, and I realise I'm going to have to add something to that statement. "She's got interfering down to a fine art."

"I'm sure she means well," Thompson says, sounding more placatory than I feel, after my conversation with her earlier.

"I wish I was. I swear to God, she never misses an opportunity to raise the subject of engagements, weddings and marriage – not to mention babies – every time Amelie comes over. And as for when she gets me by myself…" I roll my eyes.

"Would you rather she didn't care less?" he asks, his voice rather more serious now.

"Well, no… obviously not."

He shakes his head. "Then look on the bright side. At least she lives in Somerset most of the time, which isn't exactly local, and when you do get married to Amelie, and you have children, you can pack them off to their grandmother for a week, every so often. She'll be in her element, and you two can enjoy the peace and quiet."

"Ah… peace and quiet," I muse, dreamily, and he laughs, leaving me to reflect that, hearing *him* say 'when' with regard to my proposal and marriage to Amelie, doesn't bother me at all.

He parks the car behind the London Road police station and we both get out and climb the stairs to the first floor, going through the main CID office. Thompson stops at his desk, taking off his coat and I go through to my room. As I hang up my own coat on the hook behind the door, I take a moment to look around. It's good to be back. I may not have worked back here for that long – just a few weeks in reality – but it feels like I'm at home again already. I smile to myself and go over to my desk, putting down the parcel and carefully unwrapping it with my one useable hand, to reveal a framed sketch. Amelie drew it while she was staying at my mother and Aunt Issa's cottage in Somerset in October. It was one of her first attempts at sketching and I think it's wonderful. At my request, she had this one and two others framed. The other two hang in my bedroom, but I wanted to bring one in here too, and I take it over to the book case and prop it up. That will have to do for now, until I'm able-bodied enough to mount it on the wall.

I sit down at my desk, staring for a moment at the framed photograph of Amelie in front of me. The black and white image doesn't do justice to her chestnut coloured hair, or her amber eyes, or the soft pink hue of her lips, but I like looking at it, nonetheless. And that's how it should be. I am in love with her, after all.

"Stone?" I look up at the sound of a deep voice, coming from my doorway, and quickly get to my feet. The man facing me is tall, with a

7

thin, angular face and dark hair, wearing the resplendent uniform of my superior officer.

"Chief Superintendent."

He smiles and comes into my room, looking around. Chief Superintendent Webster is new to the station, having transferred from Guildford and, while we've met, that was before he officially started working here, before my injury kept me away from work. I'd been planning on going upstairs to see him later on, but he's forestalled that, much to my surprise, which I'm trying to hide. Well... it's unusual to see someone of such exalted rank on the 'shop floor', as it were.

"What can I do for you, sir?" I ask, indicating the two chairs in front of my desk.

He closes the door and comes over, sitting in the right hand one as I resume my own seat, looking across at him and wondering what I've done to deserve such a visit. "How are you?" he asks.

"A great deal better than I was, sir, thank you."

He smiles. "And you're sure you're well enough to come back?"

"Absolutely positive." The thought of another day spent at home with my mother and Aunt Dotty, while Amelie goes to work and can't, therefore, be relied upon to keep me sane, doesn't bear thinking about.

"Good..." he says a little distractedly. "I—I've got something I need to talk to you about, only I don't want to throw you in at the deep end, if you're not ready."

"I'm ready, sir. Feel free to throw me wherever you wish."

He smiles, although it's rather a weak effort. "Yes, well. Have you heard about these burglaries yet?"

"Um... no." I feel rather on the back foot now.

He shakes his head. "Not to worry. They took place last night, but I'm only really aware of them myself because..." He pauses. "Well, because I have a personal involvement."

I lean forward. "You do?"

"Yes." He looks down at his clasped hands. "I had a telephone call in the early hours from my sister. It seems two men broke into her house. They tied her up and stole her jewellery and some money."

"Is she alright?" I ask and he smiles.

"She is now, thank you. She was alone when it happened… well, apart from the maid and cook, but they slept through the whole thing, until she managed to raise the alarm at just before four this morning."

"They didn't hurt her? The burglars, I mean."

"No. She's more shocked and shaken than anything. And bloody angry about the jewels. Some of them belonged to our mother."

"You said 'burglaries'… plural, sir?"

He looks up. "Yes. Sorry. There were two further break-ins, in the same road."

"All in one night?" He nods. "Where was this?"

"Endsleigh Gardens, in Surbiton."

"And your sister's name?"

"Ruth Tierney. Her husband is a doctor."

"And he wasn't in the house last night?" I ask.

"No. There was an emergency at the hospital, I believe. It happens quite a lot these days, because the hospital is almost as short staffed as we are."

I stand up, ignoring his comment, since it's not relevant to the case. "Does Sergeant Tooley have the details for the other burglaries?"

"Yes, he does."

"Very good." He stands himself now as I go over and take my coat down from the hook, shrugging it over my shoulders and holding my hat in my hand. "I'll keep you informed," I tell him, opening the door.

"Thank you," he says. "I won't interfere." He gives me a slight smile.

"I appreciate that, sir."

I go out into the main office, followed by Webster, who walks straight out through the main door without speaking to anyone else, and goes up the stairs. Looking around, I discover Sergeant Tooley leaning over Thompson's desk and, judging from their conversation as I approach, it would seem they're discussing the burglaries already.

"We're off to Surbiton, I gather," I say to Thompson, pulling on my hat.

He looks up, surprised. "How did you know? I was just coming to tell you about it."

"You'd be amazed at the things that I know and you don't," I reply, and Tooley sniggers.

Thompson gets to his feet, rolling his eyes. "You can tell me all about your powers of genius in the car," he says, picking up his coat and hat, and following me to the door.

It's a quick drive from Kingston into Surbiton and Thompson pulls the car up outside the Tierney house, which Tooley informed us is called Brackenridge, a very large, red brick property, with a tall hedge that shields it from the road.

"Before we go in there," I say, halting Thompson's exit from the vehicle, "I should probably inform you that Mrs Tierney is the Chief Superintendent's sister."

He lets out a low whistle. "So that's why he came to see you this morning…"

"Yes."

He pauses for a moment. "Is he going to cause us problems?"

"No. He's said he won't interfere."

"And you believed him?" He turns and looks at me.

"Yes, I did. I've told him I'll keep him informed, and I will, but that's as far as it goes."

He shakes his head as we both climb out of the car. "Oh… I can see this is going to be fun."

There are three other police cars already present, parked a little further along the street, and as we walk up the pathway, a constable who's on duty at the door stands to one side, nodding his head at us. He looks bitterly cold, his cheeks and nose tinged red.

"Sir," he murmurs.

"Constable."

Thompson knocks on the door and, after just a few moments, it's answered by a young red-headed girl in a black maid's uniform, with a white lace collar.

"Is Mrs Tierney at home?" I ask.

"May I ask who's calling?" she says, respectfully.

I pull out my warrant card and show it to her, saying, "Detective Inspector Stone," at the same time, while Thompson repeats the process with his own identification.

She performs a brisk bob-curtsy and then stands back, muttering, "Do come in," and looking a little flustered.

We step inside and she closes the door behind us, then leads us through to a room near the back of the property, announcing me and ignoring Thompson, presumably having decided for herself that his rank doesn't justify such an honour, which annoys me.

Inside the room, we're greeted by a woman in her mid-forties, with blonde hair, swept back from her attractive, well made-up face. She stands as we enter, revealing a trim figure, encased in a fitted olive green dress and a beige-coloured cardigan, with a single string of pearls hanging around her neck. She may have been burgled in the early hours, but she's a picture of cultured elegance.

"Inspector." She holds out a delicate hand, which I shake, before she raises herself in my estimation, turning enquiringly to look at Thompson, who's standing just behind me.

"This is Detective Sergeant Thompson." I complete the introduction that had been neglected by her maid, and she nods her head towards him and then indicates that we should sit down, which we do, on a sofa opposite the one she's just vacated.

Once we're seated, she resumes her place, clasping her hands on her lap, and looks across at me expectantly.

"I've spoken to your brother." I decide it's best to get the family connection out of the way first, so that she can't bring it up later. "He's given me the basic facts of what happened, but perhaps I could ask you to tell me in your own words?"

She takes a deep breath, glancing at Thompson, who's got his notebook out, poised to jot down any salient details, before she begins, "I—I went to bed at just after ten-thirty." Her voice is clear and precise, even though she falters slightly, I imagine because she's remembering the events of last night.

"Your husband wasn't at home, I believe?"

She shakes her head. "No. Leo is a doctor. On Sundays, he normally plays a round of golf with a colleague of his, but yesterday he and this other doctor were telephoned at the end of their match to say there was an emergency and they had to go straight into the hospital. My husband phoned me from there, once he'd established how bad the case actually was, and told me not to expect him home."

"Does that happen often?" I ask and I can't fail to notice the shadow that crosses her eyes.

"Since the war started, yes, I'm afraid it does," she replies, with a hint of regret in her voice. "He works terribly hard at the moment. He used to have much more regular hours, but I suppose some of the younger doctors have been called up, or have gone into the medical corps, haven't they?" She looks up, although I don't think she expects an answer. "For the last few weeks," she continues, "he's had to stay on at work until ten or eleven o'clock several evenings a week."

"But this is the first time he's been away all night?"

"Yes."

"Is he here now?" I ask. I'd like to speak with him. It strikes me as interesting that the burglars should strike on the first night her husband has stayed away from home, and I'm wondering who else was aware of his movements.

"No. He's still at the hospital."

"Does he know what's happened?" I ask.

"Oh yes. I telephoned him earlier. He was quite upset about it, and told me to get plenty of rest. He said he'd try to get home early tonight, if he could." She smiles. "He's really very considerate."

I nod my head. "So, you went to bed at ten-thirty," I prompt.

"Just after," she clarifies. "I listened to *Songs from Merrie England* on the wireless, and then switched off the lights before I went up."

"And you were woken in the night?"

"Yes." She nods her head. "I felt a cold draught to start with, which startled me awake and seemed odd, because I knew all the doors and windows were locked. And then..." She hesitates. "And then I felt the man's hand on my mouth, clamped across it." She demonstrates with her own hand, placing it horizontally over her lips. "I panicked," she continues, removing her hand and lowering it to her lap again, "but he had a firm grip on me and shone a torchlight in my face."

"Did he speak?" I ask.

"Yes. He said not to scream and that, if I did as I was told, they wouldn't hurt me."

"Did he have an accent of any description?"

"No, nothing distinctive."

"Did he sound young, or old?" I ask.

"Young," she replies, without hesitation. "And I noticed there was a rather unpleasant smell to his glove…" She becomes thoughtful.

"He wore gloves?" My disappointment is almost palpable.

"Yes."

"Can you say what the smell was?"

"Something unsavoury," she says, her nose wrinkling up, "like mouldy food." That's not quite as helpful as it would have been if she'd said 'petrol fumes', but I know better than to be ungrateful for small details. They can sometimes prove very useful.

"What happened next?"

She takes another breath. "The other man knelt on the bed and tied my hands together…"

"Did they bring a rope with them?" I ask her.

"No, they used my own stockings to bind and gag me, and then they set about ransacking the bedroom. They emptied the drawers all over the floor and went through my jewellery box."

"Did they go anywhere else in the house?"

"No. They just took what was to hand in the bedroom, and left, warning me to keep quiet." She frowns. "I gave them a few minutes to leave the house, and then I started making as much noise as I could," she says. "Eventually cook heard me and she untied me and woke Ellen."

"Your maid?" I query and she nods her head. "Do you know what time this was?"

"I don't know what time the men came into the room, but I know it was ten to four when cook found me, because she told me. I knew I should have telephoned the police, but I was so upset, I telephoned

Bernard instead." She smiles a little half-heartedly. "But then, I suppose he is a policeman, after all."

I'm assuming that 'Bernard' is the chief superintendent, in which case he most certainly is a policeman.

"These men… they didn't hurt you?" I ask.

"No. I'm more upset about the jewels than anything," she says, tears welling in her eyes, which she blinks away. "All of my really valuable jewellery is locked up in the safe, but there was a bracelet my husband gave me on our wedding day, and my mother's wedding and engagement rings were in the box as well, along with a necklace which my father gave to her on their tenth wedding anniversary. They're probably worth quite a bit of money, I suppose, but that's not the point. I'd rather have the jewellery back." Her voice cracks as she speaks and she looks away, trying to compose herself.

To give her some time and privacy, I glance around the room, taking in the silverware on the sideboard, the expensive paintings hanging from the walls, and the rather fine clock on the mantlepiece. Whoever did this had no idea what they were looking for.

A slight cough from Mrs Tierney brings me back to my senses and I look across at her.

"They got in through the scullery door," she says, helpfully. "The lock was forced. There was a man here earlier, who looked at it… a very tall man…"

"Prentice?" I suggest, thinking of our fingerprint expert. He used to work with me at Scotland Yard, but decided to move out into the 'sticks', as he put it, in the hope of a quieter life. I'm not entirely sure how that's going for him, but then I've barely had time to see him since his move. "Did he dust for fingerprints?" I ask, although I doubt we'll get much, not if they wore gloves. Still, we might get lucky. They might have been stupid enough to take them off, especially if they were trying to pick up fine pieces of jewellery.

"Yes," she replies, smiling. "He took mine, and Ellen's, and cook's as well, for elimination purposes, he said."

I nod my head. "He'll probably need to get your husband's too."

"He did mention that and I suggested he contact Leo at the hospital."

I get to my feet and Thompson does likewise, closing his notebook. "We're just going to take a look around the house, and in your bedroom, if that's alright?"

"Yes," she says, standing up too. "The policeman who arrived first told us not to touch anything, so it's all still a frightful mess, I'm afraid."

"That's fine, Mrs Tierney. We'll let you know when we're finished and you can get back in there."

She shudders slightly. "Oh, I don't think I can sleep in there tonight," she whispers, almost to herself. "I think I'll get Ellen to make up a bed in one of the guest rooms."

"I'm not sure if you're aware, but there were two other burglaries in your street last night," I point out and she nods her head.

"Yes, so I was informed. I don't think I know the people concerned though."

"Well, we'll leave a constable patrolling outside for the time being, just to put your minds at rest." I'm not sure if we have the manpower for that, but in the circumstances, I think the chief superintendent will find it from somewhere.

"That's very kind," she replies, smiling slightly. I give her one of my calling cards, in case she should remember anything else, and we say our goodbyes before she sits back down in her seat. Then, I make my way towards the door, followed by Thompson.

Once we're out in the hallway, I turn to him. "It seems like kids, or amateurs to me," he says, pocketing his notebook. "They might have had the sense to wear gloves, but they took the jewels, and then left behind all that silverware in there?" He nods his head backwards towards the room we've just left.

"Not to mention the paintings and that clock."

We move towards the stairs and start climbing, finding the master bedroom with ease, being as it's the only one with an open door, on the right of the landing.

Inside, there are twin beds, one of which is pristine and undisturbed. The other has the sheets thrown back in disarray, and a pair of stockings lie across the pillow, presumably where they were left after the cook had freed her mistress. There are clothes – specifically underwear – scattered all over the floor, and the footstool, which I'm assuming once sat in front of the dressing table, is upended and is now over by the window. Essentially, it's a mess, exactly as Mrs Tierney described. Thompson and I take a look around, but there's nothing for us to see, really. We know Prentice has already done his job here, and after we've finished, we go back downstairs and take a quick look at the scullery door. As predicted, the lock is broken and the maid informs us that a locksmith has already been called.

As a result of our other enquiries, we've discovered that Mr and Mrs Horton, a couple in their mid-fifties, who live at Lilac Cottage, were the first to be burgled, at approximately one-thirty in the morning. The burglars used belts from the couple's dressing gowns to tie them up, but didn't gag them, presumably because they'd worked out that the Hortons don't have any domestic staff, and therefore alerting anyone to their predicament was going to be significantly harder for them. It took them until just before four-thirty to unfasten their bindings, by which time the chief superintendent had already raised the alarm, and thus, when Mr Horton went out to use the phone box, he found a police car already there, in the street, and was able to inform the attending officers of what had occurred. On this occasion, it appears that the burglars stole from the bedroom, but had a look around the rest of the house as well, leaving the living and dining rooms in disarray. Mr Horton was keen to point out that, not having much worth stealing, they probably decided to move on elsewhere. He was able to inform us that, while the men were searching the bedroom, flashing their torchlight around, he was able to catch a glimpse of them. They were both of medium height and slender build, and both wore balaclavas.

As for the third victim, Mrs Stokes, she probably came off the worst. A widow of approximately sixty-five years of age, living alone in a large property, she was only discovered, tied up in her bedroom, when her 'daily' let herself into the house this morning at eight o'clock. Several uniformed officers were already present in the vicinity, dealing with the other two burglaries, and it was a simple matter to inform them of what had happened. By that stage, however, poor Mrs Stokes had been lying, her arms behind her back, her hands bound together, for over five hours. As with Mrs Tierney, a stocking had been used instead of a rope, but no gag had been required – again, I presume because of the absence of anyone else in the property. Despite her ordeal, Mrs Stokes refused to be taken to hospital and we interviewed her in her guest bedroom – her own room still being in a state of upheaval – propped up on several pillows, a shawl wrapped around her shoulders, with her daily, a Mrs Mooney, fussing around like a mother hen. Mrs Stokes estimated the time of the break-in to be between two-thirty and three o'clock, apologising for not being able to be more accurate than that, and informing us that she'd been unable to see anything of the two men, because they'd made her lie face-down on the bed. She was a dear lady, uncomplaining and resolutely cheerful, more concerned that Thompson and I should be comfortable and that Mrs Mooney should fetch us a cup of tea while we conducted our interview. She maintained a strong and steady voice all the while we were there; that is, until she told us that several items of jewellery had been taken, none of which mattered, she said, except for a ring which her late husband had given her on the birth of their only child – Peter – who was killed right at the end of the Great War.

Thompson and I make the short journey back to the London Road station in silence, both caught up with our own thoughts. I suppose we should be grateful that there wasn't more violence involved. It could have been worse, and we both know it, but I think we're both going to be haunted by Mrs Stokes for some time.

"You start typing up the notes," I tell Thompson as we get to the top of the stairs. "I'm just going to see Webster."

He nods his head and I continue up to the second floor, going into the outer office, where the chief superintendent's secretary, Miss Parsons, is sitting at her desk.

"Can I see him?" I ask, nodding towards his door.

"I think so," she replies, smiling as she gets up from her desk and goes into his room, closing the door behind her. Since Webster's arrival, I've noticed that she wears lipstick, and she's changed the way in which she styles her hair, and there's also a vase of flowers on her desk, which brightens up the office considerably. I'm not for one minute suggesting that she's doing any of this to impress her boss – he's a happily married man, and she knows it. But I think she's more cheerful in herself, and I don't blame her. If I'd had to work for his predecessor, Chief Superintendent Meredith, every day, I'd have been pretty miserable too.

The door opens and she comes back out. "The chief superintendent will see you now," she says quietly, stepping to one side as I pass her.

Inside the room she's just vacated, Webster is sitting behind his desk, and looks up at me the moment I enter.

"I thought I'd come and fill you in on our enquiries," I announce, before he has a chance to ask how things are going.

"Thank you." He smiles and indicates the seats in front of his desk. I sit in the one on the right, and tell him about our interview with his sister, the details we learned and what's been done to date, in terms of fingerprinting and photographing the scenes, before moving on to tell him of the other two victims and their stories. He's visibly moved when I tell him of the statement Mrs Stokes made, and leans back in his chair.

"Do you need anything from me?" he asks.

"I told your sister that we'd leave a man on patrol," I explain. "So I suppose we'll need to arrange that." He nods his head. "Other than that, we'll just proceed with our enquiries as usual. I'm waiting for Edgar Prentice to give me his report on the fingerprints…"

"They wore gloves, you say?" he interrupts.

"Yes."

"Professionals, then?"

"No." I shake my head. "I don't think so. They didn't go equipped to restrain the householders, and they only stole small items, which suggests they were on foot. Thompson thinks they might be youngsters… they certainly look like amateurs."

He nods his head. "Thank you for keeping me updated, Inspector," he says and I get to my feet. "Let me know if anything else develops, won't you?"

"Of course, sir."

Back downstairs, Thompson is still hard at work at his typewriter.

"Shall I go and get us both a sandwich?" I suggest, going over to his desk. I could do with a break, and I've got an errand to run. It's an important one too – and it's something I need to do by myself.

"I can go if you feel like a rest," Thompson offers, looking up.

"No, it's fine. I haven't decided what I want to have yet, and the fresh air will do me good." I'm not about to tell him that I have an ulterior motive for being so obliging. I'll never hear the end of it. "Hopefully, by the time I get back, Prentice might have come up with a name and we can make an arrest before tea time."

"Does everything revolve around food with you?" he asks, smiling.

"Yes, but I don't have to bring you back anything, not if you're not hungry."

"Well, I wouldn't go that far," he says. "Are you going to the tea room?"

"Of course." 'The tea room' is just down the road from here. It's a small establishment, probably seating no more than fifteen or twenty people. They serve sandwiches, light lunches and cakes – as well as a very good cup of tea, and while they usually expect their customers to eat on the premises, they allow us the luxury of taking our sandwiches away with us. It's a perk of the job. It's not one we indulge in every day though. In fact, we quite often skip lunch altogether, but if we're here and we're hungry, why not?

"In that case, can you see if they've got any sausages?"

"I'll ask."

"Ask nicely," he says. "I could just do with a thick, juicy sausage sandwich."

"I'll see what I can do."

I go back out and down the stairs, and onto London Road. The tea room is a few doors down and I enter, and stand in the queue of people who are waiting to pay. It's waitress service in here normally, so the only people at the counter are those who've already eaten. The lady in front of me settles her bill and I step forward.

"Inspector?" Emily, the lady behind the counter, looks up at me over the top of her half-moon glasses. She's probably fifty years old and runs this place with her identical twin sister, Eleanor. "It's lovely to see you again. And looking so well. We were so worried when we heard about what happened to you."

"Thank you, Emily," I reply and she smiles. Most people can't tell her and her sister apart, but I noticed quite early on when I moved back here and started frequenting their establishment, that Emily has slightly whiter teeth than her sister. I haven't, however, revealed my secret, so I think they're of the opinion that I'm a genius, and I'm not going to disillusion them.

"What can I get for you today?" she asks.

"My sergeant would like a sausage sandwich, if that's possible?"

She smiles. "For Sergeant Thompson, I should think we can manage that." She makes a note on a small pad. "And for you?"

"Cheese, I think."

"We've got some home-made apple chutney, if you'd like some with it?" she offers.

"That would be perfect." She gives me a smile and makes another note on her pad. "And can I call back for them in about half an hour?" I ask.

"Of course you can."

"Thank you, Emily." She grins this time, showing me her white teeth, and I raise my hat, leaving the shop and turning to my right.

About half way along the road is my next port of call. It's a small jewellers I've been meaning to come to for a while now, except that my short stay in hospital and subsequent recuperation have made that impossible. But now that I'm back on my feet, I don't intend waiting much longer to propose to Amelie, and if I'm going to do that, then I need a ring. A very special ring.

I push open the door, a bell sounding above my head, and a short, rather portly, grey haired man appears through a green curtain that covers a small doorway in the far wall.

"Can I help?" he says, letting his hands rest on the counter that surrounds two sides of the interior of the shop.

"I—I'm looking for a ring," I stutter, feeling unaccountably nervous, even though I have actually done this before. I wasn't nervous that time though, which I suppose just goes to show that it means so much more now than it did then.

A knowing smile appears on his face. "Oh yes?" he says.

"An engagement ring," I clarify, as I step over to the counter towards him.

"Well… let's see what we can find, shall we?"

He moves away to the other end of the room, returning a few moments later with two full trays of rings.

"These are some of our most popular styles," he says and I scan them closely, shaking my head.

"No," I murmur. "I wanted something more… unique."

"Did sir have a budget in mind?" he asks and I look up at him again.

"Not really. If the ring is right, I don't mind how much it costs." His smile widens and he scurries away again.

"We do have these," he says, returning with two much smaller trays, featuring just six rings each – none of which are priced up, I notice.

I stare down at them. Nine of them I instantly dismiss; the stones being huge and unwieldy and nothing like the kind of thing Amelie would wear, and I'm reminded of when I did this last time, immediately prior to almost making the biggest mistake of my life and marrying the wrong woman, certain in the knowledge that all I had to do was think of size; the larger the ring, the better. Amelie isn't like that though – thank goodness. And that makes my choice so much harder. I can't just choose the most showy, expensive-looking ring in the shop. I have to choose something that's right for her; something that's perfect.

The ring in the bottom left of the tray catches my eye and I lean down, focusing on it.

"Can I have a closer look at that one?" I ask, pointing it out.

The man pulls it from its nest and hands it across to me. It's beautiful, there's no denying it; a square cut diamond sits in the centre, with two smaller, circular ones either side. However, I'd expected to feel something when I held it... and I don't.

"Hmm..." I hand it back to him, sounding as non-committal as I can. "I still don't think it's quite right."

"Did you need it before Christmas?" the man asks, tilting his head to one side.

"Why?"

"Because I'll be getting some new stock in during the first week of January. You might like to come back then?"

I don't really want to wait that long, but if needs must... I gaze down into the glass counter, which contains all manner of jewels and trinkets, and something twinkles at me.

"What's that?" I point.

"That's a necklace, sir." He obviously thinks I'm incredibly stupid.

"I know, but it's beautiful."

He smiles again, clearly sensing a sale. "Yes, it is." He opens the cabinet from the rear and pulls out the necklace in its small box, holding it out to me.

I take it from him and admire the jewel... or should I say jewels, because the pendant that hangs from a simple gold chain is made up of coloured gemstones, in the shape of a daisy. It may not be a ring, but it would make the perfect Christmas present for Amelie.

"I'll take it," I say to the man, looking up again.

"Very good, sir," he says, holding out a hand for me to give him back the box. "That will be eighteen pounds." I swallow hard and wonder if I'm being foolhardy. I've still got the ring to buy, as well as paying for a house, and furniture... but I don't care. I don't care at all.

I pick up the sandwiches on the way back to the station, feeling rather pleased with myself, even though my mission to find a ring was actually a failure.

"Did they have to bake the bread from scratch?" Thompson asks as I place his sandwich on his desk, and I glance up at the clock and realise that I've been out for nearly three quarters of an hour.

"No. I had something else I needed to do."

He looks up at me. "Oh yes?"

"Yes. I had to get Amelie's Christmas present, if you must know." I don't mention the ring, but reach into my pocket and pull out the box, opening it up and showing the necklace to him.

He lets out a long whistle. "Lucky Amelie."

"You think she'll like it?" I'm suddenly feeling a little uncertain, perhaps because I've never really been one for grand, romantic gestures – and this feels like just such a thing. I hope I haven't miscalculated.

"Well, I don't know her that well, but I can't think of a woman alive who wouldn't like it," he replies. "Just ask her not to show it to Julia, will you? I'll never live it down." He smiles up at me, unwrapping his sandwich and taking a large bite.

I shake my head, grinning, and close the box, pocketing it again, then take my sandwich through to my own office, feeling a lot more confident now.

Edgar Prentice walks through my open door at just after five o'clock, with a file in his hand. He doesn't knock, but just coughs from the other side of my desk.

"Edgar," I say, trying not to smile.

"Rufus." He lays the file down on my desk and I look up at him, noticing that Thompson has appeared in the doorway and is leaning against it, listening.

"Anything?" I ask Prentice.

He shakes his head. "No. I'm sorry, but I think we're going to have to assume that the burglars kept their gloves on. Or that the only things they touched were the items they removed from the premises."

"Absolutely marvellous." I can't disguise my sarcasm, and I nudge the file to one side, without even looking at it.

"Did you rule out Doctor Tierney as well?" I ask him.

"Yes," he replies. "I called in at the hospital on my way back here and took his prints. He wasn't best pleased about it."

"Really?"

"No." Thompson moves further into the room as Prentice thinks through his response. "I'm no detective, as you well know, but I'd say he was trying to hide something."

I glance at Thompson. "Well, I think tomorrow morning, we should perhaps pay a visit to Doctor Tierney, don't you?" I suggest. "We'll let him have a nice quiet evening with his wife, and then go and find out what he's keeping from us."

"Assuming he is," Prentice says, his cheeks reddening. "I might have got it wrong, Rufus."

"Even if you haven't, I'd still like to see him anyway."

"Well, don't blame me if I've misunderstood it all," he says, shrugging his shoulders and going back out into the main office.

Once he's gone I turn to Thompson. "Close the door, will you?"

He doesn't reply, but goes over and shuts the door quietly, returning to my desk and sitting down in front of me.

"There's another reason we're going to see Doctor Tierney," I say quietly, even though I know no-one can hear us.

"Oh yes?"

"Yes. And I haven't mentioned this to Webster yet, so keep it to yourself." He raises his eyebrows. "It may be nothing, especially considering that two other properties were burgled last night, but I think it's odd that the break-in happened on the first night that Doctor Tierney ever stayed away from home. Considering how poorly planned and impromptu these burglaries seem to have been, I'd quite like to know how many other people were aware of his change of plan, who else he might have mentioned it to, or who might have overheard his telephone call from the hospital."

"You're thinking that someone might have hatched this plan after hearing he wasn't going to be at home?"

"I don't know what I'm thinking."

"It only accounts for the robbery at his house, though. What about the others?"

"Maybe they decided to try their luck." I sit back, letting out a long sigh. "As I say, it may be nothing, but it's a bit of a coincidence… and I don't like coincidences."

"Are you going to see Amelie tonight?" My mother puts down her knife and fork, moving her empty plate away from in front of her, just fractionally, and looks up at me.

"Yes. Why?" I narrow my eyes at her, wondering what she's going to say next. When I first moved back here, and developed a very keen interest in the young lady who resides across the street, Aunt Dotty decided I shouldn't be seen entering Amelie's house at night, for fear the neighbours would gossip. She ignored the fact that the blackout makes such surveillance activities much harder, even for the most serious minded of scandal-mongers, and – more importantly – that I'm not giving up my evenings with Amelie, for anyone. As a result, now that I'm recovered from my injuries, for the last few evenings, I've been going over there for an hour or two, just so that I can stay vaguely sane.

"Oh, no reason, dear." She exchanges a look with my aunt, across the table. Dotty has a mischievous expression on her face, which isn't at all unusual and belies the fact that she is, in reality, a 'Lady', her late husband, my Uncle Sam, having been knighted towards the end of his career as a diplomat. I try to not to smile as I notice the pencil tucked into her dark blonde hair, or the specks of pale blue paint on her soft cheek. She may have removed her painting smock before dinner, but you don't have to be Sherlock Holmes to work out that my aunt is an artist. And a busy-body. In the nicest possible way.

"Okay… now I know you're up to something." I rest my hands on the table and glare at them.

"Well," my mother says, leaning forward, "we were just wondering if you'd made any plans for Christmas yet?"

"Plans?"

"Yes, dear," my aunt joins in. "You know… where you're going to be spending it; whether you'd thought about inviting Amelie over here for lunch, or anything?"

I shake my head. "No. No, I hadn't." It hadn't even occurred to me, actually, but now I come to think about it, I suppose it is something we should discuss. I don't really want to spend the day without her, but I'm sure we both have family commitments which are bound to get in the way. "I'll talk to her," I say, getting to my feet.

"Marvellous." My mother claps her hands together and I know she's already making plans of her own. God forbid.

"How was your first day back?" Amelie asks once I've released her from our first kiss of the evening. It won't be our last, I know that, and she leads me to the sofa where I sit in the corner, bringing her down with me, so she nestles against my chest, my arm tight around her.

"Tiring." I've told everyone else, including my mother, that the day went well, and I enjoyed being back, but with Amelie, I have to tell the absolute truth.

"You're alright though, aren't you?" She looks up at me and I lean down and kiss the tip of her nose.

"I'm fine, darling. It'll just take a bit of getting used to, that's all." We sit in silence for a few moments, listening to the crackling of the fire and our own harmonious breathing, before I remember my mother and Aunt Dotty's suggestion about Christmas, which I put to Amelie.

"Oh, I'd love to come and have lunch with you," she says, sounding a little sad, despite her words. "And it's very kind of your mother and Dotty to think of it, but how can I?" She moves, so she's lying along the length of the sofa, her head in my lap, looking up at me, while I stroke her hair. "It's only a couple of months since Beth died. I think my uncle and aunt will need me to be here, even if Uncle Gordon would probably rather be in London, with *her*." Amelie still hasn't grown used to the idea of her guardian's infidelity, which came to light when I was called in from Scotland Yard to investigate his daughter, Beth's, murder. Gordon Templeton's 'affair', as some people might term it, is in reality, a little more than that. During the week, while he's working at the War Office, he lives at his Westminster flat, which he shares with a young woman named Abigail Foster, who is only a few years older than Amelie herself. I'm not sure whether it's his duplicity, Miss Foster's age, or the nature of their relationship that makes it most difficult for Amelie to accept. In reality, it's probably the situation as a whole, but the fact that she and Beth grew up as sisters makes his deception so much harder to swallow, and she cannot bring herself to forgive him, or even to understand that having a wife who has confined herself to bed for more than half of their marriage has proved testing beyond words for the man. I'm not saying I approve of what he's done. I don't. But then it's not so personal for me.

"I doubt that very much, Amelie. Whatever you think of his actions, he does care about you."

"I know, but I still don't like it. I don't like what he's doing, Rufus, and I can't pretend otherwise." She moves a little closer to me, which is rather a relief, considering what happened when she discovered I was aware of her uncle's infidelity and hadn't told her about it – namely that she ended our fledgling relationship. Obviously, we worked things out again, and we did so quite quickly, I'm relieved to say, but I can still remember the utter emptiness and despair of that brief time without her.

"No-one says you have to like it," I reply, reasonably. "No-one says you have to pretend, or approve, or even discuss it with him, but you can't change it either."

She nestles closer still, which feels dangerously wonderful. "You're very fair-minded and grown-up, aren't you?"

I laugh and gaze down at her, her beautiful, innocent face a constant reminder of the fact that she is not yet twenty years old. "Well, that's not surprising, really. I am a great deal older than you."

She smiles and raises her arms, so they're around my neck, pulling herself up, so we're face to face and she's sitting on my lap. "Not that much older," she murmurs, our lips almost touching. "But old enough…"

"To know better?" I suggest and she shakes her head.

"To work out a compromise for what we should do on Christmas Day." She smirks and lets her forehead rest against mine.

I sigh into her and lean back slightly, cupping her face with my hand. "Why don't we agree to spend Christmas Eve together, being as it's a Sunday, and then perhaps we can arrange something for Christmas Day evening?"

"Wait a minute… I know," she says, suddenly brimming with enthusiasm. "Why don't we spend Christmas Eve together, as you suggested, and then you can all come over to us for tea on Christmas Day? That way we can still see each other for part of the day, I won't have to feel like I'm abandoning Uncle Gordon and Aunt Millicent, and no-one will feel left out, or offended."

"That sounds marvellous." I brush her cheek with my thumb. "See? I'm not the only one old enough to come up with useful compromises."

She grins and I lean forward, our lips touching as her sigh meets mine, in perfect harmony.

Chapter Two

My dearest Kitten,

I'm so pleased you managed to get here to see me today. I'd been on tenterhooks all morning, wondering if you'd be able to make up an excuse to leave the house, and when I saw you waiting for me, I don't know how I didn't burst with happiness.

We may have only had half an hour together, but it was a spectacular half an hour, wasn't it? And the best way to 'celebrate' that I can think of! I don't think it's ever been that good, my darling. You were wonderful, and fully deserved your little nickname. I think I shall always call you 'Kitten' from now on, just because I love to hear the noises you make. I have to admit, I hate the fact that we have to snatch our time together like this, but it does make it quite exciting and it gives us both something to look forward to when we're forced to be apart.

I'm reading your letter again now, sitting in the kitchen, because I didn't have time at breakfast, and only skimmed through it. I was so thrilled at the prospect of our meeting, I decided to save reading it properly until tonight, rather than risk being late for work and having to make up the time at lunch, which would have meant not being able to get back here to see you... what an awful thought!

Obviously, telephoning would be easier, especially as our arrangements tend to be quite last-minute – like today's – but I do understand your point of view. You have more to lose than I do, and I see the need to be cautious. The thing is, my love, that I miss the sound of your voice. I miss those naughty little things you say to me when we're together, but you're right, having those words in writing is almost as thrilling, and reading them back is extremely arousing. I wish you'd write to me more often like you did last week, and the week before that... you know? When you told me how it all felt from your perspective, without holding anything back. I treasure every word you write, obviously, but there's something about those letters that makes me come alive. I suppose it's the recollection of who you really are, and what you mean to me, and that's why, more than anything, I wish you could be here with me now, so I could remind you how good it really is. Because it is.

As for spending the night together . . . I'll give it some serious thought and try to come up with an excuse for you to stay away from the house. The prospect of having you in my bed for an entire night is a good enough incentive to put my mind to the task, I can promise you that.

I suppose I'd better get on and make my supper. And then I think I might take some of your old letters, and my memories to bed with me. I'll leave it to your imagination to work out what I'll be doing, because I know how creative you are, my purring little kitten.

Please write back soon and let me know when you think you'll be able to get away again. I know I only saw you today, but now the thought of your perfect, naked body is in my head, I honestly don't think I can wait too much longer to touch you again.

Missing you already,

D xx

———•———

As much as I'd hoped to visit Doctor Tierncy first thing this morning, it proved to be impossible. Fortunately, I decided to telephone the hospital before we left and was informed that he had appointments all morning, but would be free at twelve-fifteen. I let them know that Thompson and I would be there at that time to question him, and would be grateful if he'd make himself available. I didn't make it optional and I think they understood.

As a result of that, we spent the morning in my office, catching up with paperwork, and going over the evidence. We called Detective Constables Gilmore and Deakin in at one stage and they stood before my desk, nervous and on edge. I'd say they're both in their mid-twenties, with Gilmore being the taller and broader of the two. They both have brown hair, but while Deakin may be more diminutive, his piercing blue eyes make his features more noticeable and, I dare say, more appealing. Thompson set them the task of checking the whereabouts of known felons at the time in question, and then followed them out of my office, taking all the evidence with him to start organising it properly outside. I took the chance, meanwhile, to have a few minutes to myself, and sat back, contemplating how much I enjoyed myself last night with Amelie. I have to say, every time I'm with her is more delightful than the last; but it gets harder and harder to resist her. And I resolve that, as soon as I get the chance I'm going to go and see if any of the other jewellery shops in Kingston have anything to offer by way of engagement rings. Because I'm really not sure I can wait that much longer; and judging from the look in her eyes last night, I'm dubious that she can either.

Doctor Tierney is around fifty years old, wearing a smart grey suit, with salt and pepper hair, a square jaw and very dark brown eyes. By anyone's standards, he's an attractive man and I can easily imagine that he and his wife would make a striking couple.

"Inspector?" he stands as we enter the room and offers his hand, which I shake, and then remove my hat.

"Doctor Tierney. It's good of you to see us."

He indicates the chairs that are placed in front of his wide oak desk, and Thompson and I sit down. He copies us, and then stares at me.

"I'm a little confused," he says, his brow furrowing to emphasise the point. "I've already given my fingerprints to your colleague, and I wasn't at the house when the robbery took place, so…" His voice trails away to silence.

"Yes, sir. I just wanted to ask you about the telephone call you made to your wife."

"Telephone call?" He sounds really bewildered now and leans forward, resting his elbows on the desk in front of him.

"Yes. The one you made on Sunday informing her that you had an emergency at the hospital and wouldn't be able to make it home."

His face seems to pale. "What do you want to know?" he asks.

"Just whether anyone might have overheard you?"

"Overheard me? No, no. That would have been impossible. I was —" He stops speaking suddenly and this time, his cheeks flush bright red and I know Prentice was right; he's hiding something.

"You were what, sir?" He sits in silence, blinking a couple of times. "Where were you when you made the telephone call?" I press him.

"I—I was at the g—golf club." The words tumble out of his mouth, falling over themselves in the rush.

"Really? Your wife seemed to think you were at the hospital when you contacted her. She said you'd assessed the patient you'd been called in for, and then telephoned her." I stare at him and he closes his eyes, just for a second or two.

"Yes…" he says, opening them again. "Yes, I was here. I remember now."

I sigh and sit forward. "Shall we start again?" I suggest. "And this time, perhaps you could tell me the truth."

He goes to speak, to object to my indirectly calling him a liar, and then decides against it and lets his head fall into his hands. "Why did the burglary have to happen last night? Of all the times it could have happened, why last night?" He raises his head and looks at me, seemingly in despair.

"Where were you when you made the call?" I ask, yet again. "And more importantly, who were you with? You were clearly with someone."

His shoulders drop and he lets out a long sigh. "I can see you're not going to let the matter go," he says, "so I may as well admit it, even though it's got nothing to do with the burglaries… I was with Nurse Drummond."

"Nurse Drummond?" I prompt.

"Yes. Sandra."

"Can I assume that you and Nurse Drummond weren't working together on Sunday evening, and that you're… having some kind of relationship?" I ask.

He lets his eyes drop to the surface of his desk. "Yes," he whispers, and then looks up again. "She makes me feel alive again. Completely and utterly alive." His face lights up as he speaks, and he looks ten years younger. "Don't get me wrong," he continues, "there's nothing really wrong with Ruth, but after nearly thirty years of marriage, things do get a little stale…" He looks at me, as though he expects me to understand, but I don't, not in the slightest. The thought of spending the next thirty years with Amelie sounds like heaven to me.

"And Nurse Drummond was with you when you telephoned your wife?" I ask, getting back to the matter in hand.

"Well, not exactly. She was in the bathroom. I was in the bedroom."

"Of her house?"

"Her flat, yes." He sits back, clearly resigned to telling us the whole story. "It only started about six weeks ago," he says softly, a smile forming on his lips and a faraway look developing in his eyes. "I—I mean, we'd been aware of each other before that, and I'd admired her from afar, but... well, I am married, and she's quite young. I wasn't sure if I should..." His cheeks flush, but he continues, "Anyway, we had to work together on a very difficult case. It involved a young child and it looked like she might die, but we pulled her through. It was touch and go, though, and very stressful for everyone concerned. Later on that evening, Sandra came to give me an update on the girl's progress, and... well, before I knew what was happening, we were kissing and... and one thing led to another..." His voice fades and he runs his hands along the top of his desk, smiling to himself, his eyes sparkling. I don't think Thompson or I need him to explain any further what happened between them.

"We've been seeing each other ever since," Tierney continues. "We meet on Tuesday and Friday evenings in here." I glance quickly around the room. There's no sofa, not even an examining table, just the desk and the three chairs we're all currently occupying. *How romantic.* "I can usually stay behind for at least an hour, sometimes two, either by telling Ruth I have paperwork, or an emergency to deal with," he says. "And then Sandra and I also meet at her flat on Sundays."

"When you're supposed to be playing golf?" I suggest and he nods his head.

"What about the man you're meant to be playing with? Can you rely on him to cover for you?"

He smiles and waves his hand in the air dismissively. "Oh yes. We've known each other since medical school."

I find it hard not to shake my head in disapproval, but I'm not here to judge, in spite of the obvious provocation.

"Your wife told us that last Sunday night was the first time you've stayed away from home," I remind him.

"Yes, that's quite right," he replies, nodding his head. "I'd been with Sandra since mid-morning, and really it was time for me to leave. But she got upset about it and begged me to stay a little longer." His voice drops to a whisper and he leans forward. "She's very innocent, you see, very inexperienced." I stare at him for a moment, wishing I could find an excuse to arrest him… or just punch him. Either would suffice to wipe that self-satisfied smile off his face. "And I didn't want to leave myself, if I'm being honest, so while Sandra was in the bathroom, I telephoned Ruth and told her an emergency had come up at the hospital, that I'd been summoned from the golf course, and that I'd be here all night. You should have seen the smile on Sandra's face when I told her." He grins. "She was very grateful." I can just imagine.

"What if your wife had called you at work?" I ask, intrigued by his willingness to risk being caught.

"She rarely does that," he replies. "Especially when she knows I'm working on an emergency case. She knows I won't be able to take her call."

I suppose that explains why she telephoned her brother, rather than her husband, when their house was burgled.

He sits forward all of a sudden, his face much paler. "Will you need to tell her?" he asks. "My wife, I mean?"

"No, sir," I reply, although I rather wish I could find a reason to. His wife is sitting at home, extolling his virtues as a doctor, and praising him to the heavens as a husband, while he's using his office desk for wholly unprofessional purposes.

He sighs out his relief, and smiles. "Thank goodness for that."

"We only came to enquire, because we wondered if someone might have overheard your conversation about staying out all night, that's all. As it is, that's not possible."

"No," he replies, still beaming in the knowledge that he can continue his elicit relationship, without hindrance from either us, or his wife.

I get to my feet and Thompson follows suit, just as the door opens behind us and we turn around and see a very pretty, petite young nurse come in through the door.

"Leo," she says, then stops dead, blushing to the roots of her reddish-blonde hair, which is captured in a white cap atop her head. "Oh, I'm so sorry. I thought you said you'd be free now. I didn't realise…"

Doctor Tierney stands and comes quickly around his desk, going straight to her and taking her hands in his, kicking the door shut at the same time. "Don't worry, my dear. These men are from the police. They just came to talk to me about Sunday, but you don't have to worry, they're just leaving."

She glances up at him, fear crossing her eyes. "Sunday? You mean, they know?"

"Yes, but it's perfectly alright, they won't say anything."

She looks up at me and then Thompson, giving us both a smile. "We're not doing anything wrong," she whispers. "We're in love."

I think she honestly believes that, and I want to ask her if she actually thinks that being in love makes adultery acceptable, whether she doesn't sometimes think that Mrs Tierney might also love her husband, and consider the damage they might be doing to her, but I don't bother. They're too wrapped up in each other to even care about anyone else.

"Good day," I say with as little feeling as I can muster. "We won't need to trouble you again."

The couple step to one side, still holding hands, and Thompson and I move out into the corridor. He closes the door behind us and we both breathe out deeply, and then turn to our left and walk slowly towards the exit.

It's only once we're in the car and on our way back to the office that he speaks.

"Are you sure we can't find a reason to tell his wife?" he asks.

"Positive. I'm just as tempted as you, but it's nothing to do with us, or with the investigation. And we're not going to tell the chief super, either."

"Oh God… I'd forgotten about him."

"I hadn't." I sigh and look out of the window. "I don't want any of this in the notes."

He nods his head and we continue our drive in silence.

It's after two-thirty by the time I get back to my desk, and once I've removed my coat and hat, I go and sit down for a moment. I've met some reprobates in my time, but I think the good doctor ranks up there with the best of them. Of all the things he said to us, I think his boasting of Nurse Drummond's innocence and inexperience was perhaps the most shameful – especially given that he'd already explained the circumstances of their first sexual encounter, and I wonder for a moment whether that was how she'd imagined it might be – on a desk, in a darkened office, with a man old enough to be her father.

I wish I could pick up the telephone and speak to Amelie. I need to hear her voice, to tell her about that conversation and how it's made me feel, and to reassure myself that not everyone is disloyal. I suppose it doesn't help that my first attempt at entering into marriage ended disastrously, when my fiancée, Victoria, unilaterally decided that waiting until our wedding night to consummate our relationship wasn't all it was cut out to be. At the time, that was devastating, although with hindsight, she did us both a favour, because I've met Amelie, and I've never been happier. I know I'd never betray her, no matter what, but I could just really do with hearing her tell me that she'd never be unfaithful to me either, because I'm starting to doubt human nature at the moment.

"Sir?" I look up, the urgency in Sergeant Tooley's voice making the hairs on the back of my neck stand on end, as he comes into my office without knocking, followed by Thompson, who looks as confused as I feel.

"Yes?"

"We've just had a report come in over the telephone," Tooley says, clutching a piece of paper. "There's a little girl gone missing."

I get to my feet, my good hand resting on the table, leaning forward as Tooley approaches my desk, while Thompson takes a couple of strides and comes to stand beside him. "Where?" I ask.

"Long Ditton," Tooley says, handing me the piece of paper. "This is the parents' address, and the little girl was last seen in the recreation ground just down the road from there."

"How old is she?" I ask, looking down at the note in my hand. It says *'Mr and Mrs Sanderson, Treetops, St Mary's Road. Girl's name – Amy'*. I hand it to Thompson and he glances at it, then puts it in his pocket.

"Four, sir." Tooley's voice is strained.

"Four?" He nods. "What was she doing in the recreation park by herself?"

"She wasn't by herself. The nanny was with her."

"And she went missing?"

He shrugs. "That's what the woman said," he replies. "She was pretty upset though… not surprisingly."

"Okay…" I start to move around my desk. "Gather everyone together in the main office, Harry," I say to Thompson. "I'm just going to see the chief super. We're going to need all the help we can get."

He nods his head and we all exit my room.

Upstairs, Miss Parsons is at her desk, typing, when I enter. "Is the chief superintendent available?" I ask.

"He's got someone with him, I'm afraid. I can…" She reaches for her notepad.

"Sorry, but this is really urgent. Do you think you could interrupt him?"

She bites her bottom lip. "I'm not sure."

I lean over her desk, trying not to be intimidating, although I expect I probably am. "We've just had a report of a missing child come in," I explain and she pales and swallows. "I need authorisation for overtime, and to possibly call in some extra men from further afield, depending on how wide the search area ends up being."

She doesn't say a word, but stands up and goes over to the chief super's door, knocking once and entering. A few moments later, the man himself comes out, with Miss Parsons in tow. She closes his door behind her and sits back down at her desk, while Webster stands in front of me.

"What's happened?" he asks.

"I don't know that much yet, sir. All I've been told is that a four year old girl has gone missing." I glance out of the window. It may be only three o'clock, but because it's a dull, overcast day, it's already getting dark. "We'll need to mount a search for her, which will mean overtime and possibly using men from outside the area, being as we're so short-staffed."

He nods his head. "Do whatever you need to. I'll square it with the Chief Constable."

"I'm going to leave Stan Tooley in charge of things here, so he'll be coordinating the search teams," I tell him, "and Thompson and I will handle the family and the investigation."

"Investigation?" he queries. "You don't think she's just wandered off then?"

"I don't think anything at the moment, but we do know the family nanny was with her at the time, which seems a little strange to me. Until I can get a few more facts, I won't be able to say what we're dealing with. All I do know is it's getting dark, it's bloody cold, and she's only four years old."

He nods his head. "Go," he says and points to the door.

I don't hesitate, and walk quickly from the room and back down the stairs.

In the main office, things are surprisingly calm. Sergeant Tooley is over by one of the large noticeboards, pinning up a detailed map of the Long Ditton area, while it seems that every available man in the station is gathered around Sergeant Thompson. I go over to him, and they all fall silent, looking at me.

"We've been informed of a four year old girl, called Amy Sanderson, who has gone missing from a recreation ground in Long Ditton," I say, raising my voice just a little to ensure they can all hear me. "Sergeant Tooley is going to coordinate search parties, focusing on the area where she was last seen. We don't have much light left, so we need to start as soon as possible. Due to the blackout restrictions, once it gets dark, we won't be able to continue, so make the most of every moment you've got." A few of them nod their heads, one of two of them look at each other, their expressions grim. They all know that if we don't find her tonight, her chances of surviving in the freezing cold are minimal. "Sergeant Thompson and I are going to see the family, so that's where we'll be if anyone needs us."

With that, I take a step back, letting them know my speech – such as it was – is over. A general murmuring starts up and I pull Thompson to one side. "Phone Julia," I say to him. "God knows what time we'll get finished tonight. I'll see you outside in five minutes."

He nods his head and I return to my office, closing the door and sitting at my desk as I pick up the telephone. I'd planned to see Amelie tonight, and I really ought to let my mother and Aunt Dotty know that I won't be home, but only really have time for one call, and it's an easy decision.

"May I speak with Miss Cooper, please," I ask as soon as the operator has connected me.

"Oh, it's you, Inspector." Miss Higgins, the office manager's secretary at Hawker's Aviation recognises my voice now and I can hear the smile in hers.

"Yes."

"Just a moment," she replies, and there's a click on the line, followed by another, and then I hear Amelie.

"Rufus?"

"Yes, darling."

"What's wrong?"

I'd thought I had control of my emotions, but I suppose she knows me too well to be fooled.

"Something's come up at work," I explain and just for a second, I wonder how Mrs Tierney must feel every time her husband phones her, probably saying exactly the same thing. Still, I don't have time for that now. "A little girl has been reported missing, so I'm going to have to work late, and I won't be able to see you tonight. I'm sorry."

"Don't be," she says, sounding concerned. "But are you well enough for this, Rufus?"

"I'll be fine. I promise."

There's a moment's silence. "Please don't overdo it."

"I won't, darling. Now, can you do something for me?"

"Of course. Anything."

"Can you telephone my mother and let her know? I don't want her and Aunt Dotty to worry."

"I'll call them straight away," she says.

"Thank you. Make sure you tell them I'm perfectly well enough to handle this, won't you? I don't want them fussing."

"I will. Although I'm sure they'd rather hear from you themselves."

"I know, but I only had time to make one call, you see…"

"And you phoned me?" She sounds surprised.

"Of course I phoned you."

"Thank you," she murmurs.

"You don't have to thank me." I glance at the clock. "I'm sorry. I have to go."

"Take care of yourself, Rufus."

"I will, and I'll see you tomorrow."

"Alright. I love you." She whispers those last three words, presumably because there are other people in her office who can hear her.

"I love you too." I don't have to worry about being overheard, so I say it out loud.

The Sandersons live in St Mary's Road, in a large red brick house, well set back from the street, laid out over three floors, with twin gables, large bay windows at the front, and a central door, which is painted dark blue. At least, I think it's painted blue. By the time we arrive, it's so gloomy, it's rather difficult to tell.

"What does Mr Sanderson do for a living?" I ask Thompson, keeping my voice low as we approach the house.

"According to Stan Tooley, I think he owns a jewellers in Kingston."

I glance across at him and wonder if I'm about to come face to face with the man who sold me Amelie's necklace, and who failed to entice me into purchasing any of his rings.

"It clearly pays well," I remark, and am just reaching out for the brass door knocker, when another car pulls up into the driveway, parking alongside the black Wolseley Thompson and I used to get here. Turning, I see a man climb out, although I don't get to look at him properly, before he reaches back into the car, retrieves a briefcase, and then stands and slams the door shut loudly. He strides towards us, still not having looked up, and therefore starts when he finally does, and notices myself and Thompson standing in front of him. He may well be Mr Sanderson, but he is not the jeweller I met yesterday. He's significantly thinner and at least four inches too tall.

"Who are you?" he barks, looking up at me. "Get out of my way."

Thompson moves to his right and I to my left, allowing the man to gain access to the door, his hand delving into his pocket.

"I'm Detective Inspector Stone," I say, and the man turns to look at me.

"Oh." He seems embarrassed and pulls out a key, opening the door. "I suppose you'd better come in."

We follow him inside the house. It's unlit and almost impossible to see anything, and the man turns, putting down his briefcase, then makes a fuss of pulling the blackout curtain across the door, before switching on the light to reveal a wide, long hallway, with four doors leading off of it, and a stairway on the right hand side.

"I'm Daniel Sanderson," the man says, taking off his coat and hat, and depositing them on the end of the stairs. Now that I can see him clearly, I take in his receding dark hairline, and narrow moustache, his pale complexion and grey, rather sunken eyes. I would say he's around forty-five, or maybe a little older, but given the fact that he's probably just been told his daughter has gone missing, that's rather hard to tell. He doesn't offer his hand, and neither do I. "I assume you're here about my daughter?"

"Yes, sir."

"Why aren't you out looking for her?" he says, walking away while he speaks and heading towards the first door on the left of the hallway.

"We have other men doing that," I explain, removing my hat and holding it in my hand. "My sergeant and I have come to find out the circumstances of her disappearance."

He opens the door and turns to glare at me. "I would have thought that was of secondary importance to actually finding her," he says, gruffly.

"With respect, sir, we have done this before." I'm just about managing to keep my temper, but only because I know the man is almost certainly worried out of his wits.

He doesn't reply this time and enters the room. We follow, unbidden, and I glance at Thompson, who raises his eyebrows, but stays silent.

Inside, the room is nicely furnished, with two large sofas and two chairs, set in a square around the fireplace, together with a baby grand piano, which sits by the front window. The fire is alight, but otherwise there is no illumination, other than a single lamp, placed on a low table between the two chairs, facing the fireplace, in one of which there sits a woman, who has a white, lacy handkerchief clasped in her hands. As we enter, she turns, revealing herself to be not only extremely beautiful – in a rather classical way – but also *very* young. Her eyes lock on to Mr Sanderson, who ignores her and goes straight to an ornate, dark wood sideboard, where he takes the stopper from a decanter and pours himself a large whisky, half of which he downs in one gulp, before turning to face us properly.

"This is my wife, Lillian," he says, waving the glass in her vague direction.

She smiles, halfheartedly, and nods her auburn head in recognition.

"You are aware that it's getting dark, Inspector?" Sanderson's barking voice makes his wife jump.

"Yes, sir. As I said, we have men out looking for your daughter."

He glares at me once more. "And yet you thought it was more important to come here and question us… upsetting everyone… heh?"

I hear a sob coming from the chair and turn to see Mrs Sanderson raise the handkerchief to her face.

"See?" Sanderson says, although he doesn't go to his wife to comfort her. "See what you've done?"

"Just let them do their job, Daniel," she whimpers, and he flips his head around, his mouth opening as though to shout. But then he clearly remembers our presence, and changes his mind.

"Ask your damn questions," he says sulkily, topping up his glass and going to sit down on the end of one of the sofas – about as far away from his wife as he can possibly get.

I move a little further into the room, standing roughly between the two of them, while Thompson remains by the sideboard, his notebook in hand.

"Can you tell me what happened?" I ask, directing my question to Mrs Sanderson.

"Not really," she replies, looking up at me. "I had to go out at lunchtime," she explains. "When I got back, I had a dreadful headache and went to bed, and I only came down when I heard all the fuss."

"The fuss?"

"Yes. When Elizabeth came home and said Amy had gone missing. She was hysterical. Cook had to slap her to find out what had gone on, and then cook telephoned the police."

Mr Sanderson sits forward. "Is she alright?" he asks. "Elizabeth, I mean, not the cook."

"I have no idea," Mrs Sanderson replies, not bothering to turn her face to look at him.

"Can I assume Elizabeth is your nanny?" I enquire, before their conversation runs away with my questions.

"Yes," Mrs Sanderson says. "She's been with us for about ten months now."

"And none of this is her fault," Mr Sanderson puts in quickly. "You can rest assured of that. She's been wonderful with the children since the moment she arrived."

"I'm sure she has, sir. But I'm going to need to speak with her, nonetheless."

Mr Sanderson gets to his feet, as though he wants to argue with me and then thinks better of it and looks down at his wife. "Is she in the nursery, or her room?"

"I assume she's in the nursery," she replies a little vaguely. "Eve still needs to be taken care of."

"I'll take you up there," Mr Sanderson offers, being helpful for once.

"You don't need me to come up, do you?" Mrs Sanderson asks.

I don't actually need her husband to come with us, other than to show us the way, so I shake my head. "No, Mrs Sanderson. You rest here."

She smiles at me. "Thank you," she murmurs, closing her eyes. "My headache is really rather dreadful now."

As we leave the room, I'm struck by the fact that, while she seems upset, she's not perhaps as distraught or hysterical as I would have expected, given the circumstances, and I wonder if she's still in shock, and the reality of the situation will hit her later. I also wonder if she has anyone who will be able to help her through that, because based on their reactions to each other, I very much doubt her husband will be interested.

We climb up to the first floor and are going along the landing when Sanderson turns and says, "My wife gets a lot of headaches these days, you know?" in a rather man-to-man, knowing tone of voice.

I'm not entirely sure how to reply to him though, so I don't bother.

Up the next flight of stairs, we find the nursery door on our left. "It's in here," he says, opening it and stepping inside.

Thompson and I follow, and discover a fairly typical nursery, with a small child's bed on one side of the room, and a wooden cot on the other, a large chest of drawers between the two, and an armchair by the window. Standing by the chest of drawers, folding what appear to be baby's clothes, is a tall young woman. She has her back to us, but as we enter, she turns and I'm struck by the colour of her hair, which is black – jet black – and contrasts with the deep shade of red she's used to paint her rather full lips. She has unusually dark blue eyes and high cheekbones, and there's no denying her beauty, although to me it feels much more forced and artificial than that of the lady we've just left downstairs. The woman before us is wearing a tight-fitting pale blue dress, with an open neck and narrow belt, which highlights her tiny waist.

"This… is Elizabeth," Mr Sanderson says, as though she were a prize bloom at a flower show. The broad smile on his face, and the sparkle in his eyes reveal his true feelings – which I would say amount to a wish that the nanny might become something much more intimate than the woman who cares for his children. Whether she feels the same way, or not, remains to be seen.

"We'll manage from here," I say to him and he turns, scowling.

"I think I should remain," he replies.

"There's no need, Mr Sanderson." I step to one side and Thompson holds the door, making it clear he should leave.

"But she's one of my employees." He's digging his heels in. But so am I. I don't need the distraction of him fawning over the nanny while I'm trying to question her.

"I'm aware of that. However, your presence isn't required."

He stares at me for a moment longer, until it becomes obvious to him that I'm not going to back down, and then with a great show of reluctance, he leaves and Thompson closes the door softly behind him.

Before we've even had the chance to step further into the room, the nanny approaches.

"The baby's sleeping," she says, her voice lowered, although the sound of her master and myself talking hasn't woken the infant. "We can go to my room… if you don't mind, that is." She smiles in a rather provocative way, and I wonder how many times she's used that little trick to get her own way with the opposite sex.

"If that suits you," I reply, and she leads us from the room and back onto the landing.

I'd half expected to find Mr Sanderson loitering outside, but the corridor is empty and the nanny leads us to the right, and opens the next door along, switching on the light as she enters.

Her room is smaller than the nursery, featuring a single bed, a wing-backed armchair, a large walnut wardrobe and matching chest of drawers, with a mirror mounted on top.

Going over to the bed, she sits down, and looks up at me, her eyes widened.

"May I ask your full name?" I enquire, getting straight to the point.

"Elizabeth Sutton," she responds, leaning back and resting on her hands, in such a way that her very ample bosom is pushed forward and shown to its best advantage – a fact of which I have no doubt she is perfectly well aware.

"Miss Sutton…" I wander over to the curtained window and sit in the armchair, looking across at her. "… can you tell me what happened today?"

She blinks a few times, rather rapidly. "It was dreadful," she whispers. "I—I'd been given permission to go out Christmas shopping at lunchtime," she says, regaining her voice. "And when I got back, Amy was a bit fed up with having to stay indoors…"

"What time was this?" I interrupt.

"After one," she muses, thinking. "And before half past." I nod my head, indicating she should continue with her story. "Being as Amy had already had lunch with cook, I put Eve into the pram, and we went for a walk to the park…"

"Which park?"

"The one just down the road." She points out of the window. "Under the railway bridge. We used to go to the one further away in Ewell Road, but they're digging it up now to plant potatoes, or something. Amy liked it better at that park, because there are swings, but with the workmen being there, she's had to settle for the smaller one of late, I'm afraid." I nod my head and she continues, "We'd been there for a little while, when something went wrong with the wheel of the pram."

"What exactly?" I ask.

"I'm not sure," she replies. "It got stuck and wouldn't turn properly, like there was something caught. I crouched down to see… to try and release it, and… and…" She starts to sob. "Oh God… They're going to blame me, aren't they?"

"No-one is blaming anybody, Miss Sutton. I just need you to tell me what happened."

"Well," she sniffles, "it took me a few minutes to get the wheel to work again. I twisted it this way and that, and checked to see if a stone had become lodged, or if there was a twig stuck in it…"

"And where was Amy while you were doing this?" I ask her.

"She was running around on the grass."

"I see."

"And then, when I stood up again, Eve was fretting, because her mitten had come off, and I couldn't find it for a minute, and had to tend to her, and then when I turned around to call Amy, she wasn't there."

"So how long would you say it was between the time when you bent down to look at the wheel, and the time when you noticed Amy had gone?" I ask.

"Five minutes," she replies. "Maybe just a little longer."

"Is she normally a well behaved girl?" I enquire. "Do you think she'd have run off somewhere? Perhaps decided to hide… to play a trick?"

She shakes her head slowly. "She'd never do something like that," she says softly. "Amy was a lovely girl. She could be a little bit tiresome when she was bored, or tired, but that's normal for children of her age."

I take her word for it, being none the wiser.

"Did you notice anyone else in the park at the time?"

"Th—There was a man," she replies, stammering, perhaps a little hesitant in her reply. "He was there when we first arrived, although I can't say I noticed him later on."

"Can you describe him?"

"He was standing some way off," she says.

"Even so, you must have noticed whether he was tall or short?"

"Tall," she replies, quickly.

"As tall as me?"

"No. Not that tall, but still tall."

"Fat or thin?"

"Thin, but not skinny, if you know what I mean."

"Was he wearing a hat?" I ask.

"Yes, like yours." I glance down at my fedora. "But I'd have said it was black, not blue. And he had on a dark coat… grey, I think, with the collar turned up."

"I don't suppose you managed to notice if he had a moustache, or glasses?"

"No," she replies, thinking before she answers.

"And you didn't recognise him at all? You hadn't seen him at the park before, perhaps?"

There's a moment's hesitation before she shakes her head.

I'm intrigued by that, but suddenly there's a noise from the room next door, which starts as a plaintive whimper and quickly develops into a full-scale cry.

"I'm sorry," Miss Sutton says, getting to her feet. "I'm afraid I have to go and see to Eve."

"Just before you do, can you describe what Amy was wearing?"

The crying grows louder, but Miss Sutton remains focused on me for a moment longer. "Yes," she says, quite calmly now. "She had on a red dress, a pale blue coat and matching hat, and black shoes."

"Thank you." I nod towards the door, dismissing her and she smiles, then straightens her dress, making a point of running her hands down her skirt and wiggling her hips a little more than is necessary, before leaving the room.

Thompson sidles over and stands beside me.

"I pity the poor man who ever falls for her," he whispers and I glance up at him before getting to my feet.

"I doubt she'll be monogamous, if that's what you mean."

He shakes his head. "No, it wasn't, actually. I think she's a tease. All promise and no delivery; I think Mr Sanderson can dream, but that the most he'll ever get from her is his own fantasies."

"You think?" I shake my head.

"You don't?" he queries.

"No. If I'm being honest, I think precisely the opposite. I think she'd more than deliver and any man who fell for her would be lucky to survive."

"Well, that just shows what you know about women," he chuckles, moving towards the door and holding it open for me.

"We'll see," I muse, smiling as I pass him and go out onto the landing.

Downstairs, we find Mrs Sanderson still sitting in the drawing room, her husband standing by the fireplace, his glass in hand. He turns as we enter and takes a step towards us.

"How is she?" he asks.

"Miss Sutton?" I ask, checking that he means the nanny. He nods his head. "She's fine." I notice again how solicitous he seems for the nanny's welfare, considering he's shown no interest in his wife. But then I suppose I have no idea what's been going on between the two of them in our absence. For all I know, they may have been locked in an intimate embrace until they heard our approach, and I wonder if maybe I'm being a little cynical. Perhaps the situation with Doctor Tierney is rubbing off on me. Actually, there's no 'perhaps' about it.

"It's clear your daughter went missing in the park, or recreation ground," I explain, remaining by the sideboard, with Thompson next to me. "And that's where our search teams are focusing their efforts."

"You think she just wandered off?" Mrs Sanderson looks up from her chair.

"We can't be sure of anything at the moment."

"Nothing Amy did would surprise me. She was always difficult… right from the moment she was born," she muses, to herself, then seems to come to her senses, blushing, and then turns to her husband, who ignores her. I decide to do likewise. For now, at least.

"Your nanny said there was a man in the park when they first arrived. She said he was tall, and thin, wearing a black fedora and grey coat with the collar turned up."

"Well, that probably describes almost every man in the country," Sanderson replies sarcastically.

"I—I need to lie down," his wife says suddenly, getting to her feet a little shakily. "I—I can't be here."

The shock of it seems to have hit her all of a sudden, as I expected, and as she crosses the room towards us, I take in her pallor, the fact that even her lips have whitened, and her green eyes are duller by comparison with how they were when we arrived a short while ago.

Thompson steps to one side and opens the door, letting her out, without anyone saying another word.

Once she's gone, I turn back to her husband. "Can we have a recent photograph of your daughter?" I ask him.

He hesitates for a moment, looking at the closed door, with a worried expression on his face, which makes me feel guilty for having had so many doubts about him, and then goes over to the piano, picking up a small frame and bringing it to me.

"That's the most recent," he mumbles.

I glance down and see a cheeky smiling face looking back at me, with rounded cheeks and a smattering of freckles. Her hair is tied up in bunches at the sides of her head, but the photograph is black-and-white, so her colouring is difficult to ascertain.

"Is her hair red?" I ask.

"Yes, like her mother's," Mr Sanderson replies.

I turn to Thompson. "Go back to the station and give this to Tooley, will you? Give him the description of the girl's clothing as well, and make sure it gets circulated around."

He nods his head and leaves.

"Now, Mr Sanderson," I say, turning back to him. "I need to speak with your cook."

"My cook?" He sounds surprised.

"Yes."

"Why, may I ask?"

I sigh, wishing the man didn't see fit to question my every move. "Because when your nanny came home with the baby, she was hysterical. When people are in that condition, they tend to say and do things that they later forget. The people around them quite often remember, however. And just to be on the safe side, I'd like to ask your cook exactly what happened when Miss Sutton returned home."

He nods his head slowly and walks across the room, looking even older now; the contrast between himself and his young wife even more marked in my eyes.

"It's this way," he says and opens the door, taking me out into the hallway and towards the back of the house. He pushes open a swing door and stands aside.

"In here?" He's obviously got no intention of making the introductions this time, and after he's nodded his affirmation, I walk inside and wait for the door to swing closed behind me.

I find myself in a sizeable kitchen, with the latest appliances, a shiny linoleum floor and a large table in the centre. What's lacking, however, is a cook – or any other staff, for that matter.

"Hello?" I call.

"Just a minute," comes a reply from behind the door in the corner, and sure enough, within a lot less time than that, the door opens, and a middle-aged woman comes out. She's plump, with grey-brown hair and a kindly rounded face, which is currently smiling at me. "I'm sorry," she says, "I was just getting the sugar from the larder." She's carrying a large container in her arms, which she places on the table in front of her. "How can I help?" she asks.

"I'm Detective Inspector Stone." I introduce myself. "I'm here to ask about what happened this afternoon."

She shakes her head. "Bad business," she murmurs. "Very bad indeed." She pulls out a chair and nods towards it. "I'm Doreen Slater, the cook. I've just made a pot of tea. Take a seat and I'll pour you a cup."

She's the most welcoming and friendly person I've encountered since entering this house and I take her up on her offer, placing my hat on the table to one side.

She makes herself busy with cups and saucers, a sugar bowl and milk jug, and then settles a tea pot between us, before sitting down opposite me. "What can I do to help?" she enquires.

"Can you tell me what happened when Miss Sutton came home this afternoon?"

She nods her head. "There was all kinds of fuss," she says. "I heard the front door slam, which was odd in itself, because when she's gone out with the pram, she normally uses the back door... but, anyway, she was ranting and screaming, and I ran out to see what was going on. Lois followed..."

"Who's Lois?" I ask, interrupting her.

"She's the maid," she replies.

"Is she here now?"

"Yes. She's upstairs. The mistress rang just a minute or two before you came in here."

I nod my head. "I see. You were telling me about earlier?"

She starts pouring the tea and continues, "Yes... we went out into the hallway and there she was – Miss Sutton, that is – wringing her hands, and crying, wailing about how Amy had run off, and she didn't know what to do. She was getting more and more worked up. And then the mistress came downstairs, and that set Miss Sutton off even worse, which woke the baby, who started crying, so I stepped over and slapped her... Miss Sutton, that is, not the baby." She smiles, just slightly and adds milk to the tea, pushing the cup towards me. "Help yourself to sugar."

"I don't, thank you."

She nods and takes a quick sip from her own cup. "Once we'd established that Amy really was gone, I telephoned the police." She stops talking and looks down at the table. "I probably wasn't as coherent as I might have been," she says, "but there was such a to-do going on, it was hard to think straight, let alone answer the man's questions."

"Don't worry about that. I—"

I'm interrupted by the opening of the kitchen door, and the arrival of a woman dressed in a maid's outfit, of a dark grey dress, with a white apron tied at the waist. She looks about fifty years old, with dark blonde hair, turning grey in places, which is unwilling to be tamed by the hat that's perched on her head. "She's in pieces up there," she says, studying her bitten fingernails. "Pour me a cup out of that pot, will you, Doreen, and I'll take it up to her." She stops in her tracks, noticing me at last. "Oh, I'm sorry. I didn't see you there."

"This is an inspector... from the police," the cook says, with deference.

"Oh. Did you need to speak with me?" the maid asks.

"No, not at present."

She sighs. "That's good." I smile and she half laughs. "I haven't done anything wrong, you understand, it's just that the mistress wants a bath, and I don't really feel like I can leave her up there by herself. Not at the moment. I'm not a lady's maid, so it's not really my job to tend to her, but in the circumstances..."

"I understand."

The cook hands her a cup of tea and, with a nod of her head in my direction, she departs again.

"I take it that was Lois?" I say, turning to the cook.

"She's got a good heart," she replies, rolling her eyes. "Even if her cleaning can be a bit slapdash." She takes another sip from her teacup and I do likewise. "What were you going to ask?" she says.

"I was wondering if Miss Sutton had mentioned seeing anyone, or if she'd said anything out of the ordinary had happened?"

"No." She shakes her head. "No, she just said Amy had gone missing, that she'd looked for her and couldn't find her, and then had rushed home, hoping the child would have found her own way back here… which she hadn't, obviously."

I nod my head. "And would you say Amy is the sort of child who would just wander off?" I know I've asked the nanny this, and she refuted the idea, and that she's more likely to know the child, much better than anyone else in all probability, but it does no harm to get a different perspective.

"I think it's exactly the sort of thing that little monster would do," she replies, with considerable feeling.

I stare across at her, recalling Mrs Sanderson's outburst a few minutes ago, which I'd originally put down to her distress. Perhaps I was wrong… "Would you care to elaborate?"

She sits forward in her seat, clutching her teacup in her hands. "I know I probably shouldn't say this, given the circumstances, but that little girl is just about the most wilful, rude, disobedient creature I've ever come across. Lois and I had to give her lunch today, because Miss Sutton had asked permission to go Christmas shopping… and although she was only gone for an hour, it took me nearly twice that length of time to clear up the mess that little tike left in my kitchen." She places her hand flat on the surface of the table. "Do you know… at lunch today, she actually poured custard all over the table, when my back was turned," she muses. "There's the government sending out leaflets, telling us to be careful about wasting food, and she's tipping custard all over the place. I can't tell you how relieved we were when Miss Sutton came back and took them both out."

"And is that normal behaviour for her?" I ask. "The child, I mean?"

"Well, not the custard, perhaps," she says. "But the naughtiness, yes. Whenever Miss Sutton has an afternoon off, or is even out for just an hour or so, Lois is left holding the fort, as it were, and Amy runs her ragged."

This description, while similar to that given by Mrs Sanderson, is very much at odds with Miss Sutton's praise of her charge and has me much more intrigued than I was before.

"I understand Miss Sutton has been here for less than a year?" I say, starting to dig a little deeper.

"Yes. Before her, the master insisted that his old nanny was more than capable of looking after the children, and I think she probably was, while there was just Amy. But when the baby came along it all got a bit too much for her, having to deal with both of them, especially with Amy being as naughty as she can be. Anyway, one day she nearly dropped Eve, when she was about a month old, right in front of both the master and the mistress. He advertised for a new nanny straight away, and took on Miss Sutton just a few days later." She gives me a look and a very slight nod of her head.

"Is it usual for the master of a house to hire the nanny?" I ask, knowing perfectly well that it isn't.

"No," she replies, bridling a little. "But at the time, the mistress was… indisposed."

"She was unwell?"

Mrs Slater pauses, then leans even further forward. "I wouldn't say 'unwell' as such," she whispers. "But after Amy was born, she became very withdrawn. To be honest, I never thought they were that well suited… the master and the mistress, that is. I was quite surprised when Mr Sanderson brought her home and announced he was going to marry her, but she's very beautiful and it was easy to see the attraction – at least from his side, anyway." She smiles. "And I suppose they were quite contented to start with," she says, getting into her stride now. "And then the mistress fell pregnant within just a month or so of the wedding. The pregnancy was very difficult, though, and she had to move into the bedroom at the front of the house – where she is now. Then after Amy was born, as I say, she… well, she kind of went into a shell, I suppose. She barely spoke, and never went out. And it carried on that way for years."

"But they had another child?"

She nods her head. "Yes. And for a while everything carried on as ever it had been, with her barely saying two words to anyone, from one day to the next, and him moaning at her to make more of an effort. But then all of a sudden, about six months or so ago, the mistress changed."

"How?" I ask.

"Well, she just came out of herself. She started taking an interest in things again, and even went out – all by herself, and everything."

"Do you know what brought about that change?" I ask. She falls silent and sits back in her chair.

Her eyes shoot up to mine. "You can't say I told you," she murmurs.

"I won't."

She nods her head. "Well, I think she started seeing someone," she says. "We all do, actually."

"All the staff, you mean?" I assume she's not referring to Mr Sanderson.

"Yes. It came up just this afternoon actually, when Miss Sutton came back from her shopping trip, before she took the children out. She was a few minutes later than expected and was worried the mistress would be cross, but I told her Mrs Sanderson wasn't back herself yet, and Miss Sutton gave me a knowing look. Lois, not being known for her tact, asked outright if we thought she was with Mr Cooke, and I had to tell her not to talk about it – not in front of the child, anyway…"

"Mr Cooke?" I query, picking up on the name.

"Yes. His name's David Cooke and he's an old family friend – except he's not that old. He's only in his late twenties, I think, so not more than four or five years older than the mistress. But his family has known the master's family for years. I remember him coming here as a boy, many years ago now…" Her voice fades.

"Can you describe him?" I ask.

"He's tall," she says. "With dark hair, a slim build… and he's very handsome. Always dresses very smartly."

"Has he been to the house recently?"

"Not for a while now," she says.

"Would you say, not since before their affair started?"

She tips her head to one side. "If it is an affair, yes. But then I suppose it would be awkward for him to keep coming here, if they were…" She stops talking and two tiny dots of red appear on her cheeks.

I'm tempted to say that, after the last few days, nothing would surprise me, but I just smile instead.

"Of course, I might be wrong," she adds quickly.

"But you don't think you are, do you?"

She hesitates, and then shakes her head slowly. "No, I don't."

Thompson is waiting outside the house, having just arrived back. He's talking to a uniformed PC, standing off to one side. I recognise him as PC Adams, who came and helped dig up my aunt's garden, when I found myself incapacitated.

"Tooley's giving the men a bit longer," Thompson says as I approach, looking up into the gloomy skies. "Then he's going to call it off for tonight."

"We'll head back to the station," I tell him, then turn to Adams. "Stay here. I'll make sure someone is sent over to relieve you later on."

He nods his head and goes to stand nearer to the front door, as Thompson and I climb into the car.

"You missed all the excitement," I point out as he starts the engine.

"Oh yes?"

"I had a long and fruitful chat with the Cook, a Mrs Doreen Slater."

"And?"

"And it seems Mrs Sanderson is having an affair."

"Is she now? Any idea who with?"

"Yes. A man by the name of David Cooke. We're going to have to try and track him down."

He stares at me. "David Cooke?" he repeats. "Is that a joke? It's hardly the most unusual of names, is it?"

"Even so…"

"I'll do my best," he huffs, and engages reverse, pulling out of the driveway.

"Did you notice the other point of interest?" I ask.

He glances at me. "You mean there was only one?"

I smile, shaking my head. "Well, one that stuck out, yes."

"Which was?"

"The fact that both Mrs Sanderson and the nanny talked about Amy in the past tense."

"They did? I didn't notice."

"I did." I gaze out of the windscreen. "It might not mean anything. It could be a slip of the tongue..."

"Or it could be really quite significant."

"It could..."

We drive in silence for a while, as I try not to read too much into the actions and words of people who are clearly in shock, and aren't behaving like themselves, and then I turn to him again.

"Can you speak to Gilmore and Deakin when we get back?"

"They're not at the station," he replies. "They're out with the search parties."

"Damn... Okay, tomorrow morning will have to do."

"What am I speaking to them about?" he asks.

"Someone's going to have to take over the investigation into these burglaries," I explain. "I need you working on this case with me, so they're just going to have to manage by themselves. Tell them they're to report anything to me, or to you, if they can't get hold of me."

"Understood."

Chapter Three

My Darling,

This is just so awful. I don't even know where to start, although I suppose that by the time you read this, you'll probably have heard about it on the wireless, or read about it in the newspapers anyway.

But just in case you haven't… dearest little Amy is missing.

I'm absolutely devastated. The house was simply crawling with policemen earlier, although they've gone now, and there's just one left at the door. What he's there for, I'm not sure, but I feel as though everyone's looking at me all the time, judging how I behave, what I do and how I look. 'His lordship' came home early from work – which is understandable – but he's watching me more than anyone else, and it just makes my skin crawl.

I wish I could be with you. I know it's wrong at a time like this to be thinking of myself, and of you, but I can't help it. I think about you all the time, and wish you could be here to make this all seem so much less hideous. I need to feel the reassurance of you, my love, to feel the strength of your body and the comfort of your words. I'd love to be able to write you longer and more detailed letters, just as you asked, so I could remind both of us how much we're meant to be together and what we're missing out on, but I can't. Not right now. It's simply too hard. I'm sorry, but my mind is all over the place with worry. Please forgive me and please don't forget that I love you.

I miss you, my darling,

Your beloved,

Kitten x

The search was called off at just after five last night, but we all stayed on, continuing with enquiries and following up on the few leads we had, because it felt wrong to go home when we hadn't found the girl. But at two in the morning, I decided that some sleep was necessary, and dismissed everyone, in a cloud of disappointment.

Thompson took me home, concerned that I was overdoing it so soon after my release from hospital. I told him the same as I told Amelie... I'm tired, but I'm okay. I think he believed me. He certainly didn't argue, and then he informed me that he'd found at least thirteen David Cookes in our area and would continue looking in the morning, before starting the laborious process of interviewing and eliminating them. Feeling deflated that there were so many, I told him not to bother, and that we'd find a way to get the information directly from Mrs Sanderson instead.

I spent the rest of the journey trying not to think about Amy's fate, although I failed dismally, and I imagined Thompson, and every other officer at the station, was just as haunted as I. I kept thinking that, if Amy had run off by herself, then the chances were she'd struggle to survive in the freezing overnight temperatures. But then, if this stranger had taken her – whether it was David Cooke or not – then she was probably no better off. He may have already killed her, or she could still be alive, but facing untold dangers at his hands. None of the scenarios bore thinking about, but as we drove home in the still silence of the early morning, I knew, without a doubt, that I wasn't alone in my thoughts and I imagined that those men who'd been working late with us, who have children themselves, would be making sure to check on them before getting into bed.

This morning, we drive straight to the London Road station. Thompson is under instructions to brief Gilmore and Deakin, on the strict premise that, while they obviously have to know of the doctor's movements on the night his house was burgled, they're to keep that information to themselves. Meanwhile, I need to speak with the chief superintendent, and then we'll head over to Long Ditton, where the search parties will have already started work again, even though it's barely light.

I leave Thompson running through the burglary files with the two DCs and make my way upstairs. Miss Parsons isn't at her desk, but then it is only seven-fifteen in the morning. The chief super's office door is open, however, and I go over and tap gently on the frame, poking my head around and discovering him at his desk.

"Come in, Stone," he says. "I got in early myself. Couldn't sleep."

"I know the feeling, sir." I've probably managed an hour, maybe two, of very fitful rest, my thoughts plagued by the idea of that child, freezing cold somewhere, and by the knowledge that someone in that house knows more than they're telling. I'm sure of it. I just can't work out who, or what... or why.

"Any news?" he asks.

"No, sir. Nothing. I've actually come to see you about something else."

"Oh yes?" He leans forward, clasping his hands together on the desk.

"These burglaries... I haven't forgotten them, but obviously I'm sure you appreciate that the missing girl takes priority."

"Naturally." He nods his head.

"Sergeant Thompson is briefing DCs Deakin and Gilmore at the moment, and they'll be taking over the investigation into what happened at your sister's house, and the other properties," I explain. "They'll report to me, and I'll keep you abreast of any developments."

He nods again. "Thank you, Stone. I appreciate that."

I wonder for a moment if he thought I was going to let the burglaries slide altogether. But then, he doesn't know me.

"And now, we've got to go back over to Long Ditton," I add, backing out of the room as I speak.

"Well, let me know how it goes," he says, waving me away.

Downstairs, Thompson is still talking to the two young officers, their heads close together, leaning over a table in the main office. I walk straight past them and go into my own room, closing the door gently behind me and sitting down at my desk, before picking up the telephone.

I know Amelie will be awake, and that she won't be leaving for work just yet, so I ask the operator to connect me to her number, barely disguising my surprise when it's Amelie herself who answers.

"Hello, I didn't expect to hear your voice," I say.

"Then why did you call me?" she replies and I have to smile.

"What I meant was, I didn't expect you to answer the phone."

"Well, given that it's only twenty-five past seven in the morning, I rather assumed it would either be you or Uncle Gordon telephoning. And I answered because I hoped it would be you." I can hear the smile in her voice now. "Are you alright?" she asks, her concern obvious.

"No." I run my finger along the edge of my desk, feeling the emotion rising in my chest.

"What's wrong?" she asks. "What's happened?" She sounds afraid.

"It's nothing to do with me," I reply quickly, to allay her fears. "At least, not in the way you think. It's just this case…"

"Do you want to talk about it?" she offers.

"I wish I had the time, but I've got to go out again in a minute. I just wanted to hear your voice, that's all."

"Well, that's nice to know." She pauses. "Can I assume you haven't found the little girl?"

"You can."

"Oh. But it was freezing last night, Rufus," she whispers.

"Yes. Although we're not sure whether she ran off, or whether she was taken. A man was spotted near the place she was last seen."

"Oh God…"

"I know." I don't want to voice my worst imaginings, not until I have to. "I'm afraid a case like this means very long hours, my darling." I change the subject slightly, aware that I need to let her know how hard it's going to be in the coming days.

"I understand."

"And that means I might not be able to see you for a while."

"Just take care of yourself, and remember… I'm here, if you need to talk."

I smile my gratitude, because that emotion that was in my chest is bubbling up again. "Well, I doubt you'll want to hear from me at two in the morning."

"Is that when you finished last night?"

"Yes."

"You must be exhausted," she murmurs, then adds, "But I don't mind. If that's when you need to talk, just call me earlier in the evening, if you can, and I'll wait up for you."

"Until two in the morning? I don't think so."

"If that's what you need Rufus, then I'll do it." Her voice is firm, bordering on bossy, and it brings a broad smile to my face. "Do you remember saying you didn't like the idea of me crying by myself, and that you'd come to me if I needed you, no matter what the time was?"

"Yes, of course I do." It was a conversation we had when I was still in the hospital and I'd learned that she'd cried herself to sleep the night I'd been stabbed.

"Well, it works both ways," she says. "If you need me, then I'm here for you, and the time of day – or night – is irrelevant."

I can't argue with that, so I give in gracefully. "Thank you."

"You don't have to thank me," she says.

"Then what do I have to do?"

"Take care of yourself," she replies. "And remember to give me a kiss the next time you see me."

"That won't be hard at all. It already feels like forever since I've kissed you."

"I love you, Rufus."

"I love you too, darling."

We end our call, although I wish we didn't have to. I wish we could just go on talking and I could forget the horrible day that lies ahead.

"Ready?" Thompson knocks on my door and enters at the same time, reminding me that my time is not my own, any more than it's Amelie's.

"Yes." I get up from my desk and follow him back out into the main office. Tooley is standing in front of the wall, staring at the map of Long Ditton and doesn't even notice us passing through, and Deakin and

Gilmore are putting on their coats and hats, clearly intent on following up on something.

"Are those two okay?" I ask Thompson as we make our way down the stairs.

"They'll be fine," he says. "They know to report anything they find to you – or me – and they understand the importance of the case, being as the chief super's sister is one of the victims."

"And you stressed the need for discretion?"

"I made a point of it," he says, opening the car door. "Where to?" he asks.

"As it's still quite early, I want to go and take a quick look at this park, before we go to the Sanderson house. There's something nagging at my brain and I need to see the lie of the land for myself."

Thompson pulls up behind a police van and we both get out, walking along the pavement to the gated entrance of the recreation ground. There's a pathway running around the edge, but other than that, it's really just a patch of grass, with a fence around the perimeter and a few bushes dotted along either side, which is currently overrun with police officers.

"As I thought," I murmur, standing to one side.

"What?" Thompson says, surveying the view.

"She's not here."

He rolls his eyes. "You don't know that yet. That's why we're searching."

I turn to face him. "Look around." I wave my working arm in the vague direction of the park, then wince and quickly lower my arm again, as my wound stretches and pulls for the first time in days. I wish I hadn't done that.

"Are you alright?" Thompson asks.

"I'm fine" I look at him. "Thanks."

He nods his head. "What did you mean?"

"Other than those bushes, there's nowhere to hide, and nowhere to be hidden." I nod in the direction of the park this time, keeping my arms still. "This place was searched for nearly two hours yesterday, without a trace of the girl being found. Nothing's going to change today… she's not here," I reiterate.

He follows my gaze, before looking back at me. "Then where is she?" he asks. "Does this mean she was definitely taken?"

"How the hell do I know?" I shake my head even as the words leave my mouth. "Sorry, Harry. I'm tired and fed up, and my side hurts now."

"Do you want me to take you back to the station?" he offers.

"What do you think?"

"I think you'd probably walk over hot coals before you'd admit defeat," he says.

"Something like that, yes." I take a deep breath. "Find out who's in charge here, will you?"

He wanders off, returning a few minutes later with a constable in tow. I recognise him straight away as PC Wells. He's hard to miss, being the size he is.

"Wells," I say in greeting.

"Inspector." He nods.

"This is a waste of time. If she was taken, she won't be here anymore, and if she ran away, then there's nowhere here for her to hide."

"No, sir. I was coming to that conclusion myself, but we were ordered to continue…" His voice trails off and he stares at the space between us, clearly not wanting to get anyone into trouble.

"Well, spending any more time here is pointless. We need to broaden the search. The nanny told us yesterday that there's another park around here?"

He nods. "Yes, sir. It's just down the road." He points over my shoulder.

"Evidently it's being dug up for planting potatoes, but the little girl used to like it. The thing is, if she'd made it to that park, I imagine the workmen would have seen her and probably raised the alarm, so I can't see the point in searching there, but I suppose it's possible that she might have tried to at least make her way there by herself. The cook told me she was a rather wilful child."

"So where do you want us to look, sir?" he asks, confused.

I lead the way back out through the gate and we all stand in the road. "It seems to me that there are several streets, and probably hundreds of houses between here and this other park."

"There are," Wells confirms.

"And it's a long way away, really — if you're only four years old. In which case, she could be anywhere between here and there." I hear Thompson let out a long, slow sigh as I think he anticipates what I'm about to say. Even so, I say it anyway: "We're going to need to carry out house-to-house searches. Thorough ones."

"Yes, sir." Wells looks over my shoulder at the streets stretching into the distance, lined with properties, and his shoulders drop.

"I'll get Sergeant Tooley to come over. He'll be of more use coordinating things from here than at the station, and I'll speak to the chief super. We're going to need a lot more men than we've got now." I look up at Wells again. "In the meantime, gather everyone together and divide them up into teams of two men, then await Sergeant Tooley's arrival."

Wells nods and moves away, summoning another constable with a shout and a wave of his arm. Between them, they start to round up the men who are currently searching the park, while Thompson and I return to the car.

"This whole case is starting to feel very odd," I say, as I get in and close the door.

"In what way?"

He starts the engine and pulls away from the kerb, and although we only have a short drive up the road, he takes it slowly so we can talk.

"Someone in the Sanderson house is definitely hiding something."

"Who?"

"That's just it… I don't know. But I've got this feeling that we're not being told everything. The thought kept me awake last night."

"It certainly seems like a house of secrets and lies," he says quietly.

"Deception." He glances at me quizzically. "There's a lot of deception going on."

"You mean the affair between Mrs Sanderson and Daniel Cooke."

"Yes, but also the fact that Mr Sanderson appears to be enamoured with Miss Sutton."

"*Appears* to be?" he repeats. "You mean you don't believe it?"

"I'm not sure. I just felt like there was something a bit forced about it… like maybe he was putting it on to make his wife jealous."

Thompson huffs out a half laugh. "Well, it's not working," he replies, and pulls into the Sanderson's driveway, parking alongside the owner's car.

"I'm surprised he's still here," I remark. "I'd half expected him to take himself off to work today."

"Well, I suppose he has to keep up appearances," Thompson replies, and then bites his lip. "Or perhaps that's being uncharitable. His child is missing, after all."

"Yes, but all he was really interested in when we arrived yesterday was throwing his weight around and flirting with the nanny." I can't keep the irritation out of my voice and Thompson turns to look at me.

"Are you sure you're alright, Rufus?"

"I'm fine. Honestly. I'm just tired. And I hate cases like this."

"I don't think any of us enjoy them," he replies.

"No, I don't suppose we do." I let out a long deep breath. "We're going to pick these people apart a little more today," I explain. "We need to find the child and, if they're keeping something from me, I intend to find out what it is."

"Yes, sir," he replies and I raise my eyebrows at him as he smiles and I almost manage to smile back.

Lois opens the door to us.

"Inspector," she says, then looks over my shoulder.

"This is Detective Sergeant Thompson." I make the introductions, remembering that they didn't meet yesterday. "May we come in?"

"Of course." She steps aside and we pass into the hallway.

"Before we speak to anyone, would it possible to use your telephone?" I enquire.

"Certainly. If you'd like to follow me." She leads the way down the hall and opens a door at the end. "This is the master's study," she says. "The telephone is on the desk."

"Are Mr and Mrs Sanderson available?" I ask as she goes to leave the room.

"Yes. Neither of them ate much breakfast, but they ordered coffee in the drawing room. I've just this minute taken it in there."

"Good. Can you let them know we're here and that we'll be in to see them in a moment? We can find our own way."

She nods her head and smiles. "Certainly, sir."

Once she's gone, I go over to the desk and pick up the telephone, asking the operator for the number of the London Road station. While I'm waiting to be connected, I take in the large oak desk, with its comfortable leather chair, the book cases that line two of the walls, and the doors that lead onto the back garden. It's a smart, rather sterile room, which doesn't surprise me at all, given its owner.

I hear an unfamiliar voice answer the phone and, giving my name, I ask for Sergeant Tooley, who must be standing close by, as he comes on the line straight away, without the need for the call to be connected. "Sir?" he says.

"I'm sorry to do this to you, but can you come over here?"

"To the Sanderson house?" he queries.

"Yes. Just briefly. The search at the park is a waste of time. We're going to have to widen it to the surrounding houses and I need you here to coordinate that."

"I'll leave right away."

"Thank you, Sergeant. Before you go, can you put me though to Chief Superintendent Webster, please?"

"Certainly, sir."

This time the line clicks and goes dead, before it clicks again and Webster answers. It takes just a few minutes to explain my theory about the park where the girl went missing, the lack of hiding places therein, and the fact that she liked the other recreation ground rather more.

"With so many houses in between, most of which have garages and outbuildings, we're looking at a lot of manpower," I explain.

"Leave it with me," he says, sounding very businesslike. "I'll contact the Chief Constable straight away."

He doesn't bother with niceties and, before I've had the chance to thank him, he's gone, and I replace the receiver.

"Let's get on with this," I murmur to Thompson and, together, we leave the study and go straight to the drawing room, knocking once on the door and entering.

Inside, Mr and Mrs Sanderson are sitting on separate sofas, at opposite ends. He's holding a newspaper and she's staring into space. On the table in front of them, there's a tray of coffee things, which looks like it's untouched. As we enter, Mr Sanderson lowers his newspaper and looks up at us.

"Inspector?" he says.

"Mr Sanderson." I turn to his wife, but she's still staring, seemingly unaware of our presence. "We have some more questions."

"Really?" He sounds rather bored with the whole process, which just gets my back up.

"Yes, really. And in case you're interested, I've got men searching the houses between the St. Mary's Road park, and the one around the corner."

"Why?" he asks, looking confused.

"Because there's nowhere to hide on the St Mary's Road recreation ground. Nowhere at all. Your nanny informed me that your daughter liked to play at the other park, so we're working on the theory that she may have tried to get there by herself."

"And why not just search this other park?" he asks.

"Because I've been informed that it's currently being dug over by council workmen," I point out. "I'd like to think that, if a four year-old child had arrived in the early afternoon entirely of her own volition, they'd have reported it."

He nods his head slowly. "So… why are you back here?" he asks.

"Because, as I say, we have more questions. To start with, I'd like to know if you can think of anyone who might have taken your daughter?"

His face reddens. "Taken her?"

"Yes, sir. Can you think of any disgruntled business acquaintances? Former employees? Anyone at all who would wish you and your family harm?"

"You think this was intentional? You mean… kidnapping? But you just said you thought she might have tried to get to this other park… that's why you're searching those houses."

"I'm not ruling anything out." I stare at him. "So, is there anyone?"

"N—No," he stutters. "I can't think of anyone. Obviously, I'm quite well-off." He leans forward in his seat. "There's the income from my business, and I have a few investments, and there's also the money from my wife's family." I note that he thinks of his wealth is 'his', not 'theirs', even though some of it clearly came from his wife's family, presumably as a result of their marriage, or perhaps an inheritance. "We've received no demands though," he adds, as an afterthought.

"Not at your office?" I ask.

"Well, I don't know. I haven't been to work today."

"Can you telephone them?"

He doesn't reply, but gets to his feet, leaving the room. Mrs Sanderson doesn't move, or react in any way and, while I know I could take this opportunity to ask her about David Cooke, I can't be sure how long her husband will be absent from the room, so I remain silent on the subject – and on everything else for that matter – and satisfy myself with staring out of the window until Mr Sanderson returns, some ten minutes later, shaking his head.

"There's been nothing," he says, standing in front of the fireplace, rather than resuming his seat. "I got my secretary to open all of today's post, just to make certain."

At that moment, the doorbell rings, but we all ignore it. "And there's nowhere else that someone might write to you?" I ask.

"No."

The drawing room door opens and Lois comes in, her hands clutched in front of her.

"Inspector?"

"Yes." I turn to look at her properly.

"There's a Sergeant Tooley here to see you," she says.

I nod my head and turn to Mr Sanderson. "Excuse us, will you?"

He doesn't respond and I glance at Thompson, indicating the door with a tilt of my head, ensuring that he follows me from the room.

Tooley is standing by the front door, looking at the floor.

"Sergeant?" He raises his face as I call out, and takes a step towards me.

"Sir."

"You know what needs to be done?"

"Yes." He sighs. "But there are an awful lot of houses between those two parks, sir, especially if we're including all the side streets."

"We are," I confirm. "We need to allow for the fact that she might have tried to get to the park herself and have got confused, and wandered into someone's shed or garage to keep warm, but also I think we should bear in mind that someone who lives in those houses might have come across her and taken her. I'm trying to cover every eventuality here."

"I see."

"So, those houses have got to be searched properly. Each and every one of them. I've asked the chief super for some extra men to help out."

"Yes, sir. I know. He saw me before I left Kingston and explained that he can't get us anyone until tomorrow morning. He asked me to tell you."

"Tomorrow morning?" I can't disguise my disappointment.

"No, sir. But I'll work things out," he replies. "Don't worry."

"Keep us posted, Sergeant."

He leaves, going out into the damp morning, with a grim expression on his face.

Once the door is closed, I turn to Thompson.

"I need to speak with Mrs Sanderson alone – without fear of interruption."

"Leave it with me," he replies. "I've got an idea."

I raise an eyebrow, but he doesn't react and we go back to the drawing room, not bothering to knock this time before we enter. Mr Sanderson has sat back down again, although he hasn't picked up his newspaper and is studying his fingernails.

"Mr Sanderson," Thompson says, stepping forward. "I need to take a look at the nursery. We didn't get to see it properly yesterday."

"You didn't?"

"No," I explain, jumping on the bandwagon. "We interviewed your nanny in her own room. The baby was asleep at the time."

Sanderson nods. "And you need the see the nursery? What for?"

"To see where your daughter slept and had her meals," Thompson replies. I'm not sure Sanderson is going to fall for that, but after a momentary glance in his wife's direction, he gets to his feet.

"I'll take you up," he says, with more than a hint of enthusiasm to his voice.

I'm tempted to smile. Thompson guessed, quite correctly, that Sanderson wouldn't be able to resist the opportunity to spend some time with the nanny, and as they both leave the room, it's hard to miss the bounce in the older man's step.

I wait until the door is closed and then turn to Mrs Sanderson. She still hasn't moved, and is staring into space, sat on the end of the sofa.

"Mrs Sanderson?"

At the sound of her own name, she slowly turns her head and looks at me.

"Yes?"

"I need to ask you a few questions. Would you mind if I sat down?"

"Please do." She waves her arm towards the sofa her husband has just vacated and I sit, feeling relieved. I'm exhausted already and it's still quite early in the morning.

Looking over at her, I decide to get straight to the point. After all, I don't know how long Thompson will be able to keep her husband upstairs. "Tell me about David Cooke," I say and she jumps, very noticeably, her face paling.

"D—David?"

"Yes."

"What do you want to know?" she asks, uncrossing her legs, twisting in her seat and bringing them up beside her, so she's curled up on the sofa. She's trying to appear more relaxed I think, although the look in her eyes is anything but.

"Do you think your daughter's disappearance has anything to do with him?"

Her eyes widen, just for a second, before she sits upright, rather resentful. "Of course not. He'd never do anything to hurt me. He loves me. I just wish…" She pauses and blinks a few times, and at the same time, her shoulders sink. "I—I know it's wrong," she says, her voice dropping to a whisper. "I know I ought to feel guilty and ashamed, but I can't help wishing he could be here." She looks up at me now. "I—I can't be anything other than miserable with Daniel. He's so… so cold, and boring. David's young, and carefree, and alive. And he makes me feel the same." Her voice gets stronger as she speaks and her expression changes to one of rapturous delight – wholly inappropriate in the current circumstances, in my view. "He cares about me. He wants me and needs me. And I need him." Her defiance is breathtaking, but it's like she's suddenly realised what she's saying and her face changes again as she looks into the fireplace, the dying embers seeming to catch her attention. "I wish I'd never married Daniel."

"Why did you?" I ask, intrigued.

She startles and turns back to me again. "Sorry?"

"I asked why you married him."

"Oh… I suppose I just got swept away on the romance of it all. He was romantic at the beginning, you know?" Even she sounds surprised by that. "He's not now, of course. He's just dull, and old."

"But surely… your children?"

"What about them?" she asks.

"Well, they make the marriage worthwhile, don't they?" I wonder for a moment, whether I'm asking these questions because I want to know about the personalities of the people involved in the case, or whether it's because I can see similarities between their lives and my own. The age gap between Mrs Sanderson and her husband, and myself and Amelie, is noticeably similar. *Am I looking at my own future, right in front of me?*

She shrugs her shoulders, rather noncommittally. "They prefer Elizabeth to me. Without David, I'd have nothing – and no-one."

The clock on the mantelpiece chimes the hour and I realise I have to hurry up and get the information I need. "Can you give me his address?" I ask her.

"His address?"

"A man was seen in the vicinity. We'll need to rule Mr Cooke out of our investigations."

"It wasn't him," she persists.

"I still need to speak to him, Mrs Sanderson."

She pauses and slowly nods her head. "Very well. He lives in Thames Ditton. In the High Street." She gives me the number. "It's a lovely little terraced house…" Her voice drifts off dreamily.

"And where does he work?"

"At the bank there. He's the assistant manager." I nod my head, just as I hear footsteps on the stairs. "Don't tell my husband about this, will you?" she says, panic filling her voice.

"No."

I get up and go to stand by the window, trying to look as though I've been there the whole time. The door opens and Mr Sanderson comes in with Thompson, who remains over by the sideboard, while the master of the house resumes his place by the fire.

"Can you tell me if there are any men associated with the household?" I ask him. His wife flips her head around, staring at me. For someone who wants her affair kept secret, she's doing a fairly spectacular job of giving herself away.

"Men?" he asks.

"Yes. Your nanny told us about a man, if you remember? It's possible that he's a complete innocent and has nothing to do with Amy's disappearance. Equally, he could be pivotal to the case, and I just wondered if there was anyone who's associated with the house, who you might have failed to mention."

He glances at his wife and then frowns, as though he's thinking. "I can't think of anyone, no," he murmurs eventually.

"No regular delivery men?" I suggest.

"Well, I wouldn't know about them," he replies. "You'd have to speak to Cook about deliveries."

I nod. "And your servants don't have men friends?"

He shakes his head vehemently. "No," he replies. "I have a very strict policy about such things. That's why I employ older members of staff. Both Cook and Lois are widowed. The last thing I need is young men hanging around the house, and love-sick servants not doing their jobs properly, when I'm paying them a good wage."

"Miss Sutton hardly qualifies as 'older'," I point out, and he blushes.

"She's different," he says, then pauses before adding, "The role of a nanny is hardly the same as an ordinary domestic servant."

"But your rule applies just the same?"

His lips narrow to a thin line. "Of course." I'm not sure whether he's more angry at my line of questioning, or the prospect of Miss Sutton having a young man in her life.

In the car, Thompson turns to face me, before switching on the engine. I have to admit to feeling disappointed with events so far today. I'd hoped to find out more, to ferret out their secrets.

"I feel as though they're still holding back, don't you?" I say to him.

"Yes. But to be fair, I'm not sure whether they're hiding things from us, or from each other."

"Or both?"

He tilts his head. "Possibly."

"What was Sanderson like with the nanny when you went up there?"

"The baby was stirring," he says, "just about to wake up, and Miss Sutton needed to get something from the kitchen, so she left us to it. He seemed… disappointed." I nod my head. "Did you get what you wanted from Mrs Sanderson?"

"I've got an address for Mr Cooke, yes. He works at the bank in Thames Ditton, and lives in the High Street. Not only that, but I established in my own mind that Mrs Sanderson would probably be more upset if something happened to David Cooke than she is about her daughter."

"That's a bit harsh," Thompson replies, looking out of the front windscreen.

"You might think so, but you didn't see her face when she was talking about him. She's enchanted by him, besotted with him, and everything else can go to hell."

Thompson doesn't reply for a moment, then he turns back to me. "Do you want to go over to Thames Ditton now?" he asks.

"Yes, I do."

He starts the engine and reverses out of the driveway, onto the road. Rather than turning right and heading towards the river, past the searching men, he turns left, taking us on a more circuitous route to Thames Ditton. I think he's guessed that my mood is not good, and to see the men searching, fruitlessly, is not going to help.

"Sorry," I murmur as he drives along the edge of Giggs Hill Green. We've been on the road for about ten minutes now, and I feel something needs to be said.

"I do understand, Rufus," he says, mildly, although I don't think he does. "And I feel the same. We both want to find her... and catch whoever did this." He glances at me. "Because we both think someone did, don't we?"

I nod my head, even though he hasn't grasped the reason behind my mood at all. But then why would he? I mean, obviously I'm feeling the same way as him. I want to find the girl and return her to her parents, although with every hour that passes, that seems less likely. But the other thing that's going through my mind and weighing me down, is the realisation that I keep coming across so many people who appear to be incapable of monogamy, so many people who've made mistakes in their marriages, and who end up hurting those around them. I know that I'm about to ask a very beautiful, very young woman to commit her life to me, as I already have to her, and I can't help thinking: am I making a huge mistake myself? And is it one that she'll end up regretting?

A knock at Mr Cooke's house goes unanswered, which isn't surprising as it's the middle of the day, so we go on to the bank, where the manager tells us that he's gone out for the afternoon, to visit two important clients. He's not expected back until tomorrow. Keen to find out why we're there, the manager offers us tea, but we decline and the disappointment in his countenance, is noticeable.

"So much for that," Thompson says, himself a little moody now, as we climb back into the car. "Where to next?"

"We've got nothing else to follow up on until tomorrow," I reply. "And I don't know about you, but I can't sit at the office doing nothing. Let's get back over to Long Ditton and join the search."

"Are you up to that?" he asks.

"No, but we're going anyway."

He shakes his head and puts the car into gear, steering us back the way we've just come, but taking the more direct route this time.

At least if I keep busy, I won't have time to think. That's the plan, anyway.

Chapter Four

My dearest Kitten,

I've just received your letter and am writing before going to work.

You don't need my forgiveness. And you mustn't worry about the manner of your writing to me. Just make sure you write. Please. I need to know that you're all right. I wish more than anything that I could be with you, but I can't, and I'm dying here, not being able to hold you. So, don't feel bad about not writing the words we'd both like to hear, and just write anything. Whatever you need to say to me, just put it in your letters. I'll read them, and I'll write back. Because at the moment that's all I can do. That, and think of you all the time, of course.

I'm sure no-one is judging you, my darling. Anyone who knew you like I do, would know how much care and love you've always given to both of the children. It's all just an accident; a misunderstanding and I'm sure Amy will turn up soon.

It's not wrong of you to think about us, no matter what else is going on. You need to think of happier times, when things are so bleak. And if doing so helps you to get through this ordeal, then think about us; dream about us and all the things we like to do when we're together. Know that I love you, more than life; that I would do anything to be with you, to give you my strength and comfort. And in the meantime, rest assured, this will pass, and soon I will hold you in my arms and this will feel like a distant nightmare.

I have to go now, or I'll be late.

Please write back soon, my darling Kitten, and remember how much I love you.

D x

I've hardly slept a wink. Again. I got back at just after eleven last night. I didn't manage to stay out with the search teams for that long; I wasn't physically up to it, but at around four-thirty, Thompson and I went back to the station and, in the company of the chief super, we sat in the main office and went through all the evidence we've got so far, the various interviews conducted with the householders who live near to the park where Amy went missing and who might have seen the direction in which she wandered off – or noticed someone loitering, who didn't belong there. We went over and over everything, trying to piece something together... anything that might point to where she could be. We didn't get anywhere, of course, and eventually exhaustion got the better of all of us and the chief super suggested we call it a night. I didn't even have the energy to argue with him, and Thompson dropped me at home. My mother was still sitting up for me, although Dotty had gone to bed, and while she fussed about the fact that I hadn't eaten since breakfast – and I wasn't about to – I think she knew I wasn't in the mood to talk and just let me come to bed.

"Rufus?" My mother pokes her head around the door, coming in quietly, rather than announcing herself in her usual, jovial fashion.

"I'm awake."

She doesn't reply, but goes over to the curtains and opens them, pulling back the blackout at the same time and revealing a dull, overcast morning, which perfectly suits my mood.

"I'll run your bath," she says quietly, going straight back out again.

I close my eyes, just for a second, feeling guilty for imposing my own dark frame of mind on those I love.

"Mother?" I call out, sitting up on the edge of the bed, and she comes back in, looking down at me from the doorway. "I'm sorry."

She moves closer, and then sits beside me, the bed sagging slightly. "Don't be," she says. "I know how awful these cases can be."

I lean into her. If only it were just the case. If only I wasn't still haunted by the idea that my relationship with Amelie is doomed to end in failure. "Even so…" I murmur.

She rests her hand on my knee. "You need to see Amelie," she says softly and I wonder if she's psychic.

"I know."

"And you need some rest." She gets up again, going back into the bathroom. "Your bath's ready," she adds, coming into the bedroom again. "We've arranged that Ethel's doing you bacon and eggs for breakfast. You barely ate a thing yesterday, so we're going to make sure you at least have one good meal today."

I smile up at her and, making an effort, get to my feet and go over to her, giving her a hug.

"What's that for?" she says, looking up at me.

"Being you."

She chuckles. "That's not what you normally say or do when I'm being me."

"No, but a man can be wrong sometimes, can't he?"

Her chuckle becomes a laugh. "No, dear. All the time would be more accurate."

Once I've bathed and Mother has changed the dressing on my wound, I get dressed in the privacy of my own room, the smell of bacon wafting through the house and making me realise how hungry I am. I stand by the window, in my shirt-sleeves, my tie around my neck, wondering if I might catch a glimpse of Amelie. Just to look at her would feed my weary soul...

"Breakfast, Rufus," my mother calls up the stairs, and I sigh, disappointed, just as Amelie appears at the end of Beauchamp Road. She stops her bicycle at the junction and glances at the house, her eyes finding my window right away. I smile at her, and she smiles back. And I know I can't wait a moment longer to see her in the flesh, to touch her and talk to her. I hold up my hand, letting her know I want her to wait, and she nods her head, stepping off of her bicycle and starting to wheel it towards the pavement.

Incapable of running yet, I walk quickly to the top of the stairs and descend as fast as I can.

"Ah, there you are," my mother says, from the dining room doorway.

"I'll be a couple of minutes, no more." I glance at her as I move towards the cupboard by the door, where the coats are kept.

"Where are you going?" she asks.

"Amelie's outside."

She smiles and waves me away. "Go on then. I'll keep your breakfast warm."

I smile back, and take my coat, putting it around my shoulders, before I open the door, and go quickly down the steps and out through the front gate. Amelie is standing opposite, her bicycle resting against her hip, her navy blue coat done up tight and her grey beret settled firmly on her head. She looks adorable and I cross the road to her. I don't care that we're in a public place, or that what I'm about to do is neither becoming, nor particularly gentlemanly; I need her, more than ever, and I lean down and kiss her, letting my lips rest on hers, for longer than is strictly acceptable, but a lot less time than is necessary. Because forever wouldn't be long enough, as far as I'm concerned.

When we pull away from each other, Amelie doesn't look down the road to check who's seen our embrace. She doesn't even blush, or seem embarrassed. Instead, she looks straight into my eyes, hers filled with nothing but love and concern.

"Are you alright?" she asks.

"No."

"I didn't think you were. You look exhausted."

"I feel exhausted." I try to smile.

"You haven't found the little girl?"

I shake my head. "No. It's looking more and more as though she's either been taken, or she's dead… somewhere. Although God only knows where."

She places her hand on my arm, high up on my bicep, and I wish there wasn't the thickness of my coat between us. "Can I do anything?" she offers and I know immediately what I'm going to say.

"Yes." I move closer, cupping her face in my hand. "Do you remember you said we could talk?"

"Of course."

"Then do you think we could?"

80

"Now?"

I shake my head. "No. You have to get to work, and so do I."

"Tonight then?"

"Yes. But I don't know when. I might be late again. I can't…"

"I don't care," she interrupts. "It doesn't matter to me what time it is. I'll wait up. Just come over whenever you get home."

I lean down to her, our lips almost touching. "God, I love you," I whisper, my voice cracking slightly.

She brings her hand up from my arm, resting it on my neck. "I love you too, my darling."

As Thompson drives us into Kingston, I can feel the weight of the day pressing down on me again, and Amelie's words of love and warmth and promise are already fading into a distant memory. I'm finding it a struggle at the moment, and I don't mind admitting it. She may only live over the road, a few yards away, but it's too far. I need her beside me… right beside me; even though my doubts about our future are still looming large in my mind. And that's why I'm going to talk to her tonight. It has nothing to do with the case. I have to put my own mind at rest, to find out whether it's just her brief absence from my life that's making me feel so insecure, or whether there's any foundation in my fears, before I drive myself completely insane.

Gilmore and Deakin are waiting in the main office, looking rather pleased with themselves, and they both stand as Thompson and I enter the otherwise deserted room.

"What have you got?" I ask, because it's obvious they have something.

"A couple of young lads," Deakin replies, stepping forward. "We picked them up in a pub last night, trying to flog some of the jewellery."

"The landlord called it in," Gilmore continues. "He was going to throw them out, because they were underage, but then he saw what they were up to, and reported it."

I nod my head. "And how old are these two?"

"One's fourteen. The other says he's the same, but I think he's a bit younger."

"You haven't interviewed them, have you?"

They shake their heads. "We were going to get started this morning."

"Well don't. Not without a responsible adult in the room. They may, or may not have committed burglary, and they may or may not have been trying to get rid of the loot, but they're still underage."

"Get this bit wrong," Thompson puts in, "and the whole case falls apart."

Both men nod their heads. "I suggest you let them have breakfast," I explain, "get them a solicitor and then get started." Again, they nod, and then turn away. "Well done, both you of," I add and they turn back again, smiling.

"Bloody kids," Thompson says as he closes my office door behind him. We're not stopping here for long, so neither of us has bothered to take off our coats, although I sit down at my desk.

"Would that be our burglars, or Deakin and Gilmore?" I ask and he grins.

"The burglars," he replies patiently. "Why they can't take up a sport, or join a club or something, rather than robbing elderly people, I don't know…"

"You're starting to sound old."

"I'm starting to feel old," he says, sitting down in the chair opposite me. "I think I've had about five hours' sleep in the last two nights."

"I know the feeling."

I pick up the telephone and ask to be connected to a number in Thames Ditton. It's David Cooke's home, the number for which we found out very late last night, and I'm hoping to catch him before he leaves for the bank.

He answers on the third ring, sounding rather out of breath.

"Mr Cooke?"

"Yes," he says impatiently.

"My name is Stone. Detective Inspector Stone. I'm calling about the disappearance of Amy Sanderson. You've probably read about it in the newspapers?" I could mention that he's also probably been discussing it somehow – either by telephone, or in person, or in writing – with Mrs Sanderson, but I don't.

"Um… yes." He sounds less impatient and more uncertain now.

"I wonder if it would be possible to come and talk to you?"

"When?" he asks. "I was just leaving for work."

"Well, we'd like to see you this morning, if possible. I'm sure you appreciate the urgency of this matter."

"Of course. I'm not sure I can be of any assistance, but…"

"Nonetheless," I interrupt. "We can come to the bank, if you'd find that easier?"

"No," he says quickly. "I'll see you here… at my house." There's a pause. "I'll telephone the bank and tell them I'll be late. You can come now, can't you?"

"Of course, sir."

I hang up and look across at Thompson. "We'd better be going. He's expecting us."

David Cooke's house is exactly as Mrs Sanderson described it. A lovely little terraced property, in the high street, in Thames Ditton, and today he answers his door promptly and shows us inside, directly into his living room, which is furnished with a large, single sofa and chair, both very soft and comfortable looking, and a low coffee table. There's a deep brick fireplace, which takes up most of one wall, and a door, which seems to lead through to the kitchen, at the rear of the property. It's small, but really rather charming. The man himself is exactly what I'd expected him to be: tall, dark, and handsome. Just like Elizabeth Sutton's description, in fact. He's dressed in a three-piece suit, and appears rather flustered.

"What can I do for you?" he asks, standing in the middle of the room. He doesn't offer us seats, so we stand too, and while Mr Cooke may be tall, both Thompson and I are taller, to the point where my head almost touches the living room ceiling.

"As I said, we've come to speak to you about Amy Sanderson."

"And as I said, I'm not sure how I can help."

"Well…" I look him in the eyes. "I suppose you could start by telling me about your relationship with Amy's mother."

His eyes close, just for a second, and when he opens them again, he sighs out a breath. It's as though he's accepted his situation and he takes a step back and indicates the sofa behind us. "Take a seat," he says, and sits himself down in the chair.

Thompson and I perch on the edge of the sofa, unwilling to get too comfortable in its deep cushions, and Thompson takes out his notebook, poised.

"I assume you've already spoken to Lillian?" Mr Cooke says.

"Yes."

He nods. "In which case, you know that we've been seeing each other for some time now. You might also like to know that she's absolutely miserable with Daniel and has been since before baby Eve was born."

A thought strikes me. "I assume the baby is Mr Sanderson's and not yours?" I ask.

He shakes his head. "No. She's Daniel's. Lillian and I only started seeing each other when Eve was about five months old. And I've never been very interested in children, Inspector. Lillian is aware of that." He leans forward. "I love her though," he says earnestly. "And if she were free, I'd marry her tomorrow."

"Even though, in marrying her, you'd be taking on her children?" I ask.

He shrugs. "Well, not necessarily. I imagine Daniel would have something to say about that."

"And Mrs Sanderson wouldn't?"

He stares at me, then looks away. Is he really suggesting she'd put her relationship with him before her own children? Or perhaps he just likes to hope that?

"Is Mr Sanderson aware of your affair?" I ask him.

"We're not sure," he replies, his tone thoughtful. "Sometimes Lillian thinks he is, but at other times, she's convinced he's not even remotely interested in what she does. He's become rather wrapped up in the children's nanny, from what I've gathered…" So she has noticed, despite her apparent indifference. He smiles. It's rather a lewd, unpleasant expression, which makes his face a lot less handsome. "Sometimes, when Lillian and I are here..." He rolls his eyes upwards, indicating the bedroom, no doubt. "... she jokes that, in an ideal world, she and I could run away and go and live somewhere by ourselves – maybe on a desert island, far from prying eyes – and Daniel could stay in the house, with the nanny and the children, playing at happy families." He focuses on me and his smile fades. "Of course, this current situation... well, it changes everything."

I take a breath, swallowing down my contempt. "Can you tell me where you were on Tuesday afternoon?" I ask.

"Um... I was with clients."

"Can I have their names, please?"

Thompson turns the page of his notebook, rather purposefully.

"I'm afraid our clients' names are confidential."

"Not when it comes to a missing child, they're not."

"Well, I can't tell you."

"Then I'm afraid I'm going to have to arrest you." I get to my feet, knowing how imposing it makes me, even with a broken arm.

"W—What for?"

"Obstruction."

He sits right back in his chair and sighs. "Very well," he says. "I wasn't with a client... not all afternoon, anyway."

"Where were you then?"

I sit back down and wait.

"I was here. With Lillian." He looks up. "She managed to get out of the house and met me at about twelve-thirty. We came back here for half an hour, or maybe a few minutes longer, and then we both had to leave. She had to get home, and I had my first meeting to get to... a real one. I should have been there at one, but I was late. The manager doesn't know, and I don't want him to find out. I'd told him the meeting was due to start at twelve o'clock, which gave me time to get away and meet Lillian. The meeting was actually due to start at one, but I didn't even get there until nearly twenty past. As it turned out the client was running late himself and didn't notice, but if the manager found out what I'd been doing…"

"I imagine you'd be fired." I finish his sentence and his eyes widen.

"Yes," he breathes.

"Why didn't you just say you were seeing Mrs Sanderson in the first place?" I ask him. "We're aware of your relationship."

"I have my career to think of," he blusters, his face reddening slightly.

I want to tell him that it might have been better if he'd thought about that before he started sleeping with another man's wife, but I don't. I'm not sure I'm the most impartial judge when it comes to cheating.

Thompson turns the car around and we drive towards Long Ditton.

"You didn't like him, did you?" he says quietly.

"Did it show?"

"Only a little bit."

"Well, that's a shame." I look over at him. "What's wrong with these people?" He doesn't reply, so I continue, "Why do they get married, if all they're going to do is cheat on each other? Mrs Sanderson told me yesterday that her husband is old and boring, and dull and cold."

"That's possibly why she's cheating?" Thompson suggests.

"But then why marry him in the first place? She must have realised the age gap would show sooner or later; it's bound to, when there are more than a few years between a couple, isn't it?"

"Are we talking about Mr and Mrs Sanderson, or you and Amelie?" he asks.

I'm inclined to forget sometimes, how well he knows me.

"Both," I reply quietly.

"Well, in that case, you're being ridiculous and you need to grow up." His voice is harsh, but his comment makes me smile.

"Isn't that rather the point? I'm too much of a grown-up for Amelie. I'm being selfish, tying her to a marriage with a much older man."

"For crying out loud." With a sharp movement of the wheel, he pulls the car over to the side of the road and parks, turning in his seat to look at me. "You're about the least selfish person I know, Rufus," he says, raising his voice a little, "but in any case, the problem isn't with you, or with Amelie, or your age, or hers. It's this bloody case. You know that just as well as I do. Cases like this do strange things – they make you see the dark side of everything." He stops and takes a breath, and I take advantage.

"So you really don't think it's a problem?"

He sighs. "No. But if you're that worried about it, can I point out that the age gap between you and Amelie isn't anywhere near as big as it is between Mr and Mrs Sanderson."

"It's big enough. Amelie's thirteen years younger than me."

"So?" He raises his voice again. "At the risk of sounding soft, she's also in love with you, and you're in love with her. You're so in love, it's bloody sickening sometimes." He smiles. "Do you honestly think I believed your cock-and-bull story about going to buy Amelie a Christmas present the other day? I mean, I know you came back with one, but you were really looking for an engagement ring, weren't you?"

"How did you know?"

"Because you're about as transparent as glass. Just propose to her, will you? And put us all out of our misery."

He turns back to face the front and pulls the car out onto the road again. I can't help smiling, even though I'm still determined to speak to Amelie this evening, because only she can really set my mind – and my heart – at rest.

Lois lets us into the Sanderson house, her hands shaking, her face flushed.

"Is everything alright?" I ask.

"No. The master's in an awful to-do," she says, a deep frown on her forehead.

"What's happened?"

"I'm not sure."

"Well, where is he?"

"In his study."

I nod my head and hand her my hat, going directly to Sanderson's study door. I can hear his raised voice, and knock once, letting myself in, with Thompson close behind.

He glares at me, the phone held tightly to his ear.

"I don't care!" he's saying into the mouthpiece. "You should have contacted me right away. How could you be so irresponsible?" He slams the phone down. "Unbelievable!"

"What's happened?" I repeat my question, to him this time.

"An envelope came in the post this morning, addressed to me personally at the shop," he says, between huffed out breaths, as he paces the floor behind his desk, running his fingers through his hair. "My secretary thought it looked odd, compared to the sort of correspondence we usually receive, and was about to open it when the phone rang and she got waylaid. She's only just remembered – two hours later – and called me."

"And?" I prompt.

"And it's a ransom note," he replies, wide-eyed and pale.

"May I?" I nod towards his telephone and he pushes it in my direction, his hands shaking now, although I'm not sure whether that's with residual anger, or with fear.

Picking up the receiver, I ask to be connected to the London Road station, where my call is answered by PC Adams. I give him detailed instructions to get someone to go around to Mr Sanderson's shop, to collect the note – in an evidence bag – and bring it directly to me at the house. Immediately. Adams understands and we hang up.

"You need to sit down," I say to Mr Sanderson, who's still pacing.

He looks up again, and then does as I suggest, pulling out his chair and sitting down heavily. "Do you think this means she's still alive?" he asks, blinking quickly a few times, as though to hold back threatening tears. I'm quite surprised; it's the first time I've seen him show any real emotional reaction about his daughter.

"I don't know what it means," I reply honestly, making an effort to keep my voice much more calm and considered than I previously have in his presence. "Let's wait and see what the letter says, shall we?"

PC Adams himself arrives about half an hour later, with a small evidence bag, which he hands over to me on the doorstep, before leaving again.

I take the bag into the living room, where Mr Sanderson, Sergeant Thompson, and I moved not long after the end of his telephone call. His wife is also there and, other than a change of clothes, she looks no different to yesterday; still staring at a point in space, distanced from everything around her. This remoteness troubles me. I know now that she would have left her children for her lover, but surely she must care about her daughter, mustn't she?

Sitting down on the sofa, I take the single sheet of paper from the envelope, being careful to touch it only on its edges, and place it on the table. We all lean forward – even Mrs Sanderson, just for a moment, although she soon seems to grow bored, and sits back again – and read the printed words, which state that, for the sum of two hundred pounds, Amy's whereabouts will be notified to her parents. I check the amount again, just to make certain I haven't misread it. No, it is only two hundred pounds, in five pound notes, to be left on the park bench, near to where the girl was last seen. The time given for the 'drop' is eleven pm tomorrow night, and when the money is collected, a note will be left, giving the address where Amy can be found. Needless to say, they warn against any police involvement.

I'm surprised by how little the demand is for. My impression is that the family is worth a lot more than this, which points towards an amateur… although there's something nagging at the back of my mind, that it's another strange element to this case, another piece of the jigsaw that doesn't fit. Between the peculiar attitude of both Mr and Mrs Sanderson, both towards each other, and their situation, the fact that I'm fairly sure the nanny is using her feminine wiles to hide something, and that no-one witnessed Amy's disappearance, even though it now seems she may have been snatched by someone in the middle of the day, and now this odd ransom note, I'm as confused as I think I've ever been. If only I wasn't so tired, I could probably connect it all together, but as it is…

I glance up at Mr Sanderson, who's looking at me with a puzzled expression on his face, which isn't surprising, as I've just been sitting here for quite a while now, staring at the note, mulling things over. "Can you raise the sum of money?" I ask him.

"Yes. Easily." He speaks slowly and deliberately, and I assume he's as confused as I am by the comparatively paltry request. "I'll have to arrange to withdraw it from the bank, obviously," he adds. "I don't keep sums of money like that in the house... I don't have a safe here."

I nod my head. "Perhaps you should contact your bank to arrange that. I'd suggest you make an appointment for tomorrow morning," I say as he gets to his feet and walks towards the door. "And don't tell them what you need the money for."

He nods his head and departs.

"When he comes back, I'll have to speak to Webster," I whisper to Thompson, although I'm fairly sure Mrs Sanderson isn't listening. "I'll need to update him."

Thompson nods his head and I glance over at Mrs Sanderson, but she's staring out of the window now, as though none of this affects her. Part of me is pleased in a way that she can remain so untouched by the disappearance of her daughter, but another part of me wants to shake her and ask her what on earth is wrong with her. I know in her shoes, I'd be going mad with worry, and I'm fairly sure Thompson feels the same, judging from the frown on his face whenever he looks at her.

The door opens and Mr Sanderson comes back in. "It's arranged for ten o'clock tomorrow morning," he says.

I get to my feet. "Good. I have to go and telephone my Chief Superintendent," I tell him. "I'll leave you with Sergeant Thompson. You can start to discuss the arrangements between you, if you like."

"Arrangements?" Sanderson queries.

"Yes. Sergeant Thompson will be going to the bank with you," I explain.

For a moment, I think Sanderson is about to argue with me, but he sighs and nods his head instead, and I go out into the hallway, closing the door and going along to the study.

Webster's response to my phone call is one of surprise, even though he's heard of the ransom note already, via the station grapevine. Like me, I suppose, he didn't expect a demand to arrive so long after the girl's disappearance.

"Ordinarily, I'd say 'no' to paying ransoms," he says, his voice rather stern. "But in this instance, as it's a young child, and she's already been missing for several days… and the family can raise the money quite easily, I think you should go ahead."

"I'm rather relieved you said that, sir, because I've had Mr Sanderson make the arrangements with his bank already."

There's a moment's silence. "In that case, why are you telephoning me?"

I cough. "Because I'm going to need some additional men on watch at the drop site tomorrow evening."

"I see." I can hear the tension; actually, I can almost feel it.

"I'm sorry if you feel I've overstepped the mark, sir," I say. "But something doesn't fit here."

"What do you mean?" he asks.

"The amount for a start. It's so small."

"Two hundred pounds is a lot of money," he reasons.

"Not to this family."

"So you think our kidnapper is a bit of an amateur?"

"I'm not even sure they're a kidnapper. I suppose what I'm wondering is whether we might be dealing with an opportunistic hoaxer."

"It's a possibility," he allows.

"Either way, we have to go ahead, just in case, but it doesn't feel right to me." *None of it does.*

"Copper's instinct?" he suggests.

"Something like that."

There's a slight pause, before he says, "Very well, Stone. You have the run of things. Just keep me informed." *I thought I was.* "Just so you know, the extra men have been sent to the search area this morning. I understand Sergeant Tooley is taking charge of them?"

"Yes, sir."

"I'll get a message to him to find a few volunteers to work late tomorrow night, to cover your surveillance."

"Thank you, sir."

I put down the telephone and stare up at the ceiling, wondering whether he'll be as lenient and understanding if I mess this up.

When I get back into the drawing room, Mrs Sanderson has disappeared.

"My wife has gone upstairs to rest," her husband explains and I sit down beside Sergeant Thompson as Mr Sanderson keeps his eyes fixed on me. "Can I assume this latest development means you'll call off the search?" he asks.

"No, sir." I shake my head. "We'll keep looking for the time being."

His brow furrows in confusion. "But why?" He nods towards the note, which is still lying on the table, and I pick it up, glancing at it once more before carefully placing it back in its envelope. Reading quickly through the words, I'm struck by the correctness of the English, the spelling and the punctuation. There's not a full stop or comma out of place, and while I don't have a huge amount of experience in ransom notes, I'd have thought that was fairly unusual.

"Because we have to be certain that this is genuine," I remark to Sanderson, then I hand the note to Thompson. "Can you take this back to the station and get it to Prentice? Ask him to see if he can get anything from it, and tell him to look at the content as well, will you?"

After all his years at the Yard, I'm almost certain Prentice will have more knowledge of these things than me. He'll be able to say if this is normal, or not.

"Certainly, sir." He gets up, smiling down at me. He rarely calls me 'sir' and it sounds unfamiliar.

"Then find Tooley. Get him to leave Wells, or someone else, in charge of the searches for a short while, and bring him back here with you. We'll have to work out a plan between us and Mr Sanderson, for tomorrow morning and evening."

"Very good," he says, and leaves the room.

Mr Sanderson gets up and moves to the fireplace, standing in front of it.

"I don't understand," he says, looking down at me. "If someone has got Amy and is demanding money for her, what's the point in searching those houses?"

"Because we don't know anyone has got her," I reply and his brow furrows again. "That letter," I continue, "it could mean any one of several things."

"Such as?"

"Such as, your daughter might have been taken, and someone might be demanding money for her return."

"Exactly," he says, in a rather pompous tone.

"Or… it might mean that someone has seen the reports in the newspapers and decided to make some cash for themselves by claiming to have her."

"Really? Do people do that?"

"Yes."

He stares at me. "There's another alternative, isn't there?" he says.

"Yes." I lower my voice. "It's possible that someone did take your daughter, and that she's already… dead." I pause and watch him. He blinks rapidly again, just like he did earlier.

"B—But in that case, how could they hope to profit from this?"

"Because they'll expect to be able to take the money and make their escape before we find out she's dead. That's why they've asked for the drop to be handled in the way they have."

"S—So you think that's the most likely scenario?" he says, stuttering out his words.

"No. I didn't say that. All I'm telling you is that we're not going to give up looking for her until we know for certain, one way or the other, whether this note is genuine."

He stares at me for a full thirty seconds, and then nods his head and goes to sit down again, closing his eyes. For the second time today, I feel sorry for him.

Thompson was gone for just over an hour, but when he returned, the four of us, including Sergeant Tooley, retired to Mr Sanderson's study, where we finalised the arrangements for him and Sergeant Thompson to collect the ransom money from the bank in the morning, and – more importantly – the surveillance that will be required when Mr Sanderson makes the drop-off of the money in the evening. That was much more complicated, Tooley's knowledge of the area came in very useful and we were finished by mid-afternoon, with a sound plan set up, which guarantees in my mind that the money won't be out of our sight at any time. Tooley still had to arrange for sufficient volunteers for this operation, for which the men would be wearing civilian clothing – for obvious reasons – so he left to start on that.

I got Thompson to drive me back to the station, where I informed the chief superintendent of the plan, of which he approved, while Thompson was briefed by Gilmore and Deakin on their interrogation of the two young burglary suspects.

After that, although it's only six o'clock, we decide to go home. We don't have anything else we can do this evening, and we're both exhausted.

"What's happening on the burglaries?" I ask Thompson when we're half-way to Molesey. We've driven in silence until now, both too tired to really talk, I think.

"One of them has confessed, the other is proclaiming his innocence."

"Interesting."

He chuckles. "The supposedly innocent one isn't very bright, by all accounts."

"He doesn't sound it."

"Hmm… Even when Deakin pointed out that his chum had admitted to everything, he still said it had nothing to do with him, despite them finding some of the loot at his parents' house."

"Oh. I didn't know that?" I smile.

"Yes. Gilmore got a search warrant for both of the lads' houses. The one who's confessed turned up clean, but the other one had a bag of jewellery stashed at the bottom of his wardrobe."

"Silly boy."

"Like I say, he's not very bright. He seems determined to stick to his story of innocence though."

"Do they want any help?"

He shakes his head. "I told Deakin to keep plugging away at him for the time being – to give it another day, and if he still won't break, then I said you or I would have a crack."

I nod my head. "Sounds wise."

Sometimes just the appearance of a superior officer, especially one the size of myself or Harry, can do the trick.

My mother comes out of the sitting room to greet me.

"You're early," she says as I remove my hat.

"Yes."

She helps me off with my coat and I put both of them over the end of the stairs.

"Any news?" she asks.

"Nothing positive." We start towards the sitting room, together. "We got a ransom note, but I don't think it's genuine."

She nods. "Come and sit down."

Aunt Dotty is already in her seat, at one end of the sofa, nearest to the fire. It's her favourite place. "Help yourself to a drink, dear," she says.

"I won't. I'm going to see Amelie later."

"And that means you can't have a drink?" She's surprised.

"It means I want to keep a clear head, that's all."

For a moment, her eyes twinkle, but she doesn't say anything. I think both she and my mother have realised I'm in no fit state to cope with them meddling in my love life at present.

"Shall we have dinner now then?" Mother suggests from behind me.

"If that suits you two, then yes. I'm hungry enough."

"You didn't have lunch?" Mother's does her best to look daggers at me, even though she's not very good at it.

"I didn't have time."

"Well, I think it's lamb cobbler. I'll just check with Ethel how it's going." She leaves the room and I go and sit opposite Aunt Dotty.

"Are you alright?" she asks.

"Not really."

"An evening with Amelie will do you good," she replies and I smile across at her.

"Mother said that this morning."

"Which means it must be true."

I'm not about to deny that I can't think of anything in the world I want – or need – more than a couple of hours spent with Amelie. It's not for the reasons everyone probably thinks though. I have things I need to say to her; questions I need to ask. I just hope I don't end up regretting them.

Mother comes back in and announces that dinner will be twenty minutes – just long enough for the cobbler to brown.

She sits beside me.

"Do you want to talk about it?" she asks and we both know she's talking about the case.

"Not particularly." And suddenly I remember that I haven't had the chance to tell them Amelie's idea for Christmas Day. "But while I've got you both here, I've been meaning to tell you that Amelie and I have worked out our plans for Christmas."

She twists in her seat to face me. "Oh yes?" The excitement in her eyes is unmistakable, and I wonder how let down she's going to feel when I tell her.

"Yes. And before you build your hopes up, you have to remember that this will be their first Christmas without Beth. You can't expect Amelie to drop everything and come over here."

She sighs and glances over at Aunt Dotty, and I know that they'd planned just such a thing in their own minds. "No… I suppose not."

"But Amelie wondered whether we'd like to go over there for tea on Christmas Day."

"Us?" Dotty says, seemingly surprised.

"Yes."

"Not just you?"

"No, all of us."

Mother and Aunt Dotty exchange another glance. "A proper family gathering?" my mother says.

"Well, I don't know about 'family'," I point out. "I haven't asked her to marry me yet. I…"

"Oh, for heaven's sake, Rufus. We all know you're going to. Even Amelie's probably worked it out by now."

"I wouldn't be at all surprised," I reply, "given the number of hints you drop."

"Only because I know you need a jolly good shove."

"No, I don't. I just need to find the right ring." Oh, how I wish I hadn't said that.

A smile forms on my mother's face. "That's the only thing that's stopping you?"

"Well… no."

"Then what else is wrong?" she huffs, rolling her eyes.

"Nothing's wrong. I'd just like a little privacy when I propose to the woman I love, that's all." What on earth is wrong with me? I can only plead exhaustion… and pre-occupation with the case, and my impending conversation with Amelie.

A silence descends on the room, and then Aunt Dotty sits forward slightly. "I'm sorry," she murmurs. "We have been rather meddlesome, haven't we?"

I open my mouth to disagree – only because it's polite, not because I actually disagree with her – but my mother gets there first. "We'll leave you to get on with it, in your own way," she says.

"Really?"

"Yes," She nods her head, and looks across the room at Aunt Dotty, before turning back to face me again, leaning over and putting her hand on my knee. "As long as you don't take forever over it."

I smile down at her. "I won't. I promise."

The lamb cobbler was delicious, but once supper was finished, my impatience to see Amelie was too great and I made my excuses, to great smiles and twinkles from my mother and Aunt Dotty. I'm not sure they're going to be able to stick to their pledge to let me propose in my own time. It's been a struggle for them to avoid the topic during dinner, and being as I don't plan on proposing this evening, I think normal service will be resumed tomorrow.

Outside, it's chilly. Actually, it's really cold, and as I walk across the road to Amelie's house, I can't help but think about little Amy. I'm certain, in my heart of hearts, that she's already dead, whether through exposure to the cold, or at the hands of some other person. All I want to do now is to find her, and then find out what happened to her.

I knock on the door, feeling rather down-hearted, my head bowed.

"Hello." I look up at the sound of Amelie's voice. The light has been turned off behind her, but even in the moonlight, she's beautiful.

"Hello." I can't help smiling. "Why are you answering the door?"

"Because I somehow knew it would be you," she says, standing back and letting me enter the house, whereupon, she pulls the heavy curtain across the door and flicks on the lights.

"You did?"

She comes around in front of me and takes my hat from my head, then removes my coat from my shoulders, while I just stand there, looking at her.

"Yes, I did," she says, and then places my things on the hall table, before taking my hand and silently leading me into the drawing room.

The lights in here are dim, coming from two side lamps, set on low tables, and the glow from the fireplace.

Letting go of me, she takes my jacket from my shoulders, leaving me in my shirtsleeves – even if they are short shirt sleeves, because I can't get long ones over my plaster cast. "Sit," she says, placing my jacket over the back of the chair and nodding towards the sofa. I'm not about to say 'no', and I walk over and take a seat in the corner of the comfortable couch, while Amelie goes to the drinks cabinet, where she starts to stir the contents of a silver-coloured cocktail shaker, before pouring clear liquid from it into rather attractive cocktail glasses. She picks them up and brings them over, which gives me my first opportunity to take in what she's wearing – namely dark grey, wide legged trousers and a thin pale pink sweater, both of which combine to make her look absolutely stunning. She stands before me and hands over a glass, before she sits down, leaning into me, her shoulder against mine.

"You've made us a cocktail?" I look down at her.

"I've made us a dry martini." She smiles and holds up her glass. I clink mine against hers and take a sip of what is, essentially, cold, neat gin, with just the barest hint of sweetness from the dash of vermouth I assume she's shown it.

"That's astounding."

She takes a sip of her own and wrinkles up her nose, rather beautifully. "Hmm. It is rather good."

I put down my glass on the table, then lean over and take hers, putting it beside my own, and then I twist in my seat, just as she turns to face me and I capture her chin in my hand and cover her lips with mine. I don't think I've ever needed this more than I do tonight, and it takes us a good few minutes to pull away from each other, with great reluctance.

"Did you have that drink sitting there all evening?" I ask, nodding toward the cabinet on the far side of the room.

"No." She smiles. "I saw you coming back from work when I went upstairs to change earlier. I was just about to close the curtains, when I caught sight of your sergeant pulling up outside Dotty's house, so I knew you were home and you wouldn't be too late in coming over."

"You mean you knew I couldn't stay away." I kiss her again, cupping her cheek, my fingers twisting into her short, softly curled hair, as she breathes out a gentle sigh.

"It's entirely mutual," she says, leaning back eventually and nestling into me when I put my arm around her. "How's work?" she asks.

"Awful."

She sits up again, looking me in the eye. "You haven't found the little girl?"

"No." I reach forward to pick up my glass, but she hands it to me, and I take a longer sip this time. "We got a ransom note today, though."

"Someone kidnapped her?" She's shocked.

"Not necessarily." I explain the likely scenarios surrounding the ransom note, while I finish my drink.

"More?" she asks, nodding at my glass.

"I should probably say 'no', but I'm not going to." She smiles and gets up, taking my glass, and goes over to the drinks cabinet, returning a few moments later, with it filled up again.

"Something's bothering you, isn't it?" she says, sitting back down and passing the glass to me.

"Yes."

"Then talk to me," she says and already I feel the relief washing over me, as I lean forward and put my drink down on the table.

"We found out that the mother is having an affair," I say bluntly.

"The little girl's mother?" she clarifies.

I nod my head. "Yes. She explained to us that she finds her husband dull and boring."

"Then why did she marry him?" she asks, repeating my own question from yesterday.

"I don't know. She said he was romantic when they first met. H— He's a lot older than her though, and I think the romance has worn off."

She nods her head and leans closer to me. "And you've been worrying about whether I'll ever feel the same way?" she asks.

"Are you a mind-reader?"

"No. But I think I know you fairly well."

"Better than anyone."

She sighs and, without another word, she stands up and turns to face me, then places her knees on the sofa, either side of mine, and sits down on my lap, astride me, her hands on my shoulders, her eyes boring into mine.

"What do I have to do to make you understand?" she says. I'm rather breathless, so I don't reply, and she lets her hands wander up around my neck and into my hair. She shifts closer, her breasts just brushing against my chest, her lips touching mine, and the next few minutes are filled with heartfelt moans, deep, longing sighs and ardent whisperings, which mainly consist of each other's names, and love. When she finally sits back, I find that my hand has wandered up her back, beneath her jumper and is resting on her soft bare skin. She doesn't object, so I leave it there, looking into her eyes.

"I nearly lost you," she whispers, the break in her voice betraying her emotions. "When you were stabbed, I watched you bleeding on the pavement, I sat in the hospital, scared out of my mind, while you were in surgery, and I had a lot of time to think about what my life would be like without you. They weren't good thoughts, Rufus. They're not thoughts I want to have again. We already share so much, and one day I—I know we'll share even more." She lowers her eyes, just for a moment, then looks at me again. "But I don't ever want to share any of myself with anyone else."

I move my hand a little further up her back and pull her closer, kissing her deeply and passionately, like never before, pouring myself and my love into her, her words ringing in my ears.

"I'm sorry I doubted you," I murmur as she sits back again.

"You didn't," she replies, rubbing her fingertip gently along my lips. "You were doubting yourself. You think that as we get older, I'll find you dull and boring, don't you?"

She sees through me, every time. "It had crossed my mind, yes."

She smiles, the most sweet and beautiful smile in the whole world. "It'll never happen," she murmurs. "How could it, when you love me like you do? When you say the words you do, so often? When you make me feel like this every time we're together? When you kiss me like that, and make me want so much more…?" She lowers her eyes again, perhaps a little shy at her admission, and I bring my hand around and place it beneath her chin, raising her face until our eyes lock again and I see the glittering sparkle in hers.

"Thank you for saying that, Amelie," I whisper and she leans into me rather temptingly, which makes me groan slightly, despite my best attempts at self control, and a smile forms on her perfect lips as I let my hand drop to her thigh, resting it there and, if I'm being honest, holding her in place, because if she moves any closer, she's going to find out the effect she's having on my body. "I needed to hear it," I add.

"I know," she murmurs. "Except you didn't. Not really. You just thought you did. Deep down, you know I love you, and I'll never, ever hurt you."

"God… I love you so much." Our lips touch once more, the heat flaring between us to a fever pitch. "We have to stop," I say, when she pulls back, breathless, panting, her fingers still entwined in my hair.

"We do?" She looks disappointed, but there's that impish smile I love so much twitching at the corners of her mouth.

"Yes. You're too… tempting." Her smile widens.

"And you think you're not?"

"I have absolutely no idea, but what I am certain about is that we said we'd wait… and at the moment, with you sitting on me like this, I'm not sure I can."

She stares at me, her eyes reading mine. "Do you want me to move?" she says.

"Well, I didn't say that," I reason, and she grins. "But maybe we should try talking about something else. Something less… provocative than how much we love, and want, and need each other?"

"Even if we do… love, and want, and need each other?" she whispers.

"Yes, even then." I lean forward and kiss the tip of her nose and she giggles, which doesn't help my cause at all.

"Very well," she says, and leans back just a little. "If you insist… Actually, I have a favour to ask."

"You do?" I'm all too aware that my hand is still resting on her thigh, but I'm enjoying the intimacy of touching her, despite everything I've just said.

"Yes," she says rather dreamily as she starts to fiddle with my shirt buttons and I tilt my head to one side, staring at her.

"Is that meant to help?" I nod towards her hands, a smile forming on my lips.

"What?" She looks down to where she's twisted a button undone, and pulls away sharply, blushing. "Oh. Sorry. I was distracted."

"So am I," I point out. "I'm just trying – despite the obvious temptations – to be a gentleman."

She leans forward, her arms around my neck, and kisses my cheeks, one at a time. "In that case, I thank you," she says, full of mischief again.

"So… about this favour?" I take the coward's option and steer us to safer ground.

"Yes," she says. "I was wondering if you might be available at the weekend."

"I'm not sure." Her face falls. "I'm sorry, darling," I add quickly, "but it depends on the case."

She nods her head. "Yes, of course."

"What do you need me for?" I ask.

"All kinds of things," she replies, pursing her lips to avoid smiling.

"Are you teasing me again?"

"No. I do need you for all kinds of things… Like kissing…" And she kisses me very briefly on the lips. "And holding hands." She takes my hand from her thigh and holds it in hers, entwining our fingers, looking at them closely, as though intrigued.

"You're utterly enchanting, you know that, don't you?"

She reverts her gaze to me. "No. But everything we do is so new, I'm fascinated by it all… I mean, just look at our fingers when we're holding hands… It's like we're the same person. I can't tell which is your hand and which is mine. Not really…" Her voice fades to a whisper.

"And that's just how it should be. We are one and the same person, Amelie."

She smiles. "We are, aren't we." It's not a question, so I don't answer, but I rest my forehead against hers and savour a very special moment.

It's Amelie who sits back first, looking down at me. "It's about the Christmas tree," she says, rather unexpectedly.

"I'm sorry?"

"This weekend. I wondered if you'd be free to help me decorate it." She's looking down at our still coiled fingers and biting her lip.

"Won't your uncle want to do it with you?" I ask her and she shakes her head, not looking up at me.

"I doubt it. He doesn't usually come home during the last weekend before Christmas. He always used to tell us that he had to finish off his work in London before the festivities, but now of course, I know that what he really meant was that he wanted to spend time with *her*, being as he wouldn't see her over Christmas, because of his family duties here. What he'll be doing this year, I don't know. He hasn't said yet." Her bitterness over her uncle's infidelity is still raw and I wonder if she'll ever get past this. "Decorating the tree…" she continues falteringly. "It—

It's something I always used to do with Beth…" Her voice cracks and I take my hand from hers, pulling her close to me, crushing her tight to my chest, while she rests her head on my shoulder.

"I'll find the time, my darling," I murmur. "I promise."

Chapter Five

My darling,

I'm so grateful for your letter. Your words, your precious words, make me feel so loved, so wanted… so desired. Just knowing that you care so much, and that you're thinking of me, even though we can't be together, it means everything to me.

You won't be aware yet, because the police are keeping it out of the newspapers, but a ransom note was received yesterday morning. This has given everyone a renewed hope that Amy is still alive and I suppose they might be right. After all, a kidnapper would hardly send a ransom note for a dead child, would they? The money is due to be dropped off late tonight, so we should have her back within a few hours from now… and then the police will be gone, 'his lordship' will return to work, life can revert to normal, and I can see you again.

Is that very selfish of me?

Is it awful of me to be so desperate for your kisses, for your lips, your touch… your words, while you love me? Is it terrible of me that, when I know I should be worrying about Amy, or thinking of Eve, or trying to get on with my life, the only thought in my head is you, my darling?

Please God… let this be over soon.

With all my love, my dearest one,

Your Kitten xx

———•———

On the journey to the Sanderson house this morning, it's been very difficult to concentrate on anything at all. My mind is filled with images and memories of my evening with Amelie. Her kindness, her words, her breathless need – which only matches my own – have banished all my doubts and scattered them to the four winds.

"You seem more cheerful this morning," Thompson says, even though he's concentrating on driving.

"That would be because I am. It's amazing what an evening spent with Amelie, and a good night's sleep will do."

"Did you work everything out with her?" he asks.

"If you're asking whether I proposed, the answer is 'no'. But we talked. It was… helpful." I choose my words carefully, because around Harry Thompson, it's best to.

"Helpful?" He shakes his head, smiling. "Is that a euphemism for…"

"It's not a euphemism for anything." I cut him off before he completely lowers the tone of the conversation. "We talked. That's all." I'm not going to tell him how close we came to doing a lot more than talking – because I'm still a gentleman. Just.

He pulls onto the Sanderson's driveway and parks the car and I can feel our moods dropping. "Let's hope today goes better than I think it will," he says.

"You think it's a hoax, don't you?"

"Yes." He turns to look at me. "But we have to go through the motions, don't we?"

I nod my head, knowing that the first of those 'motions' is for Harry to accompany Mr Sanderson to the bank to collect the ransom money.

Thompson and Mr Sanderson have been gone about ten minutes. They expect their journey to take no more than three quarters of an hour, all told, so I'm waiting at the house for them, and when they get back, it's intended that we'll go over the plan for this evening's drop off of the money, and then Thompson and I will return to the station for a while.

Mrs Sanderson is still upstairs. As far as I can understand it, she hasn't come down at all yet today, and I've been sitting in the drawing room by myself, when Lois brings me in some coffee on a small tray. It's the first time I've been served any refreshments here, apart from when

Mrs Slater gave me a cup of tea in the kitchen on that first afternoon, and I find myself rather surprised by her entrance.

"Cook and I thought you might like some coffee," Lois says, putting the tray down on the table in front of me.

"Thank you. That's very kind." She's just straightening up, when there's a loud, urgent and continuous knocking on the door, and she yelps in surprise as it stops, and then starts again after a few moments' pause. I get to my feet and say, "It's alright. I'll come with you," taking in the worried expression on her face.

She nods her head and we both go out into the hall, where she opens the front door tentatively, to reveal a constable, who I don't know, standing on the other side, his helmet tucked neatly under his arm. He looks pale and slightly fearful.

"What's going on, Constable?" I step forward.

"Sorry… are you Inspector Stone?" he asks.

"Yes."

"In that case…" He glances at Lois, and then continues, "Sergeant Tooley says would you mind coming with me… right away, please, sir?"

He stares at me, rather hard, willing me to understand. And I do. Something's happened. And it's not good.

I turn, and discover that Lois is already holding out my coat and hat, which I take from her, with thanks, before exiting the house.

"Tell me you brought a car," I murmur to the constable as we walk up the driveway.

"It's parked outside," he replies.

"Good."

We climb into the Wolseley and he turns it around, driving back down the road at speed. I don't bother to ask him what's happened. Apart from the fact that I'm fairly sure Tooley will have instructed him to just get me to wherever I'm going, I've got a fairly good idea already. And besides, I'd rather just find out for myself, first hand, than have another man's perceptions of what I'm about to see.

"What's your name, Constable?"

"Beresford, sir."

"Right. Well, when you've dropped me off, Constable Beresford, I want you to go back to the house and wait for Sergeant Thompson to return. Tell him to come and find me, will you?"

The constable nods his head.

"But – and this is very important – do not tell Mr and Mrs Sanderson anything yet. Do you understand? I need to see what we're dealing with first. If they ask, just tell them that there's been a development and that I'll come back and report to them as soon as I can."

"Very good, sir."

When we get to the small park, which I'd decided wasn't worth searching, due to the lack of hiding places, Beresford turns the car left, into Effingham Road, and I keep my eyes open, wondering which house I should be looking at. After a few hundred yards, however, he turns again, to the right this time, and shortly afterwards, parks the car, behind several other police vehicles, alongside the other recreation ground. I feel a chill run down my spine, but I ignore it and climb from the passenger seat.

Tooley is standing by the gate and comes over to me, his expression grim.

"You've found her?" I don't wait for him to state the obvious and he nods his head. "Where?"

He points to the far corner of the park, away off in the distance, where there's a small shelter of some kind. A shed, perhaps? There are a couple of uniformed officers standing in front of it and I glance back at Tooley.

"Here?"

"Yes, sir."

"Bloody hell," I mutter, under my breath, and we start to walk towards the building – if you can call it that.

"We'd just about finished the house-to-house searches," Tooley explains, walking beside me. "And we got to the park itself this morning…" His voice fades and I glance at his whitened features before taking in my surroundings. Most of the grass has been dug up, with the exception of about the first fifteen feet or so, where there are some children's swings and a slide, on the far side, although they're fenced off at the moment. Walking in silence now, we stick to the pathway, until we get to the shed.

PC Wells is there, looking pale, along with another constable I don't recognise.

"Sir," Wells says, nodding his head.

I return the gesture and, steeling myself for the worst, go into the wooden structure through the flimsy door, stopping on the threshold.

"Was this locked?" I ask.

"No, sir," Wells replies.

"And who found her?"

"I did," he says.

I don't reply, but turn back into the room, letting my eyes adjust to its dimness. There are no windows, so it's hard to see, but even so, I can make out the small figure lying on the floor in the corner, her body flat against the wall. I observe the neatly piled tools and garden implements; spades, shovels, forks, and a large pile of string. I pick up a single strand, which I note is of considerable length, coiled around and around itself, and see that it has a small wooden stake attached at either end. The other pieces of string are all identical, with similar pieces of wood tied to them, and I drop the one I'm holding, shaking my head. I have no idea what that is for and at the moment I don't care.

Turning, I move across the room and crouch down by the child, recognising her straight away from her photograph. Her hair, which is peeping out from her hat, is the same shade of red as her mother's. Her pale green eyes are open and staring, and she has pouting lips, which are a blueish purple, but which I imagine would have been pink. Her nose tips up at the end and she has a light dusting of freckles across her cheeks, although one of them is bruised, quite badly. She's wearing a thick, pale blue coat, which is still fastened, but… my stomach churns and I try not to retch… her red dress has been pulled up and her underwear removed. I put my hand over my mouth and close my eyes, in an attempt to erase that image… even though I know I never will.

Opening them again and swallowing down the bile that's gathered in my throat, I notice that her legs have turned a blueish grey in colour, from the cold, and that her short white socks are dirty. One of her shoes has come off and is lying on its side and I reach over and pick it up, holding it in my hand for a moment, before putting it down on the ground.

Very gently, I rest my hand on her cold head. "I'm sorry, Amy," I murmur under my breath, and then slowly, I get to my feet.

Outside, Tooley, Wells and the other constable are standing waiting.

"Have you let the doctor know?" I ask Tooley, surprising myself by being so calm.

"Yes, sir. He's on his way."

I nod and turn to Wells. "Was the body concealed in any way?"

"It was covered with some old rags, sir," he replies. "But her foot was sticking out. I saw it the moment I went in there."

"So the workmen couldn't have missed it?"

"No, sir. Although there were no workmen here when we arrived."

"And does anyone know why they have so much string in here, with those little pieces of wood attached at either end?"

The unnamed constable peers inside the shed. "That'll be for digging the trenches," he says.

"Excuse me?" I look down at him and he stands upright, as though to attention.

"This area's being dug for potatoes, isn't it, sir?" he asks.

"That's my understanding, yes."

"In that case, when they come to dig the trenches, they'll put those bits of string along the ground, holding them in place with those wooden stakes, and then dig along them, making sure they keep in a straight line, before planting the potatoes."

"I see... And your name is?"

"PC Miller, sir."

"Well, thank you, PC Miller. Just out of interest, does anyone know where the workmen are? And why they failed to report the girl's body lying in their shed?"

They all shake their heads and I look up, noticing a small group of people standing near the gates to the park. There are two constables stopping them from entering, but I fancy I might find out more about the absentee, or unobservant workmen from the prying eyes of the local neighbours than from any official enquiry.

"Stay here," I say quietly and make my way back to the entrance. Close to the front of the group is a middle aged woman, with a pale green headscarf and rosy cheeks. She's watching my every step and I find myself addressing her directly, even though my question is aimed at the group in general: "Does anyone here know where the workmen are? Or why they're not here today?"

The woman folds her arms across her chest. "They haven't been here for over a week now," she says with a single nod of her head. "One of them told me their job was just to remove the swings and slide from the other side of the park…" She points towards the opposite corner to where the shed is situated. "Then to clear the turf away. He said a different team has to come in and do the actual digging of the trenches and the planting. And I believe a third team will come at the end to reposition the swings and slide… that's why they're fenced off at the moment, so none of the kids can use them when they're not safe."

"Completely disorganised, if you ask me," someone mumbles behind her and there's a general murmuring of assent.

"Waste of bloody time," says someone else.

I notice a car pulling up along the street and thank them for their assistance. "What's happened?" the woman asks. "Is it that little girl? The one who was missing?"

I look down at her. "Thank you for your help," I repeat evasively and she nods her head slowly, just as Thompson walks up to me. We go to move away, when another car parks up, and I see Doctor Wyatt descend, a dark expression on his face.

Thompson and I wait for the doctor and then we start walking further into the park before I turn to them.

"It's her," I say.

The doctor swears under his breath. "I've been waiting for this call," he adds in a louder voice. "Even though I hoped I'd never get it."

"Well, it's not pretty. So prepare yourself."

Thompson looks up at me, but I don't elaborate and we walk on in silence until we reach the shed. Tooley steps to one side, allowing the doctor entrance to the building and I decide to give him some space and freedom to do his job. In any case, I'm in no hurry to see the girl's body again.

"How did it go at the bank?" I ask Thompson, while we're waiting.

"Easy," he replies. "The money was ready. Mr Sanderson just had to sign for it, not that it matters now."

"Like hell it doesn't." He glances up at me. "Just because Amy's dead doesn't mean we're not still going to make the drop tonight. Whoever sent that note could still turn up – assuming it was a hoax in the first place, which I was always rather inclined to think it was. And if they do, I'm going to come down on them like a ton of bricks."

He nods. "I take it the family don't know yet? I mean, I left Sanderson to go into the house by himself once Beresford had given me the message to come down here… But does Mrs Sanderson know?"

I shake my head. "No. She was still in bed when I left, and I told Beresford not to inform anyone and that we'd go back there later on." Thompson nods. "We can't be long though. I think those people by the gates have already guessed what's going on, and the last thing we need is for the rumour mill to start."

The doctor appears at the doorway, carrying his hat in his hand, the shock obvious on his face.

"It looks like the cause of death was a blow to the back of the head," he says.

"Not exposure then?" That had been my first thought on seeing her.

"No. There's a contusion…" He puts his free hand behind his own head, indicating the place of the wound, I assume.

"Any idea of the weapon?"

"No. I'd say she's been here for several days."

"So since the day she disappeared?"

"Well, I can't be sure about that, but probably. It fits." He pauses. "And she's been sexually assaulted."

Thompson swears more loudly and with a great deal more profanity than the doctor did.

"Before or after death?" I ask.

"I can't say for sure yet, but if you wanted me to guess, I'd say after."

I nod my head, despite the nausea that's sweeping through my body, as I wonder which is worse. Clearly if it was after death, she'd have known nothing about it, which has to be a blessing. But what kind of person could do that? "Let me know as soon as possible, will you?"

"Of course. Can I take the body?"

"Give me fifteen minutes." He raises his eyebrows in question. "I want to get back to the family and break the news to them before you remove the body from here. Once you do that, the news will break like wildfire."

"Very well," he says and checks his watch. "Fifteen minutes."

I turn to Tooley. "Walk with me."

I can't afford to waste time, being as we're now on the clock and he steps up beside me, with Thompson a pace behind. "Once Wyatt has removed the body, I want that shed stripped," I tell him. "Remove everything from it… and I mean *everything*. And then get all of it to Prentice. Tell him I want it all checked for prints. And for traces of blood."

"Yes, sir."

"And then I want a fingertip search done of the entire area."

He glances around the park, which now resembles a muddied field. "Right…"

"I know it's a big task, but we're looking for the murder weapon. And for the little girl's underwear. It wasn't on the body."

He gulps. "Y—Yes, sir. I'll get right onto it."

"Are you alright?" I ask him and he nods just as we part company at the park gates and Tooley speaks to one of the constables on duty, while Thompson and I make our way back to the car in silence.

Once inside, he turns to me. "Did you know?" he asks.

"Know what?"

"About the sexual assault."

"Yes. Well… I assumed. Her underwear had been removed."

"You checked?" He's shocked.

"I didn't need to, Harry. Her dress had been pulled up."

He nods. "Sorry."

He goes to start the car, but I put my hand on his arm. "Are you going to be okay with this?" I ask him.

"With what?"

"With her being a child… and what's been done to her."

"It's no worse for me than it is for you," he reasons and switches on the engine.

"Except you have a child and a pregnant wife. And I don't. It's more… personal for you."

He looks across at me. "I'll be fine."

"Well, if you're not, I'd rather you said. Or just made yourself scarce."

He doesn't reply, but simply nods his head.

Mr Sanderson is sitting in the drawing room, and Lois shows us in immediately upon our arrival, having taken our hats and left them in the hallway. I'm surprised to find his wife is there with him. She looks up as we enter and then goes back to staring out of the window again – her usual pose, it seems.

"Where did you go?" Sanderson asks Thompson.

"He came to find me," I reply, moving into the room and standing in a space that's roughly between the two of them, as I did on the first day I met them. Thompson hangs back, close to the sideboard. "I'm afraid I have some bad news."

Mrs Sanderson turns and looks up at me. "Amy?" she says, speaking to me for the first time since our conversation about David Cooke.

"Yes."

"What is it?" Her husband stands, moving closer. "Is she…? Have you found her?"

"Yes. I'm afraid she's dead." I can't think of another way of putting it, and dressing it up with pretty words won't make it any easier to hear.

Mrs Sanderson blinks and then tears start to fall silently down her cheeks, and even though she's clutching a handkerchief in her hand, she doesn't do anything with it. She just lets the tears flow.

"Are you sure it's her?" Sanderson says, his desperation obvious.

"Yes, sir. I'm sorry."

"But it could be someone else, couldn't it?"

"No. I'm afraid not." He stares at me for a moment and then nods his head in acceptance. "I'm sorry, but we will need to carry out a formal identification of the body."

Sanderson nods again and takes another step towards me. "I'll come," he says quietly.

"We don't have to do it now," I reply, holding up my hand, and he stops and looks up at me. "We can do it later."

He turns and sits back down again, ignoring his wife's now obvious distress as tears continue to stream down her cheeks. "H—How did she die?" he asks.

"We're awaiting confirmation from the doctor," I reply, because I don't want to reveal too much in front of his wife. I can be sensitive, even if he can't.

He stands again, lunging at me, although I don't move. "She's my daughter," he spits. "S—She *was* my daughter. I'm entitled to know."

I take a breath. "We believe she died from a blow to the head, but that is yet to be confirmed."

He deflates. "A—A blow to the head? Would she have known anything? Would she have suffered."

I have no idea, but I just say, "No," because it seems like the kindest thing to do in the circumstances.

"So… what happens now?" he asks, sitting down again, much calmer.

"Our enquiry becomes a murder investigation," I say simply. I'm not going to give him chapter and verse on what that entails. He won't take it in anyway. "Once we get notification from the doctor, we'll take you to identify your daughter. That may be later tonight, or it might be over the weekend."

He nods his head and sits back, trancelike.

"And in the meantime, we'll come back here at ten-thirty tonight, as planned."

He looks up at me, confused. "Tonight?"

"Yes, sir. The ransom…"

"But surely, there's no point. Not… not now."

"We still have to go through with it, just in case. If it was a hoax, I'd like to catch whoever's responsible. I'm sure you agree…"

He takes a deep breath. "I suppose," he mumbles and then lets his head drop down onto the back of the sofa, his eyes closing. I glance at Mrs Sanderson, who's still crying silently to herself.

"Mrs Sanderson?" I move slightly closer to her. "Can I get you anything?"

She doesn't acknowledge me to start with, but then slowly raises her head. "No," she says quietly. "No, thank you."

I inwardly shake my head, wondering at how two people can be so unfeeling towards each other – especially now. Even if they no longer love or care for one another, surely in these circumstances, they can find it within themselves to at least try and show some basic humanity. After all, the life they created together is now lost. That has to count for something.

"We'll go and see your nanny now." There seems little point in standing here watching these two ignoring each other.

"Elizabeth?" Sanderson says, sitting forward all of a sudden.

"Yes." How many nannies does he have?

"Why?" he asks.

"Just to notify her of what's happened," I reply. "We'll come back tomorrow and question her again, once she's had time to recover from hearing about it."

"She'll be devastated," he says. "I—I think I should be the one to tell her." I stare at him. "She does work for me," he reasons. "I'll tell Mrs Slater and Lois as well." He's trying to sound reasonable now and I suppose I can't really argue with him. I imagine the nanny will probably feel dreadful, and possibly responsible for what's happened – rightly or wrongly. The girl was in her charge, after all.

"Tell her we'll come back to see her tomorrow, will you?" Sanderson raises his eyebrows. "This is a murder enquiry now," I remind him. "I'll need to question her again."

"Why?" he asks. "Nothing will have changed. Not from Elizabeth's perspective."

"Even so…"

He hesitates. "Very well, but this time, I'd like to be present."

"As you wish."

It might be interesting to see the two of them together.

We stop off at the park on the way back to the station, to find the search is well under way. Tooley has taken charge of it, and a dozen or more men are combing the site, looking through the hedges that surround the area, and the churned up earth. There's no doubt about it, this is going to be a painstaking task.

Sitting in the car, Thompson turns to look at me.

"Why didn't you tell Sanderson what had been done to the child?" he asks. "She was his daughter…"

"Because he still has to make the ransom drop tonight. Obviously hearing that she's dead is bad enough, but hearing about the sexual assault… well, it could be enough to push him over the edge. And I need him to act normally tonight. As normally as any man can in these circumstances."

"So you will tell him?"

"Of course." God knows how, but I will.

Back at the station, we find some of the contents of the shed have already arrived and Prentice is standing in the main office, staring down at it and scratching his head.

"I didn't realise there would be this much," he says.

"Sorry." I take off my hat and coat, placing them on a nearby table.

"Don't be. It just might take a while, that's all." He looks around. "I'll collar a couple of constables and start getting this lot shifted into my office."

I nod my head and go over to the noticeboard, where someone has helpfully pinned up photographs of the shed, and the park, beside the map of the area, with lines having been drawn to indicate whereabouts they are, geographically speaking. Down the other side of the board are several pictures of the girl's body, taken from different angles.

"Christ," Thompson whispers from behind me and I'm aware of him wandering away to the other side of the room.

I go and pick up my coat and hat and then walk over to him, tapping him on the shoulder.

"My office," I say quietly and he hesitates and then follows me into my room, closing the door.

"I meant what I said, Harry. If this one it too much for you…"

"It's not."

"I can take Deakin or Gilmore off the burglary and swap you in."

"I said I'm fine."

I stare at him for a moment and then sit down at my desk, indicating the chairs opposite me. He pauses and then walks over, sitting down in the one on the right. "We'll finalise the plan for tonight," I say quietly, "and then we'll get together the men who are going to be working on that with us." I look up at him. "I'll need you to do that. We'll explain their duties and what's expected of them. And then we'll all go home and get something to eat and a couple of hours' rest. You can spend some time with Julia and with Christopher before he goes to bed…" He nods his head, just once. "And then you can pick me up again at ten from my aunt's. Alright?"

"Yes." I get to my feet again. "Rufus?" He looks up at me. "I'm sorry. I'll try and be more professional."

I smile. "I'm not worried about that." I walk around to his side of the table and lean against it. "As far as I'm concerned you can swear and curse as much as you like, but… well, this was already a God-awful case and it just got a hundred times worse. I'll release anyone from it who doesn't think they can cope with it. They won't be helping the investigation."

"I can cope with it," he says firmly.

"Good." I smile down at him and then push myself off the desk, resting my hand on his shoulder for a moment, before going over to the door and calling the nearest constable.

My mother and Aunt Dotty are surprised when I walk in the door at just before six o'clock, although when I explain the reason – without going into details – their faces fall, and my mother takes a step forward.

"Are you alright?" she says.

"Yes."

She looks into my eyes. "Are you sure?"

"I have to be."

She stares for a moment longer. "Let's have supper, and then you can go and see Amelie."

"I have to go out again later." She tilts her head to one side in confusion and I explain about the ransom drop and why we're still going ahead with it.

"Well, you can still spend an hour or so with her," she says. "It'll do you good."

My mother knows me far too well, but in this instance, I'm not going to disagree with her.

After supper, I shrug on my coat and go over the road to Amelie's house. This time, the door is answered by the maid, Sarah, but that's not surprising, being as Amelie wasn't expecting me tonight.

"Miss Cooper is in the drawing room," Sarah says, taking my coat with a smile. For the first time though, she doesn't bother to show me the way. She leaves me to it, and that makes me smile, just a little, despite the day I've had.

I knock on the door – because it feels like the right thing to do – and when I hear Amelie call out, "Come in," I push it open and enter.

"Rufus?" She's surprised and snaps closed the book she was reading, jumping to her feet and running over to me. She's in my arms before I can even say 'hello', and I hold her close to me, relishing the feel of her soft body against mine. "I didn't think I'd see you tonight." She pulls back and looks up at me. "What's wrong?" she says, her face dropping.

"We found her." It's all I need to say.

"Is she…?"

"She's dead."

She holds my hand in hers and leads me to the sofa, guiding me into its corner and sitting me down, before she lowers herself beside me, twisting so she's facing me. "Are you alright?" she asks. I shake my head.

"It's awful." I hear my voice crack and fall silent.

"Can you tell me?" she asks. "Do you want to?"

I nod my head. "I need to... but I'm not sure I should."

She moves a little closer, holding my hand tighter still in hers. "If you need to tell me, then tell me."

The softness of her voice makes me feel more at ease than I have all day and, keeping my eyes fixed on our clasped fingers, I begin, "We found her in a workman's shed. It looks like she was hit over the head on the day she disappeared, and left there."

"Oh God," she whispers.

"And she was sexually assaulted," I add, my voice so quiet I can barely hear it myself.

"No," she says and I look up at her now, the shock visible in her eyes. "No." She's shaking her head. "She was just a child..." I release my hand from hers and pull her close to me but she leans back, preventing me, and she cups my face in one of her hands. "Did you see her?" she asks.

"Of course."

"Oh, Rufus..." She shifts in her seat and, like last night, she sits on my lap, sideways on this time, not straddling me. There's nothing sexual about this, but it's comforting, as she cradles my head in her hands and rests hers against mine, forehead to forehead.

We sit for a while, her stroking my hair and my cheek, holding me, easing my pain, until she slowly leans back again.

"Did I do enough?" I hear my own voice asking the question that's been rattling around my head, ever since Constable Beresford arrived at the Sanderson house this morning.

"What do you mean?" She tilts her head to one side.

"I got the men to search all the houses first, rather than going straight to the park. I thought the workmen there would have reported seeing a little girl by herself, so I didn't think to have the area searched..." I look up into her eyes. "That was a mistake, wasn't it?"

She shifts closer to me on my lap. "No. You said she was killed on the day she disappeared, so it wouldn't have made any difference if you'd got the men to search there first, would it? The outcome would have been the same." I know what she's saying is logical. "You did the best you could at the time, with the information you had to hand,

Rufus. You can't blame yourself for this." Her voice catches and I raise my hand, caressing the side of her cheek with my fingertips. "I won't let you."

"I love you, my darling," I murmur.

"I love you too."

"I wish… I wish I could explain to you how good you are for me."

"You don't need to. I already know, because I feel the same. You're good for me too, Rufus." I put my arm around her and she nestles down into me. "This is a little different to last night, isn't it?" she murmurs.

"Just a little."

"It's still very nice, though," she says. "I like being close to you. I like the comfort of you."

"Do you need the comfort of me?" I ask, and she looks up.

"Always."

I lean down and very gently kiss her upturned lips. "I'm yours, my darling." I stare into her eyes. "But I'm afraid this does change things."

She sits back. "How?" She looks so worried, so scared, I can't help but smile.

"It doesn't change anything between us," I say, setting her mind at rest, I hope. "It just means that I won't be here very much over the weekend." She looks confused, her brow furrowing. "You wanted to decorate the Christmas tree?"

"Oh, don't worry about that." She rests her hand on my chest and leans back into me again, her head on my shoulder.

"I'll do my best to make some time," I murmur, settling down, "but I doubt it'll be until sometime early next week."

"Well, I wouldn't worry too much about it; the weekend is already in tatters. Uncle Gordon left a message here today to say that he's coming back on Saturday evening. He's staying until Sunday night – although I'm not sure why, being as he'll only be here for a few hours."

"Why don't you decorate the tree with him then?" I suggest. "You could do it on Sunday, couldn't you? And it might give you the chance to mend some fences."

She shakes her head slowly, her hand coming up and playing with one of my shirt buttons. "No," she says quietly. "I'd rather do it with you. But we don't have to do it this weekend. The tree is already in the garden and we can bring it in whenever you have time… as long as it's before Christmas."

I kiss the top of her head and she looks up at me. "It will be, I promise."

She snuggles into me and, breathing out a long sigh, she undoes the button of my shirt just like she did last night, only this time she lets her fingers wander inside, and then I feel her hand resting on my chest, skin-on-skin. That's all she does. Just that. And we sit together for a while, intimate and comfortable. Nothing could be better.

It's nearly quarter past one in the morning. And it's freezing. And no-one has even gone anywhere near the bench in the park.

We've been watching it for over two hours, since Mr Sanderson dropped the bag containing the money underneath the seat at eleven pm as demanded, before he returned home.

The men stationed around the recreation ground, and in the roads leading up to it, must be as cold and tired as we are, and I look at Thompson in the moonlight, in our hiding place behind a bush about twenty yards from the bench, and give him a nod.

"Let's call it a night," I whisper.

"Okay." He moves forward and, once he's free of the branches of the bush, he stands and stretches. I do likewise, as Thompson makes his way towards the other side of the park, where we both know Sergeant Tooley is stationed. While he's gone, I wander over to the bench and retrieve the money bag, checking the contents are still intact, which they are.

A few minutes later, Thompson returns and, even in the dim moonlight, I can see Tooley in the distance, going around various points in the park, and men appearing behind him.

"Stan's going to round the men up and send them home," Thompson says, coming to stand beside me. "So what do we do now?"

"Firstly, we return the money to Mr Sanderson and let him know what's happened." He requested this of me earlier. Despite the fact that nothing is going to bring his daughter back, he wanted to know the outcome, and I can't say I blame him for that.

"And then?"

"We get a few hours' sleep."

"And what will happen about this?" He nods towards the bench where the money was deposited.

"Well, it was obviously a hoax," I tell him as we walk back to the car. "The question we have to ask ourselves is, was it someone who read about the girl being missing and saw their chance, but then backed down when they heard she'd been found…"

"Or?"

"Or was it the murderer, playing games with us."

He stops and looks up at me. "What do you mean?"

"Well, I know we continued the search after we got the ransom note, but they didn't know we'd do that, did they? If they knew where we were looking, they might have thought sending a ransom note would make us stop the search, and would buy them more time, to maybe move the body?"

He nods and we start walking again. "Which do you think it is?" he asks.

"At the moment, I don't know. I hope it's the former."

"Why?"

"Because that's more straightforward. If it's the latter, that means we're looking for someone who isn't scared to alter their plans, to adapt to changing circumstances. And that makes them much harder to spot. They're less likely to make mistakes… And I'd rather like them to make a mistake."

We halt by the car and he turns to me. "Because we don't have very much to go on?" he suggests.

"Try nothing at all."

Chapter Six

Dearest Kitten,

I've just read in the newspaper about the discovery of Amy's body. I'm in shock. There aren't that many details, but this is absolutely dreadful. You must be devastated, my beautiful beloved. I wish I could be with you, to hold you in my arms and kiss away your troubles.

I've got your letter from yesterday in front of me, and despite this latest news, I want to reassure you that, of course it's not awful of you to want to be with me. I want exactly the same thing, because that's how it should be, my darling. We're perfect together. And one day very soon, I hope we'll be together again. I can't wait. And you shouldn't feel guilty for wanting that too.

I miss you like mad, my beautiful Kitten. I can't wait to be with you again, and no matter what happens in the coming hours and days, remember that I love you and we will be together soon.

With all my love,

D xx

———•———

"You look exhausted."

My mother and Dotty are both watching me closely at the breakfast table, although it was Mother who spoke.

"I didn't get in until nearly three," I explain, taking some toast. "And I'm afraid my hours could be erratic for the foreseeable future."

"Were you able to explain that to Amelie last night?" my mother asks. "Or would you like me to go and see her today?"

I shake my head. "No, I explained it to her." I did. As we were saying goodnight. She was very understanding. "I've promised to help her decorate their Christmas tree," I add, "so I'll find the time for that, but…"

"Oh, that's lovely," Mother interrupts, beaming, her hands clasped together.

"Do you think you'll be back for dinner tonight?" Aunt Dotty asks, before Mother can go into further raptures.

"I honestly don't know. Why?" I glance across the table at her, while I'm spreading blackberry jam onto my toast.

"Because Issa's due to arrive this afternoon…"

"She is?"

"Yes." Aunt Dotty smiles. "She's coming for Christmas."

"Already?" Christmas isn't for another week yet. I'm surprised Aunt Issa has been willing to give up her writing for that long. I doubt she'll get much time – or peace – to do any here.

"I telephoned her yesterday," Mother explains, taking over the story. "We talked it through and she agreed it might be wise to come up early… to… to avoid any last minute rushes on the trains."

"They're unreliable enough as it is," Dotty adds.

There's something about the way they're talking that makes me wonder what they're hiding. I know they're hiding something – that much is obvious. But as to what it is, I have no idea. Still, I have no doubt I'll find out soon enough.

"I'll do my best to get back for dinner." I finish my toast and gulp down my tea. "I'm sorry, but I've just realised I need to make a telephone call before Sergeant Thompson arrives." My mother smiles and I wonder if she's thinking I'm going to phone Amelie. I wish I was, but I'm not, and I stand and leave the room, going out into the hall, where the telephone sits on the long side table.

I ask the operator to connect me to the London Road station, asking for Sergeant Tooley once the call is connected.

"Hello?" He sounds as tired as I feel.

"Tooley? It's Inspector Stone."

"Yes, sir?"

"Can you do something for me?"

"I'll do my best."

"Sergeant Thompson and I are going over to the Sanderson house this morning, but in our absence, could you put together a list of all the known felons in the area with a history of sexual assault."

There's a pause. "Against children, sir?" he asks.

"And adults. Our man may have just decided to… diversify." I can't think of another way of phrasing that. "Obviously you can ignore any who are currently incarcerated, and I'd stick to the ones who are based in the fairly immediate vicinity of Long Ditton for now. Whoever did this must have been aware of the workmen's movements."

"Yes, sir."

"If possible, can you try and have that on my desk this afternoon?"

"I'll do my best, sir."

"Get Wells and a couple of the others to help, if necessary."

"Yes, sir… While you're on," he adds quickly, "DC Deakin would like a word."

"Very well."

I wait and then hear a different voice. "Inspector Stone?"

"Yes, Deakin?"

"I'm sorry to trouble you, but I wanted to update you on what's been happening… and ask a question."

"Very well."

He explains that the second youth has now confessed in the burglary case, which is hardly surprising, considering his situation. "Alex… I mean DC Gilmore and I spent most of yesterday going through the evidence. I think they'd already sold some of it, but we've got quite a bit… What I wanted to ask was, what do we do with it?"

"You catalogue it, label it and give it to Sergeant Tooley to be locked up in the evidence room. But I'd suggest you make a separate note of all the items you've found, and then go and see the victims. Ask them to describe the things that were taken, and cross-reference them against your list. You can hopefully put their minds at rest that at least some of their possessions have been found – even if they can't have them back yet."

"Very good, sir," he says.

"With all of that in mind, can you put me through to the chief superintendent?"

"Yes, sir. Um… what will Gilmore and I do after we've finished going through the evidence and seeing the victims?" he asks.

"I'll move you over to this murder case," I tell him.

"Oh… right, sir." I can almost hear his gulp. "I—I'll put you through to the chief super."

"Thank you, Deakin… And good work, by the way."

"Thank you, sir."

The phone goes dead for a moment, and I hear a couple of clicks, and then Webster's voice.

"Stone?"

"Yes, sir."

"How are you?"

"Fine, sir." It's a lie and he knows it, but there's no point in telling him the truth. There's nothing he can do about it.

"What can I do for you?" he asks.

"I've just had a conversation with DC Deakin. He's informed me that the two suspects have confessed to the burglaries. Evidently some of the jewellery was sold before their arrest, but a lot of it has been salvaged. Deakin and Gilmore are going to catalogue it all today and will be going to visit your sister and the other victims later on to let them know. Obviously they can't have their things back yet…"

"No, obviously," he interrupts. "But it's good work, nonetheless."

"I know. I've told him that. And once they've finished what they're doing, I'll be moving them over to this murder case."

"Very good."

"I just wanted to keep you updated… as promised."

"Good of you, Stone," he says. "I'll telephone Ruth and let her know to expect a visit."

Thompson pulls the car into the driveway of the Sanderson house.

"Today's going to be hell, isn't it?" he says.

"Yes."

"Ever dealt with a case like this before?" he asks, turning to me.

"A child murder? Yes... three times."

"With the sexual element?" he asks.

I nod my head. "One of them. She was thirteen."

He huffs out a sigh, which says everything that needs saying and we both get out of the car.

Lois looks like she's been crying half the night, her eyes red-rimmed and swollen. She closes the door behind us and takes our hats and coats, before leading us to the drawing room in silence. It's hard to know what to say to her, so we don't say anything – whatever we do say is likely to upset her, and that's not going to help anyone.

Inside the drawing room, Mr Sanderson is sitting by himself, staring into the fire. There's no sign of his wife, but he looks up as we enter.

"Inspector," he says, his voice rather monotone. He doesn't acknowledge Sergeant Thompson, but I doubt Harry will mind. "My... my wife is still in bed," he continues.

"That's alright, sir." I move further into the room and sit opposite him, uninvited, although he doesn't seem to care. "I'm afraid I have to give you some information... some detail about how your daughter was killed."

He looks up at me, and leans forward. "Detail? You told me yesterday, she received a blow to the head... what else..."

"The blow to the head is the cause of death, but I'm afraid I have to tell you that something else was done to her."

"What are you saying?" he asks.

"I'm very sorry, Mr Sanderson. I'm afraid your daughter was sexually assaulted."

He stares at me for a moment, then clasps his hand across his mouth and runs from the room, clattering into the side table and knocking over the lamp that sits on top of it. We hear the front door open and then the sound of retching, followed by vomiting.

I stand and pick up the lamp, setting it back on the table again, and then sit and wait, until eventually I hear the front door close, and the sound of footsteps coming back in our direction. Mr Sanderson appears in the doorway, his face grey, his eyes haunted. He glances at

Thompson and then at me and comes and sits opposite me again, looking straight into my eyes.

"My daughter was sexually assaulted? Do you mean she was raped? Is that what you're telling me?" he murmurs.

"Yes. I'm very sorry."

"I'll kill him," he says, raising his voice, just slightly. "Whoever did this to Amy... I'll kill him."

I know I'm supposed to tell him that taking the law into his own hands isn't 'recommended' or 'advisable' and that we frown upon such things, but I don't blame him. I know, in his shoes, I'd feel exactly the same. I ignore his comments, however, and pose a question instead. "Can I ask you again, sir, whether you can think of any men who are associated with this household? Any men who'd wish you, or your family harm?"

"There is one," he says, with conviction. "There's one man who'd like to hurt me, who'd like me out of the way." He shakes his head. "But whether he'd do that..." He leaves his sentence hanging, and I notice he's gripping the edges of the sofa, his knuckles whitening.

"Who is this man?" I ask.

"David Cooke," he replies. "He's my wife's lover."

For a moment, I'm slightly taken aback, but I rally quickly. "Would he harm your daughter?" I ask.

"Well, in an ideal world, it would be me he'd rather see dead, I'm sure." A slight smile plays on his lips. "Then he could take my place as head of the family."

I want to tell him that the last thing Cooke wants to do is to take his place – the man's only designs are on his wife, not his children.

"I've known since the beginning... since the very first time she went to his bed," he says all of a sudden, the bitterness in his voice quite shocking. "She changed overnight," he adds slowly, as though he's thinking it all through, maybe for the first time. "She'd been unhappy – unwell, I suppose – since Amy was born, and things didn't really improve after Eve... She was distant, quiet, introverted. It was hard to know what to do, or say, most of the time, so I gave up trying. We muddled on through, and I kept hoping that she'd snap out of it. And then one day I came home from work and she was smiling and cheerful – completely different to her usual self. I honestly thought she'd finally turned a corner, but then she told me she'd met David, she said they'd spent the afternoon together, and how much fun they'd had. She was like a different person, Inspector. And then, I suppose about a week or ten days later, she changed again – only this time there as nothing cheerful about it. She became more secretive, and much more distant from me, and I knew then that she'd gone to bed with him. She started making excuses to go out during the day. She bought new clothes, started wearing make-up and perfume again." He looks up at me. "Sometimes I used to catch her daydreaming, with a faraway look on her face. It was so obvious what was going on, I've often wondered if she wanted me to know. Whether she was flaunting the affair at me, letting me know she'd found another man – a younger man – to share her body with."

I recall Lillian Sanderson's hurried entreaties not to tell her husband of her affair and wonder if that was just for my benefit. Based on what Mr Sanderson is saying, that seems quite likely.

"I suppose it was only to be expected really," he gets to his feet and stands in front of the fire, looking down at me. "She's so much younger than I am, after all." He runs his fingers through his hair. "But why on earth she had to choose David Cooke, I'll never know. The family connection goes back years." He stops and narrows his eyes. "Maybe that's the whole point," he muses. "Maybe she wanted me to feel worse still… knowing that she could take one of my friends and there was nothing I could do about it." He turns, resting his hands on the mantelpiece, his arms straight, the tension in his body obvious. "I know people think I'm harsh with her… that I don't care," he says quietly, so quietly that I have to strain to hear him. "But I'm not. Well, not intentionally, anyway." He turns back again, his eyes alight with emotion. "But do you have any idea what it's like, Inspector, to be married to a woman, who despises you, who makes it clear at every opportunity that she'd rather be anywhere than be with you?"

I don't reply, because I don't think he expects me to, although I do wonder whether his wife and her lover have any idea of the damage their relationship is causing. And if they think it's worth it. As Mr Sanderson gets his breath back and sits down, composing himself, I also take a moment to think about Amelie's guardian, Gordon Templeton. Did he think about Amelie and Beth, and his wife, when he started seeing Abigail Foster, all those years ago? Does anyone think about the people around them when they fall in love?

"I'm sorry," Mr Sanderson says, his words breaking into my thoughts, his voice much softer now. "I shouldn't have said any of that. It was just the… the shock. I don't for one minute believe that David Cooke would ever harm Amy, even if only because he loves my wife." He attempts a smile, but doesn't quite get there. "I can't in all honesty call him an honourable man, not when he and Lillian are conducting an affair behind my back, but I know David well enough to understand that he'd never hurt a woman he loved. Not knowingly."

That's perhaps the most fair and reasonable thing I've heard Sanderson say since we first met and it's hard not to admire his stoicism.

While I fully appreciate that nothing in life is a certainty, I'm feeling a lot more confident about my future with Amelie than I was – especially after the last couple of evenings with her. But I'd like to think that if she ever did turn away from me, I would conduct myself with similar forbearance.

However, none of that is going to help with our investigation.

"As I said yesterday," I remark, getting back to the point in hand, "we need to speak with Miss Sutton."

His head shoots up. "I'll go and fetch her," he says.

"Don't trouble yourself. Sergeant Thompson can go."

Without waiting to be told, Thompson leaves the room, although Mr Sanderson observes him closely, his eyes narrowing again, and for a moment, I wonder if he's jealous, or at least suspicious of my sergeant, who is, after all, a very handsome man… and my generosity towards Mr Sanderson wanes just slightly. *Is he really any better than his wife?*

Mr Sanderson and I sit in silence, although he doesn't take his eyes from the door, until it reopens, and Miss Sutton comes in, followed by Thompson, who looks across at me and raises his eyebrows. I have no idea what that means, but I glance at Miss Sutton and notice her red and swollen eyes, and assume that she, like Lois, has spent many hours in tears.

"Come and sit down," Sanderson says, moving along the sofa. Miss Sutton hesitates, glancing at the chair, but then goes and sits beside him, leaving about an eighteen inch gap between them.

She looks up at me, blinking quickly and dabbing at her eyes with a lace-trimmed handkerchief. I notice though, that her lipstick is still impeccable, and there isn't a hair out of place on her head.

"I know you've been informed that Amy's body has been found," I begin, and she nods her head, just once, sniffling slightly. "She was discovered in the workmen's shed in the larger park… the one on Ewell Road," I add.

Her mouth drops open. "What was she doing there?" she asks.

"Well, she didn't get there by herself," I reply, perhaps a little harshly. "Can you tell me about the man you saw in the recreation ground, when you were there?"

"I didn't really pay that much attention," she says. "He was tall…"
"And?"

Sanderson sits forward, but I ignore him. "He had on a hat, and a dark coat," she says. "I can't remember…" She turns to her employer. "I wasn't looking at him; I—I was looking at the pram, and then I saw that Amy was gone…" She starts to cry and he moves closer to her, putting his arm around her shoulder. "And then… then, once I knew she wasn't there, I just… I just ran back here," she says, sobbing more loudly.

I give her a few moments to calm down. "Do you remember telling me that Amy was a lovely child?" I say quietly. She looks up at me.

"Of course I do. She *was* a lovely child."

"She wasn't naughty, or wilful, or disobedient?"

"Not with me, no," she says. "I know she could be a bit badly behaved when I left her with Lois, or with Cook, but that's only because they're not… I mean, they weren't used to her… her ways…" She gulps down a couple of breaths and then looks back at Sanderson again. "I —I'll hand in my notice, of course," she murmurs. "You won't want me here—"

"You'll do no such thing," he interrupts. "How on earth do you think we'd manage without you?" He leans a little closer still and, with his arm still stretched across her shoulder, he places his free hand on her knee. "I told you yesterday, this is not your fault, my dear. We need you more than ever... to look after Eve." He adds that as an afterthought, and she smiles at him, dabbing at her cheeks and fluttering her eyelashes – or so it appears to me, anyway.

Sanderson stares at her for a moment, seemingly captivated, a blush appearing on his cheeks, and I wonder whether he'll stray. Or whether he has already?

My waning admiration for the man disappears altogether.

God, what a mess these people have made of their lives.

We leave Miss Sutton in the more than capable hands of her employer, agreeing that we'll return tomorrow to speak with Mrs Sanderson about David Cooke. Mr Sanderson seems more concerned for the nanny's well-being than he does over the fact that we're going to question his wife about her lover, but nothing he does surprises me anymore.

Once we're in the car, I turn to Thompson. "What was that look you gave me when you brought Miss Sutton into the room?"

He smirks. "Oh, nothing much," he replies. "She was just doing her damsel in distress bit when we were upstairs, that's all."

"Put on, or for real?" I ask.

"Hard to say." He thinks for a moment. "She'd been crying, that much was clear, but when I said we wanted to talk to her, she got all flustered and started panicking about it all being her fault, and Mr Sanderson sacking her."

"I think he's made it very clear that's the last thing on his mind."

"Hmm," he says, starting the engine and managing to put a great deal of emphasis into that simple sound.

When we get back to the station after a silent journey, Tooley has just finished putting together the list of local men with a history of sexual abuse.

"Before you go," I say to him as he starts to leave my office. "I'm sorry, but I've got another job for you."

"Yes, sir?"

"I know we asked the householders during the search whether they'd seen Amy on Tuesday afternoon, but I want you to arrange for some men to go back to the Ewell Road park and interview all the people who live in houses overlooking the area in more detail. I want to know if they saw anything unusual. I don't care what it was. Anything that didn't belong, at any time between early afternoon on Tuesday, and the time when the body was found. I've been assuming Amy was left in the shed on the day she died." At least that's what I told Amelie. "And if I'm being honest, I still think that's the most likely scenario. But it's dawned on me that she might have been killed somewhere else and dumped there some time later. We need to know if anyone saw anything."

"Very good, sir."

I look up at him. "I know it's the weekend, and I'm sorry for all the extra work."

He smiles. "None of us minds, sir," he says. "We just want to catch him… whoever he is."

I nod my head in agreement and he leaves the room, closing the door behind him, then I sit down at my desk, with Thompson taking a seat opposite me, and I look at the list which Tooley left behind. There are six men on it, which is more than I would have liked, but less than it could have been, I suppose.

"Any of these names ring a bell?" I ask, handing over the sheet of paper. It's been years since I've worked here, whereas Thompson is more familiar with the area and the people who inhabit it. I'm hoping some local insight might prove useful.

"I only know one of them," he says, pointing to the second name on the list. Albert Finch. "He's a nasty piece of work."

"In what way?"

"I arrested him about five years ago, in a domestic case."

"Really? Involving a child?"

He shakes his head. "No. We were called out one night by the neighbours, who reported a disturbance. It turned out Finch had beaten his wife black and blue. When I got there, she was being treated by an ambulance crew and he was sitting calmly at the kitchen table, nursing his bruised knuckles. He didn't deny what he'd done… admitted it right away, in fact. He claimed he'd come home from the pub and caught her with another man, the man had scarpered and he'd taken it out on her. But then, once Finch was safely under arrest, his wife changed her story. She told me there wasn't any other man involved, and that her husband had raped her *before* beating her."

"Had he?"

He shrugs. "We never did find out. She refused to go to hospital, or submit to any form of medical examination, and he denied it… the rape, that is. I wasn't sure I believed her. I thought she was probably just looking for a way to have him locked up for a bit longer, but I wanted to give her the benefit of the doubt and, to be fair, we couldn't find any trace of another man having been present in the house. Still, with no evidence, in the end it was six of one, and half a dozen of the other. He was charged with assault and was sentenced to twelve months, if memory serves."

"Is he worth talking to?" I ask him.

He thinks for a moment. "Can't hurt."

"Okay. Arrange to have him picked up with the others."

"Now?"

"Yes, now."

He stands. "I'll get that organised. Although I doubt we'll be able to start the interviews until tomorrow. Some of this lot won't be easy to find."

"Tomorrow's fine with me. Bring them in and let them stew in the cells overnight."

By the time Thompson and I are ready to leave for the day, I know four of the men have been brought in. One of them could be heard shouting the odds about police harassment throughout the entire building, I think. I fully expect that he'll keep his fellow inmates awake half the night with his rantings, but that works for me. The more tired they are, the more likely they are to slip up… assuming that any of them is guilty, of course.

My copper's instinct tells me that I'm going to find the perpetrator of this crime much closer to home, but I have to rule out the obvious, even while I'm working on the more obscure – and repulsive.

On the journey home, Thompson and I make our plans for the following day.

"We'll start with Mrs Sanderson," I tell him. "I want to get her out of the way first, and it won't hurt our wayward felons to sit in the cells for a few hours longer."

He nods. "Hopefully we'll get Doctor Wyatt's report back soon," he says.

"Not that it'll tell us anything we don't already know."

"No."

"How's the search of the park going?" I ask.

"Well, they're hampered by the lack of light," he says. It's getting dark by just after three o'clock at the moment, but then we are approaching the shortest day, and the weather is particularly grey and overcast. "I think Tooley is hoping to have it completed tomorrow."

"He's working like a trojan."

"They all are."

I can't disagree with that.

I get home at just before seven and let myself in, taking off my hat and coat and leaving them on the end of the stairs.

When I turn back, my mother is standing in the doorway to the living room.

"Come and see who's here," she says, beaming.

I know it's Aunt Issa, but I play along and follow her into the room, where Aunt Dotty is sat in her usual place, beside the fire. Next to her is Aunt Issa, wearing her country tweeds as usual, her mass of steel grey hair piled on her rounded face. She gets to her feet as I enter, but I'm distracted by the sight of Amelie, who's sitting in the sofa opposite my aunts, and who turns to face me, a beautiful smile on her face.

"Hello," I say, smiling across at her.

"Hello." She stands too.

"Well, that's a nice greeting, I must say." Aunt Issa puts her hands on her hips and glares at me, her lips twitching upwards.

"I apologise, Aunty," I say, going over to her and bending to kiss her cheek. "I was… distracted."

I turn and smile at Amelie again and she blushes.

"Understandable, dear boy," Issa replies, tapping my arm. "Completely understandable."

"Sit down, sit down," my mother urges, steering me towards Amelie, and I sit, taking her hand as we glance at each other and smile.

"This is a lovely surprise," I murmur softly.

"Your aunt telephoned me," she says.

"With two of them here, I'm afraid you're going to have to be more specific. Which aunt?"

"Dotty," Amelie clarifies. "She invited me for dinner."

I look across the room at Aunt Dotty, who's leaning against the arm of the sofa, a smile settled on her face. "Thank you," I mouth to her.

"Well, you haven't been able to see much of each other," she says by way of explanation. "And I thought it would be nice to have a big family meal to welcome Issa."

I can't help myself from smiling as she says 'family', and Amelie squeezes my hand at the same time. This is all so obvious, I feel like I may as well just get down on one knee right here and now… except I still don't have a ring, and I really would like to have one when I propose. It feels rather half-hearted making the offer without the symbol to indicate my commitment, or her acceptance.

"Issa's brought us up some pheasants," my mother says, as though we've been troubled by food shortages. Despite the issuing of ration books over two months ago, as yet, things have carried on pretty much as usual, although we all know the New Year will bring changes, so I suppose we might as well make hay while the sun shines… as it were.

"That sounds lovely." I turn to Amelie. "Do you like pheasant?"

"Yes," she replies – thankfully.

"I think we can go through in a minute," Dotty says. "But would you like a drink first?"

"I'd love one." Everyone else already seems to be catered for, but Aunt Dotty makes me a very quick, rather strong, gin and tonic – her speciality at present. It's not a patch on Amelie's dry martini, which is an abiding memory, but then nothing about that evening is likely to fade from my mind very quickly, I'm pleased to say.

As we walk through to dinner, I manage to pull Amelie back slightly, and although I'm fairly sure my mother and aunts are aware of what I'm doing, they talk among themselves and don't seem to mind.

"I'm sorry," I whisper.

"What for?" She looks up at me.

"If I'd known I was going to get home this early, we could have spent the evening decorating your tree."

She shakes her head and rests her hand on my arm. "Don't worry. Uncle Gordon got home just before I came out. I was rather pleased to escape."

"Oh…" I fake a pout. "So you didn't want to see me then?"

She glances towards the dining room door, through which my family have already disappeared, and then leans up and kisses me very quickly on the lips. "Of course I wanted to see you," she says softly, smiling.

"Good." I bend and kiss her back, taking a little longer than she did. "But you should try and spend some time with your uncle, while he's here." Her smile fades.

"He's already said he's got some work to do tomorrow," she replies. "I honestly don't know why he bothered coming home."

"Well, why not suggest you have a few hours together in the evening, before he has to go back to London?" I suggest.

She hesitates. "I suppose… Although I'd rather see you."

I smile down at her. "So would I. But I'll do my best to come over on Monday… and I'll make up for it then."

"Promise?" she says, with that lovely teasing tone to her voice.

"I promise."

We start towards the dining room, but I pull her back again. "Also…" I say, keeping my voice down, "I haven't told my mother and aunts about what was done to Amy… to the little girl. So, can you keep it to yourself?"

She nods her head. "Why didn't you tell them?"

"Because… well, I—I can't always share everything."

"Oh, you mean it's a secret… like when you couldn't tell me about Uncle Gordon's affair?"

"No. I mean I sometimes find elements of my cases hard to talk about."

"But you told me."

"I know. That's because I can talk to you, darling. I can't talk to everyone."

She smiles and I'm just about to kiss her again, when my mother's voice calls out, asking where we are, and we laugh, and go through to the dining room, hand in hand.

Chapter Seven

Dearest one,

It's simply awful.

I can't believe it's even happening. The whole thing is like a nightmare. The worst kind of nightmare, because it seems never-ending, especially when I'm away from you.

I have to agree with you, my darling, that whoever did this must have been a madman, for who else would have done such a thing to a lovely girl like Amy?

I can't bear to think about that sweet, darling little angel suffering... I just can't.

To know that you miss me as much as I miss you is the only thing keeping me going through all this insanity. To know that I'll soon be safe in your arms, being kissed by you and feeling your tender touch... Oh God... Just the thought of it is almost too much for me.

It's driving me mad being apart from you and I sometimes wonder if we could risk meeting up, even though the police seem to be everywhere and 'his lordship' still hasn't said anything about going back to work. God, I wish he would.

I wish I could get out of the house – even if only for a few minutes – to be with you and know there is still some sanity in the world.

I love you, my darling, so desperately.

Please write soon.

Your lonely Kitten xx

I know Aunt Dotty said she invited Amelie over here last night because I don't get to see her very much, but when we were sitting in the living room after supper, with Amelie's hand in mine, it dawned on me that she and I had actually spent three consecutive evenings together, despite my workload. They'd been very different, very individual evenings, but I'd enjoyed them all. Had I enjoyed them equally? Well… maybe not. That first evening, the one Amelie planned, was spectacular. It proved several things to me; that the woman I love is capable of spontaneity, that she's passionate, tempting and utterly endearing, and that I can't wait for us to be married. Our second evening showed me – as if I didn't already know – how much I need her by my side. My job can be hard at times and having her with me is only going to make it better. So much better. And last night? That was a family night, exactly as Aunt Dotty said, and it served to remind me that, even when Amelie and I are married, even when we're settled, and can be together as much as we like, there will always be time to spend with our families – idiosyncrasies and all.

Sitting at the breakfast table, I can't help smiling to myself, the memories of those three different evenings playing through my mind. Although I have to confess, it's the first one that makes me smile the most.

I also recall taking Amelie home last night, kissing her on the doorstep of her house, letting my fingers run through her hair, and wishing I'd had the use of both of my hands, so I could have held her body close to mine at the same time. I only have a couple of weeks to wait until the plaster cast comes off, but it seems like a lifetime and I'm impatient to touch her and hold her properly again.

I spent the short walk home contemplating whether I should seek Gordon Templeton's permission to marry his ward, before asking her. I know it's considered traditional, but part of me would rather ask Amelie and then seek his consent, once I know she has accepted me. Still, I suppose I should bear in mind that, considering her age, we do need to get his seal of approval. Failure to do so would mean waiting at least a year, until she's twenty-one, which I think would drive me insane – and might have a similar effect on Amelie, if the other night is anything to go by. That thought makes me smile and I resolve that, even if I'm not the most traditional person in the world, I will speak to him… I just need to find the time.

"Good morning, dear," my mother says, coming into the room. "What are you smiling like that for?"

"No reason."

She looks down at me. "Hmm… Where are Dotty and Issa?"

"They had their breakfast early and Dotty's showing Issa around the garden. They're discussing vegetables," I tell her as she leans down and kisses my cheek, before going around the table and sitting opposite me.

"Good. Then I've got you to myself."

"You had me to yourself earlier, while you were helping me bathe," I point out.

"I know, but we ended up focusing on your wound then, didn't we?"

She's not wrong. One of my mother's self-imposed 'duties' during my morning routine, has been to change my dressing, only this morning, we both decided that the wound looks so well healed that the dressing isn't really helping anymore and I'm better off without it. I can't say I'm sorry. Apart from the fact that the dressing is one of the things that 'pulls', when I reach for things, it's also one less task for me to share with my mother during my morning ablutions. And it's a sign I'm on the mend. And that's got to be good.

I look up at her. "Why did you want me to yourself?" I say slowly, wondering what on earth she's planning now.

"I wanted to ask you whether the absence of a ring is the only thing that's stopping you from proposing to Amelie," she says outright, putting her hands on the table and staring at me.

I take a deep breath. "Well, not exactly. The absence of ten minutes' privacy has something to do with it… not that it's really any of your business, Mother."

I know I'm being unfair. I've had a lot more than ten minutes alone with Amelie over the last few evenings, but I'm not in the mood for my mother's interference. Not this morning.

She sits back, looking offended, the twinkle having faded from her eyes, and I feel guilty.

"I'm sorry," I murmur. "That was rude of me."

She blinks a few times and I have a horrible feeling she's about to cry. Instead, she sits forward again. "I know it's none of my business," she says, her voice very soft and distant. "It's your business. Yours and Amelie's. I was only asking because there's something I want to give you."

She reaches into the pocket of her cardigan and brings her hand up, placing a small box on the table and pushing it across to me. "After our conversation the other evening, when you said you were trying to find a ring, I telephoned Issa and asked if she'd mind travelling up here a few days early. She said she didn't… so I asked her to go through the top drawer in my dressing table, to find this, and to make sure she brought it with her."

I open the box and then pick it up. Inside there's a ring in the form of a circular emerald, surrounded by tiny white diamonds. It's not huge, or ostentatious. It's beautiful; and it's absolutely perfect for Amelie.

I close the box again, and get up from the table, walking around to my mother and taking her hand in mine.

"Come here," I say and pull her to her feet. "I'm sorry." I look down at her. "I apologise unreservedly for everything I just said. I don't deserve you at all."

She smiles, putting her arms around my waist and holding me. She doesn't say a word, but she doesn't need to and we stand like that for a moment, until she lets me go and looks up at me again. "Do you like the ring?" she asks.

"I love it." I reach over the table and pick it up again, opening the box once more, just to have another look. She sits back down and I pull up the nearest chair, sitting beside her.

"More importantly, do you think Amelie will like it?"

"I think she will. I think it's perfect for her."

She nods and I half expect her to ask when I'm going to propose, but she doesn't. Instead, she twists in her chair so she's facing me. "It belonged to your grandmother," she says quietly. "Your father's mother, I mean, not mine. You never met her. She died a year or so before you were born and she left the ring to Alan… to your father. It had been her engagement ring, you see, and he gave it to me, when you were born. We agreed a few years later that, if you ever found the right woman, the woman you wanted to share your life with, then I would pass it on to you..." Her voice fades.

"You are aware I've been engaged before, aren't you?" I say, smiling at her.

She pats my arm gently. "Yes, dear."

"And you didn't think to pass the ring on to me then?"

"No. You weren't listening. I said that your father and I agreed that if you ever found the *right* woman, I was to give you the ring. That woman you were with before was not right for you. Your father knew that. I knew that... Even you knew that, Rufus. Otherwise you'd have introduced her to us, wouldn't you?"

"Yes," I admit.

"Why didn't you?" she asks. "Introduce her, I mean?"

"For the very reason you've said. Victoria wasn't right for me. I just wish I'd worked it out earlier."

"She hurt you, didn't she?" my mother says, looking into my eyes.

"At the time, yes."

"What happened?" she asks and I think for a moment about fobbing her off, but then I decide to tell her the truth.

"She... she slept with another man." I hear her gasp. "I found them together... well, almost."

"Oh, my dear boy," she says, letting her hand rest on my arm now. She looks terribly sad. "Is that why you left? Why you transferred to Scotland Yard?"

"Yes. I couldn't be here anymore." I don't tell her that the main reason for that is that the person Victoria slept with was Harry Thompson and that facing him every day was just too much for me at the time. Harry and I have patched up our differences, but I doubt my mother could forgive him, even if I explained that it wasn't his fault.

"Why didn't you tell us?" she asks.

"It's not the sort of thing a man boasts about, Mother."

"No... I suppose not." She leans back slightly. "Have you told Amelie about this? Because if you haven't, then——"

"I told her right at the beginning," I interrupt, "when we first met."

"Good," she says, smiling again. "There shouldn't be any secrets in a marriage."

"Well, I didn't know I was going to ask her to marry me at the time. I'd told her I'd been engaged, more by accident than intention, and I wanted to explain what had happened… so she didn't get the wrong idea."

She stares at me for a moment. "I'm not going to ask what that means," she says.

"Heavens… Are you saying you're going to allow me some privacy in my own life?"

"Well, I suppose I'll have to. After all, you'll be a married man soon."

"If she accepts me, Mother."

"Oh, don't worry about that. I have no doubts about Amelie… That's why I'm passing on the ring. I know she's right for you. And you're right for her." Her eyes start to glisten and she blinks quickly. "Your father would have loved her, Rufus, and he'd have been so proud of you."

She gets up and pats me on the shoulder before leaving the room. I've never even considered what my father would have thought of Amelie, but hearing my mother say that has made me realise that he probably would have loved her. Almost as much as I do.

Thompson and I arrive at the Sanderson house at just after nine o'clock. We deliberately decided not to get here too early, because it's a Sunday, and nine o'clock seems like a reasonable hour to both of us.

Even so, Lois informs us, Mrs Sanderson is in bed, and her master is still getting dressed.

"Can you ask Mrs Sanderson if she'll see us, please?" I ask, and Lois nods her head, leaving us in the hallway while she goes upstairs.

"What are you going to do if she says 'no'," Thompson asks, once Lois is out of earshot.

"Let her know we need to speak to her and arrange a time to come back later, I suppose." It's not ideal, but I have to keep in mind that the woman's daughter has just been murdered.

"There's something about this house." Thompson has moved closer to me, lowering his voice. "I know it sounds odd, but it gives me the creeps."

I turn and look at him. "It doesn't sound odd; I know exactly what you mean."

"Can you feel it too?" he says and I nod my head.

"It's like there's something here... something underlying the veneer... something..."

"Evil." He finishes my sentence for me.

Lois appears at the top of the stairs right at that moment, and slowly walks down towards us.

"The mistress says she'll see you. I'm to take you up."

I nod my head and we follow her back up the stairs, going around the landing and waiting by the third door on the right. Lois knocks once and we wait until we hear the quiet response to 'enter', before she opens the door, and steps to one side, allowing us to pass through, before closing it behind us.

Thompson and I both stand just inside the doorway of a rather lavish bedroom. There's an ornate dressing table in the bay window, and a sizeable wardrobe and chest of drawers lining the opposite wall, along with a couple of armchairs, neatly placed in the corners of the room, which is dominated by an enormous bed, with pale grey silky coverings, in the centre of which, lies Mrs Sanderson, her auburn hair spread out on the white pillows behind her.

"Please come in," she murmurs, indicating the chair in the nearest corner.

I pull it closer to the bed and sit down, while Thompson remains standing behind me.

Mrs Sanderson looks pale and rather fragile, not helped by the white, diaphanous gown she's wearing, and I open my mouth to speak, but before I can say anything, she raises her hand, silencing me.

"M—My husband told me last night that Amy was... that Amy was..." She hesitates. "He told me what was done to her," she continues. "H—He said he mentioned David to you?"

I'm surprised, although I try to keep it hidden and I try to imagine the scene after our departure; Mr Sanderson waiting for his wife to awaken from her sleep, telling her what had been done to Amy, and deciding to twist the knife a little further by mentioning our conversation about David Cooke, even though he'd agreed that the man was an unlikely candidate for his daughter's assault and murder. Sanderson's hatred for his wife must run a lot deeper than I'd thought.

"David didn't do it." She raises her voice to an almost hysterical pitch. "I was with him. I was with him the whole time."

She's lying about that. "No, you weren't," I say calmly. "We've already spoken to Mr Cooke and he's informed us that you were with him between twelve-thirty and one, or just after. Your nanny only got back from her shopping trip at between one and one-thirty. Then she had to get the children ready to take to the park, so she couldn't have got there before about one-forty-five, and the call came in, reporting your daughter missing at just after two-thirty. If you're hoping to provide Mr Cooke with an alibi yourself, Mrs Sanderson, I'm afraid that's not possible. Even he admits that."

"But… but… he didn't do it," she repeats, sitting up a little, her eyes wide with panic. "I know he didn't. He couldn't."

"He's told us he had a meeting after he saw you. It was due to start at one o'clock, but because he was with you, he was late arriving and got there at one-twenty. We'll be finding out who that was with to see if they can verify Mr Cooke's movements during the actual time in question… because we know he wasn't with you, Mrs Sanderson."

She stares at me, tears forming in her eyes. "You can't suspect him," she murmurs. "You just can't."

"I can – at least until he's proved to me that he has an alibi."

She lets out a sob, clutching a lace handkerchief to her mouth. "This… this is so awful," she says, between sniffles. "I know he's innocent."

I'm having to bite my tongue, to repress the urge to ask her why she seems so much more concerned for her lover, than she is for her daughter.

"How well do you know Mr Cooke?" I ask her. "I'm aware of the fact that you've only been seeing him for a few months…"

She lets her hand fall. "I've known him for years," she says defiantly. "That's how I know he could never do anything so… so… disgusting."

"So you knew him before your affair started?" I can't see any point in mincing my words.

"Yes. I've known David for almost as long as I've known Daniel."

"And yet you still married your husband, rather than the man you claim to love?"

I know I'm being harsh, but I'm not sure I care. This woman is heartless, beyond even my experience.

"I don't *claim* to love him. I *do* love him. And I told you… Daniel was romantic at the beginning. And David was a very junior banker at the time. I wasn't to know Daniel would become boring beyond words and that David would become the bank's youngest rising star, was I?"

So, this is as much to do with money and status as anything else. Somehow that really doesn't surprise me.

"Why did you want to see me?" she asks, tipping her chin in a defiant fashion.

"I wanted to ask why you failed to mention that you were with Mr Cooke on the day your daughter went missing."

"Because it's not relevant. This has nothing to do with David."

"I'm afraid it's not for you to decide what is relevant and what isn't, Mrs Sanderson. Not in a murder investigation."

"Even so… I—I didn't want my husband to find out," she adds, blushing slightly.

"Well, we both know that isn't true, don't we?"

Her blush spreads further. "What do you mean?" she blusters.

"Come now, Mrs Sanderson. Your husband has known about your affair all along."

"H—How was I to know he'd guess?"

It's all I can do not to laugh, but I manage to restrain myself. "Guess? You've flaunted it. You've made him perfectly well aware of what's been going on, right since the word go."

She sits up. "So?" she snaps. "Why shouldn't I? It's not long since I turned twenty-five. It was only a few years ago I was still in school, but my husband is rapidly approaching retirement. I'm not ready for that yet."

"So you thought you'd play games with your husband's feelings, did you?" I know this isn't relevant to the case, but she's got under my skin now.

"*His* feelings? Daniel doesn't have feelings," she hisses. "And anyway, I want to have fun. I want to be young... to be loved... to be treated like a woman, not a mother, not a prized possession, not a trophy... a *woman*." She shouts the last word her eyes wide, her chin raised.

I want to tell her that it's a shame she's being such a child, but I don't bother. Instead I get to my feet and simply nod my head.

"Thank you for your time, Mrs Sanderson," I say quietly, and Thompson and I leave the room.

"Feel better for that?" he says, once we're outside, with the door closed firmly behind us.

"No. But I'll tell you something... if we were looking for a woman, she'd be top of my list of suspects."

"The girl's mother?" He's shocked.

"Yes. She couldn't care less about her daughter. Her only concerns are herself and her lover. That's it. That's the limit of her interest."

He shakes his head. "Even so..."

"You remember I told you I'd investigated three child murders before?"

"Yes."

"Well, in one of those cases, the culprit was the mother. It happens, Harry. We don't have to like it, but it happens."

"Jesus," he murmurs under his breath, and we turn and make our way down the stairs.

"I want to speak with the cook," I tell him when we get into the hall. "Follow me." I lead him towards the back of the house.

"Why the cook?" he asks.

"Because she knows everything that goes on in this house."

I open the swing doors and we pass through, to be greeted by the sight of the cook, standing by the sink, peeling potatoes. She looks up.

"Hello," she says, smiling. "Inspector Stone, isn't it?"

"That's right. And this is Sergeant Thompson."

She stops what she's doing and dries her hands on a cloth, coming over to us.

"Can I get you a cup of tea?" she offers.

"That would be lovely, Mrs Slater," I reply and Thompson nods his agreement.

"It's terrible," she says, as she fills the kettle with water. "This news about young Amy, I mean. I know she could be a handful, and worse – as I said to you the other day…" She turns and looks at me. "But no-one could wish her dead."

She puts the kettle on to boil and sets about preparing the tea, while Thompson and I sit down at the table.

"We know the murderer is a man," I explain, hoping she won't ask how we're aware of that fact. The details will almost certainly make the newspapers soon, and everyone can find out then. In the meantime, I'd rather not have to repeat that part of the story any more than I have to. "And I wondered if you can tell me of any men who are associated with the house?"

"Men?" she says, looking confused.

"Yes. Anyone who calls at the house regularly, for example."

"Well, there's the butcher's boy," she says, doubtfully, "but he's a lovely lad. He wouldn't hurt a fly. And there's the milkman, I suppose. But I'm not sure he's ever seen Amy. He calls far too early and rarely even comes into the kitchen – and certainly not when Amy's been in here." She pauses, with the sugar bowl in her hand, clearly thinking. "Of course, there's Miss Sutton's young man," she adds, and puts the bowl down on the table, before turning to fetch the cups.

"Miss Sutton's young man?" I ask, all my nerves on edge.

"Yes. I don't know his name." She arranges the cups and saucers on the table in front of us. "And he doesn't come here, of course."

"Then how do you know he exists?" I enquire, smiling, and she looks down, tapping the side of her nose with her forefinger.

"Because I'm no fool, Inspector. And that girl, for all her pretty little ways, is no genius. She thinks we don't notice the letters that come for her, regular as clockwork, but we do." She rolls her eyes. "Honestly, between her and the mistress, writing to that Mr Cooke on a daily basis, I think they must be keeping the post office in business, I honestly do."

I can't help but wish Mrs Slater would change profession and come and work for me, but I doubt she'd like the conditions – or the lack of tea.

"So, if Miss Sutton's young man never comes to the house, he wouldn't have met Amy, would he?" I suggest and she smiles.

"Well, there's no guarantee of that, is there?" she says, as the kettle starts to whistle and she switches off the gas. "Miss Sutton takes the children out with her, doesn't she? So, who's to say she doesn't meet her young man while they're with her?"

I look up at her. "But I thought Mr Sanderson didn't like his female employees having male friends," I say, putting it as delicately as I can.

"No, he doesn't," she replies, pouring the boiling water into the teapot before she sits down opposite me. "But then that's really a rather stupid rule, don't you think? I mean, what's the sense in employing someone as beautiful as Miss Sutton, and then forbidding her from having a boyfriend?" She shakes her head. "It doesn't make any sense at all."

After we've finished our tea, we leave Mrs Slater to get on with preparing the vegetables for Sunday lunch, and we go upstairs to the top floor, to the nursery. I'm not going to bother asking Mr Sanderson's permission to speak with his nanny. Not this time.

The door to the nursery is ajar, so I push it open and find Miss Sutton, sitting in the chair by the window, gazing down at the baby cradled in her arms. For a moment, she's unaware of our presence and she kisses the infant's forehead, smiling and rocking her, humming a quiet tune. Seen like this, I'm struck by her maternal instincts, and I can't help reflect on the contrast between this scene and the one we experienced a little earlier, in the bedroom on the floor below, with the child's actual mother.

I cough, to make her aware of our presence and she startles, looking up.

"Inspector," she says, flushing. "I didn't see you."

"We've only just come in," I lie. "I'm sorry to disturb you."

"You haven't." She gets to her feet and crosses the room, laying the baby down in her cot, where she gives off a couple of plaintive cries, but the nanny hands her a rattle, which she clasps in her fist, quietening.

"We won't keep you a minute," I say, before she can remind me how busy she is, or attempt to use her feminine wiles to their best advantage. They're not going to work on either myself, or Thompson, but I don't want to waste time letting her bother. "I just wanted to ask you about your boyfriend."

She pales, and even though she's wearing a fair amount of make-up, it's possible to see the change in her skin tone. "My what?" she says, with a sterling attempt at bravado.

"Your boyfriend, Miss Sutton." I stare her in the eye, keeping a straight face.

"I don't have a boyfriend," she replies, her demeanour changing, a smugness descending over her. "Mr Sanderson doesn't permit such things."

"Even so, you receive letters, on a regular basis from someone. If they're not from a boyfriend, who are they from?"

A blush rises up her cheeks again. "A friend."

"And his name is…?"

"Who said it's a he?" she asks.

"I do." I make a show of looking at my watch. "Miss Sutton. I don't have time for this. We haven't made this general knowledge yet, but Amy was sexually assaulted…" She stares at me, and then raises her hand to her mouth. I wonder for a moment if she's going to be sick, like Mr Sanderson, but she swallows hard and lowers her hand again, blinking a few times, so I carry on, "I need to interview any men who are associated with this house – in whatever capacity. Now, *I* know you have a boyfriend. *You* know you have a boyfriend. So, you can either give me his name… right this minute, or I'll have my sergeant take you into Kingston police station and you'll be charged with obstruction. Oh… and I'll still find out who your boyfriend is."

She glares at me for a full twenty seconds, her arms folded across her chest. "Donald would never do anything to harm Amy," she says eventually.

"I'd rather be the judge of that myself," I reply. "Can you tell me Donald's full name, please?"

She pauses again, and then says, "Curtis."

"Donald Curtis." I turn to Thompson and he makes a note. "And his address?"

"This is outrageous," Miss Sutton blusters. "What happened to Amy has nothing to do with Donald."

"In which case, he won't mind answering a few questions, will he?"

"Well, no…" she says.

"So, give me his address. It'll save us all a lot of time and trouble in the end."

She lets out a sigh. "He lives around the corner," she huffs. "In Fleece Road. Above the greengrocer's."

I nod my head. "Thank you. See? It wasn't so hard in the end, was it?" I hate being so facetious, but she deserves it.

Downstairs, Mr Sanderson is waiting in the hallway.

"Lois told me you were here," he says. "Have you been talking to Miss Sutton?"

"Yes, and your wife."

He nods his head, as though it's suddenly dawned on him that he should have mentioned her first. It's too late now though.

"Did you need to see me?" he asks.

"No. We have other lines of enquiry to follow up." I turn towards the front door.

"Oh yes?" He clearly wants details, but I'm not going to give them to him.

"Yes. If we have anything to impart, we'll let you know."

He opens his mouth, I think to object, but then has second thoughts and closes it again, and Thompson opens the door to let us out.

"He didn't like that," he says to me once we're in the car.

"I'm rather past caring," I reply.

"Are you alright, Rufus?"

"No. I'm weary of their games. To be honest, I wonder why they even bothered to have children, for all the attention they seem to pay them."

He nods his head and starts the car. "I can't imagine not spending as much of my spare time as possible with Christopher, but I doubt Mr Sanderson saw his daughter from one day to the next."

"No. And Mrs Sanderson openly admits to feeling ambivalent towards her children. And that's putting it mildly."

He sighs. "As you say, why did they bother?" He reverses the car out of the driveway. "Fleece Road, I assume?" he says.

"Yes. Let's see what Donald Curtis has to say for himself."

Being as it's Sunday, the greengrocer's is closed, a brown, slightly tattered blind lowered across the inside of the window, but there's a wooden door to the left upon which Thompson knocks twice, and we wait… and wait. He knocks again, and we hear a distant, "Okay… I'm coming," from inside the building.

The door opens and a man stands before us. He's probably in his late twenties, or more likely early thirties, tall, with short dark hair and rather piercing blue eyes and is undeniably handsome, although he looks as though he's only just got out of bed, having slept in the clothes he was wearing yesterday, judging from their creased and dishevelled state.

"Yes?" he says, tucking in his shirt, rather unnecessarily, considering the condition of the rest of his attire.

"I'm Detective Inspector Stone," I say, holding out my warrant card. Thompson does the same, without revealing his name and the man leans forward, squinting at our identification. "Are you Mr Donald Curtis?"

"Yes." He scratches his head, rather confused, by the looks of things.

"May we come in?"

"Um… yes." He steps to one side and we enter into a narrow lobby area, leading to a set of stairs. "Go on up," he says.

I follow his instructions, climbing the stairs, and enter his flat through the door to my right, coming into a small hallway with four doors leading off of it, and I stand, waiting to be invited in, even though Mr Curtis is behind me. "Go straight on ahead," he says, and I do, directly into the large and very nicely furnished living room.

"Sorry," he says, picking up a jacket from the back of the sofa, which is covered with pale green material. Opposite it are two chairs, one with matching upholstery, the other with a pattered covering, that resembles peacock feathers. This pattern is replicated in the cushions that are scattered across the sofa, which Mr Curtis suddenly seems to notice, and straightens accordingly.

"I was out with some friends last night." He smiles. "Had a little too much to drink." He nods towards his jacket, which he's still clutching. "I'll just get rid of this."

"Feel free," I reply and he leaves the room, giving me the opportunity to look around. The parquet flooring is polished to within an inch of its life, but the rug we're currently standing on is thick and luxurious. On the glass topped coffee table, there is an etched silver cigarette box and lighter, and several large books, arranged for display purposes, I assume, rather than to be read, although there are two bookcases either side of the chimney breast, which are filled with leather-bound tomes, interspersed with the odd ornament or photograph. It's a very contemporary, rather elegant abode.

I turn as Mr Curtis comes back into the room. He's changed into clean, neatly pressed trousers and a shirt, which is undone at the neck, and has combed his hair, slicking it back from his face. He remains unshaven, but in the space of time he's had available, he's made a significant improvement in his appearance.

"How can I help?" he says, indicating the chairs, and taking a seat opposite us on the sofa.

He opens the cigarette box, offering it, and we both decline, although I'm reminded that it's only a few weeks since I gave up the habit myself, as he takes one and lights it, replacing the lighter on the table before getting up again to fetch an ashtray from the bookshelf, placing it on the arm of the sofa beside him.

"I understand you know Miss Elizabeth Sutton?" I ask.

He frowns, then says, "Lizzie? Yes, I know her." His lips twitch up slightly. "The Sandersons insist she calls herself Elizabeth, but she prefers Lizzie – well, she does when she's with me, anyway."

"How long have you known her?"

"About six or seven months, I suppose."

I nod my head. "Can you tell me where you were on Tuesday last?"

"At work," he says rather abruptly.

"Where do you work?"

"Sugden's Engineering."

"And what do you do there?" I ask.

"I'm a draughtsman, but I can't tell you any more than that. We're doing war work now, so it's confidential, I'm afraid."

"I see. And you were there all day, were you? You didn't leave your offices at all?"

"Well, I went out during my lunch break…"

"What time was that?"

His eyes narrow. "Look, what's going on here?" he says, putting his cigarette down in the ashtray and sitting forward. "I'm assuming you're here because of the little girl. I know she's been found dead, and while she could be difficult – well, downright annoying actually – she didn't deserve that." He pauses. "But I don't understand what any of that has to do with me? Why are you here, asking me questions? Has Lizzie said something about me?"

I'm careful not to answer his last question and reply, "We're just making routine enquiries of all the men who are associated with the household."

"'Associated with the household'?" he repeats. "Well, now I know she's told you something, otherwise how did you even know I exist? No-one else in that place knows about me. And how did you find out my address, if she didn't give it to you?" He sits a little further forward. "And anyway what do you mean 'men'? Why only men? You do realise that women are perfectly capable of killing children, don't you?"

"Yes, sir. But in this instance, we know it's a man."

"How?" he asks.

"Because the girl was assaulted… sexually."

He stares at me, his face paling significantly. Then he sits back, picking up his cigarette again, his hand shaking. "Sexually?" he says. "You mean she was…?" He doesn't finish his sentence, but the expression on his face gives away his revulsion, even as he takes a long drag on his cigarette, calming his nerves. "I like sex just as much as the next man," he says eventually, with disarming honesty. "But only with consenting adults. You think I'd do that… with a child? A four year old child? Jesus… what do you take me for?"

"We don't take you for anything, Mr Curtis. But the time at which Amy disappeared on Tuesday, could reasonably have been during the lunch hour of someone who was at work, so can you please account for your whereabouts?"

"At lunchtime?" I nod my head and he stubs out his half smoked cigarette. "I met Lizzie," he says.

"Was this while she was Christmas shopping?" I ask.

"She wasn't Christmas shopping." He looks at me as though he feels sorry for me. "She just told them that to get out of the house, because she's not supposed to have a boyfriend, let alone be meeting him for sex in the middle of the day. And before you start looking down your noses, passing judgement on that, it's a free country, last time I checked. And anyway, it's not just a fling. I've been thinking of proposing to her, so there's nothing wrong with it… not really… although she doesn't know about the proposal, so I'd be grateful if you'd keep that bit to yourselves, if it's all the same to you" He stops talking for a moment and reaches for another cigarette, although he doesn't light it, but stares down, clasping it between his fingers. "Mind you," he adds thoughtfully, "I have to say, sometimes I wonder if she enjoys the sneaking around almost as much as she does the sex. I think she gets off on the thrill of it." He glances up and smiles, then lights the cigarette, placing his arm along the back of the sofa, rather nonchalantly. "Not that I'm complaining either way."

"Can you give me details of what you and Miss Sutton did?"

"You want details? Of what we did? Is that usual?"

I tilt my head and glare at him. "I just need timings. That's all."

He takes a drag of his cigarette. "Well, she came first," he smirks, blowing smoke up in the air. "Does that help?"

"Not particularly." I refuse to be baited and sit forward in my chair, making myself as large as possible, without actually standing up. "We can do this here, or at the police station, Mr Curtis. I don't mind which."

He looks across at me. "Alright," he murmurs. "I met her at just after twelve-thirty."

"Where?"

"Here."

"And?"

"And we kept ourselves entertained for just over half an hour. She couldn't spare any longer because they'd only given her an hour or so off, and it had taken her ten minutes to walk here, and she still had to get dressed and walk back. Still, half an hour with Lizzie is like a whole night with a lot of other women. Trust me… I've tried more than my fair share." Somehow that doesn't surprise me.

"So she left here at one?" I ask, ignoring his remarks.

"There or there abouts… probably a few minutes after, I'd have said."

"And you went back to work?"

"Yes. Well, I grabbed a quick sandwich first, and then I went back. I've got witnesses for that, if you need them. Obviously I don't have any for my time with Lizzie. She's not into being watched." He smirks again. "She has her little kinks, but that's not one of them."

I know he's trying to goad me, so I stand. He does too, but he's a good few inches shorter than me, even when he pulls himself up to his full height. "You haven't been called up yet?" I ask.

"No. I've just been granted exemption."

"Medical?"

"No. On the grounds of my job. Because of the work we're doing at the moment, I've been given reserved status."

I nod my head. "I see. Well, thank you for your time, Mr Curtis. If we need anything else, we know where to find you."

"Is that it?" he asks.

"For now, yes. Did you expect something else?"

He hesitates. "No... I mean, I don't know. I've never been questioned by the police before."

"Well, there's a first time for everything, isn't there?"

"I suppose," he mumbles, and then takes a half step forward. "Was it her?" he asks.

"Was what her?"

"Was it Lizzie who put you onto me?"

I stare at him for a moment and then turn away, deliberately leaving him to mull that over for himself.

Downstairs, we let ourselves out onto the street again, where the air feels remarkably fresh, and not just because we're no longer in a smoke filled room.

As we sit back in the car, Thompson stares out through the windscreen. "Was I ever like that?" he asks.

"Sorry?"

"When we knew each other before... when I had my fair share of women... was I ever that arrogant?"

"No. Never." I turn in my seat, facing him. "Care to revise your opinion of Miss Sutton now?" I ask.

"In what way?"

"I think you called her a tease. 'All promise and no delivery' were your words, if I remember rightly."

He smiles, shaking his head. "I suppose you're going to tell me you have a complete understanding of women now, are you?" he says.

"I don't think there's a man alive who can claim that, Harry," I chuckle.

"No, there probably isn't," he agrees, then adds, "Do you think Curtis knows how much she flirts with every man she meets?"

"I doubt it," I reply. "I shouldn't think he'd be contemplating marriage if he did. But then, who knows? Perhaps he gets a thrill from her behaviour... they seem the type."

He starts the car and shakes his head slowly as he begins the drive over to Thames Ditton.

David Cooke is at home and answers the door promptly to my knock.

"You again?"

It's not the most polite of greetings, but I've heard worse, and just reply, "Yes," and wait to be invited in. It takes him a moment, but he eventually steps back, presumably because he has no desire for his personal business to be conducted on his doorstep.

We stand in his living room, but he doesn't invite us to sit, making it clear we won't be staying for long – not if he has anything to do with it.

"We've come to inform you that Mrs Sanderson has confirmed that she was with you on the day her daughter went missing," I say, breaking the silence that's starting to stretch.

"So? I hardly needed you to confirm that. I know where I was."

I'm not in the mood for him, or his tone. "And I've also come to inform you that I don't want you to leave the area, not without letting me know."

His face whitens in an instant. It's funny how using that phrase always gets a person's attention. Never fails. "Excuse me?"

"I think you heard and understood me, Mr Cooke. I'm sure you're aware that Amy Sanderson's body was found on Friday. What you won't be aware of is that she was sexually assaulted." He turns even whiter. "That means we're looking for a man in connection with her murder."

"A—And... and you think I—I..." he stutters, leaving his sentence hanging.

"I don't think anything yet, sir. I'm just asking you not to leave the area until further notice, without advising me first."

"But how could you even think I'd do something so... so vile? H—Has Lillian said something?"

"Why would you think Mrs Sanderson might say something?"

"Why else would you be questioning me and telling me not to leave the area? It has to have come from her, doesn't it?"

I don't answer him, because I don't have to. "Can you give me the name of the client you saw on Tuesday afternoon, when you'd finished with Mrs Sanderson?"

"I've already explained," he says, taking a step away and running his fingers through his hair, "my manager doesn't know I was late for the appointment. I'll get into serious trouble…"

"Listen, Mr Cooke," I interrupt, keeping my voice level and even, but slightly menacing at the same time, just for effect, "I didn't object too much when you chose to conceal your whereabouts the other day, because at the time we were investigating Amy's disappearance, which either meant she'd wandered off, or been taken, and I couldn't for the life of me think why you would have kidnapped the child, given that you have no interest in Mrs Sanderson's offspring. But now things have changed. We're investigating a murder. So, if you don't tell me precisely where you were, I'll arrest you. How do you think your manager would react to that? Especially when he knows the charges relate to the rape and murder of a four year old girl?"

"Ellison," he says quickly. "His name's Ralph Ellison."

I'm aware of Thompson making notes. "His address?"

"He lives in Watts Road. Oakley House. He's one of the bank's most important customers."

I nod my head. "We'll be discreet," I tell him and turn towards the door. "You haven't been called up yet then?" I ask, recalling my question to Donald Curtis, and feeling intrigued.

"No," he replies. "I went for my medical not long ago and they discovered I've got a heart murmur."

"I'm sorry to hear that," I say, doing my best to sound sincere.

"It's nothing serious." He shrugs. "It's not life threatening or anything. But it's enough to prevent me from being called up – or so it seems." He looks up. "I've got the letter of exemption, if you need to see it." He's being very obliging all of a sudden, but I still don't like him.

"That won't be necessary."

Thompson and I leave and walk back to the car, which is parked a little way down the road, and he turns to me as we approach it.

"I'll say something for you," he remarks, smiling. "When you don't like someone, you *really* don't like them."

Back at the station, Doctor Wyatt is waiting for me in my room, which is a surprise, given that it's Sunday, and Thompson comes in to join us, the two of them sitting opposite me at my desk.

"What have you got for us, Doctor?" I ask, leaning forward on my elbows.

"I've done the preliminary report," he replies as he places a brown file on my desk, looking worried. "But there's a problem."

"There is?"

He nods his head. "She was killed by a blow to the back of the head," he confirms. "There's no doubt about that. I've found traces of earth and concrete in the wound."

"So a brick?" Thompson suggests.

"I said concrete, not brick dust, and not cement either." Wyatt turns to him, frowning and Thompson looks at me, raising his eyebrows.

"Okay, so what are you implying?" I ask.

"I'm not implying anything, although if you want me to do your job for you, I'd say that the bruise on her cheek is suggestive of her having been struck across the face, and her falling to the ground and banging her head. But it's your job to prove that... I'm just telling you what I've found. It's up to you to work out what it means."

"Very well." I ignore his moodiness. It's understandable. He's almost certainly as tired as the rest of us; and I don't envy him the job he's been doing either. "You said there was a problem?"

"Yes." He shakes his head. "I examined her... thoroughly," he says. "And there was no trace of semen either on or in her body, or on her clothing."

I feel a little sick, but swallow it down. "Well, maybe he didn't climax," I point out. "He might have been interrupted. Or he could have used a condom, couldn't he?"

He frowns. "Do you think that's likely?"

"He might have pulled out, mightn't he?" Thompson suggests, his voice reflecting his own state of mind, which I imagine to be roughly the same as my own.

"I doubt it," Wyatt replies. "Why would he bother? And in any case, I said there was no semen. None. Usually there would be a trace, even if it was only minute."

"But what are the alternatives?" I ask. "I mean…"

He holds up his hand, stopping me from speaking. "I don't know yet. I'll need to carry out further examinations and tests before I can pass judgement and give you my final report. It might take me another day or two." He gets to his feet and looks down at me. "I'm sorry."

"Don't be, Doctor. I know you're doing your best. And I'm sorry too, but now that you've completed your initial investigations, I'm afraid we need to get Mr Sanderson to do a formal identification."

He sighs. "Very well. I'll prepare the body for tomorrow morning."

He turns to leave, just as Sergeant Tooley knocks on the door and comes in.

"Inspector?" he says, then looks up, glancing around. "I'm sorry. I didn't realise you were busy."

"That's alright, Sergeant. You can speak freely."

He comes over to the desk, standing beside the doctor. "I've just come from the recreation ground in Ewell Road," he says. "We've found traces of what I think is blood on a small area of the pathway."

"Whereabouts in the park?" I ask him.

"It's quite close to the entrance," he replies. "Just along to the right, on the edge of the path."

I turn to the doctor. "Would that account for the earth and concrete you found in the wound?" I ask him.

"Possibly." He rubs his eyes with his forefinger and thumb. "I'll go over there for myself and take a look."

I nod my head and turn back to Tooley. "Perhaps you could accompany the doctor and show him the site yourself?"

"Certainly, sir."

"And I'll send Prentice over as well, to see if he can get any samples," I add as they're leaving.

"I'm not sure there's enough blood for that," Tooley says, stopping.

"It's worth a try." They turn, but I call Tooley back. "Is there any sign of the girl's underwear?" I ask him.

"No, sir."

I nod my head. "So it looks like he may have taken it with him..." Tooley raises his eyebrows but says nothing and turns again, leaving with the doctor. "Call Prentice, will you?" I say to Thompson, once we're alone. He nods in agreement. "Ask him to go to the park. And then call Mr Sanderson and set up the identification at the mortuary for ten o'clock on Monday morning."

He stands. "Do you think we might be getting somewhere?" he says, the hope in his voice unmistakeable.

"Who knows?" I shrug my shoulders. "If there's as little blood as Tooley says, it might not tell us anything, other than where the girl died."

Thompson sighs deeply. "Yes, I suppose."

"We will find him, Harry."

He looks up and smiles. "I know."

I spend the next ten minutes quickly leafing through the files of the men we've got in custody, seeing what their offences are and deciding on the order in which we should see them. By the time I've done that, Thompson is knocking on my doorframe.

"That's all set up, Rufus," he says and comes over to the desk.

"Well, before you get comfortable," I reply, preventing him from sitting down, and standing up myself. "It's probably about time we had a word with our motley crew of former offenders."

His shoulders drop. "Must we?"

"I'm afraid we must. I think we should split up though. We'll get through them more quickly." We walk out through the door, with me ahead and I glance around. There are a few officers present, some of whom I recognise. "Pearce," I call. "And Adams... Could you both come over here, please?"

They look up from the paperwork they're sorting through together and come over, standing in front of me.

"Sergeant Thompson and I are going to start interviewing the men in custody," I explain. "I've decided it'll be quicker if we speak to them separately, so I want you, Constable Pearce, to sit with Sergeant Thompson, and Adams, you'll be with me. Alright?"

They both nod and Adams says, "Yes, sir," with a fair degree of enthusiasm. Somehow I doubt he'll be feeling like that by the time we're finished.

I hand the list of names to Pearce. "Take that to the custody sergeant. Tell him to have the men sent up in the order in which I've numbered them. I'll see Albert Finch, because he already knows Sergeant Thompson, but other than that, he's just to send each one up in order, as we call for them."

"Yes, sir."

He turns and walks down the corridor, going through the double doors at the end.

"You take room one," I say to Thompson, "and we'll be in room two. If anything comes up, just let me know. Alright?"

He nods and makes his own way down the corridor towards the interview rooms.

"Ever done anything like this before?" I turn to PC Adams.

"Interviews, sir?" he asks. "I've done a few."

"I mean interviews with convicted child molesters and rapists."

I notice his Adam's apple bob up and down as he swallows hard. "No... no I haven't... sir."

I nod my head and start walking, and he falls into step beside me. "Well..." I turn to him. "It might get a bit ugly. Try and bear it as best you can, and we'll take a break between each one."

He doesn't reply and I open the door to the interview room and step inside, taking a breath – because I know it's going to be the last clean breath of air I'll take for the next few hours.

The first man we see is John Kelsey. He's served three spells in prison – the first one at the tender age of nineteen – for exposing himself to children and young adults, although I notice that there's nothing on his record since early 1932.

"What's all this about?" he says, the moment he walks into the room. His appearance is surprising. I'd expected someone rather wretched and reptilian. Instead, I'm faced with an upright man, in a business suit – albeit one that he's been wearing since yesterday, when he was brought into the station – with glasses, and a full head of iron grey hair. I know from his record that he's fifty-seven years old and, while he looks roughly that, he's very different to what I'd anticipated.

PC Adams is sitting to my right, his notebook ready, but I stand as Kelsey enters the room. "Mr Kelsey. Please sit down."

He glares up at me. "Why?"

"Because I'm asking you to."

His staring continues a little longer and then he relents, plonking himself down in the seat opposite us.

"Thank you." I sit myself and open the file in front of me.

"You are John Kelsey?" I confirm.

"Yes. I've been rotting in one of your bloody cells overnight and I'd like to know why?"

I keep my eyes focused on the file, even though I'm not reading it. I want to make him wait. Eventually, I look up. Kelsey's face is red with anger and impatience.

"Where were you on Tuesday last between the hours of twelve noon and three pm?"

"Excuse me?"

"Answer the question."

"I was at work," he replies, taking me by surprise.

"Where do you work?"

"I'm a porter at the hospital."

"Which hospital?" I ask him.

"Kingston."

I stare at him for a moment. "You seem remarkably well dressed for a porter."

"It's not against the law to wear a suit, is it?" I don't reply and after a few seconds, he huffs out a sigh. "When your lot came calling, I was getting ready to go out for the evening…" His voice fades.

"Anywhere nice?"

"It's none of your business."

I lean forward and lower my voice. "It is my business, Mr Kelsey. I'm investigating the rape and murder of a young child. You have history when it comes to children… and that means, if I want to know what time you got up, whether you cut yourself shaving, what you had for breakfast, lunch and dinner, who you met at any and every minute of the day, and what you talked about, in minute detail, you will answer me. Do I make myself clear?"

He opens his mouth, then closes it, and then, in a quieter voice, says, "I haven't done anything… like that. Not for years. I changed my ways last time I was inside."

"Found God, did you?" I ask, sarcastically.

"No. I just… I just realised it was wrong."

"Took three spells in prison for you to work out that showing your private parts to young children was wrong, did it?"

He lowers his head, staring at his clasped hands. "I'm sorry," he mumbles.

"I'll remember to pass that on to your victims."

He looks up again. "This… this murder… it ain't got nothing to do with me." I can see the fear in his eyes now. "I was at work all day. Two of the other porters was off sick, so I didn't even get a lunch break on Tuesday, nor on Wednesday. You can check with Mr Silversmith. He's my boss."

"Oh, don't worry, Mr Kelsey. We will be checking."

I stand up and his eyes follow my movements, lightening slightly. "I can go now, can I?" he says, sounding more hopeful.

"Back to the cells, yes. You're not leaving until we've checked your alibi."

"But…"

"But nothing." I hold up my hand and go over to the door. Outside there's a young PC, leaning against the wall. I don't know his name, but he looks up on seeing me and stands to attention.

"Who are you?" I ask him.

"PC Dyson," he replies, then adds, "sir," as an afterthought, and blushes. "The custody sergeant told me to wait here."

"Right. Well, PC Dyson, you can take this man back to the cells. Then give us five minutes before you bring up the next one, please."

He nods his head and comes into the room, waiting while Kelsey gets to his feet, a more forlorn figure than he was when he entered. He doesn't look at me as he leaves, but stares straight ahead, his eyes fixed.

I turn, once he's gone and look at PC Adams.

"Alright?" I say to him and he nods.

"Did he really do that?" he asks. "Show himself to children, like that?"

"Yes."

"Filthy bugger," he murmurs.

"It's likely to get worse yet," I warn him. "I started us off with an easy one."

He turns to me and blinks a few times, but doesn't say a word.

Albert Finch is a man in his mid-forties, with light brown hair and pale blue eyes. He sits opposite Adams and I, looking around the room, resolutely refusing to make eye contact, even though he's been in here for nearly two minutes.

"Mr Finch?" I say eventually.

"Yes." He stares at the table.

"Do you know why you're here?"

He shakes his head. "No."

"You've heard about the little girl who went missing in Long Ditton?"

"Yes." He's not the most talkative soul, I'll say that.

"Well, she's been found. She was raped and murdered."

His eyes dart to mine. "You... you think that had something to do with me?"

I ignore his question, and ask my own instead. "Can you tell me where you were last Tuesday, between the hours of twelve noon and three pm?" I give myself the same latitude as I did with Kelsey, even though I know Amy was taken sometime between one forty-five and two-thirty.

"Last Tuesday?" He looks up nervously, his eyes directed to the ceiling. "I was working until one," he says, lowering his head and staring at me now, his gaze a little intense.

"What do you do?" I ask.

"I'm a plumber. That morning, I was fixing a leaky pipe in a house in Rectory Lane. And then I went home for lunch."

"Right. And what time did you finish lunch?"

"Not sure. I was at my next job by two though," he replies.

"And where was that?"

"Woodstock Lane North. Big house, it was."

"Do you have precise addresses for these properties?" I ask.

"They'll be on the work dockets," he replies. "Clara will have those."

"Who's Clara."

"She's my wife."

"Your wife? You mean the woman you beat senseless five years ago?"

His eyes widen. "No, not her. That was Pauline. And before you start feeling sorry for her, she had it coming. She made my life a bloody misery, that woman, but I didn't rape her, no matter what she said."

"So, you remarried?" I ask, not bothering to hide my surprise.

"Well, no. When I say Clara's my wife, we're not actually married… although she's a lot more accommodating than Pauline ever was, if you get my meaning." He gives me an exaggerated wink at this point and I stare at him for a full ten seconds, until he looks away.

"And Clara helps with your business, does she?"

He nods. "She does my books, takes the phone calls, that sort of thing."

"Was Clara with you during your lunch break on Tuesday?" I ask.

"Yes. I always go home at lunchtime if I can… like I say, she's very obliging, is Clara." He smirks and I get to my feet, resisting the temptation to drag him with me, by the hair.

He looks up. "Can I go?"

"No. You'll be returned to the cells until we've checked your alibi."

"You… you mean you'll be going to see Clara?" he says, standing up and facing me.

"Yes. Do you have a problem with that?"

He pales. "No… but…"

"But what?" I move around the table, getting close to him. Uncomfortably close, I hope. "Have you been using your fists again, Mr Finch?"

"No." He shakes his head, although I don't believe him. Not for one minute.

"Then I'm sure everything will be just fine… won't it?"

He narrows his eyes and his shoulders sag, but he doesn't reply and I walk to the door, opening it. "PC Dyson?" I call.

He appears in the doorway. "Yes, sir?"

"Take Mr Finch back to the cells, please, and bring us the next candidate, will you?"

He nods his head and waits while Finch shuffles across the room.

Henry Platt looks exactly how I'd expected. A man in his mid-forties, he's of medium height and slight build, with a shiny complexion and thick glasses, which are perched on the end of his nose. His hands are clasped in front of him as he walks into the room, his eyes taking in his surroundings, like a captive bird, nervous, looking for a means of escape.

"Mr Platt?" I stand and indicate the seat across the table.

He glances up at me and quickly sits, putting his hands down in his lap. "Yes," he says, as rather an afterthought.

"I'd like to know your movements on Tuesday afternoon, please, between the hours of twelve noon and three pm."

He blinks rapidly a few times. "Might I ask why?"

"Because we're investigating the rape and murder of a young girl."

He pauses, then nods his head. "I had a dental appointment," he replies simply.

"At what time?"

"I was booked in for twelve forty-five, but I got there about fifteen minutes early. Unfortunately he was running late and I didn't go in until about twenty past one."

"And when did you leave?"

"I'm not sure," he replies. "It was after two o'clock though. The man who was due in after me was complaining to the receptionist as I left. He remarked on the time."

"And after that?"

"I went home," he says. "I wasn't feeling well."

"Can anyone confirm that?" I ask him.

"No."

I don't suppose it matters, being as the vital times are accounted for. "Can I have the name of your dentist?" I ask.

"Doctor Redmond," he says obligingly. "He's got a small practice in Lovelace Road. It's part of his house, really. That's to say, he lives upstairs, with his sister."

I nod my head and stand, unsure that I need so much information.

"You'll be taken back to the cells," I tell him, even though he hasn't asked and he gets up, pushing the chair back under the table.

"Right."

"Just until we've checked your alibi."

"I see."

I go over to the door and call PC Dyson, who removes Platt from our presence.

"He was placid," Adams says, once they've gone. "I thought you said he'd be the worst."

"He is."

"Why?"

"Because he was arrested many years ago, in his late teens, for molesting two children… two young girls. It was a particularly nasty case."

"Oh my God," Adams whispers.

"Looking at the file, it seems he didn't try to deny what he'd done. In fact, he was actually quite pleased with himself. He hasn't been out of prison for very long, and I think he was placid and accommodating just now, because he expects this. Every time there's a case involving children, he knows he'll be brought in. It's going to be par for the course for him… probably for the rest of his life."

I've been back in my office for no more than ten minutes, when Thompson knocks on the doorframe and then leans against it.

"How did you get on?" I ask him, looking up.

He comes into the room. "Millard and Cowley were a waste of time," he replies. "They both had cast iron alibis."

"Same with all three of mine. What about your third one?" I look down at the list on the desk in front of me. "Douglas Coates, was it?"

He sits down, his face darkening. "He couldn't account for his whereabouts at all. Seemed rather proud of the fact, if you ask me."

"What was he like?" I sit forward.

"Shifty. Wouldn't look me in the eye throughout the whole interview."

I nod my head. "Very well. Can you get Pearce and Adams in here?"

He stands and goes over to the door again, calling the two constables into my office. They stand on the other side of my desk, looking older than they did a few hours ago, but I suppose that's not surprising, given what they've heard this afternoon.

"I've got a job for the pair of you," I tell them, and they both raise their heads expectantly. "You made notes on the interviews, so I want you to check up on the alibis of the five men who actually have them. Check every name they gave us – don't be satisfied with just one. Unfortunately, these men are entitled to their privacy, so when you're asking your questions, don't reveal what case we're enquiring about. And assuming they're telling the truth, those men can be allowed to go home."

"Do you want this done tonight?" Adams says.

"You can make a start now," I reply, looking at the clock and seeing that it's ten to five already. "And then finish off in the morning. It won't hurt our friends to spend another night tucked up in the cells."

Pearce nods his head. "What about Coates?" he says, his voice quieter than usual. "He didn't have an alibi."

"I know. Sergeant Thompson and I will speak to him tomorrow, after we've taken Mr Sanderson to identify his daughter." If I'm being honest, I'm not looking forward to either event. "Are you both alright?" I ask, as they turn to leave.

"Yes, sir."

"Well, if you're not… I mean, if you need to talk about today, or just about the case in general, come and find me." They both smile, Adams nods his head, and they leave my office.

"I made point of checking Pearce was okay between each interview," Thompson says, once they've gone. "I was pretty sure he'd never have done anything like that before."

I shake my head. "No, but they have to do it sometime."

He looks down at me. "Unfortunately, it seems they do."

By the time we leave the station, about forty-five minutes later, Pearce has already reported that Adams has checked with Mr Silversmith at the hospital, who fortunately happened to be on duty on a Sunday, and Kelsey had indeed been where he'd claimed to be, and Joe Cowley's alibi was also sound, so those two have been released, leaving us with four men still in custody overnight.

"We're going straight to the Sanderson house tomorrow?" Thompson asks as he parks up at the end of Beauchamp Road, opposite Aunt Dotty's and a little further along from Amelie's house, being as there are a couple of cars in front of Aunt Dotty's, making it impossible to park there.

"Yes. I know we're not due with Doctor Wyatt until ten, but we'll need to prepare Mr Sanderson first, and I'd rather take our time."

He nods. "I'll see you in the morning then."

"Have a good evening, Harry."

"I'll do my best."

I get out of the car and wave him goodbye, glancing over at Amelie's house, and in the bright moonlight, I notice Gordon Templeton closing up the garage and making his way back to the front door.

I know he's planning on returning to London this evening, and I'm not sure when he's coming back again, so I suppose if I'm going to speak to him about marrying Amelie, now's my best chance. I call out his name and he glances around, his eyes settling on me as I walk up the driveway. I've only ever seen him wearing a suit before now, but today he's in casual trousers and a thick sweater, and he brushes his forefinger and thumb across his moustache, as I approach.

"Inspector," he says. "Amelie's inside. Did you want me to let you in?"

"No, sir. It was you I wanted to speak to."

He looks confused, perhaps remembering the times I've questioned him in a professional capacity. "What's this about?"

"It's nothing official. It's actually concerning Amelie."

"Is something wrong?" His confusion changes to concern and he looks over his shoulder, in the direction of the house.

"No."

"Well, I was just going back in for tea. Why don't you join me? I'm sure Amelie would be delighted to see you."

"I can't." His eyes widen and I realise I'm going have to just come out with it, or we'll be dancing around like this all night. "I know that it's perhaps a little unorthodox to discuss such things on a freezing driveway in the middle of a winter's evening, but I—I'd like to ask your permission to marry Amelie." I look down at him, feeling nervous now. "I may not be the richest man in the world," I add, when he doesn't respond, "and I can't give her all the things she's become accustomed to in your household." I glance up at the enormous house behind him. "But I can promise to love her, and to keep her safe... until my dying breath." I stop talking, rather embarrassed that I just said all of that out loud.

Templeton's expression alters once more, his concern replaced with relief, and finally happiness, as a broad smile spreads across his lips.

"Of course," he says, cheerily. "I can't think of anyone I'd rather she married. I know how happy you make her and I wouldn't dream of withholding my consent."

He holds out his hand and I take it in mine, shaking his. "You won't tell her, will you?" I add, as an afterthought. "Only, I haven't asked her yet and I'd rather like it to be a surprise." I'm not sure it will be – not really – given all the hints my relations have been dropping, but I'd still prefer her to hear it from me.

"I won't say a word," he says, lowering his voice and then turning serious, his smile fading. "Do you think she'll let me walk her down the aisle?"

"Um…" That's an awkward question; one which I'm uncertain how to answer, given Amelie's feelings towards her guardian. "I'm not sure there's going to be an aisle," I say, thinking quickly and coming up with the only excuse I can. "We may get married in a registry office." I'm not a churchgoer, and I know Amelie isn't either, and although we obviously haven't discussed our options, I'm not sure I want a church wedding. If she does, then I'll go along with it, but it feels like a reasonable thing to say in the circumstances.

"I'd still like to give her away," he says, ruining my plan to put him off for the time being. "If she'll let me, that is. Things haven't been the same since she found out about my indiscretions and mistakes." He sighs. "She's polite, when she has to be, but she goes out of her way to avoid me, and our relationship has suffered." He looks up at me. "I— I had a bit of an argument…"

"With Amelie?" I interrupt, wondering if I should go to her, even though we didn't plan to meet up this evening.

"No, with Abigail." I let out a sigh and wait, assuming he's going to say more. "I wanted to come back here for the whole weekend, for Amelie's sake. I know it can't be easy for her at the moment, with Christmas coming, and… and Beth not being here." He looks down at the space between us. "It's not easy for any of us really. But Abigail wanted me to stay in London with her, which is what I usually do just before Christmas, because I obviously can't see her during the festivities." He pushes his fingers back through his dirty-blond hair. "The best compromise I could come up with was to spend Friday and Saturday with Abigail and then return here on Saturday evening. Abigail wasn't happy…" His voice fades. "But then Amelie asked me outright over lunch today why I'd bothered to come back, if I only planned to stay for a day. I—I didn't know what to say to her. I feel like I can't win." He huffs out a breath. "I would like her to at least give me the honour of giving her away though. Do you think she might consider it?" He looks up at me again.

"I'll talk to her." It's the best I can offer, although it occurs to me that, if he spent more time at home, and less time pandering to Abigail Foster and his own libido, Amelie might find it easier to accept the situation. As it is, he seems to put his mistress ahead of his family – and I know how much that hurts Amelie.

He shakes my hand again. "Thank you," he murmurs, and then takes a deep breath. "Now… being as we've got that out of the way, why don't you join us for tea?"

I shake my head. "I think it would be best if you and Amelie had an evening by yourselves." The fact that I'm having to point that out to him really ought to tell him everything he needs to know about his relationship with his ward. "And besides, my aunts and my mother are expecting me." They're not. They're quite used to me coming and going, but I wish he'd put Amelie first, just for once. I'm pretty sure if I'm there, he'll find an excuse to sneak off – probably back to London.

"I see," he says. "Well, I'll keep quiet about seeing you then, shall I?"

"I think that would be best, yes."

He nods and smiles. "Congratulations," he says, rather awkwardly.

"She hasn't said 'yes' yet," I remind him.

He smiles. "Oh, I shouldn't worry about that."

For a moment, I think about my mother and Aunt Dotty and I smile. "I'm trying not to," I reply.

Chapter Eight

I don't know what to say to you. Actually, I'm not even sure I know you – or that I want to know you.

I understood that Amy had been murdered, but not that something so utterly disgusting and vile had been done to her. I found that out when the police came to see me. I don't appreciate being suspected of such a monstrous act and I'm wondering now if perhaps we should stop seeing each other, being as I can only assume the suspicion came from you.

How could you think such a thing? After everything we've said and done, it makes no sense to me at all. I thought you knew me better than that, but it seems not.

I won't be writing, or contacting you for a while. I need some time to think.

D

———◆———

I'm fairly sure I woke up with a smile on my face this morning.

I have the ring, and I have Gordon Templeton's permission. All I need to do now is to find the time to propose. And unless anything drastic happens during the day, I may even be able to do that this evening. Fingers crossed.

In the meantime, I have work to do, and I get out of bed, opening the curtains before Mother has even come into the room. It's a grey day, rather suited to the first task in hand; taking Mr Sanderson to identify Amy's body.

I'm dreading it.

Mr Sanderson stares down the small, pale body of his daughter. Only her face is uncovered, the rest of her body hidden by a blue sheet. Her hair is tidy and all traces of mud and blood have been removed. She looks like she's sleeping, her eyes and mouth closed, her nose tipped slightly upward. It's only the grey pallor of her skin and the blue tinge around her lips that give away the lifeless quality to her body. And then there's that bruise on her cheek...

Wyatt, who chose to be present himself, rather than leaving the task to a junior, stands to one side, having revealed the girl's face, and we all look at her father. He holds himself together remarkably well and looks up at me after just a few moments.

"It's her," he says, his voice barely audible, and I nod to Doctor Wyatt, who moves forward and covers the child again.

"This way." I usher Mr Sanderson from the room and he walks out through the double doors and into the corridor, where I release the breath I've unknowingly been holding for some time."

"I don't suppose you have a cigarette, do you?" he asks.

"No, I'm sorry. I don't smoke." *Not anymore.*

"Here." Wyatt steps forward and offers an opened packet of 'Craven A'.

Sanderson takes one between his shaking fingers, nodding his thanks, and places it between his lips, leaning forward for Wyatt to light it, using a match, which he blows out and drops to the floor.

"Is that it?" Sanderson asks, looking back at me again.

"Yes. We can take you home now."

He nods. "Thank you."

"Sergeant," I say, turning to Thompson, "can you escort Mr Sanderson back to the car? I just need a word with the doctor."

Thompson inclines his head and steers Mr Sanderson back towards the main entrance as I turn to Wyatt.

"How's it going with the additional tests you wanted to do?"

"Not as well as I'd hoped," he replies. "But obviously I had to stop to prepare the body for this morning. I'll carry on now, and hopefully report back to you later today, or tomorrow morning."

"Thank you." I turn to go, but then stop. "I didn't know you smoked."

He smiles, just slightly. "I don't. I just always make sure I've got a packet on me, with some matches, when we're doing things like this. It comes in useful I've found."

My smiles widens as I walk away. It's nice to be surprised sometimes, especially in my job.

The drive back to the Sanderson house is silent, but I think we all have a lot to think about. I know I'm contemplating the interview we've got to carry out with Douglas Coates once we get back to the station, but I dread to think what's going through Mr Sanderson's mind. I know I don't envy him.

When we get to the house, Lois is standing on the doorstep, seemingly watching for us and, as Thompson parks the car, she comes out, her hands clasped in front of her.

"Thank goodness you're here." She addresses herself to both myself and Mr Sanderson. "We didn't know what to do."

"What's happened?" Sanderson asks.

"It's the mistress," Lois replies.

"What about her?" I take over the questioning, moving forward slightly.

"She's… well, she's hysterical. The post came not long after you'd left," she continues. "There were just two letters; one for the mistress and one for Miss Sutton. I left them on the hall table, and went to the kitchen to fetch the mistress's breakfast and take it up to her. When I came back the letters were both gone, and I could hear the mistress upstairs…"

"Doing what?" I ask.

"Screaming." She bites her bottom lip.

Sanderson glances at me and, together, we walk into the house, with Thompson and Lois behind us.

I can hear a wailing noise coming from upstairs, along with a loud thud, followed by another.

"I think she's throwing the furniture around," Lois says. "I did knock, but she shouted at me to go away… I didn't like to go in."

Sanderson nods. "Very well, Lois. You can go back to the kitchen."

She gives a slight curtsey and walks quickly to the back of the house. I half expect to be told our presence isn't required, but instead Sanderson squares his shoulders and starts up the stairs. I hesitate and he turns. "I think you'd better come with me," he says.

I follow behind, with Thompson bringing up the rear and we climb to the first floor, going around the landing to the third door on the right. Sanderson knocks loudly, just once, but doesn't wait for a reply, and pushes the door open.

"Get out!" His wife's voice rings out.

"Good Lord." Sanderson speaks at the same time and moves further into the room. Through the gap in the door, I can see that the bed is a mess, the sheets pulled off and thrown onto the floor, pillows scattered; all of the items on top of the chest of drawers have been swept to the floor, and the mirror in the centre is smashed, where something has been thrown at it, I presume.

I pause on the threshold, waiting as Sanderson stares across the room at his wife. "What on earth have you done?" he says.

"What have I done?" Her voice is shrill. "What have I done? I haven't done anything."

"It doesn't look that way to me." He sweeps his arm around in an arc, presumably to demonstrate the devastation of her bedroom.

"You think this matters?" she cries, a sob racking through her, and she comes into view, her eyes swollen, her hair dishevelled, her arm and hand cut – presumably from the broken glass – and her nightgown torn, with a few drops of blood splattered across the front. "My life is over."

He moves forward, holding his hand out to her, showing perhaps more affection to his wife than we've seen since this whole sorry affair began. "It's not," he says. "It just feels that way because you're grieving over Amy, that's all. We will get over this; it'll just take time…"

She looks up at him, confusion filling her eyes. "You're so stupid." A smile crosses her lips, but it's a hard, unpleasant expression. "This is nothing to do with Amy… or with you, for that matter; and stop pretending you care about me, or about us. You can't take your eyes off the bloody nanny, and don't try to deny it."

"I'm not going to. Why shouldn't I look at the nanny?" he replies, dropping his hand and raising his voice. "At least I'm only looking. Unlike you and David."

There's a moment's silence, then Mrs Sanderson screams, "You have no right to talk about him."

"No right?" Sanderson shouts. "You're my wife, in case you've forgotten, while you've been so busy with your lover."

"Wife? That's a laugh. You didn't want a wife. You wanted a trophy… Just get out, and stay out, Daniel." He doesn't move. "I said, get out!" She turns and sees me for the first time, standing in the doorway. Her face pales, and then she looks away and disappears back into the room, just as Mr Sanderson comes towards me, pulling the door closed behind him.

"I—I think perhaps we should leave her to it," he says, his face red with either anger or embarrassment, I'm not sure which. Probably a mixture of both.

I don't reply, and we're just about to descend the stairs, when I hear footsteps on the floor above, coming down to our level. Looking up, I see Miss Sutton walking towards us, clutching some folded linen in her arms, her eyes awash with tears.

"Elizabeth?" Mr Sanderson steps towards her, and she startles, only now aware of us, her eyes darting from him to me.

"It's nothing," she sniffles, raising her hand and wiping it across her dampened cheek. "I—I just can't stop thinking about Amy, that's all."

"Oh… my poor girl."

He goes to embrace her, but then remembers he's not alone and stops himself just in time, and Miss Sutton ducks past us and down the stairs to the ground floor. We wait a moment, none of us saying a word, and then follow. Only when we get to the bottom do I clear my throat and wait for him to look up before I speak. "We'll be in touch when we have something to tell you."

He hesitates for a moment and then nods his head slowly, before opening the front door and letting us out into the damp December air.

"Well, that little scene with his wife was embarrassing," Thompson says once we're both in the car with the doors firmly closed.

"For them, or us?"

"Both?"

I shake my head slowly. "Well, I suppose at least there'll be no more supposed secrets in that house. Not anymore."

"No. It's all out in the open now." He pauses, then adds. "Did you believe the nanny, when she said she'd been crying about Amy?"

"There was no reason not to. But she did seem... I don't know... distracted."

"Hmm... although I suppose that's understandable."

"Possibly, but I still feel there's something Miss Sutton isn't telling us." I turn to look at him as he starts the engine and reverses the car out of the driveway, to drive us back to Kingston.

"You don't have a very high opinion of her, do you?" he says.

"Do you?" I counter.

"No."

I smile. "Well, we can't both be wrong."

"Good Lord no. It would be unheard of."

Prentice is waiting in the main office when we get back to the station.

"Ah, there you are." He smiles as we walk through the door.

"You're looking for me?" I take off my hat and shrug my coat from my shoulders, walking towards him.

"Yes."

I nod towards my office and he follows, a folder tucked under his arm, his hands in his pockets. I hang up my hat and coat and turn to face him.

"You've got something?"

"Something and nothing," he says mysteriously. "I've been through all the items that were brought in from the workman's shed." He opens the folder and looks down at the first page. "There was a lot of it."

"Any prints?" I ask, more in hope than expectation.

"No. Well, nothing useful. I spent a good long while untangling all of that string – with some help from a couple of the uniform boys... Wells and Beresford," he adds. "And we discovered that one of the wooden pegs is missing. I doubt it means anything, although I did get Wells to go back over there and check the site to see if he could find it."

"And?"

"No luck."

"So we've got a missing wooden peg?" He nods his head. "What about the blood sample from the pavement?"

"Nothing doing. There wasn't enough of it, I'm afraid. It was little more than a vague staining." He looks up at me. "Of course, it has rained quite hard in between the girl going missing and the blood being found, so that didn't help." He turns over the page in the file. "I've also been looking at this ransom note," he says.

"And?"

"Well, there are no fingerprints, if that's what you're asking, but then I'd be surprised if there were."

I nod my head. "What do you think of the contents?"

He looks up again, tilting his head to one side. "It's all wrong. It reads like a letter, not a demand. Whoever did this was an amateur; probably someone who thought they could try and make some money after they'd heard the girl had gone missing, and then changed his or her mind once the body was found."

"It's odd that they've gone to the trouble of phrasing each sentence correctly, isn't it?"

"Hmm… that's what I mean about it being all wrong. It's too formal; too well ordered. Generally speaking, in my experience, ransom notes are written more as a series of commands, not like a letter to your Aunt Floss."

"I don't have an Aunt Floss."

He shakes his head. "No. You wouldn't."

Snapping the file closed, he hands it over to me. "I'm sorry I don't have more for you," he says.

"No. It's more nothing and nothing, than something and nothing really, isn't it?"

"I suppose," he muses, walking backwards towards my door. "But if I did all the work for you, you'd never be able to claim to be a genius, would you?"

"Claim?" I reply. "What do you mean 'claim'?" and I hear him chuckling as he walks through the main office.

I sit down at my desk, laying out Prentice's file, just as Adams knocks on the doorframe.

"Come in." I look up and he walks in, standing beside Thompson, who's on the other side of my desk, about to sit down.

"I just thought I'd let you know, Pearce and I have checked out all the other alibis," he says.

"And?"

He nods. "They're all fine."

"What about Albert Finch's supposed wife?"

"Clara Reeves?" he says.

"Yes. Was she willing to back him up?"

"She seemed to be. She was nervous, but I suppose some people are."

"She didn't look like she'd been beaten?" I ask.

"No, sir." He shakes his head firmly.

I sigh, rather annoyed. "Well, I suppose he could hit her where it doesn't show. After the way he behaved in his interview yesterday, it wouldn't surprise me. Still, there's bound to be another time… there usually is with men like him." I look up at Adams. "What's happening now?"

"Pearce is down with the custody sergeant, arranging to have them all released, as per your instructions, sir. Except Mr Coates, of course."

"Okay, Adams. Thank you." He smiles. "And good work." He nods his head and leaves the room, and I turn my attention back to the file.

"Do you think the missing wooden peg means anything?" I ask Thompson as he sits down opposite me at last.

He shrugs his shoulders. "I have absolutely no idea. I doubt it though. It's just a small piece of wood. It could be anywhere – with lots of other small pieces of wood in the park."

I pick up the top piece of paper and read it. "Hmm, except they hadn't actually used these string marker things yet, had they?"

"I don't know."

"Well, according to PC Miller, they use them as guides for when they're digging trenches for potatoes, but my understanding is that all they've done so far is to clear the turf. They haven't dug the trenches yet."

"So?" he reasons. "One of the pegs could have come loose when they were bringing the strings from their vehicle into the park, or even at the council offices – or wherever they picked it up from in the first place. It could be anywhere."

"I know." I put down the piece of paper and close the file. "I'm clutching at straws." I look across at him. "And I'm putting off interviewing Douglas Coates."

He smiles. "Well, I suppose the sooner we get it over with, the sooner we can feel clean again."

I shake my head and we both get to our feet. I doubt we're going to feel clean for some time to come.

Douglas Coates is a large man, probably around six feet tall, overweight to the point where his belly hangs over his trousers and his shirt buttons bulge, with a bald head and dark brown eyes. He sits across the table from me, leaning back in his seat, his hands in his lap, like he hasn't a care in the world. Maybe he hasn't, but his attitude is already annoying me, and we haven't even started yet.

"Douglas Coates?"

He glances at me and smirks. "That's me."

"Can you tell me where you were between twelve midday and three pm on Tuesday of last week?"

He nods at Thompson, who's sitting beside me. "I've already told him, I have no idea. I can't remember."

"I see. You are aware this is a murder investigation?"

He sucks in a sharp breath, and nods his head. "Rape and murder, I understand." He pauses. "Of a little girl?"

He says those last two words with a sneer on his lips. "Yes."

"I might've been in the pub." He looks up at the ceiling, with a ponderous expression on his face, although I'd be willing to swear it's fake.

"Which pub?"

"The Albert Arms."

"And did anyone see you there?" He shrugs his shoulders. "Would the barman remember you?"

"I was served by the barmaid," he corrects. "Lovely young girl." He lowers his face and looks me in the eyes. "Gorgeous arse on her, that one... and huge tits." He closes his eyes for a moment. "And she's gagging for it. You can tell."

"She sounds a bit old for you," Thompson says sarcastically and I turn and look at him, just as Coates starts laughing.

"Yeah, I suppose she is really. Still, I wouldn't say no... not if I got the chance."

"Mr Coates." I cut into his continued sniggering. "Do you think this young lady would remember you?"

Again, he shrugs. "Not sure. And I don't know that I'd call her a lady either, not the way she flutters those eyelids and pouts those lovely pink lips."

I open the file that's on the table in front of me. "Have you ever seen this girl before?" I show him the photograph of Amy that Mr Sanderson provided, laying it in front of him.

He stills, leaning forward a little, then he picks it up and holds it in his left hand, staring at it, tilting his head this way and that.

"Well?" I ask.

"I'm not sure." He frowns. "She does look familiar."

"So you think you've seen her?" I push.

"Don't rush me." He focuses hard on the image in front of him, bringing it a little closer to his face, as though deep in thought.

"Have you seen her or not, Mr Coates?"

He lowers the picture again, then moans softly and licks his lips in a slow, lascivious way and I reach over, grabbing the photograph back from him. His eyes flutter closed, and I'm aware of his right hand moving beneath the table, just as Thompson gets to his feet, leaning over and seizing Coates by the collar of his jacket, hauling him to his feet, and it becomes clear what he's been doing out of our sight.

"You fucking pervert." Despite Thompson's actions, and his loud, angry words, Coates continues to stroke his erection, and Thompson pulls back his arm, ready to strike.

Just in time, I grab Thompson, pulling him away, and Coates sinks back into his chair, the smile playing on his lips. "Get out," I say to Thompson, who glares at me for a second or two, and then leaves the room, slamming the door behind him.

Slowly, I turn to Coates. "Stop that. Now." His hand stills. "I mean it."

He hesitates, staring into my eyes and then slowly pulls his hand away, letting out a long sigh.

"We'll check whether the barmaid at The Albert Arms remembers you." I motion for him to stand, which he does. "If she can't, you're going to have to come up with someone else who can vouch for your whereabouts."

"And if she can?" He smiles, I presume because he knows he's on safe ground and this whole exercise was just an excuse to bask in the limelight for five minutes.

"If she can, then I'm going to have to let you go." His smile becomes a grin and I take a step closer, so I'm only inches from him. His eyes widen and I know my close proximity is making him uncomfortable. "And I'm going to make it my personal mission to ensure you are watched. All of the time. Whenever you look over your shoulder, someone will be there. Your life won't be your own. And if you so much as glance at a child, I will haul you in, lock you up and throw away the key."

He raises his chin in an act of defiance. "It's not against the law to look."

"It will be by the time I've finished with you. Trust me."

He swallows and I notice a few beads of sweat appear on his forehead just as I step away from him. "Do up your trousers," I snap, and go over to the door.

Outside, PC Beresford is walking down the corridor. "Constable? Can you take this man back to the cells?" I bark.

"Yes, sir." He stops and waits while I usher Coates out into the hallway, then I return to the interview room and pick up my file, going back to the main office. There are several uniformed men scattered around, but Thompson is nowhere to be seen.

"Has anyone seen Sergeant Thompson?"

Most of them look at me blankly, but then PC Wells pipes up, "He came through here a while ago. I think he went to the gents."

I dart into my room and leave the file on my desk and then go out into the main office and through to the corridor that leads to the stairs. The toilets are on my left and I stop, taking a deep breath, before I push the door open. Inside, Thompson is standing leaning over one of the three basins that line the left hand wall, his hands clasping its edge, knuckles white.

"Are we alone in here?" I close the door and lean up against it, preventing anyone from coming into the room.

For a moment, he doesn't respond, but then he slowly nods his head, the movement almost imperceptible.

"Are you alright?" I ask. Again there's no immediate reaction, but after a short pause, he stands and turns to face me.

"No."

"I think you should go home."

His brow creases in confusion. "Are you suspending me?"

"Good God, no. I'm suggesting you go home early for the evening, to spend some time with your family. That's all."

He blinks rapidly a few times. "You're not angry with me?"

"No."

"Not disappointed?"

I shake my head. "Of course not. I sent you out of the room for your own good, Harry – and mine. The last thing I need at the moment is you being brought up on a charge. But that doesn't mean I don't completely understand how you feel."

He nods his head. "I—I can't just leave, can I? I mean, you need me to take you home yourself."

I smile at him. "Believe it or not, I can cope. I'll get someone to give me a lift. Or I'll catch a bus if I really have to. I can manage, you know."

He runs his fingers through his hair and then shakes his head, as though he's just working something out. "No. I've let you down enough today. I'll stay."

"You haven't let me down at all, Harry. But you do need to get away from this place, and from the case. Go and give Christopher a hug. Hold your wife. Feel human again, even if it's just for a few hours." He hesitates. "If necessary, I'll order you to go." I make sure I'm smiling while I speak, just so he knows we're still friends.

"You mean it?"

"That I'll order you? Absolutely."

He smiles. "No. I meant do you mean that I can go?"

"Yes. I'm not altogether sure why you're still here."

His smile widens slightly and he moves closer. "Thanks, Rufus. I need this. I need to get away."

"I know you do."

In Thompson's absence, I set Wells and Pearce the task of following up on Coates' alibi, getting them to pay a visit to the The Albert Arms, and I also remember that we need to check on both Donald Curtis' and David Cooke's versions of events for Tuesday afternoon. So, I get Gilmore and Deakin into my office. They've finished with the burglary case now, other than tying up loose ends, so they can afford to spend a couple of hours helping me with this.

"I need you to go to this address…" I hand them a piece of paper with Ralph Ellison's address on it. "Can you check that David Cooke went to see him at approximately one-twenty on Tuesday of last week? And be discreet about it. I'd rather you didn't mention the case, so just fudge the issue and say we're investigating something to do with the bank." They nod their heads. "And then I want you to go and visit Donald Curtis' employers." I hand them a separate piece of paper. "Again, I need verification as to what time he returned from his lunch break on Tuesday."

"Very good." Deakin speaks for both of them, and they leave the office, then I sit at my desk for a couple of hours, going over what we've got so far. I have to say, it's not very much, and by the time I'm ready to go home, the only thing I'm really left with is the hope that Doctor Wyatt will come up with something – fairly soon. Just before I leave with Beresford, who's volunteered to take me home, Wells reports back that, after a brief explanation, the landlord at The Albert Arms gave him and Pearce the barmaid's home address and they went to see her. She remembered Mr Coates, mainly because he gave her the 'creeps', as she put it, which leaves me no choice other than to release him.

On the drive back home, during which I take the opportunity to apologise to Beresford for biting his head off outside the interview room, I reflect that it's been a bloody awful day.

Over dinner, I manage to keep the conversation away from the case – mainly because I'm not sure I can bear to think about it, let alone talk about it. Instead, Aunt Issa keeps us entertained with stories from the Holy Wars, which she's discovered during the research into her next book. She seems rather taken with the period and regales us enthusiastically, with some of the goriest tales I've ever heard, much to my mother's disgust, being as we're eating at the time.

As soon as we're finished, I get up from the table. "If you'll all excuse me," I say, leaning on the back of my chair, "I think I'll go and see Amelie." They all look up at me, a mixture of inquisitiveness, jollity and mischief on their faces. "She wanted me to help her decorate their Christmas tree, if you remember?" My mother's face, which had been the mischievous one, falls somewhat.

"Oh… I see," she says.

"And being as it's still only seven-thirty, I may as well make the most of having some time to myself. I'll take my key and let myself back in." I turn and leave the room, not giving them the chance to comment.

Before putting on my coat and hat, I dash upstairs as quickly as I can and go straight to my room, picking up the small box my mother gave me yesterday, placing it in my jacket pocket, and smiling to myself. I don't know if I'll get the chance to propose this evening, but I may as well be prepared.

Outside, the air has turned icy cold and I pull my hat down a little further, going out through the garden gate and across the road to Amelie's house. The door is answered quickly by Sarah, the maid, who smiles at me. I suppose I am a regular visitor these days, so that's hardly surprising.

"Good evening, Inspector," she says, stepping back so I can enter.

"Good evening, Sarah." She closes the door and, once she's turned the light back on, she holds out her hand for my hat and coat, which I give to her.

"Miss Amelie is in the drawing room," she says, nodding her head towards the door.

"Thank you."

I like that she doesn't bother to show me the way anymore. It makes me feel more at home… or at least more welcome anyway.

I open the drawing room door, to be greeted by a blanket of warm air, and the sight of Amelie, sitting on the sofa, reading a book. She looks up and smiles.

"Hello," she says softly, closing her book and getting up. She looks perfect, in her grey wide-legged trousers and a navy jumper, and I walk towards her, pulling her into my arms and kissing her deeply.

"Hello," I reply eventually and she lets her head rest against my chest. "Are you alright?" She seems a little uncertain, or insecure, her arms coming around my waist as she clings to me. "Amelie?"

She looks up at me. "I'm fine."

I lean back. "Truly?" I stare into her eyes, knowing she's not telling me everything. Even if I wasn't a detective, trained to know when people are lying, I'd still know she was keeping something from me.

"Oh…" She pulls away, huffing out a sigh. "I'm just feeling out of sorts, that's all."

"Why?" I take her hand and lead her to the sofa, sitting down and pulling her onto my lap. She nestles into me, her head on my shoulder. It's a familiar, comforting feeling.

"I took your advice," she says, her voice rather sad and wistful. "I spent yesterday evening with Uncle Gordon and we had rather a fun time together, actually."

"You did?" I recall my conversation with her guardian on the driveway, my own fears that he wouldn't give her his time and attention, and his concern that Amelie was distancing herself from him.

"We didn't do anything terribly exciting," she continues. "We just had a late tea and then listened to some music and played cards, but it reminded me of when Beth was alive. It was the sort of thing we'd have done together… she and I."

"I see."

"And then he left to get back to London. And I realised how lonely I felt, all by myself."

I lean back into the sofa, so I can see her properly. "Why didn't you telephone me? I'd have come over."

"It was after ten o'clock," she says, reasonably. "And besides, you're busy with your case. And you're tired."

I move my hand up, cupping her cheek, and look deep into her eyes. "I'm never too busy, or too tired to come and see you."

She stares at me, tears brimming and when she blinks, they fall, landing in droplets on her cheeks.

"Oh, my darling." I pull her close to me. "Don't cry." She sobs into my chest, her body shaking as I hold her. "I'm sorry," I whisper into her ear and she pushes against me, leaning back.

"Why?" she sniffles.

"I've just realised… what I said just then, it wasn't entirely true, was it?" She stares at me again, but doesn't reply. "I have been rather busy and preoccupied of late, haven't I?"

She shakes her head and places her hand on my cheek. "I do understand, Rufus. I really do."

"But you're feeling a bit… neglected?" I search for the right word.

"No," she says with absolute clarity. "I honestly can't complain about the amount of time you've spent with me. I know how busy you are, and how difficult this case is for you, and I know you've spent almost every spare moment you have with me…"

"And it's been my privilege."

Her lips twitch upwards, just slightly. "Thank you," she whispers, and then leans into me again. "I—I think it's just because it's Christmas, and Beth's not here. I—I miss her."

I hold her closer, stroking her hair. "I know, my darling. And I know I'm a poor substitute, but if you need me, then you really do only have to call. You know I'll do everything I can to get here as soon as possible."

She looks up at me, tracing along the line of my jaw with her fingertip. "You're not a poor substitute. You're perfect. And I always need you."

I lean down and capture her lips with mine, showing her that the feeling is entirely mutual.

We're both breathless in moments, but Amelie pulls away first, looking up at me through her eyelashes. "Can I ask you something?"

"Of course."

"Would you mind if we decorated the Christmas tree?"

I smile down at her. "Not in the least."

She returns my smile with one of her own – a rather shy and beautiful one. "I just think it might help to break a tradition, if you know what I mean. Doing things with Uncle Gordon is one thing, but he was always here. For as long as I've known Beth, I've known him. But doing something like this with you… it's different. It's… it's like I'm moving on. Well, trying to, anyway."

"As long as you're sure?"

She nods her head. "I'm sure. I need to make some new memories… new beginnings."

I kiss her lips very gently. "Well, I'm all for those."

We sit for a moment or two longer, and then Amelie takes a deep breath and stands, holding her hand out to me. It feels like she's taking a giant leap, and she needs me to help her along the way. And I'm only too happy to oblige.

"The tree is in the garden," she says. "It's already been put into a pot. It just needs to be carried through."

"To where?"

"Into here." She nods to the space beside the piano. "But I'll come and help you. You won't be able to manage by yourself; not with your arm."

Ordinarily, I'd object, but she has a point, and we go out into the hall, putting on our coats, and then make our way through to the back of the house, where Amelie lets us out of the door, and I see there's an enormous Christmas tree standing off to one side.

"It's huge," I remark and she looks up at me.

"That's rather traditional in this house. A huge Christmas tree." Her face is alight, smiling, and I lean down and kiss her, because I can't resist. She smiles up at me, and then, with much giggling and laughter – and a little assistance from Sarah – we manage to carry the tree through to the drawing room.

Removing our coats again, Amelie tells me the decorations are in the dining room, and between us, we carry three large, flat boxes through, and place them on the chair nearest to the tree. Amelie removes the lid from the first of the boxes and then turns and looks up at me, a smile settling on her lips. "You're very useful."

"I am?" I nod down at my arm. "I'm not as useful as I could be."

"Oh, I don't know. Being as tall as you are, at least I don't have to climb on a chair to do the decorations at the top."

"No, I suppose that's true. But if I had the use of both of my arms, I could lift you up and you could reach them yourself."

She giggles and lets her head rest on my chest. "Hmm… that might be more fun."

I put my arm around her. "There's no 'might' about it."

She raises her face to mine and stands up on her tiptoes, kissing me all too briefly. "Right," she says, turning and putting her hands on her hips, "we'd better get on."

The first job is the lights. "At least they're not tangled," I remark, smiling down at her as she unreels the flex and hands the end of the cable to me to start putting them on the tree. "Aunt Dotty is renowned for leaving hers in a mess. It used to drive Uncle Sam mad."

"No, I always insist on putting them away properly. Beth was a great one for just stuffing things away in boxes, regardless…" She blinks a few times to disperse her tears, clearly remembering something.

"Well, I'm glad you took charge of the lights." I lean down to kiss her cheek. I don't want her to dwell on her memories too much, although I think she's finding that difficult, and she puts her arms around my neck, holding on for a while, careful not to crush the lights between us, until eventually she coughs slightly and pulls away.

"Thank you," she mutters.

"Don't thank me." I raise her face to mine and kiss her again – on the lips this time – only breaking away when the need for her starts to become too much. "I suppose we'd better finish this." I nod towards the tree.

"I suppose we had." Her reluctance is as tangible as my own.

Once the lights are strategically placed and Amelie has plugged them in to check they're functioning, we work our way methodically through the rest of the decorating, with Amelie placing the baubles on the bottom branches, while I do the ones nearer the top.

"So… how is the case going?" she asks, kneeling at my feet and placing a red and blue bauble onto the tree.

"Rather badly, if I'm honest."

She looks up. "What's happened?" The concern in her voice is touching.

I look down at the glass ornament in my hand, purely for distraction, not even really noticing it. "We had to take the child's father to identify her body," I explain, letting out a long sigh. "That was bad enough in itself, but when we took him home, his wife was having some kind of fit… or tantrum. It was hard to tell which. He tried to calm her, and she turned on him. It was ugly. Really ugly. Not the sort of thing I like to witness, even on a good day, but in those circumstances, when their child has been killed in such a way as she has…" I leave my sentence unfinished and sigh, before continuing, "And then we had to interview a man."

"A suspect?" she asks, kneeling up slightly.

"We'd hoped he might be. We'd pulled him in because he had a prior record of having assaulted children."

"But it wasn't him?"

"No." I shake my head. "Talking to him was difficult though and his behaviour in the interview was – frankly – disgusting. Thompson tried to hit him, so I had to send him out of the room, and then get him to go home. He's been badly affected by all of this."

"And you haven't?" she asks.

"Yes, I have. But I think Harry's finding it especially hard. With Julia being pregnant…"

Amelie nods her head and sidles closer. Then I feel her hand on my leg, resting on the front of my thigh and I look down, to see her upturned face gazing up at me, my breath catching in my throat. "Are you alright?" she asks.

"Um… I'm not sure."

"What's wrong?" She raises her hand a little, edging closer still and I struggle to swallow. "Do you want to sit up on the sofa and talk?"

"Not especially. I mean, we can sit up on the sofa if you like, but I can think of a lot of other things I'd rather do, and none of them involve too much talking."

She tilts her head to one side, as though she doesn't understand, and then suddenly glances at her hand, and snatches it away, her face reddening.

"I'm so sorry," she mumbles. "I didn't even realise I'd done that."

I chuckle and crouch down in front of her, our faces almost level. "Don't be sorry. I liked it. I probably liked it a bit too much. And I especially liked that you feel able to do things like that. So stop worrying about it."

She smiles. "You're sure? That you don't mind, I mean."

I smile back. "Oh, I definitely don't mind." I lean forward and close the gap between us, my kiss proving the point.

We're well into the second box of decorations, having finally resumed the task in hand, when Amelie notices the fire is dying, so I naturally I offer to see to it, but she says she'll do it herself, and gets up off the floor, where she's been kneeling, and kisses me rather sweetly before going over to the fireplace. I take my chance – because I don't know when I'll get another one, and this seems like too good an opportunity to miss – and remove the ring box from my pocket, placing it carefully in one of the square cardboard compartments within the decorations box. When Amelie comes back, I'm hanging a blue and green painted glass bauble from one of the top branches.

"I've always liked that one," she says, looking up at what I'm doing before turning to the box and bending down to make her next selection.

There's a moment of silence, and then I hear a slight gasp, taking my cue and getting down on one knee behind her as she reaches into the box and turns, her face lighting up, her mouth opening in wonder as she sees my position, the tiny ring box clasped in her hand.

I speak, before she has the chance to ask, to question, or maybe even to doubt. "You already know I love you, Amelie, more than I can ever hope to express. You already know you mean everything to me and that I want nothing more than to walk through life with you by my side... so, would you please do me the honour of agreeing to become my wife?"

Without a second's hesitation, she nods her head. "Yes, Rufus," she murmurs. "Oh God, yes."

I stand and, regardless of my broken limb, I lift her up into my arms and twirl her around, holding her body close to mine.

I lower her eventually, and take the box from her hand, opening it and turning it around for her to see. "Oh... that's so beautiful," she says a little breathlessly.

"Promise you like it?"

"I love it."

I take the ring and, letting the box fall onto the chair, I place it on her finger. "You're mine," I murmur, my voice a surprisingly low growl, and she smiles, nodding her head, as I lean down and kiss her.

We're on the sofa, the decorations still only half done, the boxes scattered on the floor, and Amelie lying in my arms. And I can honestly say, I've never felt so happy in my life.

"You do realise I'm not even twenty yet, don't you?" She looks up into my eyes. "We'll need to ask Uncle Gordon's permission."

"I've already done it," I explain and her eyes widen in surprise.

"When did you do that?"

"Yesterday evening. I saw him when I got home from work. He was doing something in the garage, and I caught him on the driveway." I smile. "It was probably an unusual place for such a conversation, but he didn't seem to mind."

"And what did he say?"

I lean down and kiss her. "Well... I asked you to marry me, didn't I? So I think you can assume he gave his consent."

A slight smile forms on her lips and she nods her head slowly. "What about your mother? Does she know yet?"

I shake my head. "No. But if it's alright with you, I'll tell her either tonight when I get home, or tomorrow morning. As I'm sure you've gathered, she's been longing for this day nearly as much as I have, so I can't keep her in the dark."

She smiles. "No, I don't mind at all." I pull her closer and she puts her arms around my neck. "I like this," she murmurs, nestling into me.

"Hmm... and I love you."

Chapter Nine

Dearest,

Please tell me this isn't true? Please tell me you don't really want to break things off with me? How can you? After everything we've been to each other.

I don't suspect you of anything, my darling. I know you'd never do anything so disgusting. The suspicion came entirely from the police, I promise. All I did was confirm that I'd been with you that lunchtime. I told them that you would never have done such a thing, but it's not my fault if they don't believe me, is it?

What else could I have done? What more would you have me do?

If you can just be patient for few more days, I'll try to find a way to get out of the house, and I'll come and see you, if you still want me. We can talk it through and you'll see it's not my fault. It really isn't.

I'm crying as I write this. Please, please, my love, don't give up on me. Don't give up on us.

Your beloved,

Kitten x

————•————

"You were late home last night." My mother looks across the breakfast table at me, raising her eyebrows as she takes a sip from her second cup of tea. "We'd all gone to bed by the time you got back."

For the first time since Aunt Issa's arrival, we're all at breakfast together, which seems like an opportune moment to tell them my news, and get it over with all at once. "Yes. I noticed. Amelie and I decorated their Christmas tree." Well, we did get it finished, eventually, when sanity finally took over again – even if only temporarily, being as we stopped every few minutes to kiss, or hold hands, or just look into each other's eyes, both of us quite consumed with the thrill of knowing we'll soon be husband and wife.

"We've decided to do ours this afternoon," Aunt Dotty says, biting into her toast. She gives me a knowing smile, which I assume is her way of letting me know she's trying to be helpful; diverting the conversation away from mine and Amelie's relationship. The thing is, just on this one occasion, I'd rather like to keep it there.

"Do you still have the old angel that mother made?" Issa asks, and I start to wonder if, for once, I'm actually going to have to steer the subject around to Amelie myself. It'll certainly make a change.

"Yes," Dotty replies, smiling. "It's looking a bit battered these days, but I like to put it on the tree, just for nostalgia's sake. Sam always used to laugh about it…" Her voice fades, reminding us all that his death is still very raw for her and I glance across the table at my mother, who's blinking rather quickly, perhaps remembering past Christmases spent with my father.

This isn't quite the atmosphere I'd hoped for, and I wonder whether to postpone telling them anything until this evening. But then maybe it's just what they need. It'll give them something to look forward to… at least I hope it will.

"While I've got you all here, and I've got a few minutes to spare, I —I wanted to tell you that I've proposed to Amelie." There's a pause, which I suppose isn't that surprising, being as I've just blurted out my news, rather unceremoniously. "She's accepted," I add, to fill the silence, just in case anyone other than myself had been doubting her reaction, despite their words of encouragement before the event.

My mother is the first to her feet, almost running around the table to stand by my side and throw her arms around my neck, kissing my cheek.

"Marvellous!" she chimes. "How absolutely marvellous. I'm so pleased for you, darling." She kisses me again, just as Dotty moves in on the other side, planting a kiss on that cheek.

"Congratulations, dear boy," she says. "That's the best news we've had in… well, in years, I think."

Dotty steps back and Issa takes her place in this somewhat overwhelming procession. "You'll make a perfect couple," she says heartily, bending and kissing me.

"Of course they will," my mother adds, hugging me again. "They'll both be very happy together."

We will, if this charade ever ends. I lean back slightly, just to get some air, and Issa and Dotty return to their seats. My mother takes a moment longer, staring down at me, before placing her hand on my cheek and giving me a beautiful smile.

Once they're all seated, the conversation starts up again.

"Have you set a date?" Issa asks what I suppose is the inevitable question.

"Not yet, no. We didn't get a chance to talk about it last night." We were too busy just gazing at each other, taking in the wonder of it all. And kissing. There was a lot of kissing.

Mother takes a sip of tea, looking at me over the rim of her cup. "Well, I shouldn't take too long deciding; weddings are always more popular during wartime. Perhaps I should make you an appointment with the vicar…?"

"And there's food to think about," Issa chips in before I get the chance to reply to my mother. "Rationing's going to make that much harder."

"And what about the dress?" Dotty jumps on the bandwagon as well now. "Do you think we should offer to help Amelie with that? Let's face it, Millicent Templeton is hardly going to get out of her sick bed after the best part of a decade to go wedding dress shopping, is she?"

"I highly doubt it," my mother replies.

"Can you all stop?" I raise my voice just slightly, while trying to maintain my good humour.

They turn to face me as one, their eyes wide, their mouths open. "What's wrong?" Mother asks eventually.

"You're not going to start making appointments, or planning anything without Amelie being here. Is that clear?" They pause and then slowly nod their heads collectively. "It's her wedding," I add, hoping they'll get the message.

"We know that, dear," my mother says, patiently, "but you're both working, and we've all got nothing else to do."

"Speak for yourself," Issa mutters, but smiles at me at the same time.

"Mother." I clear my throat, my voice a little firmer this time. "No decisions will be taken without Amelie. Not one. Not the date, the venue, the dress, the cake, the food… none of it. She decides everything. Do you understand?"

"Yes, dear," she murmurs.

"I know," Aunt Dotty says, leaning forward in excitement. "Why don't we invite Amelie over for dinner tonight? I can telephone her and arrange it when she comes in from work."

My mother claps her hands together with glee. "What a splendid idea. We can celebrate properly and spend the evening working everything out."

I almost groan out loud at the prospect of an entire evening spent talking about the merits of a sit down reception, as opposed to a buffet; cars, flowers, guest lists, invitations… not to mention the venue, which I think may be a sore point, judging by my mother's mention of a visit to the vicar. Even so, I'll sit through it, and I'll ensure that my aunts and my mother don't ride roughshod over Amelie. Whatever she wants, she can have, and they will just have to learn to live with it.

I'm saved from too much more eulogising by the arrival of Sergeant Thompson, who parks up at the front of the house and toots the horn – which has become the custom over the last few days. He's never timed his appearance better, in my opinion, and I leave my mother and aunts discussing cake ingredients, of all things, under strict instructions that they are not to decide upon, order, or confirm anything until after this evening. At least that's one solace: I have another evening of Amelie's company to look forward to – even if it will be in the presence of my interfering relatives.

Thompson looks a lot better than he did yesterday afternoon, and as I take my seat beside him in the car, he turns to me and smiles.

"You're looking cheerful," he says, even though I wasn't aware of it.

"I could say the same for you." My news can wait, at least for a moment.

He pulls away from the kerb and drives towards Walton Road. "I'm feeling much better. Thanks for letting me go home early. I needed it – probably more than I realised."

"You had a good evening?" I doubt it was as good as mine, but I suppose everything is relative.

"I did," he observes, smiling a little more broadly. "It made a pleasant change to spend some time with Christopher. And it gave Julia a chance to put her feet up."

"What did you do? With Christopher, I mean?"

"We just played with his cars and trains. He's absolutely passionate about trains."

"Destined to drive one in the future, is he?"

"Oh no. He's already decided that when he grows up, he wants to be policeman."

I look across at him. "Really?"

He nods his head. "It's funny. I was already in CID by the time he was born, so he's never even seen me in uniform, and I'm not sure he actually understands what I do for a living, but that's what he's decided."

I chuckle. "Don't take it too seriously. I wanted to be a farmer until I was about seven – according to my mother, anyway."

He laughs. "I can't imagine you as a farmer."

"No, neither can I. And I don't know where I got the idea from, although I think I might have had a toy farm, so maybe that was it."

"Probably." He turns onto Hampton Court Way to go over the bridge towards Kingston. "I'm sorry about what happened yesterday," he murmurs. "I shouldn't have lost my temper like that."

"Don't worry. Coates was just trying to provoke us. We both know that."

"Well, he succeeded, in my case."

"Did you manage to talk to Julia about it?" I ask.

"Yes." His voice drops. "She's very understanding, which I suppose isn't that surprising after five years of marriage, but it's good to talk to her."

"It helps, doesn't it?"

We stop outside the palace to let a bus go past. "Do you talk to Amelie about work?" he asks.

"Yes."

"Did you tell her about yesterday?"

"I did, but not in any great detail. I didn't explain exactly what Coates was doing."

"Well, I suppose it's difficult to know how to phrase it," he says. "It's probably easier for me and Julia, being as we're married."

I smile. "Yes, it is rather awkward. But I won't have that problem for very much longer."

He turns and looks at me for a moment, then focuses back on the road. "You haven't…?"

"I have…"

"You've asked her?"

"Yes."

"About bloody time."

I chuckle. "I have only known her for just over two months. You do know that, don't you?"

"Yes. But when it's right, it's right, and there's no point in hanging around just for the sake of it, is there?"

"No, there isn't."

He turns again, smiling. "And can I assume from your general good humour that she said yes?"

"Of course she said yes."

"Her uncle agreed?" he asks, smirking to himself.

"Yes. I asked him on Sunday."

He glances at me. "Well, you kept that quiet."

"I had to. If my mother had heard about it, she'd have been hanging out the bunting. As it is, she and my aunts are already plotting and planning."

"I don't envy you that," he remarks. "I left all of the preparations to Julia and her mother."

"I wish I could do the same, but Amelie's aunt isn't going to be of much use to her, I shouldn't think, which leaves her in the hands of my female relations. She's going to need me there to back her up."

"Well…" He pulls the car into a parking space behind the station. "… as long as you don't start coming into work talking about lace and flowers, we'll be fine."

"I have no intention of doing any such thing."

We both get out of the car and he comes around to me as I'm shutting the door, and holds out his right hand. I look down at it and then take it in mine, letting him shake my hand warmly. "Congratulations," he says, with a touching sincerity.

"Thank you."

"I mean it, Rufus. You're perfect for each other, and I hope you'll be very happy together." He turns away, but then looks back. "You deserve it."

I'm a little stunned by that remark and it takes me a moment or two to follow him into the station and up the stairs. Just before we go into the main office, I pull him back.

"I'd rather you kept my engagement quiet for now, Harry. Just until the case is over. It feels a bit inappropriate to be celebrating at the moment."

He nods his head. "Will do."

We go through to my office, Thompson depositing his coat and hat en route, and I stop in the doorway, surprised to see Doctor Wyatt already there, sitting in a chair by my desk.

"Good morning, Doctor." I shrug off my own coat and put it on the peg behind the door, together with my hat, before going around the desk and sitting opposite him. Thompson takes one look at the doctor's serious face and rigid demeanour, as he turns to acknowledge my greeting, and closes the door, coming over and leaning against the window sill, behind me and slightly to my right. "What's wrong?" I ask, because it's clear something is.

The doctor lets out a long sigh. "I've finished all the tests and examinations I needed to do," he explains, nodding towards a thin file on my desk.

"And?" There's no point in me reading about it, when he can tell me.

I sense a reluctance though, as if he'd prefer not to say the words aloud. Even so, I continue to look at him. It'll be a lot quicker if he can just tell me. And I can ask questions if there's anything that's not clear.

"And…" He inhales deeply and sits back in his chair. "… and I don't think you're necessarily looking for a man. Not anymore."

Thompson steps forward, approaching my desk. "Are you saying there was no sexual assault?"

"No, that's not what I'm saying." Doctor Wyatt shakes his head slowly.

"Then I—I don't understand. If she was sexually assaulted it had to be a man."

"Not necessarily. I—I…" He's struggling to find the words.

"You think an object was used to penetrate her, don't you?" I do it for him.

He focuses on my face and nods his head. "I found minute splinters of wood and some traces of mud inside her," he says.

"So… something wooden." I'm thinking out loud. "Like the stake that was missing from the lengths of twine?"

He shrugs. "I can't be certain," he replies. "It's a park. And what's more, she was found in a toolshed in a park. I'm sure there were other objects available. Or maybe the killer came prepared."

"It's possible."

Thompson moves around the desk and takes a seat beside the doctor, his face pale now. "Just because an object was used, doesn't mean it wasn't a man wielding it." His voice sounds strained.

"No. But it does mean we have to open up our enquiries to include women as well now."

His head drops into his hands. "Surely a woman wouldn't do that. She couldn't do that," he mutters, almost to himself, and then he looks up again. "Why would she?"

"To cover her tracks?" I suggest. "To make it appear that the murderer is a man and throw us off the scent."

"Who are we looking at then?" he asks, leaning back, crossing his legs and staring at me.

"I suppose it could be anyone, but out of the family members, it would have to be the nanny, or Mrs Sanderson. The other staff were at the house the whole time."

"Excuse me... are you suggesting the girl's mother might have done this?" Wyatt raises his voice a little, incredulous at my suggestion. "That's an awful thing to say."

"You haven't met her," Thompson reasons. "She's shown barely a moment's concern for her daughter since she went missing. Her sole interest seems to lie with her lover."

Wyatt raises his eyebrows. "Her lover?"

"Yes. She's besotted."

"Even so," the doctor contends, "could a mother really do that to her child?"

"Mothers have murdered before," I point out.

"Murder, yes. But this...? Surely the nanny is the more likely suspect?"

"I'd agree," Thompson says, "if it wasn't for the fact that the nanny is the only person in the house who's had a good word to say for the little girl. She's the only one who seems to have cared for her at all."

The doctor nods his head and, with another heavy sigh, gets to his feet. "Well, I'd rather not be in your shoes when you have to question them."

I stand myself and offer my hand across the table. He seems surprised, but takes it.

"Thank you, Doctor." We shake firmly. "I know this has been a particularly difficult case. I'm grateful for your hard work."

He lets go of my hand and puts his own in his pocket. "This has been one of those times when I've really hated my bloody job," he murmurs and he turns, and leaves the room.

I have to say, I can't disagree with him.

"How are we going to handle this?" Thompson asks, once we're alone again.

I sit back down, putting Wyatt's file to one side on my desk. "For now, we're going to keep this to ourselves. We'll go over to the Sanderson house and question both women again about their activities on the afternoon that Amy disappeared. We'll try and make it seem as though we're just checking the facts again, to see if we've missed anything."

Thompson nods his head. "I suppose there's a chance it could be a stranger?"

"It could. But do you really think so?" He pauses for a minute and then slowly shakes his head. "No, neither do I." We both get to our feet and I go and put my coat and hat back on, just as Gilmore appears in the doorway.

"Sorry to intrude," he says, "but I thought I should let you know that Deakin and I went to speak with that Ralph Ellison chap last night."

"Oh yes?"

"He seemed a bit confused about why we were asking, but confirmed that David Cooke had arrived at his house at just before one-twenty. He said the appointment was for one, but that he was running late himself, so he didn't mind."

"Right. And Donald Curtis?"

"We couldn't speak to his boss until this morning," he replies. "He'd already left for the day by the time we got there last night. But he said that Donald Curtis left for his lunch at twelve-fifteen, like he always does when he's going to meet his girl, and was back just over an hour later."

"His boss knew he was going to meet Miss Sutton?" I can't hide my surprise.

Gilmore smirks. "Not by name, no, but it's common knowledge at his place of work that he sneaks off whenever he can for a bit of how's your father with his girlfriend. The boss – a Mr Pike – said he doesn't mind because Curtis is exceptionally good at his job, and he makes up any lost time at the end of the day." He looks up at me. "And he always comes back smiling, evidently."

"Smiling and bragging, no doubt," I remark.

"Mr Pike didn't mention any bragging."

"Oh, believe me," Thompson says, "Curtis isn't the type to hold back."

I pat the young detective constable on the shoulder. "Well done, Gilmore. Excellent work – again."

He grins. "Thank you, sir."

He turns and leaves Thompson and I alone. "You're full of praise," he murmurs under his breath."

"Does no harm. And it puts those two charmers in the clear – if we were still thinking in terms of it being a man – so at least we learned something."

He nods. "So, where were we?"

"Discussing tactics for interviewing Mrs Sanderson and the nanny. We mustn't let them know we suspect them," I point out to him as we start walking out through the main office towards the stairs. "We can't afford for either of them to make a run for it."

"No," he muses.

"I want to see if they slip up, make a mistake, forget a lie they've told us before, or maybe tell us a new one under pressure…"

"And if they don't?"

"Then we'll have to think again."

There's a short pause while we get into the car, and then Thompson turns to look at me. "It could still be a man though, couldn't it?"

"Yes. It could either be a complicated double-bluff, or a fetish that I don't want to think about."

"But you don't think it is? You think it's one of those two women?"

He starts the engine. "Yes. Let's face it, we've been getting nowhere with the men in this investigation. Maybe this is why."

"And if you had to choose between them?" he asks. "Who would you put your money on? Mrs Sanderson or Elizabeth Sutton?"

I take my time before answering, "My head says it's the mother. As you said to Doctor Wyatt, she's shown no interest in the child since we've been involved in the case."

"And your heart?"

"My heart doesn't want to believe a mother could do that. So my heart says it's the nanny. But I have to bear in mind that there's a huge allowance for wishful thinking in there. Still, I suppose until we have more evidence, or one of them slips up, wishful thinking is about all we have."

The temperature has dropped since earlier this morning and there's a definite feeling of overcast gloom in the air. That's perhaps more to do with my own mood than the weather, but even so, I wouldn't be surprised if we had snow soon. It's certainly cold enough.

Thompson parks the car outside the Sanderson house and we both pause before getting out.

"How do you want to do this?" he asks me.

"I'm wondering about trying something a little unorthodox."

He glances across at me. "Well, it is supposed to be your middle name," he replies, although there's no humour in his voice for once and I ignore his comment.

"I'm going to see if we can try and interview them both together."

"Mrs Sanderson and Miss Sutton?" he says. "In the same room?"

"Yes. I'm wondering if they might trip each other up somehow. It's an outside chance, but it could work."

He shrugs his shoulders. "Well, you never know."

We both climb out of the car and go to the front door, which Thompson knocks on, saving me the trouble. I glance up at the sky, which has that yellowish tinge you often get before a storm, and wonder whether I'll make it home this evening before we see the first of this season's snow.

The door is opened by Lois, who smiles up at both of us in turn.

"Is your mistress at home?" I ask.

"Yes, sir."

She stands to one side and I enter, with Thompson following behind. Once we're inside, Lois closes the door and takes our hats. "She's in the drawing room," she says and leads the way, opening the door and announcing us.

Inside, Mrs Sanderson is sitting in the same chair as she was on the first occasion when we met her, a week ago today. It feels like a lot longer than that, but cases like this can distort time, for the families much more than for us. I half expect her to blush, or look embarrassed, being as the last time we met, she was throwing things around her bedroom, but she merely turns from gazing out of the window as we enter, and nods an acknowledgement.

"Detective Inspector," she says, rather formally.

"Mrs Sanderson." I make my reply with equal restraint.

"How can I help?" Her voice is monotone and disinterested, despite her question.

I'm about to explain the reason for our visit, when the door opens behind us and Mr Sanderson walks in.

"Inspector," he says. "I've been working in my study. I heard you arrive. Do you have any news for us?"

Although he seems to have aged in the last week, he's more alert, more eager for information than his wife, who's turned away again, presumably having decided to leave her husband to deal with us.

"We've come to speak to your wife, and to Miss Sutton," I explain to him. He screws up his eyes, his brow creasing in confusion.

"My wife *and* Miss Sutton?"

It seems as though to want to speak with one of them would have been acceptable, but both is beyond his comprehension.

"Yes. We can talk to them both in here, if you could arrange to have Miss Sutton brought down? Perhaps your maid could look after your daughter for a short while?" I put forward the suggestion, while also making it clear that he doesn't really have much choice in the matter.

He pauses for a moment, glancing over towards his wife, and then nods his head, just once. "I'll go and check," he says, and leaves the room.

Mrs Sanderson makes no movement, not even a turn of her head, and I glance at Thompson, who shrugs his shoulders and makes a show of looking at the picture on the wall to our left. It's a large landscape of a field, leading down to a river, with some trees off to one side. Although I'm no great expert, I've spent enough time with Aunt Dotty to realise that it lacks any sort of focus, leaving me to wonder why the artist chose this view.

I'm just thinking about moving further into the room, when the door opens again and Mr Sanderson comes back in. He's alone.

"Where's Miss Sutton?" I ask, not beating about the bush.

"She's just waiting for Lois to go upstairs, and then she'll be coming down." He goes to the fireplace, standing in front of it, and looking rather uncomfortable. He doesn't sit and for a moment I wonder why, but then I conclude that he's probably waiting for the arrival of the nanny, so he can choose a seat beside her. God, I'm becoming cynical in my old age. "What's this about?" He turns to face me, his hand resting on the mantlepiece.

"I'd rather wait for Miss Sutton, if you don't mind," I reply, although him 'minding' doesn't really bother me one way or the other. "I'd prefer not to have to repeat myself."

"You haven't found out who did it, then?" he says, defiantly and Mrs Sanderson turns, looking at me.

"No."

Mr Sanderson tilts his head, as though he's expecting more of an explanation, but I don't offer one and, after a short silence, he sighs and looks down at the fire. His wife turns away from me and stares at him, although from this angle I can't see her face clearly enough to read her expression, and then she goes back to looking out of the window.

Within a minute or so, the door opens once more and Miss Sutton appears. I smile to myself, taking in her neatly combed hair and pristine lipstick, and wonder – again with a tinge of cynicism – whether she really has been waiting for Lois, or whether she's been using these few minutes to tidy up her appearance.

"Inspector," she says, keeping her voice low, presumably with the intention of making it alluring to the opposite sex.

"Miss Sutton." I nod my head by way of greeting and she smiles and flutters her eyes, clearly not appreciating my immunity to her charms.

"You wanted me?" She's leaning forward now in an obvious, flirtatious pose.

"I have some questions." Her rapid blinking is the only thing that gives away her surprise at my response, but she rallies well.

"More questions?"

"Yes. Perhaps you'd like to come in and sit down?"

She glances across to her employer, who smiles and waves a hand towards the sofa on his right, and she smiles at him now – using that same seductive expression she's obviously worked out is wasted on me

– and crosses the room, taking a seat on one of the sofas, and making a point of straightening her skirt as she does so.

Mr Sanderson pauses for no more than a few seconds before moving across and sitting beside her, leaving less than a six inch gap between them. After his argument with his wife, I suppose there seems little point in him pretending anything other than an interest in their nanny, and Miss Sutton doesn't seem to object to his presence, looking up at him and giving him an encouraging smile, which he returns. Well, this could get complicated…

"We've spoken to Donald Curtis," I begin, throwing the cat among the pigeons and taking a few steps further into the room, so I'm effectively between the two women. Mrs Sanderson turns to look at me, but doesn't really react, which isn't very surprising, considering she has no idea who Donald Curtis is. Miss Sutton, on the other hand, blanches and glares up at me through narrowed eyes.

"Who is Donald Curtis?" Mr Sanderson asks the obvious question and I focus on him for a moment.

"He is Miss Sutton's boyfriend," I reply. The lady in question swallows hard, then opens her mouth to speak, before closing it again, and staring down at her hands. Mr Sanderson, on the other hand, turns from me to his child's nanny, and leans back slightly.

"Is this true?" His voice is serious, strained, concerned. "Y—You have a boyfriend?"

Miss Sutton raises her face to his and I notice the tears forming in her eyes, her lips trembling. If she's acting, she's very good at it. "He's not my boyfriend. He's just a friend."

"So you deny spending half an hour at his flat last Tuesday lunchtime – when you were supposed to be Christmas shopping?" I ask and her head flips around to me. For a split second, I see the anger in her eyes, before she fixes me with a kind of frozen stare.

"I'm not denying anything," she says. "I meant to go Christmas shopping, but I met Donald on the way and he invited me in for a cup of tea." She turns to her employer. "It would have been rude to decline." She keeps her gaze fixed on Sanderson, a beseeching expression on her face and, after a slight hesitation, he nods his head.

"I suppose," he says, although I'm sure I can hear a note of doubt in his voice that wasn't there before.

"You just stopped for tea, did you?" I ask, keeping my attention focused on Miss Sutton.

"Of course." She turns to face me, twisting in her seat and raising her chin defiantly. "What do you take me for?"

"Absolutely, Inspector." Her employer leaps to her defence. "Miss Sutton has already explained what she was doing. The fact of the matter is, whether she was Christmas shopping, or having tea with this young man, she doesn't deserve to be doubted."

I turn to him, very slowly. "If it's all the same to you, Mr Sanderson, I will be the judge of that." He goes to speak, but I forestall him, continuing, "I don't appreciate being lied to."

"Who's lied to you?" he asks, raising his voice slightly.

"Miss Sutton has."

Her face pales even more, but she doesn't reply, leaving her employer to fight her corner, which he does, asking, "And how exactly has she done that?"

I pause, quite deliberately, for a sufficient length of time to enable Miss Sutton to become uncomfortable about what I might say next, being as she and I both know that her visit to Mr Curtis last Tuesday had absolutely nothing to do with tea. "Miss Sutton told me she was Christmas shopping," I explain eventually, taking in her slight sigh of relief as I speak. "But in reality, she was elsewhere… *drinking tea*." I emphasise the last two words, letting her know I don't believe a word she's said.

"Does it matter?" Sanderson asks.

"Well, lying to the police in a murder enquiry is never a very good idea."

"No… obviously not," he blusters.

"I—I only said I'd been Christmas shopping because I didn't want to get into trouble." Tears well up in Miss Sutton's eyes again as she looks from me to her employer. "I'd been given permission to go and do that, and it seemed wrong to be doing something else… but…" She covers her face with her hands and starts to sob, rather loudly.

"Now look what you've done," Mr Sanderson says and puts his arm around her, patting her shoulder and cooing, "There, there, my dear," at her. She sidles closer, twisting into him, and stutters out a big sigh, between her sobs, allowing her breasts to rub up against his chest. He sucks in a breath himself, and closes his eyes, apparently enjoying the contact.

"Oh, stop making so much fuss, will you?" We all turn to Mrs Sanderson as she raises her voice. She's still sitting back in her chair, although instead of facing out of the window, she's staring at her husband and Miss Sutton. I wonder for a moment if she's jealous, but then I take into consideration her tone of voice and the vacant expression on her face and I realise she's just rather bored with the histrionics. I'm inclined to agree with her, although I keep my thoughts to myself and turn back to Miss Sutton, who's doing her best to mop up her tears, with assistance from her employer.

"Can you just take me through what happened when you'd finished *drinking tea* with Mr Curtis?" I ask.

"Now?" Mr Sanderson says. "Can't you see she's upset. I'm sure this can wait."

"And I'm sure it can't," I reply.

"So am I," his wife puts in. "I'd quite like to know what was going on, considering our nanny lied to us."

"She didn't lie." Mr Sanderson lets go of Miss Sutton and turns to his wife, his anger apparent in his eyes. "She's already explained. She met this young man on her way to the shops. It wasn't planned."

Mrs Sanderson gives her husband a look that says she's no more convinced by the nanny than I am. "Believe that if you want, but I'd like to hear her answers to the inspector's questions."

A part of me feels bolstered by Mrs Sanderson's support, but then again, I'm also aware that if she's the guilty party here, it would make perfect sense for her to push the limelight onto Miss Sutton and away from herself, so I'm not going to be swayed by her comments.

Miss Sutton looks up at me. "What was the question?" she asks, playing for time, I presume.

"I'd like you to repeat to me what happened when you'd finished with Mr Curtis."

She nods her head and looks down at her hands. "Well," she begins, mumbling slightly, "as I told you the other day, I came back here and found Mrs Slater and Lois were looking after Amy and Eve. Amy was being a little boisterous, so I suggested I'd take them both out to the park, so she could let off some steam."

"And?" I prompt.

"And then I got them both dressed up in their winter clothes, and put Eve in the pram, and we set off."

"For the park?"

She nods her head. "Yes."

"What time was this?"

"I've already been through this," she says, plaintively. "Between one and half past. I told you."

"Well, let's see if you can be more precise, shall we?"

She pauses. "I don't think I can."

"Try and work it out," I suggest. "What time did you finish with Mr Curtis?" I already know the answer to this, but I want to see what she says.

"A few minutes after one, I suppose. He had to get back to work." Well, the timing tallies, even if the reasoning doesn't, being as he said she was the one who had to leave, because she'd only been given an hour off work herself.

"And how long did it take you to walk back here?" I ask.

"Ten or fifteen minutes at most."

"Right, so you got back here at, let's say, one-twenty."

"I suppose."

"And then it took you ten minutes to get the girls ready to go out?" I propose and she nods her head. "And another ten or fifteen to walk to the park?"

"Yes, about that."

"So you'd have reached there at... one-forty-five, at the latest?" These timings are an irrelevance. I know them all already. I just want to see if she'll trip herself up. That's the sole purpose of this charade.

That and gauging the two women's reactions – both to my questions, and to each other.

Again, she nods her head.

"And then how long had you been walking with the pram when the problem occurred with the wheel?" I ask.

"I honestly don't know." She sounds quite desperate and Mr Sanderson glares up at me, but I silence him with a hard stare of my own, before looking back at Miss Sutton and raising my eyebrows. "Maybe ten minutes," she says eventually. "No longer than that."

"And then you told me you spent five minutes or so fixing the wheel and dealing with Eve's mitten. Is that right?"

"Yes."

"And that was when you noticed Amy wasn't there?"

She sniffles loudly, and whimpers, "Yes."

"So the time at this stage would have been, roughly, two o'clock?"

"I suppose." She shrugs her shoulders.

"And yet the alarm wasn't raised until two-thirty-four. Even allowing for the fact that Mrs Slater had to calm you down before she telephoned for the police, that still leaves approximately thirty minutes between the time she went missing, and the time you got back here, Miss Sutton."

Her eyes widen. "What are you suggesting?" she says, raising her voice and sitting up slightly.

"I'm suggesting that it took you an awfully long time to return home, considering you were presumably in a hurry to report her disappearance."

"Well… I had to look around for her first, didn't I?"

"Of course she did." Mr Sanderson sits forward himself now. "She couldn't just leave the park without checking whether Amy was there, could she?"

"No," I reply slowly, as though I'm thinking this through. "The thing is…" I pause for effect, "… it's not a large space, and there's not much undergrowth to speak of; apart from a few bushes on the perimeter, there's nowhere for a child to hide. I wonder that it took more than a few minutes to search… and you could have made it back here in probably five minutes, I'd have thought, walking at speed." I stop talking and wait, but no-one says a word. "Still," I say suddenly, "if it took you twenty-five minutes to look around the park, then it took you twenty-five minutes."

Miss Sutton stares up at me for a long moment, and then turns away, her bottom lip trapped between her teeth.

"Inspector Stone," Mr Sanderson says, raising his voice. "I really —"

I hold up my hand to quieten him and turn to his wife.

"Mrs Sanderson?" She's gazing at her husband, but at the mention of her own name, she twists in her seat and looks up at me.

"Yes?"

"I know you were with Mr Cooke for half an hour or so, at roughly the same time that Miss Sutton was having tea with Mr Curtis. Can you tell me again what happened when you got back here?"

"Back here?" she murmurs, in a rather dream-like state.

"Yes. When you'd left Mr Cooke's house and returned home... what happened?"

"I—I went to bed," she replies.

"Straight away?"

"Yes. I had a headache."

"Nothing new there," her husband murmurs, loud enough for us all to hear, although no-one responds to him.

"What time was this?" I ask her, focusing on the timings, just like I did with Miss Sutton, even though I don't need to.

"I have no idea."

"Do you know what time you left Mr Cooke?" I ask her.

She thinks for a moment. "One o'clock," she replies eventually. "He had an appointment."

"I see. And how did you get back here?"

She looks up at me, confusion apparent on her face. "I—I have my own car," she says, as though the answer should be obvious to me. "It's kept in the garage."

I nod my head. "So you'd have been back here by about one-fifteen at the latest?"

"Well, no," she replies quietly. "I went to the chemists in Thames Ditton first, to get some aspirin, and then I had to walk back to my car, so…"

"You didn't mention this when we questioned you before."

She pales. "I forgot. I'm always having to buy aspirin. It slipped my mind."

"I see. So, you'd have arrived back here at, let's say, one-thirty or possibly a little later?"

"A little later, I think. There was quite a queue in the chemists."

"Did you see Miss Sutton or your children at that point? Perhaps leaving the house, or on their way to the park?"

"No. But I was concentrating on driving. My head was hurting rather badly by that stage. I just wanted to get home, take the aspirin and go to bed." Her voice is rather monotone, like she's bored with my questioning, and would really rather be elsewhere – with David Cooke, probably.

"What happened then?" I ask.

"I think I must have dozed off," she replies. "But I woke with a start when the front door slammed. And then I heard all the commotion and came downstairs to see what was going on."

"I see."

Mr Sanderson gets to his feet, stepping towards me, a bullish expression on his face. "What's all this about, Inspector? I'm sure you've asked all these questions already."

"Well, we're finished now." I make a point of not answering him and turn towards the door. "Thank you all for your time." They gaze at me, bewildered. "We'll show ourselves out."

I nod at Thompson, who puts away his notebook in his jacket pocket, and opens the living room door, allowing me to go out ahead of him. Lois has left our hats in the hallway, and we pick them up and put them on before letting ourselves out

We get into the car and sit for a moment, facing the garage doors.

"What did you make of her lies?" I ask Thompson.

"The nanny's, or the wife's?" he clarifies.

"The nanny's. I think Mrs Sanderson's omission was genuine, don't you?"

"Yes, it seemed to be, but then I suppose we still have to bear in mind that the nanny wasn't in the park where the girl was found – she was at the other one – and we mustn't forget that she's also the only one who really seems to have liked the little girl. Maybe that's why she got so upset about the whole thing."

"And that's why she lied about Curtis? Because there's no way they were drinking tea for half an hour last Tuesday lunchtime."

"No, but she could hardly admit that, could she? She'd lose her job."

I twist in my seat and face him properly. "Are you being generous to Miss Sutton because you like her?" I ask, and he turns to look at me, seemingly surprised.

"No," he says. "I don't like her. And besides, I'm a one woman man nowadays. But are you being so negative about her, because you don't? Like her, that is?"

I smile at him. "No, I'm not. I don't like Mrs Sanderson either. I treat them both with the same contempt."

He returns my smile. "Didn't you think Mrs Sanderson's level of disinterest was a bit odd?" he asks. "She seemed so bored with the whole process."

"Yes, she did."

"And, let's face it, no-one heard her come into the house. We only have her word for it that she got home when she said she did."

"Are you suggesting she went to the park and persuaded her daughter to come away with her, and Miss Sutton didn't notice?"

"I don't know," he muses. "But I suppose if Amy could have been convinced to leave with anyone, it would have been her mother."

I turn back to face the front of the car.

"You're not convinced, are you?" Thompson asks, starting the engine and selecting reverse to pull back out of the driveway.

"I don't know. That's half the bloody problem."

I'm feeling even more despondent now than I was before, I think. My ploy to question them didn't really gain us anything. Alright, so Miss Sutton lied, but as Thompson says, she had good reason to –

namely the fear of losing her position. But at the same time, I'm still not convinced that a mother could murder her child – at least not in the way that Amy Sanderson was murdered.

"She reminds me a little of my sister-in-law," Thompson says, a little wistfully as we head back towards Kingston.

"Who?"

"Mrs Sanderson."

"In what way?" I ask.

"Oh, Catherine was the same after the birth of her second child."

"What? She had an affair?"

"No, you fool," he remarks, smiling across at me. "She was detached. You know, cut off from everything. She took months and months to recover."

"And would she have done any physical harm to her child… her children?" I correct myself, remembering he said 'second child'.

"No, but she struggled to care for them both, and found it hard to cope with the newborn. If it hadn't been for Julia's mother, God knows what would have happened."

"What about her husband?" I ask. "Didn't he do anything?"

"When he could, yes. But he was at work during the day. That's when Julia's mother took over. She said it was some sort of depression… 'baby blues' or something, she called it."

I turn and face him again. "And is this a proper medical condition?"

He shrugs his shoulders. "I have no idea."

I nod my head. "I think I'd like to go and see Doctor Wyatt before we go back to the station."

"Okay."

"I want to see if he knows anything about this."

"You realise he's more used to dealing with corpses, don't you?"

"Yes, but he might have an idea… and if he doesn't, he'll probably know someone who does."

Wyatt is just leaving his office when we get there, his hat in one hand, a briefcase in the other.

"Can you spare me five minutes?" I ask him as he locks his door.

"I suppose." He checks his watch. "As long as you don't mind walking with me. I've got a meeting to get to. What's the problem?"

"I—I wondered if you know anything about... I'm not sure how to phrase this..."

"Just spit it out, man," he says, a little impatiently.

"Do you know anything about women becoming depressed after they've given birth."

He stares up at me. "Depressed?"

"Yes."

"Are you thinking about the Sanderson woman?" He stops walking and puts down his briefcase.

"Yes. She's very disinterested, disconnected from what's happening around her."

"Well, I'm no expert, but I'd say the death of her daughter might give her grounds to be both of those things... and more."

"That's fine, but I'm not sure she was that happy before Amy's death. From what the cook said, she only started to come out of her shell when she started having an affair..."

He scratches his head and sighs. "Again, this isn't my field, but doing something dangerous or out of character, like having an affair, or committing a minor crime – such as shoplifting, or something – can be considered typical behaviour of someone with a personality disorder... if that's the way you're thinking."

"I don't know what I'm thinking. Not yet."

"Then maybe you need to speak to someone who knows more about this than I do?" he suggests.

"I'd love to."

"I have to get to this meeting," he says, glancing at his watch again, "but I'll telephone your office later with the name of a colleague of mine. He's a psychologist. He'll be able to help you."

"Thank you, Doctor."

He bends to pick up his briefcase and plants his hat on his head. "Don't thank me," he says. "Just catch whoever did this. It's a nasty one."

Does he think I don't know that?

*

It's just after lunch when Doctor Wyatt calls with the name of the psychologist – Matthew Tennant – and his telephone number. I make a point of thanking him again, and then get Thompson to call Tennant and arrange an appointment for us tomorrow morning. While he's doing that, I go back through the witness statements from the people who live in the houses overlooking the park where Amy's body was found.

"I think we need to go and speak to the neighbours again," I remark as Thompson comes back into my office.

"What neighbours?"

"The ones whose houses overlook the entrance to the park," I explain, pushing the file across my desk towards him.

"Why?" He leans over and examines the pages in front of him, then looks up at me.

I point at the top sheet. "Because up until now we haven't been able to be specific, or accurate about what we've been looking for, other than it might have been something unusual."

"And we're now interested – or possibly interested – in a woman, with a young child?" he says, nodding his head.

"Or a woman behaving strangely – assuming she'd already dumped the body."

"You want to go now?" he asks.

"No time like the present. And it's not like we've got a great deal else to do, is it?" I walk around my desk and over to the pegs behind the door, where my coat and hat are hanging. "You spoke to Matthew Tennant, I take it?"

"I spoke to his secretary," he replies. "A very prim sounding Miss Butler. She's arranged an appointment for us at ten o'clock tomorrow morning." He smiles at me. "Mr Tennant can spare us half an hour. No more."

"Can he now?"

"Evidently."

He helps me with my coat, because I'm feeling rather tired and it's a struggle to pull it on over my shoulders, and we go through the main office, where he picks up his own hat and coat on the way out.

It's even colder outside, the wind having picked up, the grey clouds scudding across the sky, and we waste no time getting into the shelter of the car.

"I wish I could be at home now, with a whisky, and my feet up by the fire," Thompson says. "Preferably with Julia on my lap."

"Which of those do you wish for the most? The fire, the whisky, or Julia?"

"Julia, of course." He smiles across at me. "And don't tell me you don't feel the same way about Amelie, because I know you do."

I hold up my hand. "I wasn't going to deny it." Just the thought of sitting by the fire with Amelie in my arms is enough to bring a smile to my face.

"Oh, you really have got it bad, haven't you?" he says, grinning now, as he shakes his head and starts the engine.

"Stop talking and drive, Sergeant."

The middle-aged couple at the first house in the row of five Victorian terraced properties, let us into their hallway 'to keep the heat in'. When questioned, the woman looks worried, but says they didn't see anyone at all last Tuesday. Her husband continues, telling us that, at the time in question, they were having lunch in the kitchen at the back of the property, and then they had a cup of tea and listened to the wireless for a while, before he went and mended a puncture on his bicycle and she got on with the housework, all of which kept them at the rear of their property. I thank them for their help and we leave, closing the wrought iron gate behind us at the end of their short, narrow pathway.

"Do you think they're all going to be like that?" Thompson asks as we walk along to the next house.

"Well, it was lunchtime. I suppose it makes sense that they'd have been occupied. But it's worth a try."

Our knock is answered by an older woman, who stands, leaning against the door frame, evidently not so concerned about whether or not the heat escapes from her home.

"I didn't get back from the shops until probably about half past one," she says, in answer to my question, nodding her head. "And then I had my lunch in the kitchen and read the newspaper for half an hour or so."

"And after that?"

"I did the ironing," she replies. "I always do it on Tuesday afternoons. Washing on Mondays, ironing on Tuesdays... I like to listen to the wireless while I do it, but I remember there was some awful folk music on. I didn't enjoy it at all."

"Well, thank you very much for your time."

I touch the brim of my hat and she smiles, then turns and goes back inside, after a quick glance up at the sky.

At the next house, we're greeted by an elderly gentleman, who tells us rather grumpily that he's already spoken to the police and – in any case – he wasn't in last Tuesday; he was at the hospital. I apologise for wasting his time and he slams the door in our faces.

"How polite," Thompson murmurs and I start to wonder if this was a waste of our time too.

"I remember you," says the lady at the fourth house the moment she opens the door and focuses on me. "You're that policeman... the one who was at the park the other day."

I recognise her now. "And you were the lady with the green scarf," I reply and she gives me a smile, which I return. Without her head wear I can see that she has greying brown hair, worn in tight curls around her face.

"Come in out of the cold," she says, stepping to one side as both Thompson and I remove our hats, and she ushers us into the house. "Go on through to the lounge." She nods towards the door on the right of the hallway. "The fire's lit in there."

I glance at Thompson and smile. At least he's getting one of his wishes. We enter a small, but neat living room, rather overcrowded with furniture, but comfortable nonetheless, and the lady follows behind us.

"Take a seat," she offers, and we sit on the sofa, leaving her with the chair nearest to the fire, which she takes, sitting forward and looking at us. "How can I help?" she asks.

"I know you've been interviewed already," I reply, "but we just need to ask one further question…"

"Oh yes? What's that?"

"Last Tuesday, the day Amy Sanderson went missing… did you notice a woman in the park opposite." I nod in the direction of the window, and the green space on the other side of the road.

"A woman?" She seems surprised.

"Yes."

She frowns, although I'm not sure whether that's because she's confused by my question and it's implications – not that the public are yet aware of what was done to Amy – or whether she's just thinking.

"I didn't see anyone much at all," she replies eventually.

"What were you doing?" I ask.

"Oh, just the housework." She smiles again. "You know, dusting and such like. I try to keep busy since my Albert died…" Her eyes stray to a photograph on the mantlepiece and I follow her line of sight, noticing a picture of a rather portly man with dark hair, glasses and a pipe hanging from his mouth. "The time can drag," she murmurs.

"I'm sure it can," I reply, because I can't think what else to say, and she turns to me, smiling again.

"I was in and out of here," she says, thinking again, "but I don't remember…" She pauses again. "Except…"

"Except what?"

"There was the woman with the pram."

My skin tingles. "The woman with the pram?" I repeat.

"Yes." She speaks slowly, as though trying to remember. "The thing is, I can't recall if that was Tuesday, or Wednesday."

"Do you remember what you were doing when you saw her?"

"Dusting the ornaments on the windowsill," she replies promptly. "She came out of the park with the pram, and turned left, and she just caught my eye as I was replacing that china cat on the end there." She points to the trinket in question, a small white cat, sitting upright, and painted – rather incongruously – with pink roses.

"And do you remember whether it was Tuesday or Wednesday when you dusted the ornaments?"

She stares at me. "Tuesday," she replies and then adds, "I think."

I sigh and decide to persevere. "Did she have another child with her?"

"No." She shakes her head with certainty.

"And can you describe her?"

Again she pauses, then says, "She was quite tall, probably three or four inches taller than me. She wore a dark coat and hat… navy blue, I'd say, but they could have been black."

"Her hair?" I ask.

"Well, I couldn't see it very well, because it was under her hat, and she had her head down, looking into the pram at the time, and I only looked at her for a second or two."

I nod my head. It's almost nothing to go on. She could have been anyone. A young mother out with her infant. A nanny with her charge… or she could have been Elizabeth Sutton. In which case, what was she doing at this park, when she's maintained all along that she took the children to the one just down the road from her employers' house?

"We may need to speak to you again," I remark, getting to my feet, followed by Thompson. "I'm sorry, I didn't ask your name?"

She smiles up at me, standing herself now. "Irene Nichols," she says.

"Well, thank you very much for your assistance, Mrs Nichols. I'm Detective Inspector Stone." I realise I haven't introduced myself either. "If you should think of anything else, can you contact me at the police station in Kingston?"

"Yes," she says. "Yes, of course."

She shows us back to the front door, which she opens, to a howling gale. "Looks like snow," I comment.

"It does, doesn't it?"

"Still, we've just got one more call, and then I think we'll head for home." We step out onto the pathway.

"Oh, are you going next door?" She points to her left, to the last house in the block.

"Yes. Why?"

"Because he's not there," she says. "He's gone to stay with his daughter and her family in St. Albans until after Christmas."

"Oh, I see."

"I doubt he'd have seen anything anyway," she adds. "He's usually pottering about in his back garden most of the time. It's his pride and joy."

"Right… well, thank you again." We bid her farewell and make our way back to the car in silence.

Only when we're sat inside, in the relative warm, does Thompson turn to me.

"Could it be her?" he says.

"It could be. Or it could be another nanny, or mother."

"Do you want to go and question her?"

"No. Not yet." I lean back in the seat but turn my face to him. "It's not enough. If we go and question her now, she can just deny it and say it wasn't her – and we can't prove it was. Let's face it, Mrs Nichols is hardly a reliable witness, considering she can't even be sure what day it was. But if it was Miss Sutton, asking the question now would just put her on the alert. She'd have the chance to escape while we're still floundering around gathering evidence."

"You have a point."

"So, we need to flounder around and gather our evidence, while keeping her in the dark… just in case it was her."

"Do you think it was?" he asks.

"I have absolutely no idea. I've made no secret of the fact that, in my heart at least, I've always preferred her as a suspect over the mother, but maybe we'll learn something from Matthew Tennant tomorrow that'll change my viewpoint."

"Hmm… and maybe we won't."

Thompson drops me off at home just before six-thirty, and I let myself in through the garden gate, having already decided during the journey from Kingston to Molesey, that I'm not going to tell my mother, my aunts, or Amelie about the fact that we're now looking for a woman in connection with Amy Sanderson's death – or that we think the woman concerned may be either her mother, or her nanny. Part of my reasoning for this is that I don't want to shock them, or worry them, but I have to confess that I'm also feeling rather sickened about the whole case and would rather just spend the evening with my family, and concentrate on the future, and my marriage to Amelie. That thought reminds me that it's less than twenty-four hours since we became engaged – although it feels like a lot longer than that – and although a few hours spent discussing wedding finery still doesn't appeal, a few hours spent with Amelie is just what the doctor ordered.

I open the front door, to be greeted by the sight of my beautiful fiancée, standing near the foot of the stairs, removing her coat and handing it to my mother.

"Hello." Amelie turns to greet me, with a smile on her face as I take off my hat and deposit it on the hall table. "I only arrived a few minutes ago. We were just saying how cold it is."

I smile back. "Yes, it is, isn't it? I was just thinking about you," I reply, going over to her.

"You were?" She looks up into my eyes, both of us now completely oblivious to my mother, who I think is still standing just a few feet away.

"Of course."

I lean down and cup Amelie's face in my hand, my thumb brushing her soft cheek as I kiss her, pressing my lips to hers, and holding them there. It's only when my mother lets out a fake cough that I pull back and turn to her.

"You can't complain, Mother." I look down at her as I shrug off my coat and reach behind Amelie to put it over the end of the stairs. "We're engaged now." I put my arm around Amelie's shoulders with an air of defiance, and she nestles into me.

Mother can barely suppress her chuckle and turns away, putting Amelie's coat into the cupboard beside the door before coming back for mine. Once she's hooked them both up, Mother turns back, coming over to stand right in front of us.

"Are we ready?" she says, squaring her shoulders.

"What for… the execution?" I mock.

She slaps me on the chest. "The wedding planning," she replies, as though she thinks I might have forgotten.

"Lead on," I say, with an air of resignation and she rolls her eyes and links arms with Amelie, pulling her away from me towards the living room. "I didn't say you could take my fiancée away," I call after them.

"Then you'd better come and join in," my mother replies over her shoulder, and I follow behind.

Inside the living room, the fire is roaring and Aunt Dotty is sitting in her usual seat, right next to it, in the corner of the sofa. Issa is sat in a chair, with a drink in hand and they both stand as we enter the room.

"My dear girl," Dotty says, coming over and embracing Amelie, who looks at me and raises her eyebrows, a little overwhelmed by the attention, I think. "We're so thrilled for you."

"Thank you," Amelie mumbles and I move closer to her, feeling rather protective.

Issa steps forward now, although she doesn't hug Amelie. Instead, she stands in front of her, clutching her shoulders and kissing her on both cheeks, before stepping back slightly. "Can we see the ring on you?" she says.

"*On* me?" Amelie queries, while holding out her left hand for examination. She looks sideways up at me as my aunts hold her hand and 'ooh' and 'ahh' about how beautiful the ring looks – which it does. "D—Did Rufus show it to you before he gave it to me then?" Amelie asks and there's just a hint of disappointment in her voice.

"No," my mother explains from behind Issa and Dotty, who stand to one side to let Mother take their place, as Amelie turns to her. "No, my dear, it was nothing like that. I'm sure if Rufus had bought the ring, he'd have kept it to himself until he'd given it to you. That would have only been right and proper."

"If he'd bought the ring?" Amelie repeats, turning to look at me again. "You didn't buy it?"

"No, and I didn't steal it either." I smile down at her and she attempts a smile back, although she still looks rather doubtful. "It was my grandmother's."

She tilts her head and sighs, and then smiles properly. "Your grandmother's?"

"Yes, on my father's side."

"Did your father leave it to you?" she asks.

"Not exactly, no."

"Alan… my husband… Rufus' father, gave me the ring, after his own mother died," my mother says and Amelie turns to face her again. "And we decided that if Rufus ever found the right woman, the woman he wanted to marry and spend his life with, I would pass it on to him."

"I see." Amelie smiles, although I notice it doesn't touch her eyes.

"What's wrong?" I ask her, stepping around in front of her and placing a finger beneath her chin, raising her face to mine. Mother moves away, but I'm aware of all three of my female relations behind me, in close proximity, listening to our conversation. And I don't care. I only care that something's wrong with Amelie.

"Nothing," she replies.

"Yes, there is. Tell me."

She blinks rapidly a few times. "D—Did you use this ring for… for Victoria?" She whispers the last word, I presume in the hope that only she and I will hear it, but she hasn't reckoned on the honed listening skills of my mother and aunts.

"No," I reply, before any of them can, because this is between the two of us. "I bought the ring I gave to Victoria – and she kept it when I broke off our engagement."

"She kept it?" Amelie seems surprised.

"Of course she did. Bearing in mind what she did, that's not at all difficult to understand, really."

"No," she says, "I don't suppose it is."

"I was actually having trouble finding a ring that was special enough for you," I admit and she smiles, her eyes sparkling this time, which warms my heart. "But this… this is perfect." I take her left hand in mine and hold it, raising it to my lips and kissing the ring. "I've told you before, my darling, that Victoria, and my engagement and everything that happened with her are in the past. None of that is important anymore. You're my present, and now you are my future too. But this ring… it ties you – the woman I love more than anything – to the only part of my past that does matter." Amelie tilts her head again, evidently confused, and although I have no doubt my mother will end up in tears at what I'm about to say, I persevere, because I desperately need to erase any doubts from Amelie's mind, even if that does mean saying all of this out loud, in front of three of the most meddlesome women in the world. "My father is the only part of my past that means anything to me. And I wish that he could have been here to see this, and to meet you, because my mother is right about one thing… he would have loved you." Tears form in Amelie's eyes and I move closer. "Having you wear this ring, it's a link to him. It means he's part of our lives, part of us… and he always will be."

Amelie hesitates, just for an instant, and then throws her arms around my neck, clinging to me, and I put my arm around her, pulling her close and holding onto her. We stand like that for a brief moment until Amelie presumably remembers where we are, and that we're not alone – although for myself, I couldn't care less – and she moves away, looking up into my eyes a little sheepishly.

"Are you alright now?" I ask and she nods her head.

"Of course. How could I not be when you say things like that?"

I kiss her forehead, just quickly and then put my arm around her and turn us both to face my relations, a smile forming on my face, as I take in the sight of them dabbing at their eyes, cheeks and noses, with delicate lace handkerchiefs – except for Aunt Issa, who's using something a little more practical and masculine for the purpose.

"I thought we were here to celebrate, not weep," I remark, leading Amelie to the sofa and sitting down with her beside me, taking her hand in mine.

"How can you expect us not to weep after that speech?" Aunt Dotty says as they all follow, putting her handkerchief in the pocket of her cardigan.

"Well, I wasn't actually talking to any of you," I point out. "I was talking to my future wife."

"I know," Dotty replies. "But it was very… touching."

"And it needed to be said." I lean over and kiss Amelie on the cheek. She turns to me, blushing slightly and smiles.

My mother sniffles and I look over at her, in her seat beside Dotty. She wipes her eyes and gazes at me, wrinkling her nose and looking rather pleased with life. I suppose that's not surprising. I think it's been one of her life's ambitions to see me happy. And it's been achieved. Thanks to the beautiful woman beside me.

"We need to talk seriously about the wedding," my mother says as we sit in the dining room, with Amelie beside me and my aunts and mother around the table in front of us.

After a couple of Aunt Dotty's gin and tonics, the mood in the living room lifted considerably, but we haven't discussed the wedding at all yet – seriously, or otherwise.

"We're not discussing the dress," Dotty replies. "Not with Rufus here."

"Thank heavens for that," I remark.

"What about booking the church?" Mother says and turns to Amelie. "I offered to make an appointment with the vicar, but Rufus said I should discuss it with you first… so if you'd like me to do that…?"

Amelie glances up at me, looking doubtful again, then turns to my mother. "I—I don't know about Rufus," she says, sounding shy for the first time in the present company, "because we haven't really had time to talk about it yet, but I'm not sure about getting married in church."

"Neither am I," I add quickly and reach for her hand under the tablecloth. She clasps mine and grips tightly. "We're not regular churchgoers," I add, taking up the cause. "So it feels hypocritical."

"And it seems rather frivolous to go overboard on finery and frills, when the country's at war," Amelie remarks. "I think I'd rather get married in a registry office and have a quiet reception afterwards… if no-one minds."

"No-one minds," I say softly.

She looks up at me. "I don't need a big, expensive wedding. That's not what this is about."

"No?" I lean a little closer, teasing her, even though we're not alone.

"No," she replies. "It's about being married to you."

"Good." I raise our bound hands from beneath the tablecloth and kiss her fingers, before placing them on the table, still clasped together.

"If you're sure that's what you want?" my mother asks. She not interfering, she's just asking the question – to make sure, I think.

"We're sure," Amelie replies, and I nod my head.

"Where do you think you'd like to have the reception?" Issa says, moving us on to the next topic as Dotty starts to dish up the rabbit pie, passing the plates around.

Amelie leans forward slightly. "I don't want to sound like I'm taking control of the whole day…"

"Why shouldn't you?" I interrupt. "It's your wedding."

"It's yours too," she reasons, looking up at me.

"And if you're happy, then I'm happy. So, what did you want to say about the reception?"

"Well, I was just going to say that, Aunt Millicent is unlikely to be persuaded to leave the house, but she might be talked into coming downstairs… so do you think we could have the reception at our house?"

"Of course. If that's what you want."

I think it's a shame that she's convinced her aunt won't be talked into attending our wedding ceremony, but I have to admit – even if only to myself – that she's probably right. The mention of Amelie's aunt also reminds me that I'm supposed to be putting in a good word for her uncle, with regards to giving her away, but I think that's a conversation best had when we're alone.

"We're going to have to think about rationing," my mother says, bringing up Issa's point from this morning. "That will start early in January, won't it?"

"Yes, on the eighth," Dotty says. "But why do we need to worry about it? They're only rationing bacon, butter and sugar to start with."

"To start with," Mother repeats, knowingly, helping herself to carrots.

"You're just desperate for us to set the date, aren't you?" I suggest and she looks over at me.

"Yes… I mean, no." We all laugh at her discomposure as she gets flustered in her reply and drops the serving spoon. "I'm just pointing out that you probably shouldn't delay for too long… just in case."

I've got no intention of delaying any longer than is absolutely necessary, and that's got nothing to do with bacon, butter or sugar.

"Well, unless we're having bacon sandwiches at the reception, I don't think we need to worry too much," Issa says.

"We're definitely not having bacon sandwiches," I reply.

"You're all missing the point." Mother passes the carrots to Dotty and tries to get us to concentrate and take her seriously for a moment. "It may only be a few things on ration for now, but all that could change within a matter of weeks, and then where will we be? And with sugar being rationed, what are we going to do for a cake?"

"Oh yes." Dotty passes the carrots on to Issa. "I'd forgotten about that."

"I'm sure we'll cope," Amelie says, sensing their rising anxiety over something that doesn't really matter, not to us, anyway.

"Do we have to cope?" I ask, twisting in my seat to look at her.

"Well, we don't have to have a cake," she muses.

"I know we don't. But that's not what I meant." I turn completely, so we're facing each other. "My mother is desperate for us to name the day…"

"I'm not," Mother interrupts.

"Yes, you are," Issa and I both reply at once and we all laugh again, as I turn back Amelie.

"Bacon, butter and sugar aside, I don't want to wait, do you?" She shakes her head and her lips twitch upward. I think I know what that means, but I try not to react and just smile at her in return. "Our birthdays fall on Tuesdays next year." I'm thinking this through as I speak, working out the dates and days in my head. "Yours is five weeks from today." And mine is exactly one week later.

"Yes?"

"So why don't we get married on the Saturday in between our birthdays?"

"Which would be the…" She fishes around for the date.

"The twenty-seventh," I supply.

She smiles broadly. "The twenty-seventh of January. It sounds perfect."

"Wait…" I can hear the panic in my mother's voice. "Now, just wait a minute. I didn't mean…" She falls silent and I look over at her. "I didn't mean you had to get married that quickly, just that you should make a decision, so we can plan… that's all. I'm not sure we can get everything ready…" She looks to her sisters for support, but they're both smiling broadly. "Oh dear," she mutters.

"Be careful what you wish for, Mother. We're getting married in…" I do a quick calculation in my head. "Thirty-nine days."

"Oh, my goodness." She stares at me for a moment, but then lets out a long breath and shrugs her shoulders before she smiles and settles back in her chair, resigned.

"Thirty-nine days," Amelie says beside me, sighing.

"Yes, and then you'll be mine." I lean towards her, lowering my voice, although I have no doubt everyone else can hear me. The room isn't that big.

"Um… I think I already am," she replies.

"Well, it'll be official… Thirty-nine days… and counting."

She giggles and, not for the first time since I came home this evening, I wish we were alone. Although, if we were, I doubt we'd be counting. Or waiting.

"I think we rather shocked my mother." I close the garden gate behind Amelie and take her hand in mine as we cross the road in the moonlight. The earlier clouds have dispersed and it's even colder, than it was, but there's still no snow – yet.

"Yes, I think we might have done." She looks up at me. Even in the near darkness, I can see the sparkle in her eyes, and the twitch of her lips as she tries not to smile.

"Are you happy with everything that's been decided so far?"

"Of course." She leans into me, her head resting on my shoulder, but then pulls back and looks up at me again. "I'm sorry. I've just realised we've spent the whole evening talking about the wedding."

"And what's wrong with that? The wedding is important. Especially as we've given ourselves such a short time to prepare."

"I know, but that's not what I meant."

"What did you mean?" I ask.

"Just that I haven't had a chance to ask you about your work, and I've been meaning to." We turn into the driveway of her house and start towards the front door. "How's the case going?"

"Not very well." I feel the tension in my shoulders, which has been blissfully absent all evening and I lower my head. She stops walking, pulling me back with her, and I turn to her, looking down into her upturned, concerned face.

"What's wrong?" she says. I'm not sure where to start and, after a few moments' silence, she moves closer. "Do you want to talk about it?" Her voice soothes that tension and I realise that, despite my earlier resolution not to mention the latest developments, I do need to say something, and I need to say it all out loud, to try and make sense of the day's events.

"Yes, I think I do."

She nods her head. "Come inside. It's too cold out here."

She leads me to the door and pulls a key from her pocket, using it to let us in. The hallway is in darkness – but it's late, so that's not surprising – and once the door is closed, and the blackout curtain pulled across, she switches on a lamp on the hall table, bathing us in a soft glow. As she undoes her coat, I shrug mine off and she puts them both over the end of the stairs, then pulls me towards the drawing room.

It's still warm in here, although the fire's embers are dying, and Amelie turns on a side light next to the sofa.

"Do you want a drink?" she offers.

Considering that we had gin and tonics before dinner and a bottle of claret during it, I should probably say 'no', but… "Whisky?" I suggest and she raises an eyebrow before going over to the drinks cabinet.

"It's that bad, is it?" she says.

"Yes," I reply and she stops, the decanter in her hand and looks over at me, before pouring a finger of whisky into a cut glass tumbler and bringing it back to me. "You're not having one?" I take the glass from her as we both sit down on the sofa, with me in the corner and her right beside me.

"No. I'll never get up in the morning if I do."

I take a sip of the strong, peaty-flavoured liquor and lean into her. "If I have to go through another day like today, then I don't think I want to get up,"

She twists in her seat to face me, resting her hand on my thigh. "This isn't like you, Rufus. Tell me what's happened."

I focus on her beautiful face and wonder where to start, knowing I'm going to have to choose my words carefully. "The police doctor was waiting in my office for me this morning," I begin. "He'd been carrying out further tests on little Amy's body, and he'd got the results back."

"And?" Her voice is a whisper.

"And he'd discovered that there were no traces of her attacker having been a man."

She stares at me for a moment. "I—I thought she'd been sexually assaulted," she murmurs.

"She had."

"But surely..." Her voice fades.

"Whoever it was – and it may still have been a man – used an object, a wooden object, we think, to... to penetrate her."

She slaps her hand across her mouth, her body convulsing slightly as she tries not to retch, and I lean forward, putting my glass down on the table, before pulling her into my chest.

"I'm sorry, my darling," I whisper into her hair, feeling her arms come around my waist, as she holds onto me and starts to whimper, quietly to begin with, although her sobs quickly become louder. "I should never have told you."

She shakes her head and mumbles something I can't understand, then leans back, wiping at her face with her hand, before reaching into my jacket pocket, where she knows I keep a clean handkerchief, taking it out to complete the job. "No," she says, more coherently as she dabs at her cheeks. "I'm the one who should be sorry. I'm supposed to be here for you... to listen to your problems and comfort you. And I'm not doing a very good job, am I?"

I smile down at her and take the handkerchief, moping up the last of her tears from beneath her eyes. "You are being here for me," I tell her.

"By making you comfort me?" She shakes her head.

"You didn't make me do anything." I cup her chin with my hand, keeping hold of it as I gaze into her eyes. "I like comforting you. It's my job, and I can't wait until I can do it full time."

She blinks, and then a slow smile forms on her lips. "Neither can I," she whispers.

"And I really am sorry I upset you. I shouldn't have…"

"It's not your fault," she interrupts, putting her hand back on my thigh again. "I'm glad you told me. I'm glad I know what you're going through."

"I wish I wasn't," I murmur, letting go of her and sitting back into the sofa again. She comes with me and leans her head against my shoulder.

"How do you?" she asks. "How do you deal with a case like this?"

"I don't really know."

"Have you had to do it before?"

I change position slightly and put my arm around her, so she's resting on my chest now, her arm around my waist and she puts her feet up on the sofa. It's more relaxed like this.

"Not this bad, no. I've had to deal with three child murders in my career, one of which had a sexual aspect. The victim in that one was thirteen." I feel her nod her head.

"This feels worse, doesn't it?"

"Yes. Much. I mean, it already felt awful, because Amy was so young, but now… now we know it might have been a woman…"

"Surely no woman could do that to a child," she says, moving her arm down and letting her hand rest on my thigh again.

"I'd like to say they couldn't," I reply, "but over the years, I've come to realise that there aren't really any depths that human beings won't stoop to."

"But why?" she asks. "Why would a woman do that?"

"To make it look like the perpetrator is a man."

"Oh… of course." She sighs. "Do you have any idea who might have done it?" she murmurs.

"I have my suspicions, but I can't arrest someone based on my suspicions."

"Who do you think it was?" she asks and I hesitate.

"I have two people in mind, but would you be cross with me if I didn't say who they are?"

She leans back and looks up at me. "Because it's a secret? Something you're not allowed to tell me?"

"No, it's nothing like that. I'd rather not say, because I think you'll get upset."

"It's no-one I know, is it?" Her eyes widen in horror.

"Good Lord, no." I pull her close to me again and tighten my grip on her. "It's nothing like that, and if you really want me to, I'll tell you…"

There's a slight pause and then she shakes her head. "No," she murmurs, "I think I'd rather not know… not if you think it's best."

"For now, I do."

Bearing in mind her reaction to me telling her about what was done to Amy, if she knew that my two suspects are the girl's own mother, and her nanny – the woman charged with caring for her – I don't want to think how she'd respond. And I don't want her to be even more upset than she is now – not when I can't stay here to comfort her. Well, not for much longer, anyway. We both have to get to bed soon.

"You are sure you're alright, aren't you, Rufus?" She looks up at me through her thick eyelashes.

"I'm fine." I kiss her forehead, and she moves up slightly, so I can kiss her lips, which I do for a few minutes, savouring her sweetness, and the softness of her touch.

"Find them," she says as she pulls away from me, looking up into my eyes. "Find whoever did this to that poor little girl – no matter who it is – and make them pay."

"I will, darling. I promise."

Chapter Ten

Dear Kitten,

I'm sorry.

I've just opened your letter before going to work, and I have to write now, even if it makes me late. Reading your words and imagining how you must have felt when you wrote them, made me feel terrible about the things I said to you in my last note. I hate the thought of you crying, and knowing that it's me – and my words – that have made you so upset. I know I shouldn't have got so cross with you, but having the police come here and tell me what had been done to Amy was just such a shock. I jumped to conclusions, instead of trusting you, and I was wrong.

Can you forgive me?

Please say you can, because I miss you so much.

I know things are difficult for you at the moment, and I know you say we need to wait a few more days, but I really do want us to meet up sooner than that, if we can. I need to see you, so desperately. I think it's because I'm missing you so much, and missing all the things you do to me too, that I was so horrible. It just goes to show that I'm no good without you, doesn't it? And maybe if you can find some time to be with me, we can talk about that, and about our future together? If we have one, that is. Because I really do hope you can forget all the things I said and let us put the last few days behind us.

Write back soon and let me know when you can get away. I don't care when it is, I'll find the time. I love you too much to lose you, my darling Kitten.

With all my love,

D.

p.s. I've just realised I don't have any stamps, but I'll get one on the way home from work, so you'll still get this tomorrow and can write back to me quickly. I love you. xx

"I forgot to ask," I say to Thompson as I settle into the car beside him, "where are we going to see our friendly psychologist?"

"He's got appointments at Kingston Hospital this morning, so he's meeting us at his office there," he explains.

"Okay."

He turns to look at me as he starts driving. "Are you alright?" he asks.

"Why?"

"You look a bit tired, that's all."

"I am tired. I had a late night. And before you make any suggestive comments about that, Amelie and I spent most of it with my mother and aunts planning the wedding."

"You only got engaged two days ago. You don't have to get all the planning done in one night, you know. There's no rush."

"We didn't. Although your point about there being no rush isn't strictly true." He turns onto Walton Road and glances at me. "We've set the date," I explain.

"And?"

"It's thirty-eight days from now."

He flips his head around to me in surprise. "That's… five weeks. Well, just over."

"Yes, I know."

Again, a smile appears on his lips. "And is there a reason for this haste?"

"No." I think for a second. "Well, yes. Maybe."

"That's perfectly clear, Rufus."

I sigh. "If you must know, we're waiting."

"Not for the wedding you're not. You're ploughing full steam ahead into that, it seems."

"You can talk," I reply. "You married Julia within four months of meeting her."

"Yes, but I proposed after six weeks. We waited very nearly three months for the actual wedding, to give her mother time to make the dress and get things organised. And even then, there was an element of panic about it." He chuckles. "What did your mother say when you told her?"

"She practically had kittens at the dinner table."

"I'm not surprised." He shakes his head, smiling. "So, if you're not waiting for the wedding, what are you waiting for?"

I turn to him. "Are you being deliberately obtuse?"

He glances at me again. "Oh, I see…" The light dawns. "You mean you're waiting until your wedding *night*?"

"Yes."

"Like you did with Victoria?" he asks, as though he thinks I should have learned my lesson the first time.

"No, not like Victoria," I reply and his brow creases in confusion. "Well, sort of like Victoria."

He sighs. "You're really not making sense."

"What I mean is, the principle is the same, but Amelie isn't Victoria. She's faithful, for one thing. And waiting for Victoria was different. We decided to wait… well, I decided and she agreed – or I thought she did – only we never actually got around to setting the date. Not officially, anyway. We talked about it a couple of times, but one or other of us always found an excuse to change the subject." I huff out a half laugh. "I suppose I should have taken that as a sign and got out while I was vaguely ahead."

"You probably should," he murmurs.

I think about it for a moment. "But the thing is, it didn't bother me that much."

"What didn't?"

"Waiting indefinitely."

"And that didn't tell you something either?" he says.

"Not at the time, no. Now, I'm with Amelie… now I know how it's supposed to be, it speaks volumes."

"Victoria really wasn't right for you," he says quietly.

"Was she right for anybody?"

He chuckles. "No-one who had expectations of monogamy, no."

We wait behind a bus for a moment while a few passengers alight, and he turns to me. "So what's different? Other than the fact that your taste in women has improved significantly?"

I smile at his compliment – but only because it's true. "Well, waiting for Amelie is driving me insane, if you must know."

He roars with laughter, and I can't help but join in.

"Just as well you've only got thirty-eight days to go then," he says.

I recall how difficult it was to say goodnight to Amelie last night, in the darkened hallway, how I held her in my arms and she clung to me as we kissed deeply; how she moaned into my mouth and pressed herself against me and how I whispered my love for her, and told her how much I want her and need her as I bit her bottom lip, just gently. Remembering all of that, I know that if she were with me now, I'd struggle to wait for thirty-eight minutes. Actually, I think even thirty-eight seconds would be beyond me.

The man sitting across the desk from us is younger than I'd expected. He's probably younger than me, or maybe he just looks that way because of the rather boyish glasses he's wearing. It's hard to tell, especially as his clothes are somewhat dated. His tweed jacket and waistcoat have both seen better days, being frayed at the hems, his tie is crooked, and his watch chain is tarnished. Perhaps he's just not very interested in his appearance, a concept which his surroundings of musty books and dust laden picture frames would seem to support. I can't imagine this is where he carries out his professional appointments. It's a very small space, for a start. And there's nowhere comfortable for his patients to sit, or lie down. Instead, there's just the desk, his chair, plus the two which seem to have been squeezed in for Thompson and myself, the bookshelves behind him and a filing cabinet between the two small windows. I presume this is where he does his paperwork, and his consultations take place somewhere else – hopefully more accommodating than this. His gaze is intense as he stares at me.

"What can I do for you, Inspector?" His voice is deep, and rather more soothing than I'd expected.

"We're looking for some professional insight with regard to a case," I reply and he nods his head, waiting, while I take a breath, wondering how to explain. In the end, I decide to just begin at the beginning, giving him details of the disappearance of Amy Sanderson, the subsequent discovery of her body, and the mutilation that took place. "We're now working on the theory that a woman carried out this act, or at least that it may have been a woman," I clarify, "and have noticed, during the course of our enquiries, that the child's mother exhibits some rather strange, detached behaviour."

He raises his eyebrows. "How do you expect her to behave, given that her daughter has just been murdered?" he asks.

"Well, I didn't expect her to be cracking jokes," I reply, perhaps a little facetiously, "but in such circumstances – in my experience – mothers usually display some emotion. She doesn't."

"None?" He seems surprised by that.

"Not about her daughter, no. The only thing she seems to be interested in… the only thing that even registers with her in any way, is when the conversation turns to her lover."

"She has a lover?"

"Yes."

"Is that a recent thing?" he asks.

"I've been told that their relationship began about six months ago, at which point, her personality changed – for the better. Or at least for the more contented. She'd been quiet and withdrawn until that point, from the moment of her first daughter's birth. The arrival of a second child had no impact, but taking a lover made all the difference, evidently. And now, she positively sparks to life whenever his name is mentioned."

"Is this a serious relationship?" he asks. "Or is it just about sex?"

"I think it's a serious relationship. Obviously I can't be sure of that, but judging from the behaviour of both parties, I think they'd happily give up their current lives, if it meant they could be together permanently."

"Then I wonder why they don't?" he remarks. "Other than convention, public opinion and societal norms, what would be stopping them?"

"Money?" I conjecture. "She has a comfortable life at the moment. I don't imagine her lover is poorly paid, but he's not on the same level as her husband."

"And you think money matters?" He frowns at me.

"No. *I* don't. But I think she might. Otherwise, as you say, I can't see why she hasn't already left her husband. She claims to find him dull and boring, barely notices his existence and boasts about her lover in front of him. According to her lover, they've discussed their 'ideal' scenario, and it involves her leaving her husband and her children behind, in favour of him."

"Well, ideals are all very well, but they won't keep her in mink coats, will they?" I'm surprised by the vehemence behind his comment, as well as having found someone whose cynicism at least equals my own, and I study him as he shakes his head slowly, evidently disappointed. "So what do you want to know exactly?"

"Is it possible that she experienced some sort of… I don't know… some sort of depressive episode as a result of giving birth to her first child that might lead to her killing her daughter?"

He stares at me again, with a slightly withering expression. "Depressive episode?" he repeats.

"I'm sure that's not the correct term…"

"Not really." He sits forward, clasping his hands together on the desk. "There are many terms used to describe what I think you're talking about, but for myself, I've never seen the value in focusing on terminology. The fact of the matter is that postnatal illness – while still not recognised or understood by some in my profession – has been a sad fact of childbirth for many women, for centuries." He releases his hands and pushes his glasses up his nose slightly, warming to his subject. "There are documented cases that go back as far as the ancient Greeks. And although some say the state of a woman's mind has a direct correlation to her experiences in labour and childbirth, there is no real evidence as to this."

"I see." I'm not sure that I do, but at least he seems well versed on the subject. "And are there incidences of women with this condition who have killed their offspring?"

He sighs deeply. "I'm afraid there are. But I would say it's more common for women in that situation to harm themselves. It also seems odd that the woman in your case would wait four years… and as for the mutilation…" His brow furrows. "I can't see a reason why she'd do that."

"To throw us off the scent." I repeat the reasoning I gave to Amelie. "To ensure that we would suspect a man."

"Yes, I understand that," he says, "and I'd agree if we were talking about someone of sound mind. But we're not. That is, of course, assuming she actually is suffering from some kind of 'depressive episode'." He uses my term, raising his eyebrows again at the same time. He stands up and goes over to the window, looking down at something outside, and then turns back to face us, leaning on the windowsill. "I can't give you definitive answers," he says.

"Opinion will do."

"I'm not even sure I can give you that. I haven't met the woman, so I can't diagnose. I can theorise. That's all."

"Then theorise."

He examines his fingernails for a moment, then says, "It could be that she suffered from postnatal depression after the birth of the child – a state in which she remained, despite the arrival of a second baby, until she took a lover, and found a purpose to her life. Having found such a purpose, I highly doubt she would pay any attention at all to her children, whether for good or bad. To her, they would be reminders of the life she once had; the life her lover claims she wishes to escape." He sighs. "It could be that something happened to tip her over the edge, and drove her to murder and mutilate her child, but I'm sorry, I can't see a reason for it, not with the facts you've given me. Her current state of mind, her distraction and disengagement, could be entirely due to the fact that she can't be with the man she loves. She's stuck at home with a husband she seemingly struggles to tolerate, living a life she no longer wants. Society and – possibly – a need for the financial comforts of her marriage, dictate that she has to stay where she is for the time being, but that doesn't mean she has to like it, or be happy about it."

He pulls his watch from his waistcoat pocket and squints down at it, but before he can comment, I get to my feet.

"We've taken up enough of your time." I hold out my hand to him and he replaces his watch and shakes my hand, looking up at me.

"If you should find some evidence against her, or decide to make an arrest, and need me to speak with her, I'll be happy to oblige," he remarks. "If she were to be found guilty… well, such cases make for fascinating research."

I stare down at him for a moment, wondering how to reply to that, and decide to just nod my head, being as words have, for the moment, failed me.

"Are we any further forward?" Thompson asks as we climb back into the car.

"Possibly," I muse. "I suppose we know that this postnatal depression – or whatever it's called – is an actual illness."

"Does that help?"

"Well, it shows that Mrs Sanderson might have been suffering from it, and could have harmed her child as a result…"

"'Might' and 'could'," he repeats. "Not the most encouraging of words at this stage of an investigation."

"No. We need some evidence. Preferably physical and irrefutable."

"Back to the station?" he suggests.

"Yes. I'll let you make us a cup of tea, and we're going to wade through the files until we come up with something. Even if it takes us all day."

"I think that might require more than one cup of tea."

"Nice of you to make the offer."

We're on our second cup of tea, with which Thompson brought up some digestive biscuits, although where he scrounged them from, I have no idea. The paperwork is all scattered across my desk, but so far we've found nothing and we're both starting to feel a little disheartened.

Thompson is sitting opposite me, his cup balanced on his knee as he thumbs through his notebook. "I don't think I've ever come across a case where everyone tells almost exactly the same story. I can't find any differences between them at all…" He stops and sits forward, the cup wobbling, although he catches it before it falls and moves it to the table.

"What's wrong?"

He holds up his hand. "It might be nothing," he murmurs. "Hold on…"

He flicks back and forth through his notebook, then leans over and leafs through the papers on my desk, until he finds what he's looking for. He reads, his lips moving quickly, then he sits back and looks up at me.

"What if she's lying?"

"Who?"

"The nanny."

"What about?" I lean forward myself now.

"The child." He puts the piece of paper back on my desk and looks down at his notebook once more. "Everyone we spoke to, with the exception of the nanny, told us that Amy Sanderson was annoying, naughty, badly behaved…"

"The cook said she was a little monster," I add, remembering her comment.

"I know." He taps the piece of paper in front of him. "It says so here in your report."

"And?"

"And we've remarked all the way through that the nanny is the only one who had a good word to say about her, or who liked her at all."

"I know, but children can do that, can't they?"

"Do what?" He tilts his head to one side and picks up his tea, taking a sip.

"Turn on the charm when it suits them. If Miss Sutton was nicer to her than everyone else, then maybe the child was just better behaved for her."

"Maybe," he says slowly. "Or maybe she's lying. Maybe Amy actually was a little monster."

I think for a moment. "Even Donald Curtis commented on it," I recall and get to my feet. "And how would he have known, if…"

"If Elizabeth Sutton hadn't told him." He completes my sentence for me.

I run my fingers through my hair, trying to stay calm, and look down at him. "Does it mean anything?"

He shrugs. "Possibly not, but it's the only anomaly I can find. Anywhere."

I have to agree with him. "I think we should go and see Donald Curtis." I check my watch. It's nearly a quarter past two. Heaven knows where the last few hours have gone. "He'll be at work," I remark, "and I'd rather see him at his flat. But we could kill some time first."

"How?"

"By calling on David Cooke."

"Won't he be at work too?"

"Yes. But in his case it's less important."

"You think he'll agree to see us at the bank?" Thompson asks.

"I think so. And besides, I only want to lay a few ghosts to rest with him."

"For your benefit, or his?" he asks.

"Mine."

"Such as?" He stands, pocketing his notebook and swallowing down the last of his tea.

"Such as asking him how Mrs Sanderson behaved around the children, and confirming whether they had actually made definite plans to leave – with, or without them."

"But if we're concentrating on the nanny…?" he queries, seemingly puzzled.

"I know. I just want to make absolutely sure, before we go blasting into Donald Curtis' flat, letting him know our suspicions. Once we do that, the chances are, there won't be any turning back. For any of us."

David Cooke glares at me from the door of his office.

"Detective Inspector." His voice is a low growl. He may not be pleased to see us, but he won't make a fuss. Not here. I was depending on that, because I didn't want to wait until the end of the working day to speak to him. It would just delay our visit to Donald Curtis even further… and that's the last thing I need.

I walk towards him, with Thompson following behind me. "Thank you for seeing us, Mr Cooke."

He steps to one side, eager to usher us into his office, before I have the chance to mention why we're here, I presume.

He closes the door firmly and turns. "This is most inconvenient."

"I'm sure it is."

He doesn't offer us seats, so we stand just inside the door, him with his back to it, and Thompson and I facing him.

"So, what do you want?" All trace of civility has abandoned him now.

"I wanted to ask you about Mrs Sanderson." I keep my own voice as calm and collected as possible.

"What about her?" he asks.

"I wanted to know what you can tell me about her temperament, specifically how she is around her children."

He frowns. "Why do you want to know?"

"Answer the question, please, Mr Cooke." His frown becomes a scowl.

"I'm not sure she spends that much time with them, Inspector. You may not be familiar with how things work in homes like the Sandersons', but they employ a nanny for the very reason that they don't wish to spend too much of their own time with their offspring." He looks down his nose at me, conceit written all over his face.

"And she doesn't talk about them that much?"

"I've already explained to you, that I'm not interested in children. Hers, or anyone else's. When Lillian and I meet, we're usually quite short of time, so idle chit-chat about her daughters isn't high on our agenda. The only times we've ever discussed them in any detail is in the context which I've already described to you, whereby she dreamt of a new life…" His voice fades and he has the decency to look away.

"Without them?" I'm not about to let him off the hook.

He turns back to me. "Yes."

"Were her dreams ever more than that?" I ask him.

"What do you mean?"

"Did you formulate any plans? Did you make arrangements for Mrs Sanderson to leave her family?"

He shakes his head. "No. But I wish we had. I wish I'd taken her away from Daniel before all of this happened."

"Why? Don't you think she'll come with you now?" I can't help the scepticism in my voice.

"No, I'm sure she will, one day. But if I'd managed to get her away sooner, she wouldn't have had to suffer through all of this upset, would she?"

I stare at him, unable to believe my ears. "You're actually suggesting she'd have heard of the death of her daughter, of the murder and mutilation of her daughter, and been unaffected by it?" He doesn't reply. He fixes me with a long, hard look instead, and I can't stay silent. "I hope she does leave with you, Mr Cooke. You deserve each other."

I step forward and he obviously thinks that I'm going to strike him, because he moves very quickly to one side, inadvertently allowing me access to the door, which I open, vacating the room, before I'm overwhelmed by the temptation to raise my fists for the first time in my entire career.

"Are you alright, Rufus?" Thompson catches me up on the pavement outside the bank.

"I'm fine."

"You're not."

"Alright. I'm not."

He glances to his right, down the high street. "There's a tea room over there." He nods across the road, and a little further along. "I'll buy you a cup and you can calm down."

"I think it'll take more than a cup of tea," I point out.

"Then we'll see if they've got any buns, shall we?"

I look at him and he smirks, and I have to smile back. It's one of the best things about working with Harry again. He never lets me take myself too seriously.

Once we're seated at a small table and the waitress – an older woman with a slight limp and half-moon spectacles – has brought us our tea, and two buttered teacakes, I permit myself a really deep breath for the first time since leaving the bank.

"I should never have let him get to me like that," I say, almost to myself, although I know I'm speaking out loud.

"Well, if you hadn't have said it, I would have done," Thompson remarks. "And it's probably better that you did, being as you're the senior officer."

"Oh, I see. I can be the one to get in trouble, can I?"

He shakes his head. "I can't see there being any trouble. You didn't say anything that wasn't true, and I don't imagine for one minute that Cooke will report the conversation to the Chief Super. It shows him in a far worse light than it does you."

He's quite right. That doesn't excuse my lapse, but David Cooke is hardly going to boast about his role in it.

"So… Donald Curtis," he says, enigmatically as he stirs his tea, even though he hasn't added any sugar.

"What about him?"

"How are we going to play it?"

I shrug my shoulders. "We'll just have to ask him if Miss Sutton ever mentioned to him anything about Amy's behaviour, and see what he says."

"And make sure not to lead him in one direction or the other." He's rather pointing out the obvious, although I don't pick him up on it.

"How's Julia?" I decide to change the subject.

"Quite a lot better now." He smiles. "She's not being sick every morning anymore."

"That's good."

"Just every other morning." We both laugh. "And her mother's not coming in quite so much."

"So it's settling down?"

"Yes, the last few days have seen a real change in her." His lips twitch upwards, as though he's remembering something. "I think this bit that's coming up is my favourite part of Julia being pregnant. I really like these few months after the morning sickness, and before it all starts to become uncomfortable and she gets too big to move." His slight smile becomes a broad grin. "Although don't you dare tell her I said that."

I hold up my hand. "I wouldn't dream of it." I sip my tea. "What's so good about it? About this part of her pregnancy, I mean?"

"Well, once the sickness has worn off, she's much less tired, she gets a bit more energy back and she starts to get this glow to her. It's like you can actually see the new life she's creating. It's really quite miraculous." He's positively poetic in his admiration and I marvel at the change in him, from his wild young bachelor days, when he had a different woman on his arm – and in his bed – almost every week. Then I notice the twinkle in his eyes, before he leans forward. "And then there's the fact that she becomes absolutely obsessed…"

"What with?"

"Sex," he whispers, so that no-one else sitting in the small tea room will overhear him. I raise my eyebrows. "Don't get me wrong," he adds, "she's not exactly restrained normally, but…"

"Well, I still need you to be able to function at work, so don't let her wear you out," I joke, realising that we're very different, he and I. I'd never tell him something like that about Amelie. As far as I'm concerned, that's too personal. I'll share so much, and no more.

He smirks and then chuckles. "Oh, don't worry, Rufus. I can keep up."

"Hmm. I'm sure you can."

We take our time finishing our tea, and then pay, leaving the shop and walking back to the car. The wind has picked up again, and he has to help me with my coat, which is in danger of flying away, being as I can't wear it properly, thanks to my broken arm.

"I can't wait to get rid of this plaster," I mutter, holding it up slightly.

"I don't blame you," he replies.

"Still, only a couple of weeks to go now."

"And then you can give Amelie a proper cuddle." He smirks at me once more.

"Do you ever say anything that doesn't lower the tone of a conversation?" I ask, although I have to admit – only to myself – that the thought of holding Amelie in my arms and feeling her properly is one of my main reasons for being so eager to be free of the plaster cast.

"Rarely." He opens the car door for me, and then goes around to the driver's side, getting in himself. "It's what makes the world go around, isn't it?"

"What?" I look across at him.

"Sex."

I shake my head. "Don't you mean love?"

His lips twitch upwards. "That too. Just wait until you're married and the waiting's over," he says. "Then tell me I'm wrong."

I look out of the window to hide my smile, because I'm not about to deny a word of what he's said. Not a single word.

As we drive down Fleece Road, approaching Curtis' flat, I notice the man himself, walking along the pavement, his head bowed against the icy wind. Thompson parks the car and we climb out, just as Curtis stops to speak to the greengrocer – a portly man, wearing a brown overall – and the two of them exchange a few words, both glancing up the sky, presumably discussing the weather, before Curtis approaches his front door.

"Mr Curtis?" I call out.

He turns and looks in my direction, a confused expression on his face, which clears and is replaced by a frown as we get closer and recognises me.

"Inspector? What do you want?"

I think to myself that it would be quite pleasant to be greeted with something other than hostility, just for once, but instead I say, "Can we speak to you, please? Upstairs, perhaps?"

He pauses for a moment, then without saying a word, turns around and opens the door, letting himself in first, but leaving the door open for us to follow.

We traipse up the darkened stairs and into his flat, where he finally switches on a light and illuminates the hallway, then goes straight on into the living room. Here he enters the dark space and Thompson and I wait by the door until he's dealt with the blackout and turned on two lamps – one of which sits on the table at the end of the sofa, and the other a stylish standard lamp, which has its home beside the fireplace. Once he's done this, I take a few steps further into the room, and Curtis turns to face me.

"What's this about?" he asks, the belligerence still obvious in his voice.

"We've come to ask you some questions…"

"More questions?" he interrupts. "I've already told you everything I know."

"These are more closely connected with Miss Sutton."

"In what way?"

I take another step or two closer to him. "Can you tell me what Elizabeth thought of Amy Sanderson… how she felt about her?"

"We didn't really talk about her that much." He furrows his brow, his tone surprisingly thoughtful. I'd expected a more truculent response, but perhaps he's realised that the best way to get rid of us is to cooperate. "We had better things to do than discuss either of the children. I mean, you've seen her, Inspector. Tell me, would you bother passing the time of day, knowing full well that she'd really rather just fuck?" His face contorts into a lewd grin, but I refuse to be goaded. Again.

"So the subject never came up?"

He removes his hat and coat, throwing them over the arm of the sofa, then sits down in it and leans back, rather nonchalantly, his arm resting along the back. "I didn't say 'never'," he replies, smiling and looking up at me.

I walk around the chairs between us and stand in front of him. "Mr Curtis… I'm investigating the brutal murder of a four year old child. That means I'm not in the best of moods at the moment, and you would do well to bear that in mind when answering my questions, and stop wasting my time."

He swallows and blinks twice, the swagger gone. "Sometimes Lizzie would get into a bit of a temper about Amy," he murmurs, having decided to stop being an idiot, it seems. "She could be a brat, demanding her own way and throwing tantrums when Lizzie didn't do as she demanded. Amy even bit her once. I remember her showing me the marks, and saying how much she hated her…" He stops talking and sits forward, a shadow crossing his eyes as he looks up at me and I wonder if he's thinking that he may have just incriminated his girlfriend.

"What's wrong?" I ask. "Why did you stop?"

Rather than the expected answer of 'Lizzie didn't mean it that way', he continues to stare for a full ten seconds, before he turns away.

"Mr Curtis?"

"It's nothing."

"It's not nothing. Something occurred to you then, while you were speaking. I want to know what it was."

He shakes his head. "It was nothing," he perseveres. "It doesn't matter anyway."

"Why not?" I ask.

"Because… well, it can't mean anything. You're looking for a man, not a woman."

"Not necessarily," I reply. "Now, tell me why you just stopped talking so suddenly."

He shakes his head slowly, as though he's trying to work out exactly why we might not be looking for a man anymore, his face paling at the same time. "No," he mutters defiantly.

"Sergeant?" I turn to Thompson. "Arrest this man."

Thompson takes a step forward, without querying the charge, and Curtis leaps to his feet, holding up his hands. "Wait!"

Thompson stops in his tracks and I move closer, so I'm right in front of Curtis.

"Tell me what you've remembered. Because I know you've remembered something."

"Her letter," he whispers, so quietly I have to strain to hear him.

"Speak up."

"Her letter," he says again, more clearly this time. "She sent me a letter."

"When was this?"

"A few days ago… one day last week…" He's starting to ramble.

"What did she say in the letter?"

"She… She said Amy was a lovely girl and that she couldn't bear to think about what had happened to her. I can't remember her exact words now, but I remember thinking at the time that it didn't ring true, because Lizzie had never had a good word to say about the child when she was alive."

"So this letter came after the body was found?"

He pauses. "I think so. It's hard to keep track, being as we write to each other so often… at least until we fell out, anyway."

"You fell out?" I query and he nods his head, then sighs and sits back down again, looking at his hands, rather defeated.

"Yes. I—I thought she'd tried to incriminate me in Amy's murder… and what had been done to her. The sexual thing… you know?" I nod. "I wasn't best pleased about that and I wrote her a letter telling her so." He looks up at me. "It wasn't a very nice letter."

"Did she write back?" I ask.

"Yes. She begged me not to break things off with her. She said she was crying while she was writing." He shakes his head. "I felt pretty lousy about that."

"What are you going to do?" I ask him.

"Oh, I've already done it," he replies, brightening slightly. "I've just posted a letter to her, asking her to meet me so we can talk things through. I don't want to lose her, Inspector."

There's an emotion in his voice that I haven't heard from him yet. If I wasn't such a cynic, I'd say it could be love. But I'm a cynic.

"Do you keep Miss Sutton's letters?" I turn away from him and look at the mantlepiece.

"Yes," he replies, sounding suspicious of my motives.

"I'd like to see them, please."

He shoots to his feet again, and I turn back to face him. "No. No way. They're private; between me and Lizzie."

"I'd still like to see them."

He shakes his head vehemently. "I—I don't know what you're trying to imply with these questions, Inspector, but Lizzie is innocent. I know she is. Just because she got cross with Amy sometimes when she was playing up, and then wrote something different in a letter after the girl was killed, doesn't mean anything." He pauses. "I—It just means she was sorry the girl was dead, that's all. That's normal."

"It may well be, Mr Curtis. But I'd still like to see her letters."

"And I'm refusing to let you."

I nod my head and take the single step required to close the gap between us. "I can get a search warrant, Mr Curtis. And then I can turn your whole flat upside down. Actually, I can arrest you as well, and turn your whole life upside down." He pales. "Or you can do the sensible thing, and fetch me those letters."

We stare at each other, the pulse on his temple flickering, until he lets out a breath and backs down, going out of the room. I nod towards Thompson to follow him, which he does, and within a few minutes, they both return. Curtis is clutching a small pile of letters in his hand, which after just a few moments' hesitation, he holds out to me. I take them and remove one from its envelope. It seems to be the most recent letter, dated yesterday, in which she does indeed beg him not to end their relationship. Opening another one, further down the pile, I notice her eloquence, and wonder if I'm blushing as I read the fairly graphic content. I replace the letter in its envelope and decide I'll leave those for Thompson to peruse.

"Are these all of her letters?" I ask. There are no more than a couple of dozen here, which seems a fairly meagre quantity for a relationship of several months' duration.

"Yes," he says.

"So, if my sergeant went into your bedroom and conducted a search, he wouldn't find any more?"

Curtis glares at me, with a look of pure hatred, and then turns on his heel, leaving the room. Again, Thompson follows and, again, they return within minutes. This time, Curtis is carrying a significantly larger batch of envelopes.

"Sergeant Thompson will take those." Curtis hands them over and I add the ones I'm holding to the pile. "We'll return them to you in due course," I add, moving towards the door.

"Whatever you think she's done, she's innocent," he repeats as I pass him, and I look down at his upturned face. "I know her, and I know she'd never harm anyone."

"Then she has nothing to fear, does she?

Back in the car, Thompson puts the letters into his briefcase, which he'd left on the back seat.

"Where to now?" he asks.

"Back to the station."

"Not the Sanderson house?" He seems surprised. "I thought——"

"No. We need to read through these letters first."

"And then we'll be going to the Sanderson house?"

"Very probably."

He starts the engine and sighs. "Why do I get the feeling that tonight is going to be a very, very late one?"

"Because you've been a policeman for far too long."

"I'm not sure you should be reading these letters," Thompson jokes from the other side of my desk, a smile forms on his lips as his eyes scan the document in his hand. "But if you need any help," he adds, "any explanations of some of the things these two seem to have been up to…"

"Oh, be quiet."

Despite my earlier decision to let Thompson go through the letters by himself, I worked out when we got back here, that it would be quicker if we both did it – especially as there are so many of them. So we've divided the stack in half and are reading them as quickly as we can, commenting to each other every so often, when something important crops up. So far, in looking through her earlier missives, all I've discovered is that their relationship became physical within about two weeks of their first meeting – something which Miss Sutton claimed in subsequent correspondence wasn't like her at all, although as to the veracity of that statement, I have yet to be convinced. Thompson is going through the later letters and reveals that a few weeks ago, Miss Sutton began calling herself 'Kitten' instead of 'Lizzie'. The explanation of this seems to be that she made some very particular noises when aroused, and that Donald Curtis had given her the nickname. In many of the letters, both the older, and the more recent ones, there are reminders of Mr Curtis' comment when we first met, that Miss Sutton has her 'kinks', and I have to say, some of them are very unusual indeed.

"Good Lord," Thompson says softly, then looks up at me.

"What?"

"Well…" He tilts his head to one side. "She's describing something here which I would have said is physically impossible."

"Does it relate to the case?"

"No."

"Then you can tell me about it another time…" I struggle to conceal a smile. "Or maybe try it out on Julia?"

He shakes his head. "Absolutely not. I wouldn't want to break her."

I chuckle and get back to my reading, turning over the page in my hand. "Oh… wait a minute. Here's a passage." Thompson sits forward. "She says, *'Amy has been a little cow today. I've bent over backwards to keep her entertained, and she tipped her dinner all over the floor, and over me too, and when I bent down to clear it up, she hit me on the head.'*"

"Charming child," Thompson comments.

"Wait, there's more. *'I told her off, and the little bitch called me a slut. Can you believe that? To start with I wondered where she'd have picked up such words, but then I remembered the argument between Mr and Mrs Sanderson a few weeks ago, when he called her the same thing…'*"

"Those two have a lot to answer for," Thompson mutters quietly, putting his letter back down on my desk. "Have we trawled through enough of these yet?"

I glance across at him. He looks weary. "Yes, I think we have." I pick up the letter from a few days ago, which we've set aside, in which she describes Amy as a 'lovely girl', and put it together with the one in my hand, which is less complimentary.

"We can go and pick her up?" he says.

"Well, we can at least ask her about the discrepancies, anyway. We don't have enough evidence for an arrest yet, but we can pull her in for questioning... yes."

He sighs out his relief. "Are we going to interview her tonight?"

"Yes."

"I'm just going to phone Julia, if that's alright?" he says. "I should let her know not to wait up."

I nod my head. "I'd better call Amelie, and my mother."

He smiles and leaves the room, and I pick up the telephone receiver, asking for Amelie's number first. We're connected quickly and I recognise Sarah's voice. She clearly knows mine too, and asks if I want to speak to Miss Cooper. I smile, realising that, in just a few weeks, she'll be 'Mrs Stone', before replying in the affirmative.

"Rufus?" Amelie's voice is soothing and comforting.

"Yes, darling."

"Is everything alright?"

"Yes. I'm just calling to let you know that I'm going to be working late tonight."

"Oh?" She sounds intrigued, and perhaps a little saddened – which is gratifying, and worrying at the same time, being as I hate the idea of her being even a little sad, if I'm not there with her to cheer her up again.

"I know we hadn't made any arrangements for this evening, but I'd probably have come over after dinner, just for an hour or so. I doubt I'll be back in time now, though."

"Has something happened?"

"It might have done. We've got to question someone, and I want to at least make a start on it tonight."

"Well, I'm not going to say I'm not disappointed that I won't be seeing you, but if it means this awful case is coming to a close, then I'm relieved."

"So am I. I'll miss seeing you though."

"I'll miss you too," she whispers, although I can still hear her. "But thank you for letting me know."

I smile. "You don't have to thank me, darling. You're entitled to know where I am."

"Entitled?" She sounds a little surprised by my choice of word. "I don't think I'm entitled to anything." *How can she say that?*

"Well, you are. As far as I'm concerned, you're entitled to know everything about me. I love you and I don't have any secrets from you."

"Neither do I," she says, without a second's pause, although I can hear the emotion in her voice.

"Are you alright?" I ask.

"I'm fine." She doesn't sound it. "I'm just tired and I could do with cuddling up to you, that's all."

The need to comfort and protect her is automatic; the pull of her, magnetic. "I think I'm going to be horribly late, but I can still come over, if you want me to. We can cuddle up for a while…"

There is a pause this time, before she finally says, "You'll be tired by then. I'll be fine, Rufus. I think I'll have a bath and get into my pyjamas."

"In that case, I think I should definitely come over…" I joke, trying to cheer her up.

She giggles. "And what would your mother say to that?"

"We don't have to tell her."

"Don't worry about me. I'll—"

"Don't worry about you?" I interrupt. "How can I not? You've said you need a cuddle and I'm not there, so…"

"Well, I'm not going to cuddle up with anyone else, if that's what you're thinking. I'm not Vic—" She stops talking, although I know exactly what she was about to say.

"I've never thought you were like Victoria. Not in any way." The humour has been forgotten now. "I know I can trust you, and I do. My point is, I want to comfort you, and I can't. And that's frustrating."

"Would you prefer it if I didn't tell you how I feel?" she asks. Without being able to see her face, I'm not sure if she's upset, angry, or just asking the question, genuinely intrigued, and I wonder for a moment how this conversation got so serious.

"No," I reply, regardless. "I want to know how you feel. Always. But you have to let me respond to your feelings. You have to let me be there for you if I can, and worry about you, if I can't. That's my job. It's what I do."

"As a policeman, you mean?" She sounds confused.

"No, as your future husband. As the man who loves you and who will always put you first."

"I'm sorry," she whispers.

"Don't be." I'm not even sure what she's apologising for. "Just tell me… do you want me to come over to see you when I get home, regardless of what time it is?"

"No," she replies, keeping her voice soft, letting me know this is not a rejection. "I will be fine, Rufus, I promise."

"Okay."

"Will I see you tomorrow?" she adds, with renewed hope in her voice.

"Yes."

"What about the case?"

"I should have everything resolved by then."

"And if not?"

"Then I will move heaven and earth, and all the stars in the sky, to make sure I can get home to you. I'll stop time, if I have to, Amelie."

She sighs. "I love it when you say things like that. And I really do love you," she murmurs.

"Nowhere near as much as I love you."

The telephone call to my mother was a lot quicker and less emotional – I'm pleased to say – and by seven-thirty, Thompson is behind the wheel of the car, and I'm beside him. We drive in silence, which is a relief as it gives me time to think. I know I should be focusing on the case, and how I'm going to deal with Elizabeth Sutton, but my mind is too full of Amelie, and my need to be with her. That need has nothing to do with anything physical, though. It's so much deeper than that.

When we arrive, the house is in darkness, but so is every other building, and we get out of the car and walk slowly to the front door.

Lois answers my knock, and peers at us in the gloom. "Oh," she says eventually, "it's you, Inspector." She steps to one side, automatically, and we enter the darkened hallway, waiting until she's closed the door and switched on the light. She looks up at me expectantly, waiting for me to speak.

"We'd like to see Miss Sutton," I explain.

"Miss Sutton?"

"Yes."

"She'll be up in the nursery," she says. "Or possibly in her room, I suppose, if the baby's asleep."

I nod my head. "Would you mind fetching her down?" I ask. I don't want to do this in the baby's room.

"Certainly," she says and makes her way to the stairs, climbing up them and disappearing from view. Thompson and I remain where we are, listening to the maid's footsteps on the landing above, before she goes up to the second floor. Then there's the distant sound of voices, and finally Lois reappears by herself.

"She'll just be a minute," she says, looking flustered, and remaining with us in the hallway, as though to guard us, and we wait a little longer, until Miss Sutton comes into view at the top of the stairs.

As usual, the nanny is smartly dressed, her hair neat, and her make-up perfect. She smiles as she reaches the bottom step, then walks slowly over, looks up at me through her fluttering eyelashes, and opens her mouth to speak.

"What's going on?" Mr Sanderson's voice forestalls her speech, and I peer upwards, to where he's standing at the top of the stairs, one hand on the banister rail, looking down at the scene before him. "Inspector? What are you doing here?"

"We have some questions for Miss Sutton," I reply, looking from him, to her.

"You do?" She's positively purring now and gently bites on her bottom lip in a seductive manner. I'm aware of Mr Sanderson coming down the stairs and across the hallway to us.

"And we'd like you to accompany us to the police station," I add, speaking to her now, just before he arrives.

Miss Sutton's lip is released, her mouth popping open, and her eyes widen significantly as I notice her face pale beneath her make-up. "The… the police station?" she whispers.

"Yes." I reach for her arm, but Sanderson tries to barge in front of me, pushing my hand away, and Thompson steps forward.

"What on earth are you talking about?" Sanderson blusters.

"Please stand to one side," I tell him.

"I'll do no such thing. You have no right to come in here and…"

"I have every right." I turn to him. "Move aside. Now."

He remains where he is, staring up at me, with a startling look of defiance on his face. "You need to stand away, sir," Thompson says, very officially.

"Or what?" Sanderson turns to him.

"Or I'll arrest you," Thompson replies simply.

Sanderson takes a half step back. "A—Arrest me? But I haven't done anything. And Miss Sutton is innocent."

"If she's innocent, they'll release her." We all turn at the sound of Mrs Sanderson's voice. She's standing by the drawing room door, her arms folded across her chest. She lets her eyes settle on Miss Sutton's face, resting them there for a moment. "And if she's not… then they'll hang her." Her words fester in the air, momentarily smothering all of us, and then she turns and goes back inside the room.

"Miss Sutton?" I break the stony silence, placing my hand on her elbow.

"Can I fetch a coat?" she asks quietly.

"No." She looks up at me, bemused by my response, and I turn to Lois, who is still standing at the foot of the stairs, watching the scene before her, wide eyed. "Can you go to Miss Sutton's room and bring a coat for her, please?"

Lois nods her head and runs up the stairs, returning moments later with a navy blue coat draped over her arm. I note the colour, recollecting Mrs Nichols' description of the woman who was pushing the pram in the park on the day that Amy disappeared. Miss Sutton takes the garment, shrugging it on and looking up at me as I guide her to the front door. Thompson gets there first, having left Mr Sanderson to his own devices, and flicks off the lights, before opening the door and walking out ahead of us. I keep a firm grip on Miss Sutton's arm, leading her to the car and sitting her on the back seat, before going around to the other side and getting in beside her. She turns away, gazing out of the window. Mr Sanderson is standing on his own front step, staring at us, and as Thompson reverses the car out of the driveway, his eyes don't leave Miss Sutton. Not even for a second.

Miss Sutton has been sitting in the interview room for nearly half an hour now, in the company of PC Wells, while Thompson and I have gathered together all the paperwork, and he's made some tea, which he carries in on a tray, because I've decided we may as well be civilised. I've got the file tucked under my arm and, as we enter, Wells steps to one side and makes to leave the room, but I give him a slight shake of my head and he stays put, his hands behind his back, staring into space.

Miss Sutton doesn't acknowledge our entrance, her own eyes fixed on the table in front of her, on which Thompson puts the tea, and I drop the file, before sitting opposite her.

"Would you like some tea?" I ask her.

She doesn't look up, or reply, so I nod at Thompson and he pours a cup anyway, passing it across to her. She's in a trance and doesn't respond.

"Miss Sutton?" I say and wait. After a minute, she finally looks up. Her eyes are vacant; devoid of any emotion at all and I feel a shiver run down my spine. "We'd like to talk to you about your correspondence with Mr Curtis." I open the file and reveal the letters, lying on top of the other paperwork. She lowers her own gaze and glances at them, before returning her eyes to me. "Can you confirm you wrote these letters?" I ask, taking them out one at a time and laying them before her across the table. She continues to stare at me. "Please look at them, Miss Sutton." Her eyes remain fixed on me. "Very well." I take back the first letter, the one on the right hand side of the table and read the extracts that relate to Amy, the ones I read out to Thompson earlier. "Did you write that?" I ask her as I finish the passage. She doesn't react at all, so I take the second letter. "Let's try this one, shall we?" I lift up an earlier letter and turn the page. "Here, you've said that Amy deliberately tore her best dress, and when her mother asked about it, she blamed you? You call her a lying she-devil in that passage. Is that how you felt about her, Miss Sutton?" Again, she doesn't reply. "Very well," I remark. "Let's look at this one, shall we?" I pick up another letter. "Here you say she's a lovely, sweet darling girl." She blinks a few times, quite rapidly, but keeps her lips tightly closed.

I get to my feet and walk around the table, perching on the edge of it, right beside her. She looks up at me, doing her best attempt at a demure expression. "Can you see what I'm getting at here, Miss Sutton?" She remains silent. "Can you see the discrepancies in your letters, and how suspicious they might look to us?" I lean over and pick up another piece of paper. "When you write such diametrically opposing statements, it makes it difficult to know what's true and what isn't. So, you see, I don't know whether to believe you when you say Amy was a lovely girl, or whether what you actually mean is…" I glance down at the page in front of me. "That she was really a 'noisy, messy little brat, no better than an animal'." She sighs slightly, but keeps her eyes on mine.

"We have other reasons to be suspicious of you," I say, putting down the letters. "You've lied to us." She tilts her head to one side, evidently bemused by my statement, although she still says nothing. "You kept the fact that you had a boyfriend from us," I point out. "We discovered that information from another source. Then, when we questioned you about Mr Curtis, you initially denied that you and he were together, and only confirmed it under duress. And again, when we spoke to you in front of your employer, you told us that your relationship with Mr Curtis was just friendly, not romantic, or physical." I grab a couple of letters and drop them back down on to the desk. "These would seem to prove otherwise, wouldn't they? Your descriptions of what you do with Mr Curtis are bordering on pornographic, Miss Sutton, and are certainly not the the actions of friends."

A very slight smile crosses her face and she opens her mouth, licking her lips very slowly. "Jealous?" she murmurs, uttering her first word since we left her employer's house.

"I don't like being lied to in the course of my investigations." I ignore her comment. "It makes me suspect that the person lying to me might have something to hide."

Her smile drops and she goes back to staring at me, blank faced.

I stand again and walk back to my seat. "Let's start again, shall we?" Her brow furrows. "I'd like you to confirm that you wrote these letters…"

We continue in the same vein for nearly two hours, with me showing Miss Sutton various letters, reading her extracts, and asking for confirmations. She ignores everything I say and do, and either stares at me, or at the wall behind me. I'd hoped to break her down, to make her reveal something – anything – that might give her away. But she's sat there throughout the entire interview, as though it's nothing to do with her.

As the clock ticks around to ten-thirty, I let out a long, bored sigh and nod to Thompson, and we rise to our feet, packing away the paperwork, tucking the file under my arm, and going over to the door.

"Are you letting me go now?" I turn at the sound of Miss Sutton's voice. She hasn't changed position, but is looking across at me.

"No."

I don't give her anymore information and walk out into the corridor. Thompson closes the door behind him and joins me.

"What now?" he asks as I lean against the wall opposite.

"We're going to get another cup of tea, while she stews in there for a while."

"And then?"

"And then I'll have a think about it."

He shakes his head and I push myself off the wall again, setting off slowly down the corridor. "We don't really have anything on her, do we?" he mutters, stepping up beside me.

"No we don't. And I think she knows it. That's why she's giving us the silent treatment."

"What if we can't find anything?" He sounds very down-hearted and I turn to look at him.

"We will."

*

We've had a cup of tea and sat in my office for the last hour. We haven't talked much. Thompson has re-arranged the paperwork in the file, where I gathered it up in haste, and I've been thinking. And for once, I haven't been thinking about Amelie – well, not for most of the time, anyway. She's never far from my thoughts, but on this occasion, I've had other things to contemplate.

"Let's go back," I announce, getting to my feet.

"You're going to start again… now?" He looks at the clock.

I don't reply and, leaving the file on my desk, I walk from the room, with him following behind.

Inside the interview room, nothing has changed. Miss Sutton is still sitting at the table, and Wells is standing close to the door, although his hands are by his sides now. As we enter, Miss Sutton looks up, her eyes giving away her relief, and I think for the first time, that my ploy might work.

"Constable," I say, ignoring her and turning to Wells, who stands upright.

"Yes, sir?"

"Take Miss Sutton down to the cells, will you?"

The scraping of the chair legs on the floor makes us all turn as Miss Sutton stands, glowering, and takes two paces towards me. I'm aware of Wells behind me on one side and Thompson on the other. "You can't," she says, her voice reasonably calm, although there's a hint of some emotion beneath the surface.

"I can," I reply. "I have further investigations to carry out. And I'll need to speak to you again."

"Further investigations?" she repeats.

"Yes. I'm going to apply for a search warrant in the morning."

"A search warrant?" she parrots. "Where for?" Her skin has paled, becoming pasty in the stark electric lights.

"Your rooms at the Sanderson property," I reply, and without warning, she lunges at me, her flattened hand making contact with the side of my head, before either Thompson or Wells can react. I grab her arm and hold her off while they seize her, Wells taking charge and, once I've released her, pulling both of her arms behind her back. She struggles against him, but she's no match for his strength. Few people are, I wouldn't have thought.

I step closer, towering over her, making myself intimidating. "Something to hide, Miss Sutton?" I ask.

"You bastard," she hisses, and then sucks in a breath, before spitting directly in my face.

"That'll do," Wells says, shoving her forward and escorting her from the room.

I reach into my pocket and retrieve a handkerchief to wipe my face, while Thompson perches on the edge of the table in front of me.

"Are you alright?" he asks.

I nod my head. "I've been in worse."

He folds his arms across his chest. "She's obviously got something to hide," he muses.

"Hmm. The question is, what?"

Chapter Eleven

Lizzie,

I don't even know when or if this letter will get to you. I have no idea whether they'll forward it. But I have to write it anyway.

I was worried about you all night, because the police came to the flat yesterday. They seemed to think you were guilty of killing Amy, but I didn't believe them. I defended you. I said it was impossible. They didn't listen and they took your letters away with them as evidence of something. So this morning, before work, I went to the house. The worry had become too much for me and I wanted to talk to you. Except you weren't there. I saw the maid – Lois, I think her name was. She told me you'd been arrested last night; that the police came and took you away, and that Mr Sanderson tried to stop them, and that he was nearly arrested too for his trouble. She was in a right state, and she also let slip why he tried so hard to keep you there... that he's been sweet on you for ages. You never told me that, Lizzie, and I have to ask myself why not? Why would you keep that from me? If he's been harassing you, or chasing after you, or doing anything against your will, then surely you'd have told me, so I could do something about it. So, I'm forced to wonder, have you been fucking him too? Have all your letters to me been lies? Have you been playing me for a fool all along?

Maybe the police are right. Maybe you did kill Amy. I don't know. My head hurts just thinking about it. I don't want to think that of you. I really don't. I don't want to think you could do something like that, but then I'm starting to wonder who you even are, and if I know you at all.

One thing I do know is that I don't trust you anymore, and I can't be with you ever again.

If they do let you go, don't come back here. I don't want anything more to do with you.

And this time, I mean it.

Donald.

I'm sitting at my desk, drumming my fingers on its wooden surface. I asked Tooley to arrange a search warrant for Miss Sutton's rooms the moment I arrived and he said he'd do it right away, but these things can take time – especially when you don't want them to.

"It won't come any quicker, just because you wear a hole in your desk." I look up to find Thompson standing in the doorway.

"I know. I'm just feeling anxious about this one, that's all."

He comes in and sits opposite me. "You think I'm not?"

I smile across at him and then stand as I notice the Chief Superintendent walking through my open door behind him. "Sir," I say deferentially and Thompson shoots to his feet.

"Sit down, gentlemen," Webster says, coming over and standing at the end of my desk, between the two of us. "I hear you've got a young woman in custody in relation to this child murder."

"Yes, sir."

"A woman?" He pulls a face, as though he doesn't quite believe the outcome of the case.

"Yes."

"What evidence do you have against her?"

"Until I've searched her rooms, absolutely none," I reply with complete honesty.

He raises his eyebrows. "But you're sure it's her."

"Based on her reactions, yes."

He nods. "Very well." It seems like he's going to leave, but he stops and looks at me, and then at Thompson. "Are you both alright?" he asks, his voice softening. "This has been a horrendous case."

"We're fine, sir," Thompson replies.

"Stone?" Webster looks at me.

"I think what the sergeant means is, we'll be fine once we've got the evidence we need to lock this woman up – for a very long time."

"Hang her, surely," he replies.

I shrug my shoulders. "I think she'll try and claim it was an accident."

He leans forward, his hands on the edge of my desk. "How on earth can she hope to do that?"

"The child had a bruise to her cheek, and a blow to the back of her head. I think she was struck across the face and fell, hitting her head on the concrete pathway." I glance up at him. "Miss Sutton has a temper and a reasonable right hand," I add. "I felt both of them for myself last night."

"But what about what she did afterwards?" Thompson says, sitting forward. "That was deliberate, one might even say premeditated, to throw us off the scent. She can't claim that was accidental."

"No," I reply, turning to him. "But sexual molestation isn't a hanging offence." Both men stare at me. "And either way, we have to prove all of this before we can start talking about punishments. I need to find something physical that ties her to the scene."

"Well, I hope you do," Webster says, turning to go this time. "And then I hope they throw the book at her."

I turn back to Thompson once we're alone again. "Did you mean that?" he asks. He's paled, his eyes mournful. "You think she won't hang?"

"I didn't say that. I said I thought she'd try and plead it was an accident. And for all we know at the moment, it may well have been. Look, Harry, until we've got the evidence in our hands that she was actually there, we can't start to question her properly. Once we do, and she tells us her side, then we'll see where we go from there. But how she's punished isn't our responsibility. Remember? We're just here to find the evidence to convict."

He nods his head, leaning back in his seat. "Dear God," he murmurs to himself.

"Shall we change the subject?" I suggest. I know I want to. I'm sick of this whole case.

"Gladly." He sighs and looks across the table at me. "What do you want to talk about?"

There is something I need to ask him, and now seems as good a time as any. Hopefully, it'll cheer him up, because something needs to. "I've got a question for you."

"Hmm... what's that?" He stares down at his fingernails.

"Will you be my best man?"

His head shoots up. "Me?"

I smile across at him. "Yes. I don't see anyone else in here, do you?"

He glances around, as though to make sure we're alone. "But surely... after what happened..."

"With Victoria, you mean?"

"Yes. She was your fiancée, and I did sleep with her," he reasons.

"She was my fiancée in another life, and what happened is in the past. The dim and distant past. I thought we'd already been through this. Several times."

"We have. But... being your best man, it's..."

"It's what? Look, Harry, if you don't want to do it, you only have to say." I wonder if that's why he's prevaricating.

"No," he says quickly. "I'd love to do it. It'd be an honour."

"Then stop making bloody excuses, will you?"

"Sleeping with your fiancée is hardly an excuse, Rufus. It's a bloody good reason for you not to want me anywhere near your wedding."

"Why? I'm not marrying Victoria," I reply, shuddering involuntarily at the prospect.

"I know, but what I did... it was unforgivable." He looks down at his hands again.

"Isn't that for me to decide?" He doesn't reply. "There's nothing to forgive. Not as far as you're concerned, anyway. You didn't know who she was."

"No, I didn't."

"Then stop blaming yourself."

He glances up. "You really want me to be your best man?" A smile is slowly forming on his lips.

"Yes. On one proviso."

"What's that? Because if you're worried about Amelie, then think again. I—"

"I'm not. The proviso is that, if you get me too drunk the night before my wedding, or I'm late for the ceremony, I will demote you to constable and have you filing paperwork for the next five years."

He shakes his head, grinning. "You're actually going to pull rank on me over your wedding?"

"Too right I am. I know you, Harry Thompson." I wag a finger at him. "I know what you're like."

"Then why are you asking me to be your best man?"

I pause, just for a second. "I would have thought that was blindingly obvious by now." He tilts his head to one side and I get up, walking around my desk and over to the door to check if there's any sign of Tooley yet. "The clue's in the title, Harry. You work it out."

He doesn't have a chance to reply, as Tooley's just walking through the main office entrance and spots me by my door. He waves a piece of paper at me and I turn to back to Thompson. "We're in business," I say and he jumps to his feet. "Get half a dozen men together, will you? I want this done quickly."

He nods and goes into the main office, calling out names and gathering the men around him, while I get my coat and pull it around my shoulders. We're ready to leave within a few minutes, and I have to admit to a frisson of excitement. We're finally there. I know we are.

"What is the meaning of this?" Mr Sanderson thunders as I stand in his hallway, the six uniformed officers behind me and Sergeant Thompson to my right.

Thompson holds up the warrant, which he's removed from his pocket. "We have a search warrant here," he says.

"What for?" Sanderson looks up at me.

"To search your nanny's rooms," I reply and turn to the men behind me. "Sergeant Thompson will show you the way."

"Now wait a minute…" Sanderson moves quickly blocking the stairway in a melodramatic fashion, his arms outstretched. "I'm not letting you up there." He raises his chin defiantly.

I've had enough, and I step towards him. "Mr Sanderson," I say, my voice calm and just slightly menacing, "it's of no interest to me that you seem to be rather too fond of your children's nanny, but when that fondness gets in the way of my investigation, then I do start to take it more seriously. Now, I don't know what your motives are for trying to prevent this search, but I suggest you move out of the way, before I arrest you for obstruction."

His arms drop in an instant and he steps aside. His fascination for Miss Sutton has its boundaries, it would seem.

I nod at Thompson and he leads the way up the stairs, followed by the other officers.

"They'd better clear up after themselves," Sanderson remarks, stamping the only authority he has left on the matter.

"They know what they're doing," I tell him.

"She's innocent, you know," he persists. "No matter what you say, I won't believe it. She's always loved Amy – probably more than my wife ever did." I'm not going to argue that his wife has shown no affection for their daughter, but as to Miss Sutton 'loving' the child? That's more than arguable. He looks up at me. "She's innocent, I tell you."

I shrug my shoulders. "I'd like to have a look at the baby's pram, please?"

"The pram?"

"Yes. Can you tell me where it's kept?"

His brow creases and he points towards the back of the house. "In the boot room," he says. "Behind the kitchen."

"I'll find it."

I leave him standing there, looking bewildered, and go down the dimly lit hallway, opening the door to the kitchen, and letting myself in. Mrs Slater is standing by the sink, with Lois beside her, their heads close together. When they look up and notice me, they stop talking.

"I'm looking for the baby's pram," I say.

"Oh, it's through here," Mrs Slater replies helpfully, and comes across, opening a half-glazed door which leads out into a small lobby area, that's filled with coats, boots and shoes, and the pram, which is up against the far wall.

There's no window out here, and just a small pane of glass in the door to the rear garden, so it's very dark; too dark for my purposes anyway, and I turn to face the cook. "Is there a light?" I ask.

"No, I'm afraid not."

"In that case, can I bring the pram into the kitchen?"

She nods her head and then glances down at my arm. "Let me do it," she says and bustles forward, kicking off the brake and pulling the pram backwards into the kitchen.

I stand beside it and lean over, lifting the blanket and the sheet beneath, running my hand around the edge of the mattress.

"That comes out," Mrs Slater explains. "Would you like me to do it for you?"

I smile at her. "That would be very helpful, thank you."

She reaches in and lifts the mattress, along with the bedding, and then gasps, "Oh, dear God," staggering backwards and dropping everything to the floor.

I move quickly, taking Mrs Slater by the arm and sitting her down in the nearest chair. "I'll be back in a minute. Don't touch anything," I warn, glancing from her to Lois. Then I go out into the hallway and along to the bottom of the stairs, noting that Mr Sanderson is nowhere to be seen now.

"Thompson!" I call, raising my voice and he appears within a moment, leaning over the banister rail on the landing above. "Can you come down here?"

He runs down the stairs. "What?" he says, looking into my face. "What's happened?"

"Come with me." I lead him into the kitchen, where Lois is now comforting Mrs Slater, who has a handkerchief clasped to her nose. "This way," I mutter and together we walk over and look down into the base of the pram, at the wooden stake, its tip etched with a slight red staining, and the small pair of white cotton knickers.

I lean on the edge of the pram, trying hard to control my rage, and the contents of my stomach, then feel a hand on my shoulder. "I'll deal with this." Thompson's voice is quiet in my ear.

"Thank you." I turn to him, his face pale. "Are you sure?"

He nods. "You go and tell the parents."

I wonder for a moment which one of us has drawn the short straw, before I stand upright again. "Are you alright, Mrs Slater?" I ask, speaking a little louder.

She looks up at me, but doesn't respond. "I'll look after her," Lois says.

"Wait for me in the hall," I remark to Thompson as I turn and leave the room, going back out into the darkened hallway and along to the drawing room. I'm about to enter, when I have second thoughts and knock, just once, waiting until I hear Mr Sanderson bid me to 'come in', before I push the door open and go inside.

He's standing by the fireplace, looking tense, and turns as soon as he sees me, raising his eyebrows, with a smug expression on his face, as though he expects me to admit I was wrong about the nanny all along, and that he was right. Before he has the chance to say anything, I start to speak.

"Is your wife here?" I ask.

"No. She went out just before you arrived." He sighs. "I imagine she's with David." He sounds resigned to the situation, as though he no longer cares. "She didn't say that was where she was going, obviously, but judging from her eagerness to get out of the house, her appearance, and the expression on her face, I don't think I'll be proved wrong in my assumption."

"Then I'll leave you to pass on the information I'm about to tell you."

"Oh yes?" Again, he sounds rather complacent and I have to admit to no small sense of satisfaction that I'm about to knock the wind from his sails.

"We've found what we were looking for." His jaw drops and he reaches for the arm of the sofa, plonking himself down onto the seat.

"W—What have you found?" he stammers.

"The wooden stake that was used to penetrate your daughter, and her underwear." I can see no point in beating about the bush.

"Where?" he asks. "Where did you find them?"

"In the baby's pram. Miss Sutton must have hidden them there."

He looks up at me. "But anyone could have put them there. The pram is kept in the boot room. The door is unlocked during the day."

"You're clutching at straws, Mr Sanderson. Your nanny is guilty. We both know it."

He shakes his head, slowly to start with, and then with increasing speed. "But she can't be. She can't. It's not possible." He stares up at me. "That would mean I—" He stops speaking abruptly, covering his face with his hands.

"You what?" I ask, even though I know what he's about to say. Except in reality he doesn't say a word. Instead his shoulders start to shake and he throws his head back and howls, his face a picture of contorted agony. "You slept with her, didn't you?" I ask. He doesn't respond. "Didn't you?"

Eventually he calms enough to nod his head. "What have I done?" he whimpers. "Oh God, what have I done?"

"When did this happen?"

He looks up at me. "The first time was the night before last," he murmurs and pulls a handkerchief from his pocket, using it to wipe his face as he calms down.

"The first time?"

He nods. "I'd been worrying over what you'd said... about the young man she'd been visiting on the day Amy disappeared. I wanted to speak to her about it, just to make sure she doesn't really have a boyfriend." He pauses and looks down at his hands. "We spoke on the landng, so as not to wake the baby, and she told me again that she'd just gone in for tea with him, and then explained that she couldn't possibly have a boyfriend..."

"Because of your rule?" I suggest.

"No." He shakes his head. "She said it was because she was in love with me."

I sigh and stare down at him. "And you believed her?"

He shrugs. "Why not?"

"And I suppose one thing led to another, did it?"

"Yes," he whispers. "She kissed me, and I kissed her back... and the next thing I knew we were in her room and we were—"

"And the second time?" I interrupt, because I have no desire to hear the details. "Or has it happened more than twice in the last couple of days?"

"No… just the twice. It was last night. She came down and saw me in my study, about half an hour before dinner."

"You had sex in your study?" I can't hide my surprise.

"No. Of course not. She couldn't leave Eve for that long, and my wife could have walked in on us." He huffs out a breath. "Elizabeth… Miss Sutton asked if I'd go and see her in the nursery after dinner. She made it clear what she had in mind."

"I'm sure she did."

"I went to her immediately after we'd finished eating. We were still upstairs together when you arrived. Lois almost found us together… I had to hide behind the nursery door when she knocked." He at least has the decency to blush.

"Can I get this straight?" I ask, taking a couple of steps closer. "You're saying, you didn't go to Miss Sutton's room? You had sexual relations with your nanny, in your baby's nursery, while your baby was present, and your wife was downstairs?"

"We meant to go to Elizabeth's room, but we got carried away… and the baby was asleep," he says, attempting to justify himself.

"Oh, well that's alright then." I look away for a moment, my revulsion threatening to overwhelm me. "I'll be leaving now," I say, turning back to him.

"What will happen?" he asks.

"We'll be charging Miss Sutton with the murder of your daughter."

He gulps and takes a deep breath. "Will she hang?"

"I have no idea. That's for a jury to decide."

I turn and make my way to the door. "Inspector?" he calls and I stop, looking back at him. He cuts a pathetic figure perched on the edge of the sofa, his handkerchief clasped between his hands. "Does my wife need to find out about this? About Miss Sutton and I?"

"I would suggest you tell her. I think it's quite likely it will come out during the course of the trial."

"But… but I'll be ruined," he murmurs.

"Then perhaps you should have thought about that beforehand."

I can't stand to look at him any longer, and open the door, stepping out. Thompson is waiting in the hallway and, I lead us both to the front door, and outside into the fresh air.

The interview room looks less sinister somehow in the daytime, not that the windows are very large, or afford much light, but the starkness of the single lightbulb in the middle of the room does make it a more haunting space at night. Wells has been replaced by Constable Beresford; a less formidable sight, but a sufficient caution against any attempt to cause trouble.

Miss Sutton looks exhausted, presumably from lack of sleep. Her make-up hasn't worn well, her lipstick faded, her eyes lined with black from her smudged mascara. She still stares across the table at me though, defiant as ever.

"Miss Sutton," I say quietly as put down the file in front of me. She doesn't reply. "Are you planning on staying silent again?" There's still no response and I nod my head. "Very well. In that case, perhaps I should talk, and you should listen?" She stares at me, tilting her head, but I continue, "We obtained a search warrant earlier today, and went to your place of employment." Her eyes widen this time, but she still says nothing. "And when we looked in the baby's pram, we found the following items…"

As I finish speaking, Thompson lifts the wooden peg, and the white knickers up onto the table. They've been tagged, but removed from the evidence bags, so she can see them clearly.

"These items have already been examined," I point out. "And although we're awaiting the results, I think we all know that the blood on the end of this piece of wood will have come from Amy… from where you used it to penetrate her body, after you killed her."

"I didn't kill her," she says, sitting forward, her clenched fists hammering on the table, the outrage in her eyes and voice clear for all to see and hear.

"Then what happened?"

"It was an accident."

"Really?"

"Yes."

"Would you care to explain that statement?"

"Certainly." She sounds very sure of herself all of a sudden. "Where would you like me to begin?"

"Let's start with your fictional account of the time you spent with Mr Curtis at his flat on the day Amy disappeared, shall we?"

"Fictional?" Her eyes widen. "What do you mean 'fictional'?"

"We both know you didn't accidentally run into Mr Curtis, and neither did you go there for tea. Did you? You went there for sex."

"No I didn't," she folds her arms across her chest, sitting back in her chair. "Ask Daniel. He'll tell you."

"Mr Sanderson? How can he confirm anything about your visit to Mr Curtis?" I ask. "He wasn't there with you. All he can tell me is what you've told him, and being as you were having sexual relations with him as well, his testimony could hardly be called reliable."

"But…" she flusters. "But…"

"But nothing, Miss Sutton. I know you thought that, by seducing Mr Sanderson, he would support you and back up your story, but that's not going to work, I'm afraid. The only chance you have now is to tell us the truth."

She looks down at the table for a full minute, before raising her face again. When she does, I can see all the fight has gone out of her. "It really was an accident," she mumbles.

I turn to Beresford. "Can you get us some tea?" I ask and he nods, leaving the room, as I turn back to Miss Sutton. "Tell me what happened. Don't leave anything out… and don't lie to me."

She nods her head and takes a deep breath, and then she starts talking.

*****

Thompson clinks his pint glass against mine and takes a long drink. I sip at my beer and put the glass down on the bar again. The Dog and Duck is busy tonight, mainly with our fellow officers, many of whom are celebrating the fact that this awful case has finally been brought to a successful conclusion.

"I don't think I've ever been so relieved to get to the end of a case," he says quietly.

"I couldn't agree more."

"And at least she confessed, in the end," he adds. "Although I was surprised she admitted to sending the ransom note."

"Why?"

"Because I honestly thought that was the work of a chancer. I didn't believe it really had anything to do with the case."

"Well, I suppose we have to accept her explanation; she did it to put us off the scent, just like she gave us the false description of the man, who never even existed. The ransom money had nothing to do with it."

"I suppose we should be thankful it was her – at least we don't have to waste any more time looking for the supposed hoaxer; and I'm almost comforted to know there wasn't a stranger out there, prepared to hold up the search, and jeopardise the little girl's life for the sake of a couple of hundred pounds… it was all Miss Sutton, and her games."

"Yes," I muse. "I'd like to say that has restored my faith in humanity. But I'd be lying."

He takes another drink. "Try and put it behind you, Rufus," he suggests. "You've got so much to look forward to. We both have; between your wedding, and Julia and I having another baby… we've both got a lot to be grateful for."

I smile across at him. I know he's right. I really do. I just can't get rid of the foul taste in my mouth, and I have a feeling it'll be a while before I do.

"Go and see Amelie," he says, interrupting my train of thought. "Talk it through with her."

"I should probably go home first."

He shakes his head. "Amelie's going to be your wife in about five weeks' time. She's going to have to get used to how this feels… that sometimes we just need to let it all out." He has a point. "Come on," he says, "I'll take you." He finishes his pint, and I take another few sips of mine, and we wish everyone else a good evening, and go back to the station, where he opens the car door and waits for me to get in.

"Thanks for your help on this one," I say quietly, with one foot inside the car.

"I think you'll find it was mainly down to you," he remarks. "I found it harder than usual – much harder. You were right about that."

"You seem surprised." I say, my lips twitching upwards.

He smiles. "That you were right? Of course I'm surprised. It doesn't happen very often…"

"Oh, be quiet and drive me home." I get into the car and make myself comfortable as he closes the door and comes around the other side, getting in beside me.

"No. I'll drive you to Amelie's, and then I'll pop over the road and tell your mother where you are, so she doesn't worry. You need to see your fiancée."

I turn to him. "I'm not going to argue with you there."

"Well, that makes a change…"

The door to Amelie's house opens to my knock, and she throws herself into my arms, taking my breath away. I manage to catch hold of her, pulling her close as she nestles into me, and I walk her backwards, indoors, and kick the door closed behind me, savouring the feeling of her body against mine. I don't think I've ever needed anything as much as I need this and I bask in the warmth, the softness, the allure of her.

"I'm sorry," she murmurs and turns on the light, flicking the switch on the wall beside us.

"For that?" I marvel. "You're sorry for *that*?"

She smiles, shaking her head. "No. I'm sorry for the telephone call, yesterday."

"Why?" I still don't understand the need for an apology, any more than I did last night.

"Because I was being silly, and childish… and jealous." She lowers her eyes. "You only telephoned to let me know you weren't going to be home in time to see me, which was very kind of you, considering how much work you've got to do at the moment, and I turned it into a three-act drama."

I smile. "No, you didn't."

"I was tired," she reasons, as though I haven't spoken. "And I was missing you, and trying not to let it show… which I think I failed at rather miserably."

I place my hand on her cheek and raise her face to mine. "You don't have to hide your feelings from me, darling."

"I know, but it doesn't help you if I'm constantly telling you how much I miss you, does it? You need me to be stronger than that."

I frown at her. "What are you talking about?"

"Well, as your wife, I'm not much use to you, if all I do is think about myself, am I?"

"You don't. I know that. I know you think about me, just as I think about you. Constantly. And as for missing me… well, I rather like the fact that you do. Because I miss you too."

"I know, but you don't need me wasting your time telling you about it, do you?"

"Yes, I do. And you're not wasting my time. I need to know how you feel. If you miss me, I want to know, so I can try and do something about it, and if I can't, at least I know I'm not alone. At least I know I'm not the only one who feels lonely when I can't be with you."

"You feel lonely?" She stares into my eyes.

"Of course. You're part of me. If I can't be with you, I'm lost." She sucks in a breath. "You don't have to pretend with me, Amelie. And you don't have to be anything you don't want to be. Not ever."

"But surely, a policeman needs a wife who's supportive."

I shake my head, my lips twisting up into a smile. "You are supportive. That's why I'm here…" My voice fades to a whisper and her brow furrows.

"Something's happened, hasn't it?"

"Yes."

She pulls away. "Come with me." Her voice is firmer now, and she takes my hand and leads me into the drawing room. Once inside, she takes my coat and hat, along with my jacket, which I'd just shrugged over my shoulders, placing them all over the back of the nearest chair, then guides me to the sofa, sitting me down in the corner, and perching on the edge of the seat beside me, looking closely into my eyes. "Tell me," she says.

"We've made an arrest."

Her eyes widen. "Who?"

"The nanny."

Amelie claps her hand to her mouth in shock. "The nanny?" she repeats. "The children's nanny?"

"Yes."

"You're sure it's her?"

"She's confessed."

"Oh my God. Did she do… did she do the… the thing… the thing that was done to the little girl, after she was killed?"

"Yes. She's admitted that."

Tears form in her eyes, but she blinks them away, trying to be strong for me, I think. "How could she?"

I shrug my shoulders. "Self preservation, I suppose." She tilts her head to one side. "She claims the child died by accident, but didn't think anyone would believe her, so she came up with the idea of making it look like a man had killed her."

"Accident?" I can hear the scepticism in her voice, which mirrors my own.

"Yes."

She sighs and sits back into the sofa, leaning up against me, as I put my arm around her. "Are you allowed to tell me about it?" she asks.

"Of course. If you want to hear it. Parts of it aren't pleasant."

"I know." She twists and looks up at me. "But I think you need to talk, don't you?"

I nod my head. "Only if you want me to."

She settles back into me again. "As long as you hold me, yes."

"Oh, I'll hold you." I tighten my grip on her. "I don't ever want to let you go."

She puts her arm around my waist, clinging to me. "Then don't."

We sit like that for a while, just holding each other, letting the horrors of the last few days wash over us, but then Amelie shifts and lies down, her head in my lap, looking up at me. "Tell me," she repeats. "Get it over with…"

I nod my head, my arm resting across her slender waist as I start to tell the story.

"The biggest confusion was with the parks," I begin, because it seems like the most logical place.

"The parks?" she queries.

"Yes. The nanny had maintained all the way through the investigation that she'd taken the children to the small park, just up the road from the Sanderson house."

"And she hadn't?"

"No. She'd taken them to the larger park on Ewell Road. The one where the body was found. It may have been being dug over, but the workmen had removed the swings and slide from the back corner, leaving them to one side to be re-installed nearer the front at a later stage, and they'd left a small area of grass for the local children to play. It wasn't much, but it was something, and the nanny took the children there, and walked the pram up and down the pathway, while Amy ran and played on the grass."

"I see," she muses, although I'm not sure she does.

"That meant all of our enquiries were centred around the wrong place," I point out. "We spent hours searching the wrong park; carried out house-to-house interviews in the wrong roads, and searched the properties between the two parks over several days, because we'd assumed the girl had tried to make her own way from one park to the other, when in reality, she'd been at the second park the whole time."

"So what actually happened?" she enquires, nestling into me a little, which feels comfortable, like she's where she belongs – which she is.

"Amy was misbehaving. She was a demanding child, it seems, craving attention and playing up when she didn't get it. The new baby didn't help with that, being as she took up a lot of the nanny's time herself, and from what I can gather, Amy could be difficult to control."

"So?"

"Well, while Amy was being tiresome, the wheel of the pram got stuck – that much of the nanny's story was true – and she was trying to mend it. But Amy wouldn't give up. She kept demanding that the nanny stopped what she was doing and focused on her. She made a grab for the nanny and almost toppled her over, and the nanny saw red, stood up and struck the child." Amelie gasps and I tighten my hold on her.

"She hit her?"

"Yes, across the cheek. Amy fell backwards and banged her head on the concrete path."

"Why didn't she go for help? The nanny, I mean?" Amelie asks.

"I don't think it even occurred to her," I reply. "She said she knew straight away that the little girl was dead, and she panicked."

"She panicked?"

I nod my head slowly. "Yes, I know. I spent some time explaining to her that her actions were not those of someone in a panic. She behaved in a very calculated fashion, but she maintains it was all done on the spur of the moment, in a state of a confusion." I shrug my shoulders. "That will be for a jury to decide."

"So she hid the body?"

"Yes. She checked there was no-one around, and then picked up Amy's body and laid it over the pram, then wheeled it to the far side of the park, to the workmen's shelter. She left the pram outside and laid Amy's body in the far corner…" I let my voice fade, because I know what comes next in the story.

"And then she…?" Amelie clearly can't say the words.

"Yes. She said she took a few moments to decide that her best chance of getting away with it, was to make it look like a man was responsible. She came up with the idea of saying she'd seen a man in the park, but she didn't think that would be enough… and then she saw the wooden pegs, attached to the string. She untied one and removed the child's underwear…"

"Don't," Amelie says, interrupting the story. "I can't hear this part."

I lean down and kiss her, just gently, pulling her closer to me. "It's alright, I wasn't going to say exactly what she did."

"Did she tell you?"

I nod my head. "Yes. I had to make her tell us."

"What was she like when she was explaining it?"

"Quite matter of fact, really. I—I think that was the worst part. She didn't even think about Amy. Her sole concern at that stage was to protect herself."

Amelie shakes her head. "And how did you feel?" she asks.

"Sick."

She puts her arms around my neck and pulls herself up, so she's sitting on my lap, leaning against me, her head on my shoulder. "My darling," she whispers into my neck.

As much as I love having her sit with me like this, I need to finish the story. I need to tell it all, so I can begin to put it behind me, and start to look forward. "What happened next?" Amelie asks, just as I'm about to start speaking again, as though she's read my mind.

I smile, just lightly, at her perception, and continue, "Once she'd finished, she covered the body – although she didn't do a very good job…"

"Was that intentional?" Amelie asks.

"I don't know. She said she'd covered the body, but when it was found, there was a foot sticking out, which made it easy to spot. Maybe she missed that in her haste to get away."

"It's just that you'd think, if she was trying to delay the discovery, she'd have taken more trouble."

"I suppose… but you have to bear in mind that, contrary to the version of events she gave us, she went to that park frequently with the children. She was well aware of the fact that the men had finished their digging. Admittedly, she had no idea of when the next team would come in to do the planting, but I imagine she felt fairly safe in the knowledge that Amy's body probably wouldn't be discovered for a few days at least."

"I see," Amelie says, leaning back slightly and looking at me. "So what did she do then?"

"She hurried home, just as she said she did. During the walk, she worked out her story, that the girl had been playing and had disappeared while she was fixing the pram, and dealing with Eve's glove. She remembered that, when she'd got home earlier, from her visit to Donald Curtis, the cook had explained that Mrs Sanderson was still out of the house herself, and they'd conjectured about the fact that she was probably with David Cooke. The affair was common knowledge among the household staff... well, her husband knew as well, but that's..."

"Her husband knew?" Amelie's shocked.

"Yes. Mrs Sanderson begged me not to tell him, but that was just an act. She wanted me to believe the whole thing was a secret, that her husband was impossible to live with, and that she was justified in cheating on him, so I wouldn't think badly of her. Not that I could really care less, but I suppose she was worried about how it might look. Anyway, it transpired the whole house was aware of her infidelity, and the downstairs servants had been discussing it on the day of Amy's disappearance. Miss Sutton revealed that she'd met Mr Cooke once, not long before his affair with Mrs Sanderson had begun, when he was still calling at the house, and she'd decided to give us a description of a man that vaguely matched him, in the hope that suspicion would be well and truly diverted from her."

"How calculating," Amelie comments, quite taken aback, I think.

"That's not the best of it," I remark. "Not when it comes to Miss Sutton's ability to manipulate."

"Why? What else did she do?"

I hold her a little closer. "Firstly, she wrote letters to her boyfriend, Donald Curtis, describing how upsetting she found the whole thing, in the hope, I presume that he'd take her side when questioned. And she made a point of telling him how much she missed him, reminding him of the times they'd spent together, presumably so he wouldn't forget the... um... benefits of their relationship." I struggle to phrase my sentence and look down at Amelie, hoping I'm not blushing. She smiles up at me and nestles into my neck.

"It sounds like they weren't waiting?" she murmurs and I chuckle.

"No, darling. They most certainly weren't. But even if we hadn't read about it in their letters, Donald Curtis had already made the nature of their relationship very clear."

She leans back a little. "Really? He told you?"

"Yes. He didn't leave much to the imagination."

She blushes herself now. "Do… do men always talk about things like that?"

"Some men do." I recall my conversations with Thompson.

She leans back, and sighs. "Do you?"

"No. What happens between us is personal. I wouldn't dream of talking about anything that we might do together with anyone but you."

A smile forms on her lips and she leans up and kisses my cheek. "Thank you," she mutters.

"You don't have to thank me."

She shakes her head. "Based on what you've just told me, I think I probably do." She leans into me again. "Was that all she did?" she asks. "She wrote to her boyfriend?"

"No. She also started playing up to Mr Sanderson."

"Playing up?' she repeats.

"Yes. Flirting."

"With her employer?" I love how innocent Amelie can be sometimes. It's beautifully refreshing. "But he's married."

"Yes. He's also never disguised the fact that he's keen on the nanny… not if the arguments between him and his wife are anything to go by."

"Good Lord…"

"I know."

"So what happened?"

"I think Miss Sutton worked on the theory that, if she could hook him in, he'd protect her should the need arise. Being as everyone knew Mrs Sanderson was having an affair, she obviously thought Mr Sanderson might be open to a little flirtation. He was – quite clearly – because in the early stages of our investigation, he did his best to interfere every time we tried to interview Miss Sutton. And then, after we went back the last time, and started to ask more questions, she… she persuaded him into bed."

"He slept with her?" Amelie sounds disgusted.

"Yes. Twice."

"Twice?"

"Yes. The second time was literally minutes before we arrived to arrest her."

She leans back and looks up at me, her eyes wide with shock. "How could he?" she mutters. "That woman killed his daughter… mutilated his daughter. How could he do that?"

"Well, he didn't know what she'd done at the time. That realisation only came later. At the time, I imagine all he was thinking about was that the woman he'd been attracted to for months, was finally going to be his. Of course, once I told him what she'd done to Amy – and that she'd used him for her own ends – he broke down."

"Good," Amelie says, her remark more cutting than anything I've ever heard her say before. "It serves him right." She looks up at me again. "What an absolutely horrible bunch of people."

"I couldn't have put it better myself. Do you know, I don't think it dawned on any of them that, if they'd just spent a little more time with the child and focused more on her and less on themselves, she wouldn't have been so demanding in the first place. She wouldn't have been so wilful, or so badly behaved. And then none of this would have happened. I've spent a lot of time during this case, asking myself why on earth Mr and Mrs Sanderson ever had children. Actually, I've spent quite a bit of time, asking myself why a great many people have children. David Cooke remarked to me that the reason people like the Sandersons have a nanny is so they don't have to spend any time with their own offspring – so why do they have them in the first place?"

Amelie shifts on my lap, sitting forward and looking back at me, her face a picture of confusion. "Can I ask you a question?" she says, her voice rather quiet all of a sudden.

"Yes."

"Do you like children?"

I tilt my head, staring at her. "Yes, I do. That's the whole point. I don't understand why people who don't like them and employ someone else to look after them, bother to have them."

"So… so you want us to have children of our own?" she murmurs, and I smile.

"Yes, of course I do." I pull her back towards me, holding her against my chest. "I'm sorry. I'm being very cross and crotchety, aren't I? Of course I want us to have children, one day."

She sits upright again, very abruptly. "One day?"

I let out a sigh. "There's no rush, is there?" I reach out and caress her cheek with my fingertips. "You're not even twenty yet, although you will be by the time we're married… but even so, I—I'd like us to have some time to ourselves first."

She smiles and leans into my touch as I cup her face in my hand. "You would?"

I struggle to suppress my grin. "Yes, I would. I haven't waited all this time for you, just to start sharing you with someone else straight away."

She gasps, and then takes my hand, kissing the palm, in an action that makes my skin tingle. "You'll never have to share me," she whispers, locking eyes with me.

"When we have children, I will. And that's how it should be. That's why I want to wait – so that when children do come along, we can shower them with love and attention."

"Does that mean you won't shower me with love and attention anymore?"

"Of course not. But I know you'll be busy and pre-occupied with them, and I'll understand if you don't have so much time for me."

She shakes her head slowly. "Rufus," she says, seriously, "I'll always have time for you."

Her words fill me with love and hope, and I place my hand behind her head and pull her closer, crushing my lips against hers. Without breaking the kiss, Amelie twists around and moves her legs, straddling me, like she did the other night, my body responding to the nearness of her as we groan and sigh in mutually ascending arousal.

"Whoa." I lean back, breathing hard. Amelie stops, panting, her fingers still twisted in my hair, her eyes alight with a need I haven't seen before. "We have to stop."

"We do?" She bites her bottom lip and I reach out, pulling it free.

"Don't do that. You're teasing me."

I trace along the outline of her lips with my thumb, her eyes widening. "And you're not?" she whispers, then captures my thumb between her teeth and sucks it into her mouth. I'm mesmerised by the sight and stare at her soft full lips surrounding the tip of my thumb. She must know what she's doing, surely? And yet, the look in her eyes tells me she probably doesn't. Even so, I know I have to regain control of the situation before I'm completely undone, so, regardless of my broken limb, I lift her off of my lap, shifting forward in the seat at the same time, and tip her back onto the sofa beside me, laying her down, and moving on top of her, my weight supported on my good arm. She squeals and giggles her pleasure as I lean down and kiss her. Thoroughly.

I halt, suddenly, aware of her hands on my skin... on my back, and realise that, while we've been kissing, she's pulled my shirt from my trousers.

"What are you doing back there?" I ask, leaning up and looking down at her.

She flushes bright red. "Um... exploring?" she suggests, smiling lightly.

"Oh..."

"Well, you did it the other day. It seems only fair."

I nod my head, because I can hardly argue with her reasoning. "And have you found anything you like?" I tease, although I'm not sure teasing is very sensible at this point.

She nods her head. "All kinds of things."

"Such as?"

She smiles. "Such as the fact that your skin is softer than I expected, especially on your sides. And your muscles flex when you move..."

She shifts her hand from my back, down to my side. "Careful," I warn.

"Why?" She looks up, wide-eyed.

"Because that's where my wound is... the knife wound. It's just above where your hand is."

"Oh God." She removes her hand altogether and I feel it on my shoulder, on top of my shirt now.

"I didn't say you had to stop."

"I completely forgot about your wound," she says, looking guilty now.

"So do I, most of the time. I just didn't want you to run your hand over it…"

"Neither do I," she interrupts. "I might hurt you."

I shake my head. "That's not what I was thinking. It really doesn't hurt that much anymore, but I don't wear a dressing, and you might have felt it and been shocked."

"You don't wear a dressing?"

"No. I stopped a few days ago."

She tilts her head. "Can I see it?"

"The wound?"

"Yes."

"You want to?" She nods her head, and with great reluctance, I sit up, missing the feeling of her body along the length of mine. Amelie twists in her seat, so she's sitting beside me, as I pull a little more of my shirt out and raise it above the wound.

"Gosh," she says, sounding fascinated as she leans over, studying it. "It looks just like a cut."

"That's because it is just a cut. A deep cut."

"And it honestly doesn't hurt?" she says, still staring.

"No, as long as I remember not to stretch too much."

I feel the gentlest touch from her fingertips, tracing around the outside of the knife wound. "The skin's all puckered here," she remarks.

"I know."

"Will you have a scar?"

"I imagine so."

I let my shirt drop again as she sits up and looks me in the eyes. "It's not as bad as I expected," she says softly.

"Few things are," I tell her and lean over to kiss her cheek. "Your imagination can always build something up to be a lot worse than the reality. That's how fear works."

She nods her head and I glance down at my dishevelled clothing. "And now, I suppose I'd better re-arrange myself," I add, smiling and getting to my feet.

Amelie stands beside me. "Would you like a hand?" she asks.

I grin down at her. "I'm not sure that would be appropriate, are you?"

"Well, I did pull your shirt out. It only seems fair that I should put it back."

She reaches forward and I grab her hand, halting her. "Yes, except there's a world of difference between pulling a shirt out, and tucking it back in." I point out the obvious.

She stares up at me and blinks a couple of times. "Oh yes." She flushes bright red yet again. "I suppose there is." I'm rather relieved she seems to have understood that without me having to explain, because I'm not sure where I would have begun.

"In which case, I think you'd better let me do this."

"Yes, I suppose I had. Sorry." She bites on her bottom lip again and I reach out and pull it free with my thumb.

"Don't be sorry." Her eyes glisten and her lips part slightly. "Don't ever be sorry."

I straighten myself out eventually, with a little difficulty, and Amelie rings the bell and orders coffee, which seems like a good idea and a reasonable distraction, considering the turn of our conversation, and the heightened emotions in the room.

"I have something I need to discuss with you," I say, as Amelie passes me a cup of coffee. She turns and leans back, gazing into my eyes.

"Oh yes?" She looks so beautiful, and so alluring and I wonder if I've made a mistake bringing this up now, because I'm pretty sure that what I've got to talk about might well take the edge off of our evening. Still, I did promise... and it has to be done.

"Do you remember me telling you that I spoke to your uncle?" I say and her face falls slightly.

"Yes. You said you asked his permission to marry me. You're not going to tell me now that he refused, are you?"

"No, but he did ask me to speak to you about something else."

"What's that?"

"He wants to give you away." She sucks in a breath and moves back from me slightly. "Hey... don't do that." I put my coffee down, bringing my arm around her, pulling her back again. "I'm the messenger, that's all."

"Sorry," she mumbles.

"I told you; don't be sorry. And in any case, I'm the one who's sorry. We were having a lovely time and I feel like I've spoiled it. I just thought I ought to mention it while I had the chance, that's all. I did promise him I would."

"I don't understand why he wants to do it," she says, ignoring most of what I've just said.

"Because he knows you feel let down by him. He wants to make amends, to show you he's not the man you think he is."

"Isn't he?" she asks, raising her voice slightly. She leans back. "He came home last weekend, claiming it was because he knew I'd be lonely without Beth, but he only stayed for a day, before rushing back to *her*. What was the point?" She blinks a few times and sighs. "God, I sound like a jealous wife, or at least a resentful daughter, when the reality is I'm neither of those things. I'm nothing to him..."

"That's not true, Amelie, and you know it. He cares very much about you." A tear falls onto her cheek and I brush it away with my thumb, moving closer to her again. "He's not a bad man. Not really. He's just a man who's made bad choices. Trust me, after the last few days of investigating this case, I appreciate the difference more than ever."

She swallows down her tears and stares up at me. "What do you think I should do?" she whispers, her voice thick with emotion.

"It's entirely up to you, darling."

"That's not very helpful, Rufus," she says patiently.

"I know, but I can't make this decision for you. Perhaps you should talk it through with your uncle."

"You don't think that might end in an argument?" she says. "I think I'll find it difficult if he brings his mistress into the conversation."

"I doubt he'll do that. He's not that insensitive. And besides, even he appreciates that Miss Foster can be overly demanding on his time."

"Then why does he give in to her?" she laments, her shoulders dropping. "Does he love her?"

"Yes, I think he does."

"Then why does he stay with Aunt Millicent?"

"Because he loves her too. Just in a different way."

Amelie sighs, a frown forming on her face. "You think I should speak to him about it? About the wedding, I mean, not his mistress…"

"Yes. I think you owe him the right to put his case, and to listen to him."

"Why?" she asks. "Because he took me in when I had no-one else? I was a child then, Rufus…"

I hold her tighter. "I know, and that's not what I meant. The reason I think you should listen to him is because – regardless of Abigail Foster – he's never actually let *you* down, has he?"

"But what about Aunt Millicent?" she pleads. "What about how she'd feel if she knew?"

I shake my head. "I know it's hard, but you have to take her out of the equation. The problems in their relationship are nothing to do with you. This is about you and your uncle, and nothing else. If you don't at least hear him out, you'll regret it. If you listen to what he has to say, and you still decide you don't want him to give you away, then no-one can argue with you. And I'll support you, whatever you choose. I'll even be there with you, when you speak to him, if you want."

"You don't think he'd object to that?" she asks, sounding doubtful now.

"He might, but if you want me there, he'll just have to put up with it, won't he?"

She pauses for a moment or two, then slowly nods her head. "Alright, I'll speak to him," she murmurs and then leans into me, putting her arms tight around my waist. "I'm sorry."

"What on earth for?"

"For being so grouchy."

I chuckle. "You're not grouchy. You're beautiful, and adorable… and mine."

"Entirely."

Chapter Twelve

Dearest Donald,

They've given me permission to write to you.

I haven't heard from you since that awful letter you sent, where you doubted me and broke up with me. I have no idea whether you've written since, but then I doubt the family will forward any letters to me, not after what I've done. Even so, I can't not write to you, although I know you might not want to hear from me.

I suppose you'll say you were right to doubt, but I beg you to believe me, I didn't mean for any of this to happen. It was an accident – a dreadful accident. And it wasn't my fault.

Amy was being an annoying brat and she tried to push me over, into the baby's pram. I was so angry with her, I turned and hit her, hard, across the face. She toppled and fell to the ground and struck her head on the edge of the pathway, and I knew immediately that she was dead. I panicked, Donald. I couldn't think what to do. And then I saw the shed in the corner of the park, and realised I could hide her there.

It was only when I was covering her over that I worked out that the men might come back at any time, and she'd be discovered. I needed a way of throwing suspicion away from myself, and then I caught sight of the wooden stakes out of the corner of my eye. The plan just seemed to pop into my head, and I'd done it before I even knew what had happened. It was the work of moments really, and she didn't feel it, did she? She was dead, after all. I hid the stake and her knickers in the pram and went straight back home.

I promise, my darling, it was never my intention to involve you, and certainly not to incriminate you. I deliberately gave the police the description of a man who looked like the mistress's lover, so that if they found out about us, they wouldn't suspect you of any involvement. You have to believe me about that, if nothing else.

The police might tell you that there was something between Mr Sanderson and myself, but you mustn't believe them. They're only saying it to stir up trouble between us. I promise, you're the only man for me, Donald, and I hope you'll remember that, especially if you're called as a witness. I hope you'll remember how much I love you and how how much we've meant to each other over these last few months.

I don't know if I'll ever seen you again, but if I don't, try to think of me fondly.
All my love,
Your little Kitten
xxx

———————◆———————

It's been a very busy three days, most of which has been spent re-interviewing Miss Sutton, getting her statement finalised, then closing down and clearing away the case files, and making sure everything is completed, so that I can take a few days off over Christmas. I even worked late on Saturday, just to finish off the last few bits and pieces, so no-one can claim I've left anything hanging over.

Amelie's been busy too, although I've found the time to pop over and see her in the evenings. We've kept it brief, as she's been helping with the Christmas preparations and her aunt has been making a fuss – which Amelie assures me is perfectly normal whenever she feels she isn't the centre of attention.

The brief moments I've had to myself have only served to reinforce my own feelings that I can't wait until Amelie and I are married. Partly, this is for the entirely selfish reason that I'll have her to myself, and won't have to share her with anyone else – not most of the time, anyway – but it's also because that last whole evening we spent together, the one when I told her about Miss Sutton's confession, was a moment of revelation for me.

It wasn't surprising to discover that we want each other, with a breathtaking need. I think we both already knew that, being as every time we're together, we can't keep our hands to ourselves. It also wasn't news that feeling her touch directly on my skin was arousing beyond words, and that I can't wait for more of the same. It didn't come as a shock to sit and hold her, to look at her, and to feel the pull of her, the desire for her, or to see that reflected in her eyes. I wasn't taken aback by the fact that talking to her, telling her about the case, and how I felt about it, made me feel so much better about all of it. She has that knack; to just make everything better. No matter what it is. No… the revelation came in the knowledge that, after we'd finished discussing Amelie's forthcoming conversation with her uncle about the wedding, we were able to just sit. And we did. For a very long time, in each other's arms, not saying a word, our breathing naturally synchronised as we stared into the flickering flames of the fire and did absolutely nothing. We didn't need words. We didn't need actions. We just needed each other. When I got home, I realised that there are going to be times in our life together, when we won't necessarily be able to say how we feel, or even show how we feel, but we'll have each other. And that's all we need.

Today is Christmas Eve and I'm having breakfast with my mother and aunts, who are busy discussing our plans for later. Amelie is coming for lunch, and will be spending the rest of the day with us. I have no doubt the wedding will be discussed at length, and I don't mind – not as long as she doesn't, anyway. I'm just looking forward to a whole afternoon and evening with her, so much so, that I can't stop myself from smiling.

"You're looking cheerful," my mother remarks, pouring me a second cup of tea and passing it across the table.

"I'm feeling cheerful."

"Is this because your case is finally over?" Aunt Issa teases, because I'm fairly sure they all know why I'm so happy.

"No. It's because Amelie's coming for the day." I may as well say it before they do. "*And* because the case is over. It's been a horrible one." I've explained it to them all now, over the course of the last couple of evenings. They were appalled by what had been done to Amy Sanderson, and I think a little cross with me for keeping it from them, 'bearing it all myself', as my mother put it, until I pointed out that I hadn't. I'd told Amelie. She smiled when I said that, and only just stopped short of preening herself.

The telephone rings, but we all ignore the shrill tone, knowing Ethel will answer it. "Do you want some more toast?" Mother offers, holding out the rack in my direction.

"No, thank you. I'm sure we've got a big lunch and tea planned. I think I'll save myself for that."

"Well, being as they'll probably have rationed everything by next Christmas…" Aunt Issa's doom laden prophesy is interrupted by Ethel entering the room, her eyes finding mine straight away.

"There's a telephone call for you, Mr Stone," she says and I feel my heart fall to my boots. *Not today… please.*

I put my serviette down beside my empty plate and get to my feet, going over to the door and out into the hallway. Ethel has left the telephone receiver on its side, on the hall table, and I pick it up, putting it to my ear.

"Stone," I say, dreading hearing either Thompson, or the chief super on the other end of the line, telling me I've got another case to investigate.

"Rufus?"

"Amelie? What's wrong?" I can hear from her voice that something is, and besides, I'm due to see her in a few hours. Why would she be telephoning?

"Nothing," she says. "But can you come over?"

"Now?"

"Yes. Is that alright?"

"Of course. I'll come straight away."

"Thank you."

We end the call, and I go back into the dining room, where my mother and aunts turn to look at me, worry etched on their faces. I can only assume their thoughts had run the same way as my own, and I smile, hoping to allay their fears. "That was Amelie," I tell them, and they smile back at me. "She's asked me to go over there."

"Instead of her coming here?" Dotty says, looking panicked, presumably at her lunch plans being spoiled.

"No. She didn't say why. But she didn't mention cancelling lunch. I assume something's come up. I'd better go."

My mother waves me away. "We'll see you later on," she calls.

"I'll be back soon," I reply over my shoulder and dash across to the cupboard by the front door, pulling out my coat and shrugging it over my shoulders, before running over the road.

Amelie answers the door herself and looks me up and down, her eyes shining, as she steps to one side to let me in. She takes my coat, putting it over the end of the stairs, and then turns to me.

"You look lovely," she remarks, smiling and resting her hand on my chest.

"So do you." I let my gaze roam over her dark green long-sleeved dress, which accentuates her waist, and I'm about to kiss her, when the door to her uncle's study opens and he steps out into the hallway.

"Er-hem…" He announces himself with a fake cough and we turn to face him, my arm around Amelie's waist. I don't care if he does or doesn't approve; we're engaged, we're together, we're in love, it's Christmas and we're happy. To hell with it… "Can you both come in here?" He indicates the room behind him.

Amelie looks up at me, smiling slightly, and then moves forward as requested. I follow, wondering if we're about to have 'the conversation', and steel myself for the awkward situation that might follow. It won't be easy to hear their argument, I'm sure. Still, I said I'd be here for Amelie, to support her, and I will.

We enter Gordon Templeton's study, and turn, waiting for him to close the door behind us. Once he has, he crosses the room, and sits behind a large oak desk.

"Take a seat," he says genially, indicating the two chairs in front of him and I take Amelie's hand, leading her over and letting her sit before I do, and then clasping her hand again, partly as a demonstration of my support, but mainly because I want to. The room is more of a library than a study, three of the walls being lined entirely with bookshelves, and the third being taken up with a large bay window. Other than the desk and chairs, there is a small drinks cabinet to one side of the window, and a wireless, mounted on a very attractive cupboard on the other.

Amelie's uncle leans forward, his elbows resting on the desk, his smiling face settled on his ward, before he turns to me. "Before we get down to the main purpose of this meeting," he says, as though addressing a committee in the House of Commons, "I feel it would be helpful if you and I could work out what we're going to call each other." He takes a deep breath. "It seems rather formal for you to keep addressing me as either 'sir' or 'Mr Templeton', and thinking about it, I believe I've only ever called you 'Inspector'."

I can't help chuckling. "Yes, I think you have."

"Well, I can't possibly call you 'Inspector' for the rest of our lives, so in the circumstances, I think it would be easier, if you'd call me Gordon," he says. "And perhaps I can call you Rufus?"

"Of course, sir." He stares at me. "I mean, Gordon," I correct myself.

He leans back, laying his hands flat on the table. "Good," he says. "I'm glad we got that settled. Now… as I'm sure you're aware, being as I asked you to speak to her about it in the first place, Amelie and I had a small matter to settle." I notice his use of the past tense and turn to my fiancée, who's looking at me.

"You spoke to him already?" I ask and she nods her head.

"I know you said you'd be here with me if I needed you to be, but I decided this was something I had to do by myself."

"We had a very full and very frank talk," Gordon says and I turn back to face him. His expression is more serious now, his eyes fixed on Amelie, not me, even though it's me he's talking to. At least I think it is. "Amelie said her piece and I said mine… and, after I'd convinced her that I love her just as much as I loved Beth, and I always will, she agreed to let me give her away to you… my future son-in-law."

I notice his careful use of terminology, presumably to reinforce his reasoning with Amelie, that although there's no blood tie between them, she's his daughter, just the same as Beth ever was.

I turn in my seat to face Amelie and she looks up at me. "You're happy with this?" I say, because I have to make sure, even though the man is sitting opposite me.

"Yes," she says and nods her head, smiling, just to make certain I've got the message.

"You're positive? Because if you're not…"

"I'm happy, Rufus. Honestly." The sincerity in her voice is unmistakable and I take a breath, turning back to look at Gordon Templeton, who's staring at me, rather disgruntled.

"Just doing my job," I point out to him, giving Amelie's hand a squeeze. His brow creases in confusion.

"Your job?"

"Yes. It's my job to make sure Amelie is happy. In everything. And if she isn't, then it's my job to put that right."

"So, if she'd said she wasn't happy?" he asks.

"I'd have put it right. Sir."

He stares at me for a moment – quite a long moment – and then smiles and slowly nods his head, leaning right back in his chair. "Well, while we're on the subject of putting things right, I—I have a few things to make up for." His voice falters and he looks down at the table for a moment. "You both know I've done things in my past that I'm not proud of, and you both know that the current situation, between myself and Miss Foster, isn't ideal. Not for everyone, anyway." Two small dots of red appear on his cheeks and he coughs, covering his mouth with his clenched fist to conceal his embarrassment, I think. "I want to do something to… to make amends for at least some of those wrongs," he continues eventually. "I want to give you a wedding present."

"You don't have to do that," Amelie says, before I can.

He holds up his hand, preventing either of us from speaking, and opens the drawer to his right, pulling out an envelope, which he places on the desk in front of him. "I want to," he repeats. "I need to. Believe me, this is for my benefit as much as yours." I can see the emotion in his face and hear it in his voice and I turn to glance at Amelie. There are tears forming in her eyes and I move my chair a little closer to hers, just as Templeton says, "I—I want to give you a house."

I turn back to face him. "A what?" The words spill out of my mouth, unbidden.

"A house," he repeats unnecessarily, being as I heard him the first time. "I want to give you both a head start."

"Even so…" He holds up his hand again.

"Ordinarily, I'd have suggested we could go and look at properties together, so you could choose something to your tastes, but you've... um..." He fumbles over his words. "You've decided to get married a little sooner than I'd anticipated."

"Yes," I reply simply, before Amelie feels any obligation to admit a reason for our haste.

"Unfortunately, that means it's going to be difficult for me to buy you somewhere new," he says, sounding disappointed. "However, I do already own several properties in the village..."

"But they're rented out, aren't they?" Amelie says, showing she was aware of this much at least, even though it's news to me.

"All except one," he replies, smiling. "I own a couple of terraced houses in School Road, one of which has just become vacant, literally a couple of weeks ago. It's not big. It's got a sitting and dining room, a small kitchen, and the bathroom beyond that, and then two bedrooms upstairs. It'll give you a start though, so if you want it..." He pushes the envelope across the table. "It's yours."

"You'll seriously give us a house?" Amelie's breathless.

"Yes. It needs some work," he says, with a cautious tone to his voice. "I'm afraid the last tenant didn't take very good care of it, which is why I moved them out. I'll get it fixed up for you..."

"Can we be involved in that?" Amelie leans forward.

"Of course, my dear." He smiles. "I'll take you to see it after Christmas, if you'd like, and you can start making plans."

Amelie turns to me, her eyes alight. "What do you think?" she asks, and I smile my gratitude that she's asking me.

"I'm not trying to steal your thunder, Rufus," Templeton says, before I can reply. "I appreciate that you want to provide for your wife, like any husband. I'm just trying to make that easier, I suppose..."

"I understand," I reply. "And I'm grateful." I get to my feet, and Amelie joins me, our hands still clasped together. "Can we agree a compromise?"

He stands himself and looks up at me. "A compromise?"

"Yes. I'll accept the house, if you agree that I can pay for the work to be done."

He thinks for a moment, and then nods his head. "Very well," he sighs. "I'm learning not to argue with you."

I release Amelie's hand for a moment, and hold mine out to him, which he accepts and we shake hands before he offers me the envelope. "The documentation is all in there," he says. "The house is yours, and I hope you'll both be very happy there."

"Thank you," I reply, as Amelie dashes around the desk and hugs him.

"Thank you, Uncle," she says. "Thank you so much."

"You're very welcome, my dear," he replies, looking down at her, a contented smile on his face as he brushes his fingertips down her cheek. "Just make a better job of marriage than I have," he murmurs and leans down, kissing the spot where his fingers just touched her. I feel a pang of jealousy, remembering how I felt when I first saw them together, but I quash it down quickly as Amelie comes back to me, her face a picture of happiness.

She links our arms, my hand being occupied with holding the envelope, and with a last 'thank you' to her uncle, she leads me back into the hallway.

"Are you sure you're alright with this?" she asks once we're alone, nodding down to the envelope.

"I'm happy if you're happy," I reply.

She tilts her head to one side. "Tell me the truth, Rufus. If you don't want this, we'll go back in there and give him back his envelope. And his house."

"I am telling you the truth, darling. It's a bit of a shock, that's all." I smile, because I can't help it. "To be honest, I hadn't even considered where we were going to live once we were married. I mean, I knew we'd have to live somewhere, and I'd considered having to save up, but when we decided to get married so quickly, the thought of where we'd live didn't even cross my mind." I hold up the envelope. "This solves that, doesn't it?"

"It does rather." She smiles. "I hadn't thought about it either," she admits. "It's silly isn't it? My head's been so full of the excitement of it all, of the engagement and the wedding plans, I hadn't really thought about anything beyond that."

"Hadn't you?" She shakes her head and I put my arm around her, pulling her close to me, as I whisper in her ear, "I'd thought as far ahead as the honeymoon," and I lean back again, looking down at her as the blush spreads up her beautiful cheeks.

"Oh… well, I'd thought about that too."

"In a good way?" I ask.

"Yes… mainly."

"What does that mean?" I feel a shiver of fear creep up my spine.

"We can't talk here," she murmurs, glancing at the door to her uncle's study.

"No, we can't." But we're going to talk somewhere. "Come with me," I murmur and lead her to the end of the stairs, folding the envelope and putting it in my coat pocket before draping it around her shoulders. It swamps her, but that just means she looks even more adorable than usual.

"What are you doing?" She looks up at me.

"Taking you outside for a minute."

"But you'll freeze."

"No, I won't."

"I have my own coat, Rufus…" she reasons.

"I don't care." I take her hand and lead her to the door, opening it and dragging her outside onto the doorstep, then pulling the door to behind us.

"Tell me what you you meant?" I ask her. "Tell me why you said 'mainly' just now? Aren't you looking forward to being married?" I thought she was. I thought she felt the same as I do.

"Yes… but sometimes I feel nervous."

"What about? Marrying me?"

"No." She smiles and shakes her head. "About the… the wedding night."

I sigh out my relief. "You're nervous? After all the things we've already done? After all the kisses, the touches, all the words we've said to each other?" She nods her head.

"I know it sounds ridiculous, considering all of that, but…"

"No, it doesn't." I lean down and kiss her lips, just briefly. "But surely you know I'll… well, I'll make it alright. I'll take care of you."

"Yes, I do."

"Then you must also know you have nothing to be nervous of. I promise."

"It… it feels like such a big step."

"Well, we don't have to make it in one go," I remind her, kissing her again and hearing her slight moan. "We can take it slowly. We've got our whole lives, remember?"

"Good Lord, Rufus…" she says, leaning back in my arms and staring up at me, her eyes wide, "I may be nervous, but I'm not waiting that long." I throw back my head and laugh, and she joins in, as I capture her perfect giggle with my kiss, holding her close, until we're both breathing hard. "I do like it when you do that," she sighs, pulling back at last, her eyes sparkling with that familiar need.

"So do I." I cup her cheek with my hand. "Do you think your sudden bout of nerves might have something to do with the fact that I haven't been able to spend much time with you over the last few days? You don't normally seem nervous around me, and our moments together since the case ended have been rather brief and snatched, haven't they?" She tries to bow her head. "Look at me, Amelie." She raises her eyes again. "Do you think that's what it is?"

"Possibly," she murmurs. "I can't help missing you."

"I can't help missing you either. But please try and remember… you have nothing to worry about, and nothing to fear. Not now. Not on our wedding night. Not with me. Not ever."

We're all together in the sitting room, with Christmas music playing on the wireless in the background, enjoying some very exotic cocktails before lunch. I have no idea where Aunt Dotty got hold of the ingredients and I'm not going to ask either, simply because I'd hate to have to arrest her.

Amelie is beside me on the sofa, with my mother and Aunt Dotty opposite, and Issa sitting on one of the chairs.

"What was the emergency this morning?" my mother asks, and Amelie turns to me.

"You didn't explain?" she says, looking surprised. I got back here over an hour before Amelie arrived, but decided this was something the two of us should tell my relatives together, and made a silly excuse for my visit to Amelie this morning. Obviously it wasn't an excuse my mother was going to believe.

"No. I thought we should do that together," I explain.

"Now I'm really intrigued," my mother replies, sitting forward slightly and clasping her hands together.

"Gordon Templeton wanted to see us." I take a sip of my cocktail, letting the alcohol works its magic. "Amelie's agreed that he can give her away."

"That's good news." Aunt Dotty smiles across at us.

"Hmm." My mother narrows her eyes. "But that's not the reason you went over there, is it?"

"No… and if they still burned witches at the stake, they'd be building a fire as we speak," I remark and she does her best to look affronted. "Gordon wanted to give us a wedding present as well."

"Already?" Issa remarks.

"Yes. He's given us a house."

My mother's mouth drops open and I stifle a laugh at the sight of her, lost for words, for once in her life.

"A house?" It's Dotty who speaks first. "Where?"

"Not far away. It's in School Road."

"Oh, thank God for that," she breathes, taking a swig of her drink. "I was worried you were going to be moving away."

I shake my head. "No. You're stuck with us for the foreseeable future, I'm afraid." I smile across at her and she returns the gesture, her eyes sparkling. "It's a property he already owns, and it needs some work doing – which I'm going to pay for – and he's going to take us to see it after Christmas."

"That's very generous of him," my mother remarks, smiling.

"Yes, it is." I don't tell her his reasoning, because as far as I'm concerned, that's between the three of us. "The really ridiculous thing is, that until he made the offer, neither Amelie nor myself had even considered where we were going to live after the wedding. Can you believe that?"

"Yes," Issa replies, smiling. "You're both far too wrapped up in each other to think of anything sensible."

"Thank you," I say, nodding to her and she nods back. She didn't mean it as a compliment, but as far as I'm concerned, being wrapped up in Amelie is the best place for me to be, and as she looks at me, I know she understands that too.

"I'd thought about it," Mother remarks and we all turn to her.

"You had?" I ask.

"Oh yes."

"And what conclusions had you drawn?"

"I'd assumed you'd stay on here," she says and for a moment, I wonder if there's a hint of sadness to her voice and behind her eyes, that we won't be. "Still," she says, squaring her shoulders, "this is much better."

I look at her and she smiles. I smile back, but I think we both know she's putting on a brave face.

"We'll only be down the road," Amelie says, possibly sensing my mother's disquiet as well. "And I'll be coming back here all the time." I turn to look at her, surprised by this revelation.

"You will?"

"Yes." She glances up at me. "I'm going to need help."

Now I'm really confused. "What with? I'm not that difficult to live with, you know."

She struggles to control a giggle as she leans into me. "I know... but you do realise I can't cook, don't you?"

"No, I didn't realise that."

"Want to change your mind?" she asks, teasing. At least, I hope she's teasing.

"No. Never. And anyway, I can cook."

"I know. But you also have to go out to work... and your hours are hardly regular. And that means I'm going to have to learn to cook."

"And you want my mother and my aunts to teach you?"

"Well, Mary's offered to help," she says, referring to the cook who's employed by her uncle and aunt, "but I thought your mother and your aunts might join in too… if they don't mind."

"We'd love to," my mother blurts out, grinning.

"It seems like a good idea to me," Amelie continues. "Because, believe me, I'm going to need all the help I can get, and they know the things you like to eat, after all."

"I'd agree…" I remark.

"But?" She looks at me doubtfully.

"I'm just worried about the trouble they can get you into in my absence… that's all."

Amelie grins. "All sorts, I imagine. It'll be such fun."

Oh dear God…

"While we're on the subject of life altering experiences, like me learning to cook," Amelie continues, even as my imagination is going into overdrive, "I wanted to ask you a question."

"Me?" I turn to her.

"Yes."

"What do you want to know?"

"Nothing. I just wanted to ask you how you'd feel about me giving up my job."

I smile. "Well, again, I have to admit, it's not something I've even thought about."

"You've been distracted, have you?" she teases.

"Yes." She bites her bottom lip, looking up at me in a beautifully tempting way, although after our conversation this morning, I have my doubts she's even aware of what she's doing, or what she does to me either. "But in answer to your original question, it's entirely up to you. It's not for me to decide whether or not you continue working once we're married, Amelie. That's something only you can choose. If you want to keep working, then I won't expect you to do everything around the house. I'll do whatever I can to make things easier for you… I am used to taking care of myself, after all, so taking care of you at the same time won't be a hardship, I can promise you that."

She stares at me for a moment, and then leans over and kisses me, regardless of my mother and aunts. "I do love you," she says, loud enough for them to hear.

"I love you too." I smile at her, feeling rather flushed with pride at her outburst.

"I think, in that case, if it's alright with you, I'd rather stop working."

"As long as that's what you want."

"It is. I want to look after you," she murmurs, leaning into me again.

"And I want to look after you too." I kiss her forehead. "How much notice do you have to give at work?" I ask her, thinking of practicalities now.

"A week," she replies.

"Then why not resign right after Christmas? That way you can devote your time to planning the wedding and overseeing the work on the house, to make sure it's exactly what you want it to be, and not have to worry about working at the same time."

"That's a good idea. And later on, once we're married, if I want a change, I can always volunteer to do something to help the war, can't I?" Amelie suggests.

"Yes. As long as you don't volunteer to do anything that takes you away from me."

"Never," she replies and leans her head on my shoulder.

"This is just perfect," Aunt Dotty flusters, her eyes twinkling with delight. "Just perfect."

I, for one, cannot find a single reason to disagree with her.

It's late and we've had a marvellous day together, and just to make it complete, as I open the front door to walk Amelie home, we notice it's snowing. It must have been for some time, because it's settled on the ground, forming a layer of white dust over the hedges, walls, paths and the naked branches of the trees.

"Oh… it's beautiful." Amelie turns to look at me, as I pull the door closed behind us and hold her hand to steady her down the path and out of the garden gate.

"Mind your step," I warn. "It's icy." She lets go of my hand and links arms with me instead.

"At least we'll fall down together now," she remarks, smiling.

"And I can break my other arm."

She giggles. "I'll look after you."

"I think I'm supposed to say that, aren't I?"

"We can say it together." We get to the other side of the road and she leans up and kisses my cheek. "Thank you for a wonderful day," she whispers. "You've been…"

"What?"

"You."

"I've been me?" I shake my head. "What does that mean?"

"It means you've been kind, considerate, loving, gentle, funny, romantic… and all the other special things that make you who you are."

I nod my head. "If I am any of those things, my darling, it's because of you." She looks down, seemingly embarrassed, as we turn into her driveway. "And before we say goodnight, can I do one last thing?" She leans in closer, presumably expecting me to kiss her, which I do, just gently, before reaching into my pocket and pulling out a small box, wrapped in brown paper. "I know it's not yet Christmas Day… well, not quite anyway, but I wanted to give you this while we we're alone."

She glances down and then pulls off her gloves and reaches into her own pocket, revealing a tiny box, wrapped in similar paper, which she holds out to me. "I love you, Rufus," she whispers. "Merry Christmas." We swap gifts, and she looks up at me. "Shall we open them now?" she asks, her eyes twinkling in the moonlight.

"I don't see why not." She smiles and starts to tear into the paper and I have to chuckle at her childish delight as I open my own present, with a little more care, to discover a black box, with the name of a jewellers on the outside.

"Open it," she murmurs, looking at me, holding her own dark blue box in her hand.

"You first. I'm so nervous about this."

"You are?" She seems surprised and looks down again at the box in her hand, pulling open the lid and gasping.

"You can't see it clearly, but the stones are all different colours." I point to them with my little finger. "And in the light, it sparkles like… well, like your eyes." She swallows and I notice tears forming. "Don't cry," I whisper. "You're not meant to cry."

"Even if you've just made me so happy it's all I can think of doing?" she says and I pull her close to me and kiss her tenderly.

"It's my job to make you happy, remember? But I don't expect you to cry every time I do it."

"Really? Then I'm afraid you might be disappointed, if you keep doing things like this."

She chuckles, looking down at her necklace and smiling. "It's your turn," she says, nodding to the box I'm still clutching, and I pull open the lid, to reveal a pair of cufflinks. "They're gold," she says, taking one out, and holding it for me to see more clearly. They're square, with a bevelled edge and a small stone set in the corner. "And this is a garnet. It's the birthstone for January… which we share."

"They're beautiful," I say, with utter honesty, because they are. Like her. "We share so much more than a birthstone, Amelie."

She gazes up at me. "I know."

"And very soon we'll share everything."

The End

The Rufus Stone Detective Stories will continue in Book 4, *The Nightingale*, due out in Autumn 2020.

Printed in Great Britain
by Amazon